Elisabeth McNeill is a history graduate of Aberdeen University and a regular contributor to *The Scotsman*. She has had five novels published by Headline. She has four children and lives in Roxburghshire.

St James' Fair

Elisabeth McNeill

HEADLINE

First published in 1992
by Random Century Group

First published in paperback in 1992
by HEADLINE BOOK PUBLISHING PLC

10 9 8 7 6 5 4 3 2 1

ISBN 0 7472 3851 0

Printed and bound in Great Britain by
HarperCollins Manufacturing, Glasgow

HEADLINE BOOK PUBLISHING PLC
Headline House
79 Great Titchfield Street
London W1P 7FN

To my dear grand-daughter Iyunadi

PROLOGUE

There is nothing to show that a bustling town once occupied a long spit of land between two rivers on the outskirts of Lauriston. A green meadow stretches in a gentle sweep to a rising hillock at one end with a scattering of trees along its surface, but unseen beneath its undulations lie streets and alleyways; vanished churches, convents and a hospital; a royal mint and the cellars of the homes of prosperous merchants and busy journeymen. For what is only a field today was once Roxburgh, the capital of Scotland, a more important place than Edinburgh and a mecca for kings, papal legates and other important travellers.

No one knows for certain what happened to the town. It may have been abandoned because of the plague, or perhaps its buildings were razed to the ground to prevent it being taken again by invaders from south of the border. It could have been gradually deserted because it became a place of ill omen after James II, King of Scotland, blew himself up by the misfiring of a cannon when trying to blast an English garrison out of the town. Whatever the reason, soldiers and courtiers, clerics and journeymen left Roxburgh; the fine houses and churches fell into disrepair and then ruin. By the beginning of the 17th century the site had become a pasture. Today only a crumbling and haunted-looking castle broods on a hill above the vanished town and sheep graze over its sunken streets.

Until the 1930s, there was an annual reminder of the glory that once filled the empty field. This was a fair, named after St James, patron saint of pilgrims, to whom Roxburgh's chief church had been dedicated. Churches dedicated to that saint dotted the pilgrim routes of Europe, culminating in the magnificence of St Jaime de Santiago in northern Spain.

Roxburgh's fair was started in the 12th century and even after the town disappeared, it continued to be held on the first Monday in August every year. During fair-time, life surged back into the deserted town; voices rang over it once more and feet trod its hidden streets again. The ghosts of its dead mingled with seekers after pleasure at the fair.

This is the story of what happened during a particular St James' Fair in the year 1816.

CHAPTER 1

Lauriston, the most elegant and prosperous town in the Scottish Borderland, was in a ferment. Its inns and lodging-houses were filled up with people flooding into town for the Fair; fleshers and provision merchants were rushed off their feet coping with orders from housewives catering for large family parties. All the livery stables were full and the big grain mill in the middle of the town was working day and night to supply the bakers with enough flour for the extra bread that needed to be baked. Money clinked in pockets and faces were smiling because the sun was shining and the weather promised to stay fine. Good weather always made fair-goers better humoured and more prepared to spend and although some people in Lauriston grumbled about the annual disruption of their peaceful routine, most of them looked forward to St James' Fair.

In his office overlooking the town square, Andrew Elliot, a sharp-faced man of the law, was reading aloud a letter that lay spread out on the desk in front of him to Canny Rutherford, a plump, grey-haired man, who leaned forward in his chair listening intently with his blue eyes fixed on the lawyer's face. When the reading was over, Elliot raised his head and stared at his client in silence for a few moments. At first the object of his regard nodded without speaking, then suddenly, like a jack in the box, did something very unexpected. Leaping from his chair he executed a jolly little dance in the middle of the carpet, rubbing his hands together and bouncing up and down on his stout legs as he cried in exultation, 'By Jove, who would believe it! My girl'll be a Duchess!'

Delight made him swell like a puffball and his bright

eyes glittered and gleamed like chips of lapis lazuli. He was beaming so broadly that his scarlet cheeks bulged out like ripe apples and the rising colour in his face and neck made Elliot put out a restraining hand, fearful that his client be carried off by an apoplexy in his hour of triumph. But Canny had no intention of succumbing to a fit. As suddenly as he had started, he stopped dancing and leaned, panting heavily, across the desk to pump his lawyer's hand rapidly up and down. 'What a triumph, eh? What a sensation this'll cause. The gossips will have something to make their tongues wag when they hear about this.'

The lawyer, as lawyers often do, felt it necessary to pour a little cold water on his client's enthusiasm and counselled caution. 'Do sit down, Mr Rutherford. You must remember it's not definite yet. He's written to say he's interested, that's all . . .'

But all efforts to induce calm were in vain because Canny only laughed more joyously and cried out, 'He's made the first move, hasn't he? He's strapped for cash. Everybody knows there's bills out against him all over the countryside. He's seen my lovely daughter and he's been struck by a brilliant idea . . . who'd believe it? I ask you that, Elliot, who'd believe it?'

Who indeed, thought the lawyer, looking across his desk at the delighted man. Canny Rutherford had earned his bread as a boy by filling water buckets at Lauriston's town pump for local housewives. No one then could have predicted that time would transform the water-carrier into a fabulously rich man with a daughter who was sought in marriage by a Duke.

'What is Miss Rutherford going to think about this? It will be quite a surprise for the girl. How old is she now – seventeen?' asked Elliot, carefully folding up the letter which had caused his client so much enthusiasm.

'She's eighteen. I've been wondering about finding a suitable husband for her – but even I never thought about this,' exulted Canny.

Elliot shook his head dolefully. 'There's quite a difference in their ages. We all know what young girls are like – romantic. Do you think she'll agree?'

Canny was not in the least deflated. His excitement was impossible to quench. 'Oh, that'll be all right. Of course she'll agree. She'll be delighted. What girl wouldn't jump at the chance of becoming a Duchess?'

He stood in the middle of Elliot's carpet looking like a jubilant Toby jug with his booted legs apart and his round stomach bulging out beneath a long white waistcoat. Even Elliot, who knew Rutherford's history better than most, found it hard to remember that in spite of the apparent innocence of the blue eyes, steel lurked behind them. Canny might look like a pottery jug but he was a fiercely astute man who had proved his ruthlessness in a hard world. The water boy, who left Lauriston when he was eleven years old, had amassed a fortune in the West Indies – through brigandage, it was rumoured. When the ex-brigand had come home, transformed into what was almost, but not quite, a gentleman, he brought with him his only daughter. Even the lawyer was struck by the girl's dark and exotic beauty and was not greatly surprised when the Duke's letter arrived suggesting that a marriage might be arranged between Miss Rutherford and himself. For as well as being lovely to look at, Canny's daughter was an heiress with a greater fortune than any other young woman between Lauriston and London and the Duke was not only an appreciator of women but he was also hard up and greedy.

Elliot thoughtfully fingered his watch seal as he gazed through the window of his office which overlooked the town's cobbled square, half-shadowed by the old Town Hall that bore a blue-faced clock on its tower. The hands stood at fifteen minutes to three and women were out shopping in the sunshine. A ragged boy was earning a few pence by filling buckets of water at the stone-walled pump and the lawyer permitted himself a wry smile as he thought that his client had once done the same thing. He switched his gaze back to Canny's face and said

11

slowly, 'Can I take it that you are in favour of accepting this offer?'

'Don't be silly man. Of course I am,' was the sharp reply.

'But before we accept, we have to be sure that Miss Rutherford is in agreement,' warned the lawyer.

Canny snorted. His impatience with Elliot's ultra-cautious attitude was growing uncontainable. Elliot was a good enough business adviser, he thought, because he was as cunning as a monkey, but his caution made him slow and slowness irked the fat man more than anything. Canny's given name was William, but from childhood he had been known by the nickname, bestowed on him as a joke like many in the Scottish Borders, because of his impetuous nature.

'I didn't make my fortune by hanging around when opportunity offered,' he said impatiently, 'I want you to reply at once and say we're interested – more than interested, in fact. I want the Duke to know that I regard this letter of his as a definite offer. He's not to have any room for backing out.'

In these peremptory tones Elliot heard the voice of a man who once went cruising in a black-painted ship on the dangerous waters of the Caribbean. He picked up his pen and prepared to begin transcribing but, for the last time, he warned his client, 'Now, remember there's no guarantee that Miss Rutherford will be marrying the Duke. Things are very much at the negotiating stage and if you run around talking about this affair, you could ruin it. I'll reply to his letter exactly as you wish but I hope you're sure there'll be no hitches, because once you've accepted his offer, there can be no backing out.'

Like everyone in Lauriston, except Canny Rutherford who was too rich to care, Elliot lived in mortal terror of the Duke of Maudesley who ruled the lives of the locals like a feudal overlord. He owned most of the property in and around the town, including Elliot's own house and office building; he employed the majority of the working people; he was like a king to them and his power was absolute. Anyone who annoyed him knew their only course was to pack up and leave Lauriston. It was this potentate who had selected Canny's daughter as a possible consort. Although the Rutherfords and the Duke had never met socially, he knew everything that went on in the town and had spied her on the street. His informants would have told him who the girl was and how much she was worth.

'Write the letter, write it!' snapped Canny, hopping up and down impatiently on his plump-calved legs. The lawyer shrugged. He'd done his best. He dipped his quill in the inkpot and prepared to begin writing.

'Neither of us are foolish men. We know it's her fortune that interests him more than her beauty. He'll want to know how much you're prepared to give her as a dowry,' he said.

Rutherford pulled out a chair and sat down, biting on the silver knob of his cane as he thought. After a few moments he announced, 'I'll give ten thousand as an earnest to begin with. Then another ten thousand on the day of the betrothal, and, when they marry, she'll have a dowry of a quarter of a million. . . . We'll bait the hook for him!'

In shock Elliot laid down his pen again. Even he was surprised at this largesse. Rutherford must be richer than rumour made out. He shot an awed glance at the man before him but before he could say anything, Canny met his eyes with a hard stare and added, 'Make sure he knows that when I die, she'll fall heir to another half a million at least – possibly more. I want him to realise that my Odilie's an heiress of the first rank. I doubt if there's a better in the whole of the kingdom. So when you draw up her wedding contract it'll have to be water-tight. She'll keep control of her own money because I've heard about this Duke and I don't want him wasting her fortune on wine and loose women.'

A short while later Mr Canny Rutherford stood in the doorway of Elliot's law office, staring around his native town with pleasure so sharp that it seemed to him he was seeing lovely Lauriston for the first time. The town had a Continental look – it could have been somewhere in France. The houses and offices facing onto the square all looked clean, freshly painted and prosperous. Flowers bloomed in pots on window sills and a bent-backed old man was sweeping up litter from the cobbles with a long-handled broom. The pump which Canny knew so well was shaped like a Roman altar and stood in the middle of the square. Looking down over all, the cock on top of the Town Hall tower was glittering so brightly in the sunshine that it seemed to be made of real gold.

Canny stared across the square at the town's two main streets – the Horse Market and the Corn Market – which ran off parallel in an easterly direction. He knew that the people bustling around would have noticed him standing proudly in his lawyer's doorway and that they'd be thinking, 'Yonder's Canny Rutherford who used to be such a poor wee laddie. My word, he's changed!' He longed to cup his hands around his mouth and give a yodel as he used to do when a boy. Then, when he'd caught their attention, he'd startle them with his news, 'My daughter Odilie's going to marry the Duke!' How annoying it was to have to remember Elliot's injunction to keep his secret for a little longer, for the joy that bubbled up inside him hurt with the pent up force of a capped volcano. If he did not hurry home and break the news soon, he would surely burst.

With a lordly air he settled his tall grey hat on his head and patted it into position with a ringed hand. Flourishing his cane, he stepped into the roadway where he almost collided with a mournful-looking man who came out of Oven Lane that led down to the river from the side of the lawyer's building. Canny drew back when he saw that he had bumped into Jockie Cunningham, another one who'd grown up with him. Normally he would not bother to waste time conversing with the gloomy and envious fellow but today's good humour made him beam and call out in a friendly manner, 'Isn't it a grand day, Jockie?'

'Fine enough I suppose, Canny. Let's hope it doesnae

rain for the Fair,' said Cunningham in a lugubrious voice, for he was rarely known to make a cheerful comment on anything and could be relied on to search out the black side of every happening. Canny's optimism was unquenchable however and he replied, 'Don't you worry. It's set fine. It'll no' rain for the Fair. Try looking on the bright side for once.'

'If you say so, *Canny*. You were aye one for the bright side,' was the reply as Cunningham wandered on up the street. Canny looked after him with annoyance showing in his expression for he knew that his nickname had been deliberately stressed in a mocking way just to annoy and to make it obvious that he was still thought of as a poverty-stricken laddie in spite of his wealth and display. Jockie Cunningham and other people of his sort in Lauriston did not take Canny seriously even now. Frowning with pique he hurried off up Bridge Street heading for his home, Havanah Court.

When Canny Rutherford returned from forty years in the West Indies, he built his dream house choosing the site with extreme care. It had to be in Lauriston because he wanted everyone in the town to see it and gasp in admiration.

'Why don't you buy a big estate? You can well afford it,' friends asked, amazed at his decision to build a mansion in the middle of a town, but there would have been no satisfaction for him in hiding behind a high stone wall or in the middle of a landscaped park. Canny was out to impress the people who had once disdained him as a pauper's son.

After long and expensive negotiations with the then Duke, brother to the present incumbent of the title, the best situation in town was secured on the north bank of the River Tweed at the edge of the town and backing onto Bridge Street opposite the ruins of the ancient abbey. The recently built Rennie Bridge came to an end at the left of the property and meadows of velvety green stretched westwards along the river bank while to the south the

15

outlook was across a broad sweep of river towards the smudged purple shadows of the Cheviot Hills.

Little by little over a period of several years, Canny's house had taken shape till it finally emerged from its scaffolds imbued with an assurance and elegance unequalled in the entire Border country. It was built of pale honey-coloured sandstone, long and low and shaped in a wide semi-circle like arms spread out to embrace the sun. There were no walls around it and the beautiful gardens could be seen through a line of metal railings by people passing to and fro in the street or strolling along the banks of the river. Canny had given as much care to the planning of his gardens as to the house itself, and fountains spouted over quaint grottoes constructed beside pergolas of roses. Seats were placed beside sweet-scented bushes and everywhere the ear was filled with the sound of softly running water. At the end of each outspread wing Canny had built a pavilion – the one on the west was an orangery, while on the east was a tropical greenhouse built for the delight of his daughter Odilie who missed the lushness and warmth of her birthplace in Jamaica.

He was thinking of Odilie now as he hurried along Bridge Street towards the lion-surmounted pillars of the front gateway which acted as lodestars for the hurrying man. When he reached the tall ornamental metal gates, he paused and peered through them as if he was a stranger. The smoothly-raked gravel of the drive swept in front of him in an elegant arabesque to a pillared front door where a sweep of front steps gleamed white with holy-stoning and the panes of the windows glittered and spark-led with the frequent polishing that was insisted on by Martha, his sister who was his housekeeper.

Martha drove the servants hard for she'd spent most of her life in service before he returned with his fortune from foreign parts. She knew how to catch maids out if they were inclined to idle. The Rutherfords had started life as Poors' House bairns and had never forgotten the shame of being raised on the parish. Even now, at nearly sixty, Canny was always overcome with gratitude on cold or rainy days when he looked down and realised that his feet were encased in stout shoes, for as a boy he'd gone barefoot.

The black servant Joe Cannonball had seen his master coming and opened the front door the moment Canny set foot on the bottom step. He was grinning broadly as he adroitly caught the hat that Canny tossed towards him while he bustled across the floor laid with tiles of black and white. The walls of the entrance hall were faced with pink marble and the domed roof was held up by slim pillars of grey veined stone. Canny had brought a team of Italian stuccoists up from London to embellish the ceilings of his house and in the hall they had excelled themselves, creating an icing sugar confection of heavily embossed decorations – tropical birds with outspread wings, pineapples and palm trees in honour of the place where their patron had made his fortune. 'You all right, sah?' asked Joe with a familiar air and Canny smiled back.

'More than all right, Joe, more than all right,' he exulted. He and Cannonball did not pretend at conventional master and servant formality because they were old shipmates who had enjoyed many adventures together. Although there was no question of servility on Joe's part, he was very much Canny's 'man' and a deep friendship and mutual reliance existed between them which would have surprised people outside who regarded Joe as only the same kind of black servant as the coloured boys who were popular with fashionable households in the south.

'Where's Mattie, Joe? Where's Miss Odilie? I've news for them,' cried Canny, rubbing his hands together as he headed for the drawing room. Before he reached its door, however, it opened to reveal his sister. Martha was as thin as her brother was plump and as untidy as he was dapper. Her grey hair straggled from beneath a lace cap that perched on the top of her head and a large white apron was tied round her waist. She looked ill at ease posing as a lady, for she had not yet recovered from her rapid transition out of the kitchens of other people's houses into stately living.

Canny paused at the sight of her and his smile flickered a little. 'You're wearing that damned peeny again, Martha!' he said disapprovingly. 'I've told you not to wear a peeny – what if somebody called?'

Mattie peered myopically at him through round, gold-rimmed glasses and lifted the corner of her apron unapologetically. 'Don't be so daft, Canny. Who grand is going to call on me? Anyway it's a clean peeny and if I didn't show thae maids of yours how to do things, nothing would ever be right. They're an idle lot.'

Her brother groaned. 'I'm tired of trying to make you into a lady, Matt, but you should try for Odilie's sake, especially now. And don't call me Canny! I was christened William. I met that long creep Cunningham in the square just now and he was Canny-ing me as if I was still a laddie. Do folk never forget anything in this town? You could at least set them a good example by calling me by my right name.'

Mattie was unimpressed by her brother's pretensions. 'Och, you'll aye be Canny in Lauriston. If you want to be called William you shouldn't have come back here to live,' she told him briskly, pulling a checked duster out of her apron pocket and flipping it at the furniture making tutting sounds with her lips as she did so. 'Look at this dust! Thae maids are clarty besoms. They dinna ken how to work and that Joe's as bad as they are.'

She succeeded in irritating her brother, who grabbed her duster in mid-flick and ordered, 'Stop it, Matt! You can't go about doing the dusting when we've ten maids to do it for you. Come in and sit down and listen to what I've got to tell you. It's grand news. Really grand. You'll be pleased.'

She looked suspiciously at him. 'What's happened? What're you up to now?'

He went up on his tiptoes and adopted a high-class voice. 'We're going into society, to mingle with the nobs. You'll maybe have a Duke for a nephew yet.'

Martha laughed. 'Not that again. You're always on about finding some nob to marry Odilie. What Duke? Some foreigner, I suppose. Some Frenchman that didn't get his head chopped off maybe.'

But then she looked harder at her brother and her hilarity died a little. 'You're really up to something, aren't you?' she asked in a different voice.

'Up to? What should I be up to?' He was enjoying himself as he wagged a finger at her in admonishment. 'You'd better start learning how to behave with the aristocracy, Mattie. You might have one of them in the family. Where's Odilie?'

'She's upstairs. What's going on? I hope you've not done something daft.'

'Am I in the habit of doing daft things?' asked her brother with a wounded air and taking his sister's arm he said with unconcealed glee, 'Let's go up to her. I can hardly wait till she hears this.'

Meanwhile Joe Cannonball was smiling broadly as he popped his head around Odilie's boudoir door and told her, 'Your Papa's back, Baby. My word but he's in some fizz. He's coming up here quick quick.'

Odilie looked up from where she sat on a fragile-looking sofa in the sunny window, her pet dog Scamp, a pampered brown and white spaniel, on a cushion beside her. The room, one of the prettiest in a house of lovely rooms, overlooked the river and the brilliant light of the summer's day flooded in making her bask in its warmth like an open flower. Sunshine always cheered her up. On dull, wet days Joe thought she drooped like a wilting lily but the stretch of fine weather they were enjoying had enlivened her and assuaged the longings she still felt for the brilliance of Jamaica where she had been born.

'What's he up to?' she asked, for like her father she adopted no superior airs towards Joe.

He shook his head and said, 'Don't know, but he's dancing around as if he's found a guinea in the gutter.'

They both laughed at that idea and Odilie laid aside the book she was reading and smoothed down the skirt of her pale muslin dress with careful hands. Today she was wearing a gown decorated with a line of blue satin ribbons down the front and Joe's eyes were full of unhidden love and admiration as he looked at her. He had been part of Rutherford's household since Odilie was born and as far as he was concerned, she was as much his child as she was Canny's for he had looked after her and watched her growing up with awe-struck wonder. Now that she was a woman, she was a walking miracle to him.

His admiration was justified, for Odilie was very pretty indeed – small, slim and graceful with a curving form and a wide-jawed head that sat like an open flower on the long stem of her neck. Her dark hair was abundant with wanton hair-spring curls escaping from the combs that vainly tried to hold it back from her pert face. Wide-spaced eyes and a short nose gave her a startled, faun-like look and though her mouth was too wide for classical beauty it was so humorously curved that when she was happy – as she was today – everything and everyone glowed in her radiance.

She liked to be surrounded by colourful things and the room was filled with flowers, pictures, scattered lengths of multi-coloured silks, an embroidery frame and a painting easel that bore a sketch of Scamp, half-finished because he refused to keep still for very long. A straw hat with multicoloured flowers tucked into the brim lay on a table beside her and a gilded harp stood in the corner. On the floor at her feet were a pile of books bound in red leather and lettered in gold. They looked very scholarly tomes for such an apparently frivolous young woman.

Before she had time to question Joe further, Canny and Martha came bustling up the stairs and her father rushed towards her with both hands outheld, exulting, 'I've something wonderful to tell you, my dear!'

He lifted her book off the sofa seat and glanced at the title, which made him raise his eyebrows a little. *The Breeding of Bloodstock: Volume 1*, it said. His daughter moved along to accommodate him while Martha perched opposite in a gilt-framed chair. As he settled himself on the sofa Canny was suddenly aware that four pairs of eyes were regarding him attentively – Odilie's, dark-fringed and the colour of caramel; Martha's as blue as his own; Scamp's golden and greedy; Joe's black as ebony, dancing with amusement and curiosity.

Under their scrutiny he shifted in his seat and coughed awkwardly but the eyes went on staring fixedly. In order to make his announcement as theatrical as possible, he rose to his feet again and took a little turn on the carpet. Then he paused and told Joe, 'Off you go, Cannonball. There must be plenty for you to do downstairs.'

Everyone was thunderstruck. This announcement must indeed be serious if Joe was not to hear it. The black man was far from pleased at his abrupt dismissal and Odilie looked extremely surprised too but neither of them made any protest for something in Canny's voice told them that he was not in the mood to be trifled with. Joe contented himself with slamming the boudoir door closed while, assuming a serious expression, Odilie folded her hands and sat back, waiting for her father to begin.

He smiled lovingly at her. 'You're eighteen now, my dear. It was your birthday last week, wasn't it? You've done with schooling and it's time we were thinking about a suitable marriage for you.'

Odilie sighed. 'Oh, not that again, Papa! You've talked of nothing but marrying me off for the last three months though I've only been home since Christmas. You must be very anxious to be rid of me.'

Canny hastened to reassure her. 'Oh, no, my dear. I don't want rid of you at all. I want you to stay as near to me as possible even after you marry – that's why I'm so pleased . . .'

She went on staring at him with a half-smiling, patient look on her face. Speculation about whom she should eventually marry had become a sort of game between them, a running joke.

'Who have you picked out for me this time?' she asked in a teasing tone. 'It can't be the Prince of Wales – he's married already!' Then her smile faltered when she

21

realised that her father's attitude was not the flippant one he usually adopted if they talked about this subject.

'Please listen to what I've got to say, Odilie. This is a serious business,' he told her and the words sounded peremptory even to him. She sank back surprised among her cushions. Martha was also eyeing her brother in slight alarm for she had never seen him take such a firm line with his daughter before. When Canny sensed that he had their complete attention he announced in a solemn voice, 'Today I received an offer of marriage for you, my dear.'

Odilie abruptly rose and walked across to the window where she stood with her back towards the others as she gazed over the garden. When she spoke her voice sounded distant. '*You* received the offer. Why didn't my suitor approach me first? I can't imagine who can be offering for me because I know no one I'd want to marry.'

Her father adopted a placatory tone. 'My dear girl, you're my only child and you're very rich, a considerable heiress. Any marriage you make will be a matter of business. It's only correct that I should be approached first. I'd want it that way because you're not aware of the wickedness there is in this world or how many fortune hunters are about. There's always been a lot of them but it's even worse now with all those half-pay officers looking for well-off brides.'

His daughter swung round towards him and Martha was startled by the resemblance to Canny in the girl's face. She snapped, 'You underestimate me. I'm not a fool, Papa. I'm not going to fall for any half-pay officer.'

Taken off guard, her father floundered slightly. 'I'm not suggesting you're a fool, Odilie, but things can happen that are out of your control. You might not have a choice. I heard the other day about the daughter of my old friend Thomson, the Savannah merchant. He's living in London now and some young blade ran off with his girl, took her to Gretna Green and married her!'

Odilie didn't look shocked. 'I remember that girl – she's very foolish. Perhaps she wanted to go,' she suggested.

Her father shook his head. 'Well, if she did she's rueing the day because he's left her already. Her father refused to give her an allowance of two thousand a year as the new husband wanted, and he disappeared. The girl's ruined. You're worth far more than two thousand a year, Odilie, so that's why finding the right husband for you is very important.'

Odilie sighed for this was a theme that she'd heard many times before. 'Money! I wish I was poor and could be left to find a husband for myself.' Canny swept that aside as being beneath consideration. He knew what it was like to be poor, to dine on potato peelings gathered from someone's rubbish heap and he had fought to ensure that his daughter need never have the same privations.

'You should thank God that you're rich,' he told her, 'but because you are, a marriage for you needs careful arranging.'

His daughter frowned. 'Left to you and the lawyers, you mean? That sounds a very cold way. Doesn't it matter that I might want to fall in love, Papa?'

Canny shook his head, made uncertain for a moment as his memory went back to his first sight of his daughter's mother, the lovely Jacqueline, at a ball in a plantation house on a balmy night when the air was sweet and smelt of flowers. Odilie sensed she had a momentary advantage and pressed it home. 'Perhaps I should find myself a rich husband like my mother did,' she said but though her tone was light, her shoulders were tense and she was beginning to feel frightened.

Canny walked closer to her and tried to coax her into a better humour. 'I asked your mother's father for her hand first. He wouldn't have allowed us to marry if I'd not done it that way or if I'd been a poor man, my dear. Now don't be angry, just listen to what I'm trying to tell you. This offer is truly magnificent. It's been made in a letter to Elliot, my lawyer. It's all been done in a very business-like manner.'

Odilie groaned. 'Business-like! Love isn't business-like! You make my marriage sound like an investment. Am I to be disposed of to the best prospect?' she flung at him. Her eyes were flashing dangerously as they used to when she was thwarted as a child.

' "Disposed of" is the wrong way to put it,' he protested. 'You'll always have a choice and you can refuse this man if you really don't like him but I want you to consider it seriously. This marriage is as good as any girl can get.'

'As I said, the Prince of Wales is spoken for,' snapped his daughter.

Canny's impetuousity made it impossible for him to stand the strain of their verbal battle any longer and he riposted sharply, 'But the Duke isn't!'

A stunned silence greeted this announcement. Odilie gazed, eyes wide in astonishment, while Martha clamped both hands over her mouth and stared too, but not in admiration as he had hoped. Her eyes showed consternation, making it obvious that she thought her brother had gone too far this time. Slowly Odilie's gaze went from her father's face to that of her aunt, noting every reaction and her voice was disbelieving when she asked, 'Which Duke?'

Angrily Canny jerked a thumb over his right shoulder in a backwards direction. 'Him up there. Our Duke. The Duke of Maudesley.' He was disappointed that his triumph was falling so flat with the people he most hoped to please.

His sister and his daughter both shuddered and gulped.

'Oh no, Canny, not a Fox,' gasped Martha.

Odilie's eyes were stricken as she cried out, 'He's awfully old, Papa. I've heard a lot about him. People say he's louche and bad-mannered, very arrogant. You can't mean that you think I ought to marry him!'

Canny threw out his hands and pleaded, 'He's not old, he's only forty. And you'll be a Duchess, Odilie!'

She recovered her fight. 'I don't care! I don't want to be a Duchess. I thought all your talk about a titled husband was only a joke.' Then she surprised herself by bursting into tears.

Martha ran over to hold the sobbing girl in her arms, and turned to scold her brother. 'This is all just talk, isn't it? The Duke wouldn't marry a Rutherford. You've made a lot of money, it's true, but our father was a drunken ostler at the Cross Keys, and everybody in this town knows it. Tell the lassie you've just been daydreaming. He can't have offered for her.'

Canny was seriously angry now. 'He has! Even Dukes have their price and this one's hard up. Odilie's rich.'

Martha fixed him with cold eyes. 'You've not accepted,' she whispered. 'Oh, tell me you've not accepted . . .'

He blustered in reply, 'I've been aiming as high as I can for her. I never guessed she'd not want to be a Duchess.' He was telling the truth for until now his daughter had always gone along with his half-playful suggestions about an advantageous marriage. 'What woman turns down a title?' he asked his sister, who was still hugging the weeping girl.

Odilie extricated herself from her aunt's embrace and cried out at her father, 'You should have asked me first, Papa. I should have had some say in this. Surely you're not serious.'

He nodded grimly. 'I didn't refuse him but I didn't accept, either. I said we were interested, that's all. We're still at the negotiating stage.'

Her face was shocked. '*Negotiating*? Does that mean you're prepared to pay him to marry me? He's not even seen me. We've never met. He can't care about me! All that interests him is my fortune. How shaming!'

'He has seen you,' protested Canny desperately. 'His letter said he's seen you in the town.'

Martha spoke up behind him. 'He'll have spied her out all right. He's an awful man. Not a maid at Sloebank Castle is safe from him.'

Canny shot her a look. 'Be quiet,' he ordered. 'That's servants' gossip, all talk. They say things like that about every Duke.'

Martha shook her head but held her tongue. Odilie was beyond caution, however. She was shouting, 'I'll not be bartered for with such a man. How much is it going to cost you to buy a lecherous Duke for my husband?'

There was no support for Canny. Even his sister's face was hard and he could see she thought he had been actuated by overweening ambition and that this marriage only appealed to him because it would stun Lauriston. He felt angry and misunderstood because neither of the women appreciated his true motive, which was to raise his beloved Odilie to a rank of society that even his money could not buy. He snapped, 'Plenty. It's costing me plenty. But I thought you'd be pleased. I'm prepared to pay if Odilie is able to move in the highest circles.'

The girl stepped closer to him and looked earnestly into his face as she whispered, 'He hasn't even seen me properly, Papa. Does he know what colour I am? Does he realise that I'm black?' As she spoke she pushed up her loose-flowing sleeve and held out a bare arm towards him, turning it slowly under his gaze. The matt skin was a glorious copper colour and looked as soft as satin.

Martha gave a stricken sob but Canny cried out, 'Oh, my bairn! Oh, Odilie, you're not black. Who told you that lie? Joe's black, you're not the same colour as Joe.'

The girl shook down her sleeve again and stared bleakly at him. 'As far as snobbish white people are concerned, I'm black. I never told you about the girls at that horrible school in London you sent me to because I didn't want to upset you. They teased me all the time and called me the Negress. They used to recoil from me because they said if I brushed against them I'd make them dirty . . . now you want to pay a Duke to marry me and set me up in their kind of society where I'll face sniggers and talk like that all my life. I'll be called the black Duchess! How could you do such a thing if you love me?'

Desperately her father reached out and hugged his child to him. 'I never think of you as being any colour, Odilie. You're my lovely daughter, who has the same beauty as your mother and she was a Creole with skin like polished gold. In spite of what they say about him, the Duke's got eyes in his head. He can see that you're the most beautiful

26

girl in the whole countryside. Any man would be proud to marry you.'

Odilie allowed herself to be comforted, sobbing in her father's arms, 'Oh, you don't understand. I hate the taunts, I really hate them. . . . That's why I miss Jamaica so much.'

Canny groaned for this was a revelation to him. His dusky-skinned wife had been an acclaimed beauty and having lived for many years among coloured people, he was totally without prejudice. He genuinely loved Odilie and it pierced his soul to realise that she could be hurt by cruel and unthinking people.

'Don't take on my dear, don't upset yourself. I'll make sure he knows about your colour and we'll go about this affair carefully. You don't have to decide one way or another till you've met him properly and that can be arranged during the celebrations of St James' Fair.'

'She hasn't very long to wait, in that case. The Fair's next Monday,' came Martha's disapproving voice.

CHAPTER 2

It was impossible to keep a secret in Lauriston. After Canny Rutherford left the lawyer's office, Andrew Elliot appeared in his counting house on the ground floor and laid a sheet of paper on the top of the high desk at which his senior clerk was sitting. 'Copy this letter out and send it up to the Duke at Sloebank Castle,' he ordered. Before he left the room a thought struck him and he turned back to add, 'And keep what's in it to yourself.'

When, a few minutes later, he hurried down the stairs again and strode off in the direction of Roxburgh Street and his home, Viewhill House, the clerks all clustered around their senior's desk and craned their heads over his shoulder to decipher what he was writing.

It was so interesting that Elliot was hardly out of sight when the youngest clerk went running across the square to the shop of Tom Burns, the provision merchant, to break the astonishing news that Canny Rutherford was going to marry his daughter to the Duke.

Soon every shop around the square was buzzing with the news as the townspeople discussed this sensation.

'I mind Canny when he was a wee laddie – a poor wee white-faced thing like a ghostie. Aye starvin' of hunger he was. Who'd have thought his lassie would become a Duchess!' exclaimed Mr Burns to Mrs Pringle, the minister's wife, who had just popped in for two ounces of China tea. She raised a disapproving eyebrow because Canny was not a member of her husband's congregation nor of any congregation come to that.

'I suppose it's quite an honour for the town even though the girl's a half-caste. I wonder if any children will be – er – coloured,' she asked delicately.

Tom laughed uproariously. 'That's a good one, Mrs

Pringle, that's all we need. Our next Duke might be a black!' he cried.

In the butcher's shop next door Elliot's clerk was being cross-questioned by the customers. 'What dowry's being paid?' they wanted to know. He looked knowledgeable but cagey. 'It's confidential so I cannae tell you exactly but it'll be in six figures by the time he's finished.'

The excitement was everything that Canny would have desired. 'Six figures!' they chorused and the butcher said with satisfaction, 'That's going to pay my bill, anyway. It's been running on ever since the Duke inherited from his brother two years ago. He's wanting to rebuild the Castle they say and he's brought an architect chappie doon frae Edinbury. Maybe he'll get started on it now.'

'A lot of folk'll get paid. My word, Canny's a hero. He's doing the hale toon a bit of good marrying off his lassie to the Duke,' agreed a customer. They were all hard at work discussing the news when Canny Rutherford's black servant was spotted sprinting over the square to Elliot's office. After a few moments he reappeared and went dashing on up the hill in the direction of the lawyer's house. The gossips looked at each other and nodded their heads. 'Something's up. You dinna see that black yin running unless it's important,' they agreed.

Elliot's home was a bleak, tall and narrow house with a flat grey façade set behind a rank of sharply pointed iron railings at the side of the busy street. A long narrow strip of steeply sloping garden ran down from its hidden front to the river. Viewhill House resembled a prison because the wood of the front door was studded with big metal bosses and all the windows facing the road were stoutly barred. Cautious Andrew Elliot was very concerned about burglary although it was not a common crime in the town.

When Joe Cannonball rapped on the door knocker, it was opened by a tall, thin, fair-haired girl who was anxiously wiping her hands on a sacking apron. She looked surprised at the sight of the Rutherfords' servant but she knew Joe well and recovered enough to smile with appealing sweetness as she ushered him into the dank-smelling passage.

He asked her, 'Where's your father, Grace?'

'He's upstairs in the parlour with Hester,' she said. 'What's wrong? You look awfully excited, Joe.'

He rolled his eyes. 'My word, my word, there's terrible trouble down at our house. Miss Odilie's going to be married.'

The girl called Grace gasped. 'But I saw her yesterday and she didn't say a thing about it then.'

Joe shook his head. 'She didn't know then! It's her father going off like a minute gun again. Fetch your father, Grace. Canny wants to see him.'

Grace was looking worried as she turned to do his bidding. She walked away lurching heavily to the left, for she was lame. It seemed as if one leg was considerably shorter than the other.

Her father and his second wife Hester, a high-coloured woman with hair of flaming red, sat side by side at a round table in their small sitting room with their heads together and nodding in eager conversation. When Grace entered the room Hester was saying, 'But she's black. The Duke can't marry a black woman.'

Her husband quelled her with a glance and turned to ask his daughter, 'What do you want, my girl?'

She looked only at him and ignored the woman by his side. 'Joe Cannonball's downstairs. Mr Rutherford's sent for you. He wants you to go down to Havanah Court immediately.'

Elliot stood up rubbing his hands and pulling down the points of his waistcoat. 'I'll be down directly,' he instructed as he mentally totalled up the fees he was likely to earn over this affair. The thought made him rub his hands again. He rarely showed emotion but today he looked almost happy.

When Joe and the lawyer returned to Havanah Court, Canny was pacing the floor of his library, very concerned. 'What a problem, what a problem,' he exclaimed as soon as Elliot stepped through the door. 'I've never denied

30

Odilie a wish before – no matter how preposterous. I don't know what to do with her.'

Elliot looked patient. 'Start at the beginning. You've told her about the marriage idea, I presume.'

Canny nodded. 'And what a fuss she made! You'd think I'm trying to send her into a nunnery or something. She says she doesn't want to marry him. What am I going to do?'

Elliot walked up to Canny's desk and carefully aligned some pens on the blotter before he said, 'I did warn you that you should have spoken to her first. The letter has already been despatched by now. You've been very rash . . . but you were so certain she'd be pleased. What's her objection exactly?'

'She says he's bad-mannered and arrogant. And she says he's louche – where did she hear that word, I wonder? Martha's filled her head with all those stories about the maids at Sloebank Castle being scared of him.'

Elliot nodded. 'Hmm. True, I suppose, but not grounds for refusing an advantageous offer of marriage, or many of the men I know would remain bachelors for life. Tell her that matrimony changes men. Don't worry, she's at a foolish age when girls read stories and imagine themselves heroines. They dream about love but they grow out of it.'

Canny groaned, pointing with his head to the first floor. 'Odilie doesn't read novels, she prefers bloodstock books apparently. She won't listen to me. She's up there now weeping her heart out.'

Elliot frowned. 'Silly girl. It's a problem but you'll overcome it, I'm sure.'

'I'm almost ready to call the whole thing off,' said Canny, who'd faced up to more dangerous adversaries than the Duke in his time, 'The most I can lose is only ten thousand pounds, after all! Write again and say my letter was a mistake.'

Elliot stopped fiddling with the pens. 'Don't talk nonsense, man. What better marriage than this could you possibly get for the girl?'

'She says she doesn't want to be a Duchess.'

31

Elliot sighed heavily. 'Do you want me to speak to her? I can point out the advantages of this match better than you, perhaps.' He meant, she won't get round me so easily.

Canny brightened. 'You could try, but I don't think she'll listen to you. She's very strong-willed is my Odilie.'

The lawyer fixed his client with a steely eye. 'You should be more firm with her. Girls are not improved by soft handling. You're her father, you should tell her you know what's best for her. Stand by your decision about whom she's to marry and don't weaken. She'll come round in the end.'

But the other man's face was still doubtful. 'I don't like to see her upset,' he said.

'We'll all be upset and worse if she's allowed to play the fool. Let me handle this,' said Elliot and after a short discussion Canny agreed to remove himself while his lawyer interceded with Odilie alone.

The interview took place in the large salon where Odilie was sitting with her dog at her feet. There was a challenging look on her face when she watched the lawyer enter the room. It was very clear to him that this girl did not like him very much, but he decided to play her at her own game and kept his face expressionless as he carefully closed the double doors behind him, leaning back on the gilt handles as he did so. Then he stared hard at her. Neither of them spoke.

She was a beauty all right, and it was no surprise that the Duke had offered for her. For a moment Elliot wondered how many races had mingled their blood to create Odilie Rutherford. As he walked towards her however he was slightly intimidated by how stonily bleak and flat her eyes looked. It was as if she had dropped a shutter behind them in order to make it impossible for him to read her mind. She pointedly did not ask him to sit down but he took the initiative and said cordially, 'Good afternoon, Miss Rutherford,' as he pulled out a chair and settled himself in its cushioned depth.

She said nothing but let her hand drop as if for comfort

on to the head of the dog whose stare was as hostile as that of its mistress. Elliot felt rising anger that this chit of a girl was succeeding in discomfiting him and there was a cold note in his voice when he said, 'I imagine you know the object of my visit.'

She nodded and answered, 'Yes, I can guess why you're here.'

'Your father tells me that you're not happy about the marriage he's trying to arrange for you.'

She lifted her dark arched eyebrows. 'Should I be?' she asked.

'Indeed you should,' he told her as he looked levelly back.

'I've never met the man. I don't know if I want to marry him or not,' she protested.

'A meeting will be arranged. The Duke is as anxious for that as you. This is not a one-way contract. Both parties have to be satisfied.'

He detected a flush creeping into her golden cheeks and wondered if her vanity was affected by the thought that the Duke might reject her in the end. He decided to press that point. 'There's always the possibility that *he* may not wish to continue with the projected marriage, of course,' he told her.

The eyes that stared back at him were still totally enigmatic and it was impossible to tell whether his words had made her worried or hopeful. 'To please your father you should at least make no objections at this stage, not until we arrange a meeting anyway,' he pressed on.

She nodded and sighed. 'All right. Providing it's understood that I won't be forced into anything.'

Elliot continued implacably, 'I can't imagine your father forcing you over the most trivial matter. He is the most indulgent and fond parent I have ever encountered. Fond to a fault, I'd say.'

She did not reply to this and he went on, 'So, I can take it that you will meet the Duke? And that you understand this is not a frivolous matter, Miss Rutherford.'

She was rattled. 'It's far from being a frivolous matter for me, Mr Elliot.'

The lawyer permitted himself a wintry smile. 'I'm glad of that. It's a great honour and a compliment, you know, to have a man like the Duke of Maudesley even to consider an alliance with you. If you become a Duchess you'll have the world at your feet, for it's one of the highest positions in society, second only to royalty . . .' He sighed. 'You should be thankful to your father for his generosity on your behalf. The dowry is princely and he's trying to ensure a wonderful future for you. You're young, not yet old enough to appreciate the potential of this affair, but I predict that if you turn away from this opportunity you'll live to regret your hastiness. You'll repine for the rest of your life.'

Her eyes went wide as she stared at him, and for the first time they showed animation. 'But I don't love the Duke, and from what I hear I doubt if I ever will. He has a bad reputation.'

Elliot made an irritable gesture with his hands. 'Gossip! Gossip and envy, my dear girl. I've lived my whole life in this town and there have been three Dukes in my time. Nobody has had a good word to say about any of them. As for love, it's a delusion. When you're older you'll find that it only lasts a short time and when it's over people must live with the consequences of having yielded to it.'

A bleak note in his voice made the girl look into his face intently. When he saw that he had caught her interest he added, 'Your father knows your future's far too important to be wagered on the vagaries of *love*. In my experience it causes more harm than good.'

She shook her head in disbelief. 'But surely, even if you don't love someone you should at least like them a little before you enter into marriage with them? I know affection can grow into love between a couple but what if I don't even like this man? What if I actively dislike him?'

'On what basis? What could you know about him except what you've heard? All you must consider are the facts: he's a gentleman; he's not too old – barely forty;

34

he's been well-educated and has travelled widely. They say he was a little wild in his youth but most young bucks are the same. Besides, marriage changes men. So what are you afraid of? You're a strong-willed girl. You'll bring him to heel. No one would dare to ill-treat you.'

She stared at him, lips parted. This idea was obviously a new one to her. 'Ill-treat me? Good heavens, of course not! I never imagined anything like that.' No one had lifted a hand to Odilie in her entire life and few had even dared to scold her.

Elliot continued to reassure her. 'Your father has instructed me to make sure that any marriage contract to be drawn up on your behalf will be very rigorous. You'll have control of your own money. Your husband won't be able to squander it and if he leaves you, your future and your fortune will be safeguarded.'

She put a hand to her forehead. 'You're already thinking about what will happen if the marriage breaks down and we've not even met each other yet!'

'I'm employed to anticipate every eventuality,' said Elliot smoothly and triumphantly, feeling he was beginning to break her down.

While Andrew Elliot was in Havanah Court interceding with Odilie, his own daughter Grace was limping dejectedly around the dark kitchen of Viewhill House. The news Joe Cannonball had brought made her sad, because in the eight months since Odilie's return from school in London, the two girls, who were almost the same age, had become close friends. Although the circumstances of their lives were very different, they had taken to each other at once and Odilie's high spirits provided welcome frivolity and amusement for Grace, who had never been close to anyone with such a light-hearted attitude to life before.

If Odilie was to be married, however, their budding friendship would no longer be allowed to grow and Grace unhappily contemplated a return to her old loneliness. Before Odilie arrived she had not known what it was to have a companion or a confidante and she did not relish going back to that isolated state. She wondered who had been suggested as a husband for her friend. Her only hope was that Odilie's new home would not be too far away and they would be able to see each other from time to time.

Grace's position in the Elliot household was that of an unpaid servant. The only other domestic kept was a kitchen maid called Kelly who was half-witted and unable to tackle any task other than the simplest. It was impossible to entrust Kelly with a message or to tell her to do anything that required moving from one simple thought to another. She scrubbed floors and swept the step, carried coal and riddled the ashes but that was all. Everything else was done by Grace.

Walking slowly, the girl lifted a wooden bucket from behind the door and went out to fill it from the well at the basement area. When she stepped outside, the brilliance of the afternoon surprised her because the kitchen in which she spent much of her life was always dim and hardly any light came through its sunken little windows. She blinked in the sunlight and wiped her sweating brow with the back of her wrist as she stared over the garden wall to the meadows by the river where people were strolling or playing with their children.

Her heart was heavy as she lugged the bucket back into the stifling kitchen. Lifting a ladle, she scooped some water on to a wide deal table that stood in the middle of the floor. She had done this job hundreds of times before and as she worked she asked herself, 'Am I going to live like this forever? Oh, I'll be lonely without Odilie.' She took a cake of coarse yellow soap out of a drawer at the end of the table and rubbed it on to the wet wood before she began scrubbing, holding a stiff bristled brush in both hands and pushing it rhythmically to and fro, using the weight of her body to propel it over the table top.

The work was almost hypnotic and she became lost in it so did not hear steps on the stairs behind her or know anyone was there until the voice of her step-mother cut into her reverie, making her jump. 'Look, you've missed out that corner! See that you scrub it clean.'

Hester, sweating and dishevelled in a cotton gown that was crumpled because she'd been sleeping on the sofa while wearing it, stood behind Grace pointing at the far side of the table. There was an ill-natured scowl on her face as she began prowling the kitchen like a tigress looking for trouble.

'That grate needs blackleading,' she scolded, pausing beside the enormous open fireplace. Then she ran her finger along a stone shelf beside the sink. 'And this shelf's sticky. Scrub it too when you're at it. I don't know what you do down here. Idle your time away, I expect . . .'

Grace went on scrubbing without speaking, for long ago she had learned that it was safer to ignore Hester's bouts of bile and not answer back because that only brought worse trouble on her head. Although her face was impassive, however, her thoughts were chaotic. 'I hate you, Hester, how I hate you! Oh, what's going to happen to me? Will I have to live with this terrible woman forever?' she silently mourned to herself.

The sight of her submissively lowered head made a tide of cruelty rise in her tormentor. Hester had never liked her husband's daughter, although she had no reason for jealousy because Andrew Elliot was quite indifferent to the plight of the only child of his first marriage.

'You've missed out a bit,' she jeered again, pointing at another corner which was difficult for Grace to reach from where she was standing. Without protest the girl limped around the table with the scrubbing brush in her hand and cleaned the offending place. Goaded beyond endurance now, Hester looked around and then reached up for a bag of flour that stood on a shelf beside her. With her eyes fixed on Grace's face and wearing a teasing smile, she pulled open the neck of the bag and poured most of its contents into the middle of the table. Rubbing it in with her hand she said, 'Oh dear me, look what's happened! The bag must have burst.'

Grace stared bleakly at the grey mess in the middle of

the table but still said nothing. Then Hester turned around and grabbed a jar of jam from another shelf. Like a woman possessed she emptied its contents too into the floury paste and stirred it around with her fingers. 'I'm so careless,' she exulted. 'Look what I've done. Clean it up, cripple.'

With difficulty Grace fought against an impulse to burst into tears but when she blinked her eyes the tearfulness passed and instead of feeling ill-done by, she was suddenly filled with anger and burned to scream in fury, to sweep all the china off the shelves and stamp the pieces into the stone flags of the floor before attacking Hester with a carving knife. She tightened her fists into knuckles and had to fight to retain her composure, knowing that if she did let her temper loose, it would only end with a beating for her because Hester was bigger and stronger than the girl. When her stepmother finally flounced away, Grace scrubbed the table clean again and swept the debris from the floor. Then she heard her father come back. The front door banged, and his footsteps crossed the floor of the room above her head where she knew Hester was sitting. A few minutes later she heard him calling her name. 'Grace! Where are you, Grace?'

She stopped working and stared apprehensively at the kitchen doorway. What did he want? Had Hester been complaining about her again? She was even more afraid of her father's wrath than of Hester's and she stiffened as she listened to his footsteps in the passage. The kitchen door swung open and to her relief he sounded almost friendly when he said, 'Oh, there you are. Go upstairs and tidy yourself. I want you to go down to Havanah Court and have a word with Rutherford's daughter. Go and talk some sense into the silly girl.'

Grace was genuinely astonished at being given a commission by her usually indifferent father. 'Hester told me to do this before I went out,' she protested.

'Don't worry about that just now. Kelly can do it. Go to Havanah Court straight away. The girl's more likely to listen to someone of her own age. Tell her how fortunate she is to have such a good marriage arranged for her.'

It was news to Grace that Odilie might object to any alliance and her head was in a whirl. 'Why should she listen to me? Who's she going to marry?' she asked in a bemused way.

Her father frowned as if she was being completely stupid. 'The Duke's made an offer for her and her father's as good as accepted. Now the stupid girl's sticking her toes in. When she sees you, she'll realise how lucky she is.' He waved a hand at his daughter and she flushed scarlet because she knew what he meant. She was to be used as an object lesson for rebellious Odilie who needed reminding of her blessings.

Half an hour later Grace was shown into Havanah Court by a solemn-looking Joe Cannonball. She found her friend walking up and down the boudoir carpet with Scamp clasped in her arms. The dog's brown and white fur was wet where she had laid her face. When Grace appeared Odilie cried out, 'Have you heard the news? Have they told you?'

'My father said something about you getting married to the Duke,' gasped Grace, half in disbelief.

Her dark-haired friend groaned, 'What's the honour in being a Duchess when the Duke looks like a fat warthog?'

Remembering her father's instructions, Grace demurred, 'He's not as bad as that.'

Odilie grimaced furiously. 'Not you too, Grace! He *is* as bad as that. In fact he's worse, everyone says he's horrible. But in spite of that, they don't think I've any grounds for objecting. All they consider is *rank*. It wouldn't matter to them if he had a tail with a fork at the end as long as he was a Duke. It makes me so angry. If he told the people in this stupid town to lie down in a line so that he could walk on top of them, they'd do it.'

'Lauriston people aren't the only ones like that,' said Grace.

'I don't suppose they are, but it's idiotic. Because he comes from the right family he can do no wrong. Even my father's impressed because he's offered for me, and I thought he had more sense. I can't believe it. I can't believe this is happening to me, Grace.'

'But you're really very lucky. Your father only wants the best for you. He's so kind to you. You'll be a Duchess, imagine that! You'll go to Court and have a house in London . . .' protested Grace.

'Surely you wouldn't want to marry him, Gracie?' asked Odilie.

'No Duke's ever going to offer for me. Nobody is,' sighed the other girl.

'My dear, I'm sorry. I'm being selfish thinking about myself all the time.' Odilie grasped her friend's hand. 'It's just that I can't think of anything except how terrible this all is. The idea of marrying him makes me go as cold as ice, and yet everybody – even you – is saying that I should. I'm so angry at my father that I simply will not speak to him. He's running around frantic.' A faint smile appeared on her face as she said this.

Grace sat down on the day bed and said softly, 'I was sent down here to persuade you to do what they want but I wouldn't if I didn't think that you're really very lucky. When you're a Duchess you'll be able to do what you like. You'll be rich and you'll be free. High society marriages aren't like ordinary ones. Dukes and Duchesses can go their own way. If you want, you'll be able to take a lover. No one'll worry about it.'

Odilie stared at her friend with amusement glimmering in her eyes. 'Listen to you advising me to take a lover before I'm even married! For shame, Miss Elliot!'

Grace smiled too, happy that Odilie was beginning to brighten. 'Make a bargain with the Duke – I've read of such things in stories,' she suggested but Odilie was solemn again.

'I don't want a marriage like that, Grace. I'd want to love my husband, really love him – but perhaps that only happens in books as well.'

The girls were interrupted at this point by the arrival of the tea tray, followed by Martha who surveyed her niece with a critical but loving eye and asked, 'Are you feeling calmer? Your father's up to high doh about you.'

'I hope it's his conscience that's bothering him,' said Odilie smartly.

'That's not fair. You ken fine he dotes on you.' Martha might be hard on Canny when they were together but she brooked no criticism of him from anyone else, not even from her dear niece who became contrite at once.

'Sorry, Aunt Martha. It's just that I'm so upset. I've been telling Grace about it.'

Martha looked at the other girl and asked, 'And what do you think about all this, Grace?'

The blonde girl looked down at her feet. 'I think Odilie's been offered a great opportunity, but I understand how she feels. It's not very romantic, is it?'

Martha bustled over to the tray and poured tea from a silver pot into fragile cups, handing one to each girl before she said, 'What's romantic got to do with it? You girls read too many books. She'll have to marry somebody some day and her father thinks it might as well be a Duke.'

Her niece stared at her in disappointment. 'Oh, Aunt Martha, I thought you'd be on my side in this. You don't like the Duke much, do you?'

'I've nothing against him,' said the older woman in a neutral tone.

Odilie gasped, 'That's strange. Only last week you were telling me about how he chased all the maids in Sloebank Castle. And you always say how ugly he is. When I think about having children by a man like that I feel sick!'

Martha sipped her tea. 'Huh, the idea of having anybody's children makes some women feel sick. Anyway, you mightn't have to put up with him for long. He's a Fox and they're not a long-lived family.'

'He's only forty. He could live for years and years,' said Odilie hopelessly.

'Oh, not all that long. What you should do is have a son as soon as possible. Then you'll know you won't have to put up with him forever.

41

There'll be a time limit on it,' said Martha mysteriously.

Both girls stared at her and it was Grace who asked, 'What do you mean, Miss Rutherford?'

'Don't you know the story, Grace? I thought everybody knew it. There's a curse on the Fox family. If Odilie has a son within a year of marriage, she'll be a widow well before she's forty.'

'Why?' the girls chorused together.

'Because none of the heads of that family have ever lived to see their sons reach the age of twenty-one. In fact, most of them die when the laddies are still bairns. It's because of the curse.'

Odilie's eyes snapped with interest. She had been brought up by black servants who practised voodoo and had knowledge of curses and magic, so belief in the black arts had been instilled in her early. 'What curse?' she asked her aunt. 'Tell me.'

Martha folded her hands in her pinafored lap and said, 'I'll tell you if you don't go talking about it outside. None of the Foxes like it to be discussed and little wonder! It must be hard living with a curse like that on you.'

'We won't. Go on,' cried the girls.

'Well, when the monks were being driven out of the abbey over there, it was a Fox who led the attackers and an old woman living in the town cursed him for sacrilege. She said he and his descendants would never see their sons reach majority – and none of them has. Not one of them!'

The girls stared at each other and Grace gave a superstitious shiver but Odilie was quite brisk as she said, 'Even if it's true, twenty years is a long time. Too long, I think. I still don't want to marry him.'

Odilie had a resilient nature however and could never remain melancholy for long. After they had taken tea, she rose and told her friend, 'It's a beautiful evening and it's not going to do any good sitting here worrying about this marriage business. Come with me for a walk in the gardens.' It was obvious that she wanted a heart to heart

42

chat with her friend, away from Martha's ears and taking Grace by the elbow, she guided her out of the room and downstairs to the stone terrace which was glowing and still warm in the radiance of the setting sun.

When they were seated side by side on a bench gazing over the river towards the road on its south bank, Odilie sighed, 'Isn't life strange? This morning I was so carefree. I'd no idea what was going to happen to me.'

Grace smiled. 'Some people might think what's happened is wonderful. You'll be envied by every unmarried woman in the countryside. Aren't you ambitious, Odilie?'

The other girl shook her dark head. 'I can't be, can I? I just keep imagining that man as my husband. He's not what I dreamed of at all.'

'But you've not met him yet and you don't love anyone else, do you?' asked Grace.

Odilie shook her head. 'Oh no, nothing like that. If I did I'd be fighting even harder than I am. It's just that I've dreams – you must have dreams too, Grace.' She turned towards her friend and saw with a pang of remorse how Grace's face changed again. Care seemed to cloak her once more.

'I'm too plain to be married,' said Grace.

'That's nonsense. You're a very pretty girl,' protested Odilie with a rush of sympathy.

Grace shook her head silently and Odilie studied her, seeing a tall girl, five foot six at least, and thin – too thin, she thought as she saw how starkly her friend's collarbone showed inside the scooped neck of her cheap cotton dress. Grace's skin was palely translucent and her fine boned face was dominated by large, well-shaped eyes of a striking shade of blue enhanced by fringes of long lashes. It was her hair however that was her greatest glory – a mass of palest gold which she wore knotted tightly at the nape of her neck without artifice or conceit. The trouble was that her delicacy and style were not immediately noticed because of her timidity and acute awareness of being crippled.

'You shouldn't be so sad and retiring. You're really

43

very pretty,' Odilie told her friend again in a firm voice but Grace only flushed.

'Don't tease me,' she said shortly.

'I'm not teasing. I wouldn't be so stupid. Your hair's beautiful. It's such a wonderful colour and your skin's like cream. You should stop worrying about your limp. It's not nearly as bad as you imagine and when you're nervous you make it worse. Besides, everybody has something about themselves that they want to change. Did I ever tell you how the girls at that awful school called me names and said I was dirty because of my colour?'

Grace stared at her friend in genuine surprise for she thought of Odilie with the same awe and admiration that she would have given to a princess in a fairy tale. The idea that anyone could find fault with such a paragon was unthinkable. 'But your colour's glorious. You look as if you've been dusted with gold,' she protested.

It was true. The rays of the setting sun made Odilie glow as if she was burnished.

'I've been called a negro, a black, a half-caste and worse. It hurts. When they meet me for the first time some people either look embarrassed or laugh – as if I'm a joke. I hate that most of all,' she said bitterly.

'Oh, Odilie, I'm sorry. I know how you feel. When I see people looking at my leg, I burn up inside. It doesn't matter if they're sorry for me or if they only dismiss me as a cripple, the hurt's the same. Isn't life cruel? Sometimes I wish I was dead,' Grace said in a rush. It was the first time she had felt able to unburden herself of her feelings about her lameness to another person.

Tremendous sympathy engulfed Odilie, who realised with a chastening shock that even in the midst of her own troubles, there was always a little inner island of hope and happiness in her heart to console her. Even if she had to marry the Duke, she'd still be Odilie Rutherford who'd been surrounded with love from her earliest day and it would never occur to her to wish herself dead. Hurriedly she took Grace's hand and whispered, 'Oh, no, my dear, not that. You don't mean that.'

44

Tears glittered in Grace's eyes as she nodded and said firmly, 'I do, Odilie. I've thought about it often. What is there for me to look forward to? I'm crippled and I'm poor. I'm alone in this world, quite alone, for no one loves me and no one ever will – except you, that is. I've no dowry so I won't get married and I'll have to stay in that dark house with Hester who hates me until one or other of us dies. It might as well be me and as soon as possible.'

'Hester's cruel to you, isn't she?' asked Odilie, who had always suspected that Grace's life at home was miserable although this was the first time the other girl had actually talked about it.

Grace's face was bleak as she nodded. 'She goes out of her way to make my life a misery and always has. If I annoy her she beats me or locks me up, with only water and dry bread to eat – she's often left me for two days at a time. Sometimes I don't even know what I've done to offend her. If any of the other children do something wrong, she finds a reason to take the whip to me. If I did die no one would miss me. I sometimes think I must be a really hateful person because no one – not even my father – likes me.'

Odilie was urgent in her protestations of reassurance. 'But I like you, I like you very much. Don't I matter? You mustn't say such terrible things.'

Grace was inconsolable, however. 'Perhaps you're only sorry for me because I'm pathetic and crippled. The nice young man who helped me over the bridge at the Fair last year felt the same. He was sorry for me, too. I could see it in his eyes.'

'What young man?' asked Odilie curiously.

'Oh, just a man who helped me when I nearly fell on the bridge last year. It was so embarrassing . . . I really wished I was dead then.'

Odilie grasped her friend's hand firmly. 'Don't talk like that. You're a lovely girl, and a sweet person. I like you very much. Martha likes you, she's told me she does. She says Hester's hard on you because she isn't your real

45

mother and is jealous. I expect you remind her that your father loved another woman before her.'

Grace shook her head. 'I can't imagine Father ever loving anyone. He knows what Hester does to me and he doesn't care a fig or try to stop her.'

Odilie looked shocked. 'Isn't there someone else in your family you can talk to about Hester? Haven't you any relations on your mother's side?'

Grace shook her head. 'No, I don't think so. I used to be taken by an old maidservant to visit my grandfather but that stopped when I was about eight – he died then, I think. I remember him very vaguely and I seem to remember my mother too, or perhaps I only dream about her. I think she used to sing to me.'

'What happened to her?' asked Odilie.

Grace shook her head. 'That's just it – I don't know. She must have died when I was small because Hester's been my father's wife for as long as I can remember. I asked Father about my mother once and he was very angry. He shouted at me and said that I wasn't to mention her ever again. I didn't even know what her name was until a few months ago when I found an old Bible in our house with her signature in it. Now I know she was called Lucy Allen but absolutely nothing else about her.'

Odilie was genuinely astonished. 'But this is Lauriston! This is a town where everybody knows everybody else's business. There must be somebody who remembers your mother and your grandfather. If you were eight when he died, that's only ten years ago – yesterday, as far as this town's concerned.

Grace's brows furrowed. 'I know, but if I ask about my mother, people go strange. We used to have a maid called Jessie – she was the one who took me to see my grandfather and I'm sure my father and Hester didn't know what she was doing – but even Jessie would go all silent if I wanted to know about my mother. She's dead now so I can't ask her any longer.'

Odilie sat up straight on the bench and announced, 'I know what to do. Aunt Martha's always talking about things that happened forty or fifty years ago as if it was yesterday. I'll ask her about your mother. She's sure to know all about her because she's lived in the town since she was born and she has a memory like an elephant's. I'll do that when you've gone home and I'll tell you exactly what she says. Now come on, cheer up. We came out here to make ourselves feel better, not worse! Look over there at all those people. What do you think they're doing?' She pointed across the river to where a large group of men could be seen straggling along the road heading for the Rennie bridge.

Grace gazed out too, shading her eyes against the sun with her hand. 'Oh, that's the carpenters,' she said.

'What are they doing over there all in a bunch?' asked Odilie.

'They're building a wooden footbridge across the Tweed from the Cobby to the field where the Fair's held. They do it every year and then people pay a penny to cross it because it's a short cut into the fairground.'

Odilie was interested. 'Of course! I'd forgotten about this famous Fair that everybody's talking about. It must be a wonderful event.'

Grace smiled. 'Oh yes, it is. Everybody goes. Even my father takes a day off work. People come from all over the Border country, from the Cheviot Hills and the Yarrow Valley, from Selkirk and Melrose and Lauder. They even come up from England and foreign parts.'

Her eyes were shining again as she spoke and Odilie laughed. 'At least the thought of it cheers you up. Are you meeting a beau there or something? Maybe the fellow you met last year!'

Grace shook her head, embarrassed again. 'Of course not! But I like the Fair because of the crowds and the excitement. People are always in such a good mood – at least till night-time when the gypsies start fighting. You'll love the Fair, Odilie, because there's all sorts of stalls and sideshows, medicine sellers and pedlars with velvet and lace for sale and fortune-tellers and a circus.'

'When is it? We'll go together,' Odilie declared.

'It begins at noon next Monday but your father might not want you to go – it can be rowdy.'

Odilie smiled ruefully. 'My father won't dare to try and stop me doing anything. I've got him in my pocket over this marriage. You and I will go to the Fair and enjoy ourselves. It may be the last time I can go out as an ordinary girl.'

By this time the carpenters had reached the end of the bridge and it was possible to see that there were about twenty of them, some carrying tools and others with leather aprons looped up around their waists. As they drew nearer the girls could hear that they were singing as they tramped along and Grace held up a finger while she told her friend, 'Listen, Odilie, they're singing the Fair song . . .'

Odilie cocked her head slightly to catch the sounds that came floating over the water. The tune was catchy, like the music for a country dance, and she strained her ears to hear the words.

> '*St James' Fair, St James' Fair,*
> *I'll be there, Oh, I'll be there,*
> *Tae see my lass wi' the curling hair.*'

The men sang the short refrain over and over again, their voices rising up in the gathering dusk. Odilie repeated the lyric to Grace who nodded and smiled, 'That's right, that's it. You've got it. St James' Fair is said to be a wonderful place for lovers meeting.'

When evening was well advanced, Grace left for home and Odilie went back into the house where she sought out her aunt who she found mending a pair of Canny's silk stockings. He could well afford to buy new ones when they laddered and he probably would not wear mended ones anyway but the old habits of thrift were too deeply ingrained for Martha to give them up.

Odilie sat down beside her aunt and lifted a skein of silk, running it gently through her fingers as she sighed. 'Poor Grace, she's so unhappy. It makes me ashamed of moaning about my own situation when I hear what she has to put up with . . .'

'And what's that?' asked Martha, stitching away.

'That father and step-mother of hers. They sound dreadful.'

'I hope it makes you appreciate your own father then,' said Martha in a reproving tone.

Odilie nodded. 'I do, really. I know he's only in favour of this marriage plan because he loves me, but . . . I'm not going to argue that all again, Aunt Martha. It's Grace I want to talk about. I wish I could help her.'

'I doubt if there's much you can do except to be her friend,' was Martha's advice.

'Hasn't she any family? When we were walking in the garden she told me about her mother,' Odilie ventured and was rewarded by seeing that Martha's needle faltered but her voice was still level as she replied noncommittally, 'Did she?'

Although she was disappointed by this lack of encouragement from her aunt who usually loved to gossip, Odilie pressed on, 'She said she knows hardly anything about her mother and can't find anything out. Would you believe that no one had even told her what her mother's name was but she found it written in an old Bible. Her father's very secretive about it all, apparently.'

Martha knew that she was being pumped. 'Her mother's name was Lucy Allen,' she snapped shortly.

'Yes, Grace knows that now but she's longing for more information. I said I'd ask you because you may know something about Lucy Allen.'

'I knew her by sight but she was much younger than me,' said Martha.

'Tell me about her. What did she look like? Was she a local girl?' This is like drawing teeth, thought Odilie.

'She was born and brought up at a place called Bettymill, a mill by the Tweed along the road to Maxton.'

'That's interesting. Grace doesn't know that. Is there anything else?' Odilie persisted.

'There's naething much to tell.' Martha stood up and

started gathering the mending together as if she was anxious to make her escape but her niece put out a hand to detain her.

'I don't believe you, Aunt Martha. I've never known you without something to tell, even about the most uninteresting people. For instance, you haven't told me what she looked like.'

Martha sat down again and sighed, 'Grace has a great look of Lucy. She was tall, too, and she had the same kind of hair – yellow and curly, the kind lads like.'

'Yes, Grace's hair's her prettiest feature. Was her mother pretty? Maybe it's because she reminds him of her mother that her father's so hard on her. Maybe he still mourns her.' Odilie was delighted that she was getting somewhere at last.

'I doubt if he mourns Lucy,' said Martha in a hard voice.

'Why?'

'Because Elliot's no' the sort to mourn anybody – and because . . . Oh, let it be, Odilie. It's a sad story.'

Odilie, however, was deeply interested by now and scented a mystery. 'Oh, please tell me more. If there's anything Grace shouldn't know I won't tell her.'

But Martha was looking grim. 'Like I said, let it be, Odilie. Some things are best left alone – anyway, there's nothing to tell. Grace's mother was called Lucy Allen and her father was old David Allen, the miller at Bettymill. She was his only child, a very bonny lassie with bright yellow hair and a laughing face. She's dead now. She's been dead a long time.'

There was something so very chilling about the way the last words were spoken that Odilie was sobered. 'When did she die?' she asked softly.

'Long ago. I don't remember.'

'What did she die of?'

'She died because she had another bairn after Grace.'

'Like my mother! She died of childbed fever, too.'

'No, not like that exactly – it wasn't childbed fever. But she died just the same,' and Martha would be detained no longer but scuttled off, determined to bring the conversation to an end. She left behind a niece puzzling over her aunt's strange behaviour. Any chance of following Martha and pressing home her advantage was removed by Canny, who came in brandishing a letter that carried an enormous green wax seal.

'It's from the Duke,' he told her. 'He wants us to go to dinner at Sloebank Castle on Friday night. He has a party of friends up there for the Fair. It's a very civil letter, Odilie.' He held it out to her to read but she brushed it away.

'I don't want to read it. I suppose you're going to accept anyway. I can only hope that if I don't pass muster, if my table manners are bad or if I burp or pass wind perhaps he'll send me packing.'

She saw the look of consternation on her father's face at this and was immediately contrite, adding, 'Oh, don't worry. I won't do anything like that.'

Canny assured her, 'I never imagined you would,' but in secret he wouldn't put it past his wayward daughter to behave like a hoyden in order to escape this marriage.

'Didn't you? Wait and see,' she teased wickedly. 'But remember, though I'll go to this dinner with you, if I don't like him, if he doesn't suit me, I'll turn him down. Goodnight, Papa.' And she swept from the room leaving him staring forlornly after her.

CHAPTER 3

Thursday, 30 July.

The sun rose from a bank of clouds like someone rising from bed and rubbing his eyes. The first light glimmered over the roofs of the town and gilded them with gold. Birds rustled in their night-time roosts and then, in a burst, they began singing a glorious chorus. The sound wakened a sleeper in a curtained bed in the fine house overlooking the river. He turned on his side and slowly came back to wakefulness. As soon as light began creeping through the bedroom window, Canny Rutherford pulled his watch off its hook on the wall behind his head and consulted its face. It was still only a quarter to six and there were two hours to endure, alone with his troubled thoughts, before breakfast-time. He was worried, anxious in his mind; not in the blissful state that he should have been with his daughter on the verge of marrying a Duke.

'Elliot's right – I shouldn't be so lenient with her,' he told himself crossly. 'I ought to tell her what she must do and then she should do it.' But then he remembered he was dealing with Odilie, who made up for her lack of stature by spirit and dogged determination. He had always indulged her and hated to see her unhappy. When she wept, as she did when thwarted, each tear had the power to scald his soul.

By half-past six he had decided that the loss of ten thousand pounds was endurable. By seven o'clock he'd changed his mind again. The girl didn't realise the value of the opportunity he was handing to her. As the birds outside his window poured out their morning orisons, he decided that for her own sake Odilie must be persuaded to go through with it. He also decided that he'd buy her a new horse, for horses were her chief passion and she

52

had recently been agitating about a mare that was for sale near Coldstream. It could jump like a cat, apparently. If he was as tender-hearted as Elliot said, he'd probably buy the mare and anything else she wanted to soften the disappointment of having to agree to a loveless but socially advantageous marriage.

Lying back against his pillows, Canny rehearsed how to be firm with Odilie; he thumped one fist into the open palm of the other hand emphatically as he prepared what he was going to say to her: 'It's your duty to do this. You'll be a Duchess, dammit.' Hold that idea, he thought. Hold it and persist in it. Don't weaken even if diamond tears begin to slide down her cheeks. Above all, don't weaken!

When shafts of sunlight falling across his bed told him morning had fully come at last, he jumped up, threw on his clothes and hurried down to the stableyard where Stevens the head groom and his small army of stable lads were bustling about.

'Stevens, get yourself over to Coldstream and buy that mare you were telling my daughter about. I don't care what it costs but don't come back without it,' said Canny shortly.

The birds also wakened His Grace the Duke of Maudesley, whose Christian name was James. He got up and stood in his nightshirt in front of the empty fireplace of his vast bedroom in Sloebank Castle, yawning and stretching his arms above his head as he looked at his favourite picture, a Zoffany painting of a cockfight in the court of an Indian prince. My word, he thought as he did every morning, there's a lot going on in that picture. The chap who painted it knew a bit about cockfighting.

Crowds of natives in long robes and tightly wound turbans were watching British officers in the colourful uniforms of the East India Company Army as they matched their fighting cock against the bird of an Indian prince. The detail was excellent and the Duke, who was a keen enthusiast of cockfighting himself, always found something new to examine in the scene. He liked to imagine the progress of the fight that followed – the excited shouting of the men, the noise of scraping in the dust as the cocks clawed the ground, the furious beating of their wings and the ripping sound of their beaks as they tore each other apart. Most of all he liked to imagine the smell of blood in the sawdust.

In the bed behind him a girl stirred and sat up against the pillows. Her hair was tangled and her eyes looked bleak as she stared at him. He didn't even know her name and had not enough interest to find it out. 'Get out,' he said shortly, and gestured to the door. She gathered up her shift and ran naked for the doorway. He watched her plump thighs and round little belly go without regret or sympathy. If he saw her later carrying hot water to the guest bedrooms he wouldn't even recognise her.

When she had disappeared, he walked over to the window and pulled aside the long brocade curtain. The lawns were sparkling with dew in the sunlight and on their far expanse he could see a young man wandering about. He leaned forward and stared a little harder before he recognised Playfair, the young architect, out there dreaming of building a new castle no doubt. The Duke smiled and felt exhilarated by the awareness of his privi-ledged status in life. Sometimes he found it difficult to believe that he, a younger son who had been born with no prospects except to join the Army and look for a rich heiress to marry, had actually inherited a Dukedom – and now the dark-skinned little beauty with a dowry as big as a treasure trove had come along for him. Good thing I didn't marry any of those women in the past, he thought to himself. His brother, the last Duke, never married but that was because he was afraid of the curse. He thought he'd avoid it by staying single, poor fool, but witches' curses meant little to James.

He'd marry and take his chance – a nice chance, too, with a dowry of a quarter of a million and more to come. Until now there had not been enough money to live the life he wanted but then he'd seen Miss Rutherford, the rich merchant's daughter – from a distance it was true –

but even if the girl was cross-eyed or half-witted, he'd still marry her.

With a happy look on his face, he stared across the rolling acres of his park towards the gleam of the River Tweed making its peaceful way through his green meadows. Water brought this to me, he thought. His brother had drowned while boating in Italy and if that wasn't the hand of Fate he didn't know what was. He'd never expected to be possessed of such power as he now enjoyed.

From the window he could see piles of planks in a distant field. They were for the Fair footbridge, of course. It was a damned nuisance having crowds of people and tents over on the meadow facing his house and spoiling his view every year, but it was only for a short time and it brought in money; nearly ten thousand was expected this year if the fine weather held. During the French Wars, takings at the Fair had dropped but now peace had come again and commerce was thriving. It was worth putting up with a few days' inconvenience for ten thousand pounds. James Fox rubbed his hands and turned back into the room, planning how to spend the revenue – on some good bloodstock, clutch of fighting cocks and a stock of claret for the cellar he thought.

When he was dressed and breakfasted he went down to where young Playfair was still staring along the river towards the town of Lauriston. Soft curls of pale greyish-blue woodsmoke were rising from its chimneys, showing that preparations were being made for the cooking of many breakfasts there.

'Good morning, your Grace. I've been thinking that your new house should look towards the south,' said Playfair in an eager voice. He was a keen-faced young fellow in his early twenties, so keen that even at this time of day he carried a large roll of drawings in his hand.

'Damned right. I don't want to see their chimneys. I'd move the whole town out of sight if I could. One of my ancestors shifted a village out of the park, but it'd be more difficult to move a town!' The Duke gave a short bark of a laugh when he spoke but his expression remained heavy and unattractive. His mouth was tiny and red, pursed as if he was perpetually displeased while his skin was sallow and his body, though tall, was ponderous and ill-proportioned with a broad chest, a protruding belly and awkward legs. To Playfair his manner was discourteous and disdainful, as it always was with anyone he considered his social inferior – which was almost everyone else on the earth.

The architect however was unabashed. 'I've made some drawings for the new façade . . .' he said, unrolling the top sheet of plans and laying them down on a stone balustrade at the end of a grass-grown terrace where they fluttered slightly in a mild breeze coming up from the river on the valley floor.

'Let's see.' The Duke snatched a sheet and studied it for a long time while the other man anxiously watched his face. If the plan for rebuilding Sloebank came to fruition, it would be William Playfair's first major architectural commission, and a ducal client would make his future secure.

When the verdict was delivered it was not unfavourable. 'It'll do, I suppose. At least it looks more like a proper castle than the place does now, but it ought to be bigger. Give it another two wings, one on each side, and put more of those little turret things along the top. I like them.'

Playfair looked doubtful. 'Don't you think more turrets might be a little excessive?' he asked.

'Nonsense – what do you mean? Nothing's excessive for a Duke.'

'Of course not, but the cost of two more wings will be very high.'

Playfair was having a sore task in being paid for the plans he had already prepared. Sometimes he wondered if all his work would earn him as much as a penny piece in the end. Yet he laboured on because the honour of building a new castle, especially one in such a wonderful setting, could only be good for his reputation and would bring in shoals of other clients not so sticky about paying.

'You chaps are always on about money,' said the Duke testily, 'but don't worry. I've had a windfall. Look in at the factor's office on your way out and he'll let you have something on account. Then get to work and build me the biggest and best castle in the country. I want more windows, more turrets, more salons, more marble, more plasterwork and more carving than anywhere else. I want a place that'll be the wonder of everyone who sees it. Go to it, Playfair! That place over there isn't good enough for me now.' He waved a hand back at the old house, a grey-coloured, four-square Georgian mansion which, albeit only seventy years old, had been allowed to become delapidated and streaked with damp slime that stained the pillars of the front entrance like wreaths of falling seaweed. 'It's too damned plain,' announced the Duke, surveying his ancestral home.

Playfair made noises of agreement but he could not honestly condemn outright the work of the man who had designed it and was regarded as the master of Scottish architecture. He had to say, 'It has a good line, though, sir. William Adam knew his business.'

The Duke was not so discriminating. 'It's too ordinary. Everybody has a place like it. Adam built half the big houses in Scotland and they all look the same to me. Even Rutherford, that merchant down in the town, has a finer place than I do now. It's not right. It's time I had a proper castle. You're lucky to get this commission, Play-fair.'

The young man agreed. 'I know that, your Grace. Don't worry, I'll build you a house fit for Oberon.'

The Duke looked quizzically at him but eventually decided the fellow was harmless and stumped off indoors leaving Playfair alone gazing down the slope of hill towards the River Tweed. His heart was singing with delight at the opportunity that had been given to him. What a magnificent site for a house! He would build it on the level part of the breast of a hill and surround it at the back with a park full of fine trees, but there must be nothing in front to hide his façade which would be viewed

57

best from the other side of the river. He closed his eyes and imagined it – the lines of windows, surmounted by fairy turrets, extended wings, pillars and porticos, shaded walks and stately rooms.

He stared across the Tweed to a long rolling meadow dotted with fine trees and noticed what a fine view would obtain from the salon windows. On the horizon before him rose a spectacular mound topped by the crumbling ruins of an ancient fortification which he knew to be the castle of Roxburgh. It stared down over meadows and the river. No finer setting could be imagined for his projected mansion for it had everything the romantic imagination required – rural peace, trees, water, grazing cows, romantic ruins and mystery. Nothing he'd seen on his travels through France or Italy could match it. He rubbed his hands together, knowing that his name would be famous forever if he succeeded in building the residence to harmonize with this lovely setting.

As he gazed over the lawns to the river, Playfair suddenly noticed with disquiet the huge pile of planks. He panicked – Surely there were no plans to build anything there? This threat of disruption to his idyllic setting upset him, and he turned on his heel to hurry off towards the kitchens where he had made friends who provided him with all the gossip from the Duke's household. He quickly found the butler and pointed down towards the meadow as he asked urgently, 'What's going on over there? Surely they're not building something, are they? They can't. It'll spoil the view from the new house that I'm planning.'

The butler laughed. 'Ock, dinna fash yersel', Mester Playfair. It's only the bridge for the Fair. It's held over there in that field every year and carpenters from the town build a bridge across. Folk from the town pay a penny to cross it – it's a short cut.'

Playfair asked anxiously, 'Do they take it down again when the Fair's finished?'

The answer was a nod. 'Of course they do.'

'I'm surprised the Duke allows it. It's facing his house and it spoils the view,' said the architect fussily.

The servant pulled a face. 'No Duke'll ever stop the Fair and couldn't even if he wanted to, because it's been going on far longer than the Foxes have been around. It's been over there since before the time of the monks. That big field used to be a town: the King had a palace in it and hundreds of folk lived there.'

Playfair walked to the kitchen door and stared across the river to the empty meadow that stretched for about a quarter of a mile along the river bank. It was fairly flat for most of its length except for one bit of sharply rising ground topped by a cluster of trees at the far end. The young architect had a lively imagination and the notion of a vanished town lying beneath the green turf intrigued him. His eyes were full of interest as he turned back and exclaimed, 'What happened to the town? Was it the one that a former Duke had moved away?'

The butler shrugged. 'No, that was later. Roxburgh was abandoned and everything fell doon. Only the castle's left and it's falling down too, but the Fair's still going on in the same place.'

'When does it start? How long does it last?' Playfair had intended to return to Edinburgh soon but the idea of visiting such an ancient event took his fancy.

The butler told him, 'It aye starts on the first Monday of August – that's next Monday. In my father's time it used to last for eight days but now it's only about two. Folk start moving on by Tuesday. Even the gypsies don't hang about either because the townspeople don't like them.'

The mention of gypsies intrigued the young romantic from the city. He raised his eyebrows and asked, 'Do many gypsies come?'

'In their hundreds,' was the none too enthusiastic reply. 'They flood in from far and near, the thieving buggers. We've to lock up everything that's movable, even the buckets. They bring some fine horses, though. Folk come to the Fair specially to buy horses from them.'

'I could do with a new horse,' mused Playfair, remembering the Duke's promise to give him money on account. 'I think I'll stay in Lauriston a little longer and visit the Fair.'

The rising excitement in the town was palpable as Playfair walked along Roxburgh Street on his way back to his lodgings in the Cross Keys Inn overlooking the square. An unusually large amount of traffic was wending its way down the road beside him – carts loaded high with sacks and bundles; carriages with ladies and gentlemen riding inside them; dust-stained travellers walking with the stride of people accustomed to covering long distances. Many of them were pedlars who carried tall staves in their hands and bore oddly shaped bundles on their backs. All this, Playfair realised, was the first eddies of the tide of humanity that would flood into town for the Fair.

The inn was packed when he walked in and the din was deafening. All the local gossips knew who he was and had long ago found out what he was doing in Lauriston. One or two looked knowing when they saw him and an old man called Cunningham raised a hand in greeting and called out, 'How's the Duke taking to getting married, then?'

Playfair rustled the banknotes in his pocket and grinned. 'I didn't know he was getting married but he's in good mood right enough. Who's the bride?'

The men around him all spoke at once. 'It's Canny Rutherford's lassie!' Cunningham leaned over to say in confidential tone, 'I grew up wi' Canny. Didnae have anything in his belly in those days, as shilpit as a gutted herring and white-faced as a bogle. You'd never think he'd grow into the big braw-looking man he is the day and you'd never dream his daughter would be marrying a Duke. It just goes to show it's a funny old world, doesn't it?'

Playfair was interested, for he wondered what sort of woman would become the mistress of the fine mansion he planned to build on the top of the hill. He hoped she would be a woman of discrimination for it would be hard to create a palace and have to walk away from it, knowing that the people who lived there were not able to appreciate what he had done. 'What's the girl like?' he asked, and a positive burst of comments surrounded him but the one he first heard was a hoarse whisper at his ear, 'She's bleck.'

'What?' The surprise made him choke on his beer.

The answer was repeated more loudly. 'She's bleck, she's a blackamoor. Her mother was a native of some place or other. It's costing her father a pretty penny to get the Duke to marry her.'

Playfair's face took on a dazzled look for he was a romantic young man and the idea of a poor man's black daughter catching the eye of a Duke thrilled him. His vision of the right house for such a girl became even more magical.

As he sat listening to the bar-room gossip, more and more people were arriving in town, drawn there by the lure of St James' Fair. Every road that led to Lauriston would be busier than usual over the next few days, with people coming down from Edinburgh, up from the port of Berwick and from Peebles and over the ridge of the Cheviots from England.

One of the busiest roads wended its tortuous way from Carlisle, through Longtown and Langholm to Hawick and Selkirk and then on to Kelso. It was a favourite route for people with big waggons and heavy loads because it had a good solid surface except in the wettest weather and, because it was busy, there was less chance of being robbed in the wilder places like the narrow defile called Mosspaul.

At the Lang Toon, as Langholm was called, a cavalcade of carts had spent Wednesday night under a grove of trees by the riverside. This was the travelling freak show – *Archer's Marvels Renowned Throughout Europe and the World*, its placards announced. Some of the carts had slogans painted on their sides. *The World's Smallest Married Couple* said one; *Long Tom – A Genuine Giant* proclaimed another.

There was also a bearded lady, three pig-faced women who did a dance for the customers, a display of stuffed two-headed calves and chickens with four legs, and *Battling Billy – The Strongest Man in the World*.

All these attractions were housed in a selection of vehicles, some of them solidly roofed, half-moon shaped structures like real houses on wheels while the others were only carts with shaky canvas tents built on their platforms. The conveyance that carried the pig-faced women had bars on its windows and so did the one that proclaimed itself the home of Battling Billy.

By mid-morning on Thursday, 30 July, all the carts were being packed up for another day's journeying and Jem Archer, the man in charge of the cavalcade, was bustling about making sure that everything was firmly tied down and ready for departure.

Jem was a tall, portly man of fifty-odd whose once tightly muscled body was beginning to run to fat. At first glance he looked formidable because of his size and by the fact that his tanned face was disfigured by a badly broken nose, but the wrinkles that marked his eyes and mouth were the signs of habitual smiling and his tough appearance was only a cover for his true gentleness. When he smiled, good nature and affability radiated from him. Yet people on the road knew that Jem was no simpleton or soft touch and treated him with great respect, for he had been one of the most famous bare-knuckle boxers of his generation and was still handy with his fists when the occasion demanded.

'Come on, stow those tents! Come on, get your bairns aboard! Come on, get the horses harnessed if you don't want to be left behind. We've a long way to go today,' he was calling out as he toured his little encampment.

'What's the hurry? The Fair's not till Monday,' protested a scolding voice. The objector scuttled like a crab from behind a green-painted cart and scowled at Jem. She was a tiny woman, a little over three feet tall, with uncombed hair and a face like an evil gnome.

He folded his arms and stared down at her in a tolerant

way as he said, 'Come on Meg, get aboard. Alice wants to be there early.'

'*Alice!* Of course it has to be the precious Alice. So that's why we're being hurried along the roads. I might have guessed. What's wrong with taking our time like we usually do? We could set the show up here in Langholm tonight and make a bit of money if it wasn't for your fancy Alice,' spat the dwarf.

Jem said gently, 'If you want to stay in Langholm you're welcome, Meg, but we're moving on and if you're coming with us you'd better get your pony harnessed.'

The dwarf knew she was beaten and lurched off muttering. Soon Jem saw her and her equally tiny husband lifting their baby in its cocoon of blankets on to their cart. As he knew they would, they had decided to come along.

At last he was ready to line up his cavalcade. When the horses' heads were all turned towards the road and he was satisfied that nobody had been left behind, he walked to the front of the line where his own caravan waited with two big bay horses between its shafts. It was the biggest caravan of all, dome-roofed and dark glossy green in colour with a wreath of brightly coloured flowers painted around the door. On the driving seat sat his Alice. He was smiling fondly as he walked towards her. 'Ready then, Alice? Everything stowed away?' he asked. She nodded and smiled back at him. Alice was a tall, slim woman with an unmistakable air of refinement and elegance although her blue dress was only made of cheap cotton and on her head was a countrywoman's yellow straw bonnet. There were scarlet poppies wreathed around its shallow brim in the artistic way that only Alice could achieve. Jem had watched her picking the flowers that morning along the burnside.

'Everything's ready and I've seen to Billy. He's asleep – I gave him a draught. Long Tom's driving his cart,' she told him in an educated voice that was a marked contrast to Jem's own Cockney accent. He climbed on to the pole-shaft of the caravan, picked up the reins of his horses and settled himself happily beside his woman but

Alice's face wore a troubled look as she turned towards him and said, 'Poor Billy. He didn't want to take the draught today. He's been funny since we started coming north and very bad since Carlisle. Do you think he knows he's in his native country?'

Jem shrugged. 'Who can tell? Maybe he smells the land or something. People can, you know. Some folk have a strong sense of place.'

Alice nodded and said, 'I know. I'm feeling a little strange myself. It's like rising excitement in a way so I can understand why Billy's on edge. I know you don't usually come so far north, Jem. It's good of you to travel so far for my sake.'

He smiled, showing broken teeth. 'I'd do anything for you, Alice. You've only to ask.'

She smiled too and leaned back against the wooden wall, raising her face to the sun. His eyes as he looked at her were yearning. Jem was not sure of Alice and was always afraid that one day she might leave him.

The road along which they were travelling was fringed with trees that cast a dappled shade on to their faces. As the temperature rose Alice untied the ribbons of her bonnet and took it from her head, resting it on her lap. The poppies were dying already and she slowly plucked them out of the ribbon and threw them down one by one on to the dusty surface of the road. Jem felt sad to see the pretty things drooping so piteously and he sighed as he glanced across at her. Suddenly he asked, 'Why did you dye your bonny hair, Alice?'

She sighed and said, 'Because it's going grey. My age was showing.'

'I didn't notice any grey. And even if your age is showing, what does it matter? I'm fifteen years older than you are anyway.'

'But you've worn well,' she teased him.

'Still Ajax, eh?' he responded, making the muscles of his upper arms jump. Ajax had been his fighting name. They both laughed and Jem said, 'Oh no, I can't take on

64

any young challengers any longer. I'll have to content myself with running a freak show.'

'You don't want to settle down, do you?' asked Alice, eyeing his face carefully.

He grinned at her. 'You know I don't. I was born on the road and so was my mother and my father before me and their people before them. All my brothers are on the road, too. We'll maybe meet my brother Simon at Lauriston. He goes there most years and it's a long time since I saw him. I'm looking forward to a meeting. We always used to go with our father to St James' Fair when we were nippers and I've not been back since then.'

'Did you go to the Fair? When was that?' Alice asked curiously.

'Let me think – forty years ago. Before you were born, my love. It must have been in the 1770s. This road was wild in those days. My father carried a broadsword in the van and sometimes he had to use it.'

'I hope you don't have to use one again,' she said.

Although she was smiling there was a doubtful look on her face and Jem assured her, 'Don't worry, lass, there'll be no trouble and anyway, I have a pistol now, not a sword.' He leaned forward and cracked his whip over the backs of the ambling horses, crying out, 'Get a move on, lads! We've a long way to go.' then he told Alice, 'We'll camp on the haugh outside Hawick tonight and by tomorrow we should be near Lauriston. We'll be in plenty of time for you to look around and see your old friends before the Fair starts.'

She nodded with a solemn look on her face. 'It won't take me long. I don't expect there are many people I knew still there. I want to see the old places, that's all, and find out what happened to some friends. A lot can happen in twelve years.'

'Don't be disappointed if it's different and people don't remember you,' Jem warned her.

'I won't be disappointed at all by that,' she assured him with a little laugh.

There was a long pause while they trundled along but

after a bit Jem asked, 'You'll not leave me, Alice, will you?' I'm afraid that when you see your old place you might want to stay.'

She shivered and put out a hand to pat his. 'Oh, don't worry about that, Jem. I won't want to stay there. Oh no, I wouldn't want to do anything like that.'

As the waggons of the freak show were trundling up the road from the south, an even more eye-catching attraction was wending its way down from Edinburgh. This was the Circus Royale which was owned by Jem's younger brother Simon. With strings of multicoloured flags flying from the roofs of the caravans and led by a long line of slowly pacing horses, greys and roans and cream-coloured palominos, the cavalcade passed through the towns and villages that lined the route. In Little France and Dalkeith, in Fala, Ford and Pathhead, children and adults rushed out of cottages by the roadside to gaze round-eyed at the wondrous sight as it trailed past, heading for the inn at Blackshiels where there was a big field in which to camp for the night.

In the first waggon, hauled by four horses, sat Simon Archer who was Jem's junior by about ten years. Beside him proudly sat his tight-muscled little wife Bella was was a rope walker and, like Simon, the member of a family that had been travelling performers for many years. Their children, a troupe of four young tumblers, were in the waggon behind their parents playing with Jacko, a tame monkey, and listening to their mother scolding their father. Though he was twice her size Simon cowered beneath the lash of Bella's tongue. She was giving it to him hard as they drove along. 'You're nothing but a big fool, Simon Archer. Why didn't you get rid of him long ago? You knew what he was like. You shouldn't have trusted him after the last time and now he's done this. What a fool you are!'

Her husband attempted to halt her flow, to little avail. 'Hold hard, Bella. You can't say El Diavolo meant to break his leg. It wasn't his fault.'

She refused to be mollified. 'It *was* his fault. If he hadn't been full of brandy, he wouldn't have fallen off that horse in Leith – and in front of the audience, too. The last time he got drunk in Penrith you should have sent him packing. I told you at the time but not you, you're a big soft fool. He pleads with you to forgive him and you're taken in. "I'll give you another chance, Diavolo," says you! So what does he do? He goes out and gets drunk again but this time, instead of breaking his arm, he breaks a leg and now we've got him lying back there in his van groaning fit to bust and no trick rider in the circus. It's St James' Fair on Monday and we've only that equestrienne wife of his – some equestrienne! I've seen better riding a pony in the park on Sundays – and a few lads that can do nothing but turn somersaults. The rest of the season's still to come and we've our winter money to make. You've spoilt everything.'

Simon tried again. 'I didn't do it, Bella!' he protested but she slapped him on the arm and her hand was hard. 'Be quiet! Listen to what I'm saying. We've got to find another trick rider or our tent'll be empty at the Fair and so will our bellies. What are we going to do?'

Rubbing his face with his hand Simon suggested, 'We could try to hire somebody from another circus. There'll be some at Lauriston, I expect.'

Bella snorted, 'So you want your throat cut, do you? There's only Perry's on the road up here at the moment and if you tried hiring their man, they'd string you up. Where's your brothers? One of them might have somebody.'

'Four are in England but I heard that Bartle's going to America soon. Jem may be up this way though because I met a friend of his at Leith and he said Jem's thinking of coming to Lauriston.'

Bella furrowed her brow, 'But Jem's in boxing, isn't he?'

Simon shook his head, 'Not any more. He's got freaks now, his friend said.'

'Then he won't have any rough riders,' said Bella dismissively.

'But he might know someone who does,' suggested Simon. His wife nodded in agreement, 'Yes, he might. Let's hope he's there.'

Seeing that she had calmed a little, Simon shot a look at her from under his eyebrows and remarked, 'Jem's friend told me something else interesting. He said Jem's got a woman travelling with him now.'

Bella sat up straight, obviously interested. 'Has he? Is she from one of the families?'

'I don't think so. His friend didn't know her. He said her name's Alice and that Jem dotes on her.'

Bella smiled. 'He's as soft as you are, is big Jem. I wonder where he found her. He's not been one for running after women, has he? He's been on his own since his wife died.'

'That was more than ten years ago, Bella. He must've got over it by now,' protested Simon.

'So this Alice isn't from a travelling family . . . Did his friend say what she's like?'

'She's some kind of lady, apparently. There was a tale about Jem meeting her a long time ago and losing touch with her but finding her again recently. He first met her when he was running the boxing ring but they've only just teamed up again.'

'The boxing ring!' Bella sounded shocked. 'She can't be much of a lady if she had anything to do with boxing. That's a bad game. Most of their women are the kind that walk the piazza at Covent Garden. I hope she's not one of those.'

'If she is, that's his business,' said Jem's brother. 'By all accounts he's happy enough. Good luck to him, is what I say.'

By this time the big inn at Blackshiels could be seen looming up at the side of the road ahead of them. There were carts and carriages crowded into its yard and ostlers ran in every direction yelling and shouting at each other. Simon drew on the reins of his horses with gratitude in his heart because he knew that once he's settled his circus he'd be able to enjoy good ale and good fellowship, swopping news in the bar parlour with other travellers before nightfall. The beer at Blackshiels was famous as far south as York and he was thirsty after a long hot day.

Mercifully the field was empty and the circus filed slowly through the gate. The siting of the waggons was supervised by Bella, who leaped lightly to the ground and bounced on her feet as if she was made of rubber before starting to rush around, marshalling the cavalcade. She was the real boss of the operation and everyone knew it. Simon, moving more slowly, unharnessed his horses and slipped nosebags over their muzzles. Then he walked over to the inn yard and started to fill the water buckets. It had been a hard day and watering all the animals – his horses and monkeys, his dancing bears and a mangy tiger with sad golden eyes that rejoiced in the inaccurate name of the Barbary Lion – was a long job.

As he walked to and fro among the vans he could not avoid hearing the anguished moans of his injured trick rider El Diavolo coming from the second caravan but he decided against going in and commiserating with the man who was sure to be drunk, for brandy was the only thing that could dull his pain.

After Simon had been stoically carrying water for the best part of an hour, the mistress of the inn took pity on him and called out from the raised back kitchen window. He walked up to her and saw that she had pushed a mug of beer through in his direction.

'I thought you looked as if you needed that,' she said.

'I do indeed,' he told her, drinking it down gratefully. 'You're busy yourself missus. We were lucky to find your field unoccupied.'

'You were that. We've a full house tonight and they're doubling up in the beds. Everybody's going to the Fair. You'll be headed there yourself, I expect.'

Simon wiped his mouth on his sleeve and nodded his head. 'We are but we might not make it. Our best trick rider's injured and we're making slow progress because he can't be jolted about.'

'That's bad luck. Do you want to leave him here?' asked the host's wife.

'No, we won't be coming back this way. We're heading south to Newcastle after Lauriston. He'll just have to keep on going, poor devil.'

She frowned for a moment and then said, 'You might be in luck. A party's just arrived in a chaise from Edinburgh and one of them's a famous doctor. I'll ask him to take a look at your man if you like. He might be able to do something for him.'

'That would be a mercy but what El Diavolo needs is a new leg, I think, and I doubt if a doctor can give him that,' said Simon and gave her the sweet smile that was very like his brother's and which made people forget his formidable height and strength.

The landlady laughed back and flirted with her eyes. 'I'll speak to the doctor anyway,' she promised.

When Simon ran back to tell Bella that a doctor might be coming to look at their trick rider she regarded him with a measure of respect as if he'd done something very clever. 'Well done. How did you arrange that?' she asked. Then she bristled a little and asked, 'But did you find out how much it would cost for a doctor to look at his leg?'

'I haven't seen the doctor yet. It was the landlady who offered to ask him to take a look at Diavolo.'

'Well these doctors don't work for nothing, you know. I hope she tells him we've no half-guineas to throw away,' grumbled Bella.

Simon's temper snapped. 'Oh, give over, woman! It'd be worth a half-guinea to get him in the saddle again, wouldn't it? Like you were saying, the best of the season's still to come.'

This evidence of a flash of temper from her normally placid husband quietened Bella. 'I expect it would,' she agreed in a humbler tone.

They had almost finished their meal when the sound of strangers' voices were heard outside their waggon and

Simon looked out to see two well-dressed gentlemen wandering about among the caravans.

'I love a circus,' one of them, a grey-haired fellow in very fashionable clothes was saying. 'When I was a lad and the animal show came to Lauriston I used to want to run away with it.'

'Instead of which you joined the Edinburgh menagerie, Thompson!' laughed his companion.

'Yes, I became a lion . . . a medical lion,' agreed the first man and gave a pretend roar that started all the performing dogs barking.

Amid the cacophony of noise, Simon jumped down to the ground and approached the strangers. 'G'day gents. Do you want something special?' he asked.

They stared at his mountainous shoulders with respect and the man called Thompson said, 'The landlady told me you needed a doctor. Apparently somebody's injured, is that right?'

Simon smiled. 'That's right, sir. My trick rider broke his leg four days ago and it's giving him gyp. He's in the waggon back there. Are you gents surgeons?'

'I'm a doctor but it's a long time since I set broken legs. I'll take a look at him though if you like,' said Thompson and his friend laughed, telling Simon, 'And if the man dies, Thompson here'll give you a good price for the body. He's an anatomist, Professor of Anatomy at Edinburgh in fact.'

The first man shot a warning glance at him and told Simon, 'Don't listen to him. I'm the Professor of Anatomy but I'm a doctor right enough and I might be able to help. Let's have a look at him anyway.'

Bella had now joined the group and walked in Simon's shadow as they all went towards the injured man's caravan. When they knocked on the door it was opened by a slatternly woman who was obviously reeling drunk. Without speaking, she held the door open and ushered them in. The light was dim and there was an overwhelming smell of horse liniment, unwashed human bodies and brandy. El Diavolo, whose real name was Patrick

71

Murphy, lay on his tumbled cot with a bottle on the floor beside him. His wife Selina, the equestrienne, came back from the door and sank down on the other bunk with a glass in her hand and her disordered hair tumbling round her shoulders. Untidy as she was, she looked neat compared to her husband who was half-naked and deliriously drunk. His broken right leg lay disjointedly on the top of his blankets like the limb of a broken doll.

Simon, who was a fastidious man, scowled at the squalor in which the pair were living and turned back to fling the door of the caravan wide open so that fresh air could enter and clear some of the stench. Then he bent down and took the bottle off the floor as he told the sick man, 'This gentleman's a surgeon and he's very kindly said that he'll look at your leg.'

El Diavolo only muttered and waved a hand. 'Doesn't feel a thing,' said the surgeon's friend and laughed.

Bella glared at Selina who gave a fatuous grin back and said in a broad Irish accent, 'Sure, brandy's the only way to take away the pain.'

Professor Thompson drew back the dirty blanket and bent over the patient. When he tried to straighten the leg, the sick man groaned and ground his teeth alarmingly so Thompson looked around for something to give him to bite on. He found a leather glove on the floor and handed it to the moaning man. 'Bite on that,' he instructed, 'because I've got to straighten this leg up or it'll never mend.'

The scream that issued from the caravan while this operation was going on made the hairs stiffen on the backs of all Simon's animals. In the Archers' caravan Jacko the monkey clung to Simon's eldest son and gibbered in terror. Even revellers in the bar parlour heard the scream and looked at each other in wonder and dread.

Fifteen minutes later Professor Thompson was back in the open air and telling Simon, 'It's not good, I'm afraid. The left femur's badly broken and he's in a fever.'

Everyone, even Selina who was hanging out of the

caravan door, looked solemn at this. 'Will he be able to ride again?' Simon asked.

'He might – it'll probably be easier for him than walking but not for a long time. I doubt if he'll ever be much use as a trick rider again, though, and he's not going to make any recovery at all unless he stops drinking and starts eating properly,' Thompson warned them.

'He's my speciality rider and he used to be good – before the brandy got him. We're on our way to St James' Fair and we're without a horseman. The crowd always expects at least one. I hope they don't get nasty,' said Simon mournfully.

The Professor laughed, 'I'm a Lauriston laddie myself and the people there are usually pretty peaceable – until it's dark anyway. Don't give a late show, that's all. But there's usually good gypsy horsemen at the Fair. Why don't you look out for one and hire him to perform with you? A gypsy in the cast would at least stop his friends from breaking up your show if they don't like it.'

Simon brightened when he heard this suggestion and he became even more cheerful when Professor Thompson refused to accept a fee for his treatment of Diavolo. 'I can guess what a financial loss this is for you,' he said. 'Keep your guinea in memory of the good times I had at the circus as a lad. And don't forget to find yourself a gypsy – they're all great riders. I'll come and see you on Monday night and give you my opinion of your acts.'

Simon was beaming when he said, 'That's a good idea, sir. I'll look for a hard riding gypsy. It shouldn't be too difficult to find one of those.'

At the same time as Simon was watching Professor Thompson setting El Diavolo's smashed leg, Odilie and her father were in the stable of Havanah Court examining the new chestnut mare which he had bought for her.

It stood in its box, gazing nervously around with its glossy skin shivering slightly like moving silk. Odilie went into the box and ran her hand down the mare's neck, which calmed the animal and it turned its head to nuzzle her arm.

The girl smiled slightly but her eyes were shadowed and thoughtful as she looked across at her father and said, 'I know why you've bought her. It's to make me feel guilty for behaving so badly. You shouldn't try to bribe me.'

Canny raised a hand in an unspoken gesture of peace and asked, 'Do you like the horse, my dear?'

'She's beautiful, so fine and strong too,' said Odilie but her voice was still mournful.

'She's a beautiful goer. Covers the ground like a charger and jumps anything. Try her out, miss,' chimed in Stevens who was watching the interchange between father and daughter and feeling sorry for Canny.

To his disappointment Odilie shook her head. 'Not now, it's too hot. I shall take her out tomorrow.' Then seeing the look of dejection on her father's face, she took his arm and led him from the stables. 'You're very kind to me – too kind, perhaps. I said that I'd go to dinner with the Duke and I won't let you down. I'll keep an open mind about him till then.'

Canny groaned, 'This is all for your benefit – everything I've done has been for you. I know Martha thinks I'm wanting to show Lauriston how much I've risen in the world but it's not true. I'm doing this for you . . .'

His daughter paused and looked at him. 'You're really a remarkable man, Father, aren't you? You've come a long way. Is it true you were born behind the Cross Keys over there?' She gestured with her hand in the direction of the square.

He nodded. 'In a bothy at the back and so was Martha. Our father was an ostler and he drank something terrible. Our poor mother had to beg food for us. Then one day he was killed in a carriage accident on the way to Sprouston. He was drunk at the time of course and folk said it was his own fault. They put us in the Poors' House.'

Odilie gripped her father's arm harder. 'How old were you?'

'Six or seven, I suppose. Martha was a year older. I remember how angry I felt at the way my mother was treated . . .'

'She died young, didn't she?'

He shrugged. 'Yes. She got consumption and couldn't fight it. That was when I ran away to Berwick and joined a ship and Martha went into service. I was eleven and she was twelve.'

There were tears in Odilie's eyes when she leaned forward impulsively to kiss his cheeks. 'I'm sorry, Papa. I'm really sorry. I'll behave myself from now on, don't worry. If you want me to marry the Duke, that's what I'll do. When I hear stories like yours and Grace's it makes me feel very fortunate.'

Canny looked at her with love and then, to change a subject that touched him deeply, too deeply, he asked, 'What's Grace been telling you?'

'About *her* mother, how she never knew her and how cruel her father is. I'm surprised at you having that man for your lawyer, Papa.'

Canny shrugged. 'He's a good lawyer. Sometimes pleasant, kind fellows are not as good as the villains.'

'You must have been away from Lauriston when Grace's mother died,' said Odilie and was surprised to see a shifty look come over her father's face. So he did know something about it.

'I didn't know her but I knew her father, old Davie Allen,' he conceded.

'What was he like?' asked Odilie, who was anxious to find out as much as she could for her friend.

'Oh, a grand man, a good man. They say he was awfully fond of his lassie . . . He tried to do the best for her.' Canny's voice trailed off and a strange look crossed his face again. No matter how much Odilie urged he would say no more.

A short time later a little boy went running through the town carrying a hastily penned note from Odilie to Grace. He pushed open the gate of the Elliot house and found the girl in the garden playing ball with her youngest half-sister, six year old Amelia.

'Note from Havanah Court,' he said shortly, pushing it into her hand.

Grace was about to walk into the house with it and lay it on her father's desk when she noticed that the superscription bore her own name. Ignoring Amelia's whines about the cessation of their game, she split the seal open with her thumbnail and read the words written in Odilie's sprawling hand . . . *'There's some mystery about your mother. Even my father acts strange when I ask questions, but I've found out some things. Come as soon as you can and I'll tell you. P.S. Have you ever heard of Bettymill?'*

Every word was like a golden nugget to Grace, who read the note over and over again, then stood hugging the piece of paper close to her chest with an abstracted and faraway look on her face. Amelia totally ignored, gave up tugging at her skirt and ran indoors to whine at her mother instead.

Slowly Grace followed her into the house but not to Hester's sitting room. Instead she headed for her father's study where the family's books were kept. The big Bible was there on a dusty shelf and she pulled it down, turning to the flyleaf. *Lucy Allen* was written in a girlish hand and beside it was a pair of double lines to denote a marriage pointing to *Andrew Elliot*, also written by the same person. There was a date *'797* in brackets and a little arrow led down from the sign of union to one word written in different coloured ink. It said *Grace* and beside her name was another date, *1798*.

Her eyes slowly filled with tears as she gently spread her open palm over the page. 'Grace – that's me,' she sighed and imagined her mother dipping her quill in an inkpot to write the five letters – *G-r-a-c-e.* Perhaps the baby that was Grace herself had been lying beside her when she did so. Lucy must have been happy when she wrote her daughter's name. The girl had a sudden surge of emotion and a sense of identity because now she felt some link with her lost mother. Even if Odilie's aunt was acting strange, she at least knew something about Lucy Allen. Martha probably carried a picture of Grace's mother in her mind's eye. As soon as she could Grace was determined to leave Viewhill House and hurry to Havanah Court where Odilie was waiting with her information.

Before she could leave however, Hester came storming into the library and said accusingly, 'Amelia tells me a boy brought a letter and you opened it. You've no business to read your father's letters.'

'It wasn't sent to my father. It was for me.'

A look of disbelief crossed Hester's face. 'And who was writing to you, pray?'

'It was from Odilie,' said Grace, folding up the letter and pointedly putting it in her pocket.

Hester snorted. 'Oh, from the grand Miss Rutherford, your special friend. But don't you worry. She'll soon drop you when she moves into Sloebank Castle and makes finer friends. You won't be having notes from her then. She'll not need a crippled maidservant hanging on to her skirts when she's the Duchess.'

Grace felt a tide of anger rise in her. She wanted to attack Hester so badly that the effort of controlling herself was almost unendurable. Instead she took a deep breath and said, 'Where's Bettymill, Hester?'

The question stopped her stepmother like a blow. 'What? What did you say?'

'I asked where's Bettymill?'

'Why?'

'I wondered if it was the old mill where Jessie used to take me sometimes when I was little. Her brother the carrier used to let us ride out there on his cart.'

'She took you out to Bettymill . . .' Hester sounded amazed but recovered herself quickly and added, 'Jessie came from Bettymill, that's why she took you there.'

'I remember there was an old man living there, who was he?'

Hester gobbled like a turkey, 'Your father would have sent Jessie off if he'd known she was taking you there.'

'Why shouldn't I go? What's all the mystery? Has it something to do with my mother?'

Hester advanced on Grace with her fists clenched. 'Your mother was a whore,' she hissed, 'and you'd probably be one too if you weren't crippled and ugly. Get up into your room and stay there till your father comes home and hears about this.'

All evening Odilie waited impatiently for a visit from Grace but none came and there was no answer to her note. She sent Joe Cannonball out to find the boy who'd carried the message to Viewhill for her and he came back with the information that Miss Grace had received the note and read it in the boy's presence.

'I hope there's nothing wrong with Grace. I was sure she'd come down when she got my note,' Odilie told Martha.

Her aunt only clicked her tongue and said, 'She's probably got things to do up there. That step-mother of hers keeps her busy. Hester won't get her own hands dirty because she doesn't like remembering she was once a servant.'

'Elliot married a servant after his wife died?' asked Odilie in surprise.

Martha gave an irritated shrug as if she'd inadvertently let something slip. 'He did that. He married his wife's maid,' she said and bustled off in her newly acquired evasive manner.

After supper Odilie sat alone in her boudoir looking out at the moonlight on the water and wondering about Grace. She did not know that the object of her concern was also spending the evening alone but in Grace's case, supperless and locked in an attic room. Being locked up without food was not an unusual punishment for Grace and she had come to accept it without protest for it was at least better than a beating and she always kept a book and an apple hidden in the room to pass the time.

Tonight however she did not want to read for she had much on her mind as she sat staring up at the tiny square

78

of window glass in the roof with her chin in her fists. She was thinking about Lucy Allen. 'Your mother was a whore,' Hester had cried and her face had gone scarlet and her eyes looked deranged when she said the horrible word. Was she driven by malice? Grace hoped so because she had a mental picture of an idealised mother with a smiling face and tender hands. She was sure Hester was only being wicked because from the deep recesses of her memory she could almost summon a gentle vision of Lucy, a figure that was misty and without definition like someone walking ahead of her in a dream.

The mention of Bettymill had obviously thrown Hester into a panic. Was it the place where Jessie used to take me, wondered Grace? Judging by Hester's reaction, she was certain it was. She concentrated her mind and found herself vividly remembering the old man who lived there. He smelt of snuff and had a long grey beard and trembling hands. She used to be upset because he always wept when he saw her . . . She remembered his tears and how scared she'd been of him though he was gentle and kind. If Bettymill was the name of his house, she remembered it as warm and welcoming. They used to sit in a big room with a leaping fire in the grate and lots of pretty things to look at around the walls – pictures and coloured plates, shining brass and gleaming copper. The house had been bowered in trees and everything was very green and quiet with only the sound of running water and the creak of a slowly turning mill-wheel to break the silence. She also had a vague memory of going into the mill itself and being transfixed in wonder by the sight of the huge, ponderously rotating cogwheels and the air hanging above her head like a veil enmeshed with millions of motes of grain floating in it. Her ears had been filled with the sound of gentle creaking that lulled her like a lullaby or the rocking of an infant's cradle . . . creak, creak, creak, so slow and so rhythmic. It was amazing how much she could remember when she really tried. Her last memory before she fell asleep was of the smell of Bettymill, a moist and mossy scent that came back to her so strongly that it seemed to fill her little room.

When she woke, it was almost dark. She had apparently been forgotten for no one came near her. From below she heard the sound of her father's voice and the clatter and din of the children going up to bed. Her tension gradually eased as she realised that she was being left to cool her heels. Her father was not coming up to her as Hester had threatened and she wondered if her step-mother had fulfilled her threat of reporting to him what had happened that afternoon. Probably not – but why not, she wondered?

She could not fully relax however until she heard her father and Hester making their way to bed. Grace was fully awake but her window did not give a view of the ground for it stared into the sky and as she gazed upwards she saw a skein of swifts dashing across the glass searching for their night-time roosts. Then, a little later, the bats came out, swooping past on their way to skim over the surface of the river below the house. Finally the moon rose, sailing slowly across the skylight like a huge blood orange, pillowed among long narrow clouds. The fascinated girl was almost hypnotised by the smiling face on its surface. Its glory, its mystery and magic entranced her, for it was a lover's moon. How lucky for some people, she reflected, that such a moon should be shining at the time of the Fair.

The magic of the moon made her at last bring forward the subject she had been pushing into the background of her mind ever since she realised that Fair Day was so close. She had not allowed herself to discuss it even with Odilie, although she had tentatively mentioned the young man who'd helped her across the wooden footbridge last year. She had not told her friend what a fine young man he was – tall and straight and very gentlemanly in his ways although he was dressed like a countryman. He'd seen her stagger and almost fall in the pushing crowd on the narrow bridge and had put out a hand to steady her. Then he helped her down the steep steps and when she was safe on the grass, he smiled at her in such a way that her heart turned over. She remembered the feeling still and for a long time she'd lulled herself to sleep with the memory of his smile. She treasured it like a gift.

The wonderful thing about the young man was that her lameness did not seem to repel him. He did not hurry away from her in embarrassment but walked along with her, chatting about the various attractions on display and measuring his steps to hers. They had spent almost an hour together before she told him that it was time for her to return home, which was not true really but she did not want to be a burden and expected him to be relieved to be rid of her. She thought that he was only being kind in not breaking away himself. By taking her leave, she was trying to make it easy for him but he had actually looked disappointed to lose her.

'Can't you stay a little longer?' he'd asked.

Flustered, she shook her head. 'I have to go. My step-mother will be waiting . . . There's things to be done at home.'

'I'm sorry you can't stay. My name's Adam Scott. I'll look for you at the Fair next year,' he told her when they parted.

Now, a year later, Grace looked at the moon and thought about Adam. Would he remember her this year? Would he really be looking out for her at the Fair? Don't be silly, she told herself. It's not likely that he'll give you a single thought, for you're only a pathetic cripple and there are dozens of much prettier girls to catch the eye of such a handsome fellow. But she had thought about him so much and she had so little self-regard that she was afraid to risk disappointment. If she went to the Fair and saw him with another girl on his arm, her secret dreams would be shattered. She would lose them; they would crumple like an eggshell in her hand. Rather than risk that it would be better not to go to the Fair at all. She decided to make some excuse to Odilie and get out of going. Most important of all, she decided that she'd stop dreaming about Adam Scott.

*

The moon that entranced Grace and filled her with romantic longings was having a similar effect on Odilie, who sat wrapped in a Paisley shawl in her bedroom window brooding about love and marriage. Her thoughts were bitter, however, because it seemed it was to be her fate to marry a man who did not sound like the sort of husband of whom she had dreamed. Try as she might, Odilie could not bring herself to the state of mind that would accept such a marriage, despite the huge advantages it would bring. As a consolation, she tried to imagine the reaction of the girls who had teased her so cruelly at school when they heard the news – Odilie Rutherford, the negress, a Duchess! She would become someone they would have to curtsey to and defer to in status. She would walk before them all in precedence and have them over her but she would despise them and herself for it. Perhaps this is what it means to grow up, she thought sadly as she sank her dark head on to her hand. Perhaps this is the first realisation of reality. Perhaps love as it's written about in books of poetry is just an illusion.

The moonlight was shining just as brightly over the huddled houses of two tiny villages called Kirk Yetholm and Town Yetholm that were tucked away, half a mile apart, in a fold of the Cheviot Hills seven miles south of Lauriston. The villages were almost on the border between Scotland and England in an area long known as the Debateable Lands because for centuries they belonged to no one in particular and had changed hand at intervals, Scottish for some years before reverting to England, but neither monarchy was ever able to establish official government there. The people of these lands lived by their own rules and the result was little in the way of law. The most lawless community of all were the gypsies of Kirk Yetholm.

For a hundred years they had made this village their winter base because they had been granted the right to live there rent free by a local landowner for whom one of their number had performed a great service – he'd saved his life in a foreign battle. With the protection of such a powerful man, the Romanies, who were hated and feared by the population in general, moved in and made their homes in a huddle of dilapidated cottages known as Tinkler's Row. Over the years they increased their numbers until by the early 19th century there were four main families, almost two hundred people of 'Egyptian' blood living in Kirk Yetholm.

For most of the summer, farmers and villagers in the district round about breathed easily because, from the coming of spring until the frosts of autumn, the gypsies abandoned their hovels in Kirk Yetholm and went wandering over the face of the countryside in horse-drawn waggons, but they made an exception for the time of St James' Fair. A few days before it began they all came straggling back home to prepare for the event which was a high point in their annual calender. It was there that they made enough money – by fair means or foul, by horse-dealing, fortune-telling, selling horn spoons and tin pots, by thievery and trickery of all kinds – to provide for themselves and their families over the winter.

On the night when the two girls in Lauriston were staring at its smiling face, the moon also cast its silver radiance over the ragged thatches of the gypsy houses of Kirk Yetholm and, one by one, it lured shadows out of broken front doors. Men met beneath the overhanging eaves and lounged about with their hands in their pockets, whispering each other in a language that was incomprehensible to people not of Romany blood. The Kirk Yetholm gypsies spoke a sort of bastard Romany muddled up with local words and never talked it unless they were sure that no Gorgio could overhear them.

The men gathered in the shadows, carrying thick cudgels in their hands and with skinny and predatory hounds lurking at their heels. Only males gathered in the darkness for the women and children, who did most of the day to day work and the selling of gypsy wares, were abed and asleep by the time the moon rose. Its radiance delighted the men, however, for it lit the way when they went poaching or lurking around farmyards looking for ways of helping themselves to feed for their horses.

Local farmers always dreaded the days before St James' Fair because it was then that the gypsies had their greatest need for hay and corn. With no land of their own on which to grow food for their animals – and no desire for a life of drudging husbandry even if they had owned land – it was unthinkable for them to purchase any hay and corn but they had an insatiable need for horse fodder and so they stole what was required. There was little anyone could do to stop them and it was better not to try because, if they had no reason to dislike a farmer, they only took a little on a regular basis from his barns and haystacks. If he did something to annoy them however, they plundered him like rapacious Vikings. Farmers soon learned to accept their losses with good grace for fear of worse reprisals.

This year the gypsies' need for fodder was even greater than usual because they had gathered together an unusually large number of horses. The end of war with France had meant that returned soldiers up and down the countryside were selling off their old chargers, some of them fine animals with a lot of life left in them. On the grassy spread of common land in the middle of Kirk Yetholm village, twenty hobbled horses were pegged out in lines, an unprecedented number which had been gathered from far and near over the summer to sell at St James' Fair. There were plenty of fine horses available in 1816 and the gypsies had taken their pick of the best of them.

Overlooking the green was a tumbledown house belonging to a gypsy family called Faa and there the men were gathered waiting for their leader. At last the door opened and a tall man stood framed in the doorway. One of the lingerers whistled and cried softly, 'We're here, Gib. Where's Jesse?'

'With his blewre probably,' said the new arrival. The moonlight showed him to be a tall, well-built man with a crest of snow-white hair that sprang up vigorously on his proudly carried head.

His silver-grey sideburns were thick and uncut so that his brown face was edged by a bushy fringe that almost met on the point of his chin. It gave him the look of a lion and he had a lion's kingly air too, which made all the other men defer to him. He gestured to a young lad at the back of the crowd and said, 'Run over to Thomassin's and see if Jesse's there.'

After a few minutes the messenger came back alone. 'He's not there. She hasn't seen him all day and she says she's spoiling to chin his curlo if she finds him.'

The white-haired man called Gib laughed hoarsely. 'She'd better not cut his throat. We need him at the Fair. He's the best horseman in the whole Border. Anyway she's no claim on him, she's not rommed to him – not yet.'

'If they're not wedded yet it's not for want of her trying, and she's a grasni shantu. He'd better marry her before somebody else does,' said a dark-haired, shifty-looking man called Abel who stood at the back of the group.

Gib replied shortly, 'That's his business, Abel. Thomassin should remember that the harder you try to force some men, the more they stick in their heels – like horses. Come on, the dude's bright up there in the sky and the merryfeet are running. I fancy rabbit stew tomorrow.'

Soundless as shadows they drifted off towards a cluster of trees that could be seen spread out like a carpet on the side of a hill that rose behind the village. While they were climbing the last slope, another man emerged from the wood in front of them and ran down towards Gib, who greeted him with an uplifted hand and asked shortly, 'Where've you been, Jesse? We sent the chal to Thomassin's looking for you.'

'Just wandering about,' was the casual reply. Jesse's dark hair fell down at the back of his neck in thick, luxuriant curls like a girl's but that was the only effeminate thing about him because he had a strong and striking face with a high-bridged nose and daring dark eyes that could make women feel strangely weak when he chose to exert his power on them. It was generally acknowledged among all the Yetholm folk that Jesse Bailey was a very taking man.

'You've been doing a bit of faking, I hope. What did you pick up?' asked Gib. He was the 'king' of their community and had already decided that although he had sons of his own, his successor should be this wayward but favourite nephew. He was grooming Jesse as his inheritor and the young man had a lot of learning to do yet.

'I've not stolen anything so far. I was just wandering about looking at things,' was the disappointing reply to Gib's question.

'And you've probably got a book in your pocket,' said the uncle in disgust. He looked at Jesse with a despairing expression but the young man only patted the pocket of his short blue jacket and laughed as he asked, 'Can you see through cloth, too? Don't dukker me, Gib.'

'I don't need to be a fortune-teller to know you've a book. That minister in the village didn't do you any favours when he taught you to read, my lad. He only filled your head with rubbish.'

Jesse sighed. There was no use protesting to Gib Faa, his mother's brother, who knew him well. His uncle was the head of their community and guardian of their traditions. Illiterate himself, Gib scorned scholars and put far more stock in gypsy lore and in a man's adroit ability to survive in arduous conditions than in anything that could be read in books. But when Jesse was eight years old he had been ill, victim of a virulent typhus fever that killed many of the gypsy children that year. The local minister, a saintly man who worried about the immortal souls of the pagans in his parish, noticed Jesse's mother's anguish about her melting eyed boy and saw to it that nourishing food was sent to the Bailey hovel every day. Miraculously the child recovered, although he was still very weak when summer and the travelling time came round. Then the minister persuaded Jesse's mother to let her son stay with him and his wife in the manse instead of going wandering. When she came back in the autumn, her boy, fed all summer on eggs and cream, vegetables and slices of roast beef by the doting childless couple, was not only strong and healthy again but he had been taught to read and write. A new world had been opened up for him although the gift of learning that had been given him was in time to prove a mixed blessing. It introduced him to a morality very different from the Romany code, to a new way of thinking about and looking at things. It put longings and questions into his mind that were making him deeply unsettled. The gypsy part of his nature, which was strong, fought with this enchantment for books that enthralled him and he was unable to break this strange addiction.

'Thomassin's after you. Rake tute,' warned Gib.

Jesse shrugged. 'That's all right, I'll look after myself. She'll cool down. She's too hasty.'

'She wants you for her rom,' Gib told him.

'I'm not ready to marry yet,' was the short reply.

'You're twenty-two. That's old enough for marrying and she's nineteen, a fine chavi – her mother's my mother's cousin.'

'I know all that. I'll probably do it in the end but I don't want to be hurried,' said Jesse curtly. He wondered what point there would be in trying to explain to Gib how he dreamed of escape, how much he wanted to see the world beyond the gypsy routes. How could he tell his uncle that he wanted to leave behind the established routine of stealing and gambling, fighting and drinking. The thing he loved best beside books was the horse and his skill as a rider was renowned far outside Yetholm. Jesse knew that this ability could be exploited as a passport to the world where it would help him escape from the clutches of his gypsy culture and travel to where his talent would find him new opportunities. But that was only a dream, for he knew that Gib had fingered him as the next gypsy leader and it seemed as if his destiny was cast. Nothing was going to change it.

By now they were in the depths of the wood and with

low whistles, the gypsies were setting their dogs on to carefree rabbits that skipped about in the grassy glades beneath the trees. It was not long before the men had a big enough catch to fill their capacious pots at home and they turned to trek back down the hill. As they left the wood, Gib took his nephew by the arm and pointed over to a farmsteading surrounded by a circle of tilled fields in the next valley.

'Go over to Turnbull's and take a few sheaves out of his stack,' he instructed.

'But we took from him yesterday,' protested Jesse.

'Oh, he'd be disappointed if we passed him by,' laughed Gib and pushed the young man off in the required direction.

Though he made no objection to his uncle's order, as he slipped soundlessly along in the shadow of a stone dyke, Jesse reflected on how little he enjoyed stealing. During that boyhood summer of his illness the old minister had drummed into him that stealing was a sin and not only punishable by law – which he knew already – but by God as well. This was a concept that had never occurred to him before. The idea that there was an omnipotent God in Heaven watching everything men did was deeply unsettling to Jesse.

'I'm tired of all this,' he said to himself as he slipped into the silent farmyard. He wasn't only afraid of being caught but was also tired of doing something that had become second nature to him. He'd done it so often that it was too easy but there was always danger, for every time he filched a bale of straw or a spare bridle off a saddleroom hook, he knew there was a chance of some farmer sticking a gun in his back or worse, for if he was hauled before the law, he was in danger of being strung up on the gibbet. Magistrates did not think twice about hanging gypsies: it was an inevitable end for them. Only three months before, Jesse's own older brother had been strung up for sheep-stealing near Dumfries. He remembered how he'd felt as he watched, bitter-faced and stoical, while the corpse swung to and fro on the rope's end. His predominating thought had been, 'What a useless way to end a life!'

He was not caught in Turnbull's yard that night, however, for he was as silent as a ghost and knew his way around the yard almost as well as the man who owned it. He'd been there so often that the dogs knew him and did not bark. Filling a sack from the corn kist he heard midnight strike from the church clock in the village below him and then he turned and ran back to Kirk Yetholm with a bale of hay on his back and sack of corn over one shoulder.

Jesse was the last of the men to return to the village and while he was stacking the hay and pouring the corn into a bin at the back of Gib's home, he did not know that a pair of dark and flashing eyes were watching him from a window on the other side of the row. Thomassin Young wondered if she should step out and speak to him but caution held her back. Jesse was difficult to handle and she was determined to snare him in the end. She'd kept herself for him, she'd put it around that they were bespoken to each other and she was intent on snaring him with ropes of silk, but she knew that her task would be difficult – he would take a lot of careful handling before she had him to herself.

CHAPTER 4

By the time most people in Lauriston were stirring in their beds, in the hills that formed the border with England, two men were making their way back home after finishing their morning's work. Mist drifted around them like fairy hair as, with the long easy strides of people accustomed to walking in rough country, they descended from the top of Woden Law. Deep in the valley below their feet, the Kale Water twisted and turned with a thin fringe of scrubby trees of hazelnut and rowan along its banks.

The men were Tom Scott and his twenty-one year old son Adam. Both looked satisfied, for though it was not yet seven o'clock they had covered a thousand acres of hill and 'taken tent' of the eight hundred sheep that were in their care. The Scotts were hired shepherds employed to take care of a rich man's flock in the hills where their ancestors had lived and worked for centuries before the land was enclosed by their overlords and sold off as farms. At one time the Scotts had earned their tenancy of those lands by their swords but when the fighting years were over, the country was divided up among richer men and by an unstoppable movement, the Scotts found themselves servants to an owner whom they rarely saw. They were proud and valuable men nonetheless because they knew the hills around them like no one else and they were loyal to the man who paid their wages.

They rarely spoke while they walked the hills, only pausing now and then to whistle orders to the three black and white collie dogs called Jess, Birk and Rab that were running at their heels. The dogs moved eagerly, bellies low to the ground, heads down and scarlet tongues lolling in anticipation of the hot meal that awaited them in the huddle of greystone buildings which could be seen far away on the valley floor beside the river. Every now and again men and dogs all lifted their heads and took a bearing on the biggest house that gave out as an enticing signal a trickle of smoke curling up from its chimney. This was the Scotts' home, Fairhope, an ancient steading that had once seen Roman legions march past its front door. Today, however, it stood isolated and lonely by the side of a narrow track, all that was left of the broad Roman roadway that could be followed all the way to York from their little valley. As far as they were concerned, its importance was that it was their only link with the village of Hownam four miles away.

Time stood still in their deep and mysterious country of rounded hills and hidden valleys between England and Scotland. The men, their dogs and the birds that flew up before them uttering wild cries had the universe to themselves, a world that had remained unchanged and untouched for aeons. As the sun rose it revealed a landscape of fold upon fold of land of sensual curves. The crowded hills, rising one after the other in a never ending perspective, looking like sleeping giantesses lying on their sides with their heads pillowed on outflung arms and their hipbones and shoulders jutting up into the sky. Their flanks were marked by an occasional boundary wall or a circle of stone. These enclosures were shelters into which the sheep were herded during bitter weather or when the shepherds wanted them all together for shearing or lambing. The hillsides were tinged with streaks of lavender and purple where the heather was beginning to flower and from a distance, as the sun rose and cast its radiance over the world, the universe looked as if it had been washed by the brush of a celestial painter.

In those lonely hills there was an immense empyrean of sky, pale blue and marked today by no clouds. It gave the promise of another brilliant day which rejoiced the men as they walked through their paradise. Both father and son had an air of remoteness that cloaked them with an impressive dignity and set them apart from the hired men on lowland farms, for the isolation in which they lived had invested them with an extra dimension, expanded and glorified them as if they were party to a secret that other people never learned.

The impression they gave, looming out of the mist, was of a pair of heroes from a Greek myth and this illusion was enhanced by the tall crooks topped by curved finials which they carried. The Scotts were both tall and lean with erect shoulders and proudly carried heads. Tom's hair and beard were grizzled and his face deeply tanned and wrinkled by exposure to all kinds of weather over forty years of shepherding but his son was brightly blonde, fresh-skinned and cleanshaven. Black and white checked plaids were loosely draped around their shoulders and Tom wore a black cocked bonnet with a grey heron's feather stuck into the headband.

As they strode down the hillside towards Fairhope, Tom Scott gave a piercing whistle and the dogs ran back towards him, clustering at his heels. He led them to a low-roofed shed, opened the green-painted door and ushered them inside. Catherine his wife had been watching for her men coming down the hill and on the shed floor she had laid out three big pans of steaming meal with a few scraps of vegetables on top. Each dog knew its own dish and went straight for it.

The shepherds then carefully scraped their boots on an iron boot cleaner at the cottage door, hung their crooks on a metal hook that stuck out of the stone wall and, after washing their hands in the stone water butt and slinging back their plaids, bent their heads in order to enter the low doorway of their home.

Fairhope was an ancient bastle house, once fortified like a castle with walls so thick that no frost ever penetrated them. The living quarters were on the first floor while the animals were stabled at ground level. In winter it was always warm inside and in summer the temperature stayed pleasantly cool. In the kitchen, the windows were tiny with only four little greenish panes set in deep embrasures and they were fringed by fluttering curtains of white hung from polished brass hoops on a cane pole. The interior walls were whitewashed every year and the floor was laid with broad stone flagstones that shone a pale cream colour, whitened by centuries of regular scrubbing. In the blackened cavern of the fireplace, a copper kettle was boiling merrily from a 'swee' hung over the flames, and something delicious was sizzling on an open griddle.

The men paused at the top of the narrow little staircase from ground level and smiled as they savoured the smell of frying ham and baking scones. Then, nodding to Catherine, they drew back their chairs and sat down at the table where a little girl in a long white nightgown was eating porridge with a horn spoon. She looked up to say to her father, 'You're early. Mam's baking a ham for Monday. Aren't you awful excited?'

Tom Scott ran his fingers through his beard and smiled fondly at his baby. 'Aye Leeb, I am that. Are you excited about the Fair, too?'

The child almost jumped out of her chair. 'I can't sleep at night for thinking about it,' she cried.

'You're a wee fibber,' said her brother. 'I heard you snoring fit to shake the house when I went out this morning.'

She made a face. 'Och, you! You're never excited about anything.'

Adam leaned back in his chair. He enjoyed teasing his little sister. 'I wouldn't care if they stopped the Fair altogether. I'm going to look out for the Duke this year and tell him so. It's nothing but an excuse for a lot of silly folk to spend money they've had to slave all year to earn. I'd rather stay up here in the hills than go all the way down there to walk about with the dafties.'

'The Duke won't listen to *you*. Anyway, I like the town. You and your hills – there's other places as bonny,' said the little girl.

'No there isn't,' said her brother solemnly and he wasn't teasing this time.

'Eat up and stop your gabbing,' came the voice of Catherine, the mother of the family. 'I'm like the bairn, I'm wanting to get everything ready because there's a lot to do if we're going fairing on Monday. Adam, you write a letter to Mary and tell her to be waiting for us at the Teviot toll bridge. It's a six-month since I saw her and I'm fair longing for a sight of my lassie.'

'Oh, Mary'll be fine. She likes her place. She's on a good farm and she's with your brother,' consoled Tom, who knew how his wife missed their eldest daughter, seventeen year old Mary who was working as a bondager, a female farm labourer, on a place near Morebattle. She'd been away from the family home for almost two years but her mother was not yet reconciled to having one of her brood out of her sight.

The eagerness of Catherine and Leeb made the men hurry at their breakfast and after it was finished, while the women bustled about tidying up the house, Adam went into the other room next door which was the family parlour and used only on special occasions. There he laid a sheet of paper on to the top of the family Bible and penned a short letter to his sister.

When he emerged with it in his hand, his mother read it and approved. Then she told him, 'Take it to the carrier in Hownam, won't you lad? I want her to get it as soon as possible. Oh, I hope she can get away for the Fair.'

'Mary'll not miss the Fair. Don't you worry about that and she's working for a good man. He aye lets his people go fairing. She'll get away, Mother, don't worry,' her son consoled her.

It was a four-mile walk to the carrier's cottage at the head of the valley but that distance was nothing to Adam Scott who strode along, accompanied by a dog as usual, admiring the countryside as he went. Crab apple trees fringed the road into Hownam and though the crop was still green, it looked promising. He knew that come October, Catherine and Leeb would walk along with their wicker baskets and gather fallen apples from the roadside to make the jelly that they put on their bread throughout the winter. Adam stopped to watch a dove-grey heron fishing in the Kale Water and the bird was so unafraid that it did not attempt to fly away even when it spied him.

Excitement rose within him as he thought about the Fair. In spite of what he had said to his little sister, he was eagerly looking forward to it. Only two more days to go! St James' Fair was one of the few occasions in the year when Adam left the hills and every moment away was treasured, to be recalled later in isolation. He thought about the crowds and the din; the mingled smells of roasting meat, beer and freshly boiled toffee; the surging excitement of galloping horses and the sight of strange folk from foreign places, some of them talking a different language or at least what sounded like a different language to him. He remembered how music came blaring out of tents housing sideshow attractions and how the buskers tried to out-bawl each other.

But most of all he thought about the girl with the yellow hair whom he'd met on the wooden footbridge last year. He first noticed her clinging to the handrail, obviously frightened in case she was swept off her feet by the press of people. When he saw the panic on her face, he'd hurried up and put a hand on her elbow to steady her and something magical had happened at that moment. She'd clung to him like a child and then smiled, such a sweet smile that it transformed her frightened face.

It was only after he helped her down the steps of the bridge that he realised the girl was lame. One leg seemed to be shorter than the other and she walked haltingly, but instead of making him pity her, this infirmity was infinitely endearing. It made him tender: he wanted to look after her, to shield her from the world.

All too soon she'd announced that she must go home, and only when she had disappeared did he realise that he didn't even know her name – but he'd thought about her since then. He still remembered the blueness of her eyes and the exquisite paleness of her skin, and was determined to search the whole fairground for her this year.

Because of the girl who so badly needed looking after, Adam Scott was longing to go to the Fair as much as his little sister Leeb.

Bonny Mary Scott was feeding a large pen of dappled pigs in Mr Wauchope's farm outside Morebattle when the local carter drove into the yard and whistled at her. 'Here, Mary. There's a letter for you. It's from your mither. She says . . .'

Dropping her bucket, Mary ran up to him and snatched the piece of paper from his hand. 'At least let me read it for myself,' she snapped angrily, for it was very rarely that she received a letter and she did not want her pleasure spoiled.

The carter was unabashed and sat on top of his load of boxes grinning broadly. 'Is there any message back? Just tell me and I'll pass it on up the valley. It'll no' cost you anything,' he told her.

'There's no message,' said Mary primly as she tucked the letter into her skirt pocket. She was a big, well-built girl with nut brown hair, a fine specimen of womanhood, the sort who would breed a houseful of children without any trouble. Like all the other five bondagers on Wauchope's farm she wore the traditional costume of a long, yellow and black striped skirt over heavy working boots and topped by a big apron, a printed cotton blouse and a large hat. Because it was summer her hat was the 'ugli', a face-shading poke bonnet of cotton stretched over a bamboo frame. In wintertime, the bondagers wore large shiny black straw hats like plates, bent over and tied on to their heads by squares of printed cloth made from the same material as their blouses. Mary preferred these straw hats because they were more becoming than the sunbonnets but her Aunt Lily, who was the forewoman of the bondager squad, was a stickler for protocol and insisted that each girl turn out in the same costume like a well-drilled army squad. She also required that they were all clean and tidy every morning with their boots greased to a high shine, no matter what sort of dirty task they were called upon to do.

Mary was bonded – or promised as a worker for a year at a time – to her Uncle Sandy, Aunt Lily's husband and Catherine Scott's brother. Sandy was a slow-spoken and kindly man who did not work his niece too hard and, because he had no children of his own, he was glad of the opportunity to keep her. It was easier to find a good place on a farm if you had a girl as well as a wife to share the work because farmers liked to have as many workers as possible in each of their cottages.

When she had become old enough to go to work, Mary's mother wanted her to be a serving maid in some well-off household but the girl rejected that idea. 'I've lived all my life in this valley and I'd miss the open air,' she said. 'I don't want to be shut up in a house all day.' Unlike some girls she did not resent the bondager arrangement because it was not onerous for her, she got on well with her aunt and uncle and life on Wauchope's farm where her uncle was head ploughman was very easy-going. The farmer Wauchope himself was fat and good-natured, as well as being famous in the locality for the generosity of the spread he put on at his harvest kirns. A place at Wauchope's was regarded as one of the plums of the district for all local labourers, and there was always a happy atmosphere in his farm toun.

On the morning she got her letter, it had been Mary's bad luck to draw the job of feeding the pigs and she grumbled to Aunt Lily as she filled the bucket of foul-smelling swill from the big wooden barrel in the food shed.

'Aw Auntie Lily, why did you gie me the pigs? I'll be stinking and I'll never get the reek washed out of me before Fair Day. It gets into my hair and takes days to wash away. I'm meeting my folk at the Teviot Bridge on Monday and I'm wanting to look my best. They'll be able to smell be as far away as Hownam!'

Lily only laughed. 'You'll no' reek if you have a good wash, Mary. I cannae gie all the nasty jobs to the other lassies and let you off, can I? They'd say it was favouritism. Just get on with it and finish quick. Then you can run home and have a wash. I've left a kettle of water boiling on the fire for you and I made some fresh soap last week. It's in the crock behind the door. Don't worry, you'll look bonny enough to your mother – she'll be longing to see you. And what about that young lad you were dancing with in the road the other night? He wouldn't care if your face was as black as a sweep's. If looks are anything to go by he's fair daft about you.'

Mary bridled and the normal healthy glow of her cheeks deepened to scarlet. 'Oh, him! That's Jockie Armstrong. Well I'm no' daft about him. He's just a big red-faced loon and he aye stands on my feet when he dances with me. He doesn't ken his own strength either and throws me about as if I was a sack of wool when we're doing a reel. He'd better stay away from me, that one.'

Lily laughed. 'You wait. He's after you and he's a determined lad – I can tell by his eye. You'll have to run fast if you're to get away from Mr Armstrong. Who is he, anyway?'

'His father's the blacksmith down in Eckford. I'm no wanting to marry any blacksmith, Aunt Lily.'

'You could do worse. A smith's his own boss; he doesn't have to keep flitting all his life like we do,' said Lily more solemnly. 'But hurry up now and feed those pigs. They're fair squealin' wi' hunger.'

When Mary finished tipping buckets of swill into the big stone troughs in the pig pen, she stood back, pushed up her sleeves and surveyed the farm around her. It was a big, well-looked after place with neat fields rolling softly off towards the horizon in every direction. Their hay had been cut in all the five hayfields two weeks before and was now safely stacked in tall ricks in the cobbled yard behind her. Mary smiled as she remembered the fun of hay-making, for the weather had been good this year and there was much jollity and horseplay between the lads and lassies, as well as a good deal of drinking home-brewed beer. If this fine spell holds, she thought, the corn and barley harvest will be even better. These fields were not yet fully ripe but they were growing more golden with every day of glorious sunshine. When they were ready for cutting they would glow like molten gold beneath the sun.

Mary contemplated the coming harvest with pleasure. It was hard work but she was not afraid of that. She liked the ache of her tired muscles when she walked home at night and she loved the camaraderie of work in the corn-fields. She enjoyed the singing of the reapers as they cut the corn and she laughed at the sometimes blush-making jokes of the countrywomen who came in to help tie up the stooks, but most of all she looked forward to the harvest supper which was laid out in the big barn behind the farmhouse. The food at the supper was always abun-dant and the evening ended with noisy dancing to a fiddle band. Mary loved to dance.

Her face sobered a little when she reflected that Jockie Armstrong would be sure to turn up at the harvest supper and he'd head for her with the look of firm determination on his face that Aunt Lily had recognised and which Mary herself had learned to spot even from a distance. It was most certain that he'd be at St James' Fair as well and looking for her, because he'd asked her at the Saturday dance if she was going.

What did she think about Jockie? She wasn't sure because he said little but sometimes he irritated her and at other times she felt herself go all soft and funny when he took her hand. Not that she gave him any encouragement . . . She had no intention of settling down yet.

When she walked back to the big barn she met up with her friend Elsie, another bondager who was a couple of years older than Mary and a high-spirited girl. She called out, 'Looking forward to going fairin' are you, Mary? I hope this fine weather holds.'

Mary nodded. 'Yes, I'm looking forward to it right enough. I've had a letter from my Mam. She says they'll be waiting for me on the Teviot Bridge at twelve o'clock and it'll be grand to see them all again. I've not been home since the spring and then it was only for Mothering Sunday.'

Elsie gave her a friendly push. 'Och, you're no' going to spend all the Fair Day wi' your family, are you? You'll have to meet up with us lassies. We're out for a grand time. I'll look for you in the fairground and get you away from your ma. Then we'll show you some fun. Last year I drank so much beer that I had a headache fit to split my skull. I couldnae thole wearing my hat for three whole days after the Fair but what a laugh it was! It was worth it.'

Mary, feeling greatly daring, said she'd look out for Elsie although she privately wondered how she was going to give her mother the slip. In the meantime the first thing she wanted to do was go to the cottage and take the opportunity of washing herself all over while there was no one else at home.

Aunt Lily came in when she was almost finished and sitting in her shift on a wooden chair under the window drying her feet on a coarse towel. 'My word Mary but you're looking bonny and you dinna smell of pigs a bit,' said Lily, still laughing as she walked up to her niece and gave her a big sniff like a nosy dog. She's aye laughing, thought Mary in an exasperated way.

When Lily saw that the girl was offended she stopped teasing to say, 'Och, dinna take on. I've something you'll like. It's in the top drawer of that dresser over there. Go and bring it out. It's in a wee bottle.'

Mary stood on tiptoe and put her hand into the drawer. It was so high up that she had to feel around with her fingers for quite a while before a little bottle met her fingers. When she brought it out, she read on the faded label *Eau de Lavande*. A picture of a sprig of lavender was drawn beside the words.

'Oh, my word Aunt Lily, it's perfume,' she exclaimed.

'Aye, it's perfume and I've never used it though I've had it for years. A lady I used to work for gave it to me when I was getting married,' said Lily, 'but you can have it now as a reward for feeding the pigs for the rest of the week! It'll make you smell really bonny.' Then, unable to resist a joke, she added with her characteristic giggle, 'And it'll drive poor Jockie Armstrong fair mad!'

The question of fairtime finery was exercising the ingenuity of girls all over the countryside that day but Grace Elliot was one of the few exceptions. Hester had unlocked her door early in the morning so that she could start her day's work and, surprisingly, nothing more was said about their trouble of the previous day. It seemed as if her stepmother was trying to pretend the whole thing had never happened and she was no more surly than usual when she gave Grace a handful of coppers and told her to go down into town to buy some vegetables. The girl took her shopping basket from its hook in the pantry and walked to the square where she saw that crowds of women of all ages, encouraged by the long spell of good weather, were out buying new bonnets, lengths of ribbon and artificial flowers for last-minute trimmings. Her mind was full of speculation about what Odilie had found out about Lucy Allen from Martha but she dared not take time to go to Havanah Court until she'd carried out all her chores. Hester's rage, reactivated, could mean another day spent under lock and key.

Although she would have liked to linger in front of the haberdasher's window and watch the excited crowd inside handling the pretty things, Grace hurried past. Anyway, the money she clutched in her hand was not hers to spend and she reminded herself that because she had decided not to go to the Fair, she had no need of finery.

While Grace was lugging her basket back up to Viewhill, in Kirk Yetholm Thomassin Young had washed her scarlet shawl in the stream that ran behind her house and spread it out on a grassy bank. She pegged its edges with pieces of stone and sat down beside it to keep wandering dogs and staggering infants off until the sun dried it.

Her head was lowered and her thick curtain of straight

101

black hair fell around her like another shawl hiding her sharp, high cheek-boned face with the slanting enigmatic eyes that had the power to chill the blood of credulous people on whom she turned their power. Beautiful though she was, Thomassin already looked dangerous and capable of casting spells. As she sat barefoot in the sun wearing her ragged clothes, she was thinking about Jesse.

'I'm nineteen years old and I want to be rommed. I must bring him to the point . . .' Since childhood they had been promised to each other, an arrangement made early by their families but Jesse seemed reluctant to marry. He was always putting her off with excuses, saying first they should wait until spring and now, until autumn, though Thomassin knew there was no other girl in their community that had taken his eye more than herself for she was the most striking looking of them all. How to secure him for her own, she wondered. If she could get him into her bed, she would have won for the gypsies had a strict moral code that regulated relations between their men and women. Once Jesse slept with her, he was hers. There was no way that he could avoid marriage then.

She stretched out a hand and felt the cloth of her shawl. Already it was nearly dry because the sun was very hot. She'd wear it with her green skirt and the new black shoes with the flashing buckles that she'd stolen out of a lady's house near Berwick last week. She'd adorn herself with her late mother's golden jewellery, plait her hair and pile it up on her head. She'd look magnificent. A faint smile crossed her face as she planned how she'd slip her arm through Jesse's and lean her head against his shoulder. She'd wait till evening when he'd sold a few horses and had a few drinks with Gib and his friends, then she'd single him out and separate him from them like a collie dog cutting off a special ram from the flock. 'I'll get him this year,' she silently swore.

While she lifted her shawl from the grass and folded it up carefully, an old woman, walking with the aid of a knobbled stick, came limping over the grass towards her. 'Going to look bonny for our Jesse, are you?' his grandmother Rachel asked in her cracked voice as if she could read minds – which everyone in the community believed so there wasn't any point lying to old Rachel.

'I am. It's time we were properly rommed,' said the girl shortly.

'You've waited long enough,' agreed the old woman, eyeing the girl. 'You're ripe and ready for bairns now.'

'He's not though,' retorted Thomassin.

'No man ever is,' said Rachel with a wicked grin. 'They've got to be persuaded. You'll have to cast the glamourie on him.'

The girl looked up from beneath the falling sheet of hair. 'Tell me how, Rachel,' she said.

'There's ways. But they're costly.'

'How much?'

'To a Giorgio, the cost of a golden ring. To you, because I like you, nothing. Just give the firstborn girl my name.'

'I promise. What can I do about Jesse?'

Rachel was famous among the gypsies, and outside as well, for making up spells and potions. She could concoct draughts that enabled people to see into the future; she could dose sick animals and drive out the demon of sickness from people too; she could re-awaken a straying husband's affections, kindle love in someone indifferent or bring a rain of misfortune down upon an enemy's head. She knew how to make an impotent man rampant and a barren wife fruitful. No one talked about it but she also knew how to eliminate rivals and leave no trace of the deed. The girl was staring at her intently as she pleaded, 'Make me a potion that will bring him to me.'

The old woman sank down on to the bank and patted the grass beside her as she said, 'Sit here and listen. On sunrise of Fair Day, if it promises well – and it will – stand outside your door and say the word "Temon" three times.'

'Is that all?' Thomassin did not sound convinced.

Rachel shook her head. 'No, but that's the start of it. It means that during the day a man will fall deeply in love with you . . . it's up to you to make sure it's Jesse.

I'll make you a cordial to slip into his ale: five drops are enough. You'll have to gather the ingredients for me.'

'What do you need?'

'A phial of blood from a newborn baby. A woman in the last cottage in Town Yetholm had a bairn yesterday. Prick its finger when she's not looking. And you'll have to go out on to the hill and catch a snake. When you've got it, put it into a silk bag and bring it to me. I'll need a church candlestick too and a fresh goose quill.'

Thomassin did not ask where any of these things were to be acquired. She would find them, of that she was determined. With a smile she jumped to her feet and held out a hand to help Rachel up, 'I'll bring them tonight,' she said.

While Thomassin was out on the hill searching for an adder, Grace was frantically hurrying through her work because she was anxious to get down to Havanah Court and hear Odilie's news. It was after midday before she could make her escape and hurry all the way downhill, forgetting her worries about how awkward she must look in her limping run.

She found Odilie sitting on the boudoir floor surrounded by a froth of gowns with ruffles of lace, silk and muslin in every possible colour – pink, blue, mauve and cream, pale green and emerald, scarlet and midnight blue. Martha was in the corner sorting through a mound of artificial silken flowers which were so artistically made that they looked real. She peered up distractedly when Grace was shown in and cried, 'Oh Grace, come and help this girl decide what she's going to wear tonight. She's changed her mind four times already.'

'Where are you going?' Grace asked in amazement looking at the piles of beautiful materials.

'It's tonight that Father and I are having dinner with the Duke. Did you forget that?' said Odilie, listlessly picking up a strand of red ribbon and running it through her fingers.

'Yes, I did. I'm sorry,' said Grace, sitting down on the

floor beside her dispirited friend. She picked up the skirt of a pale blue gauze creation with tiny seed pearls stitched around the hem. 'Wear this. It looks lovely,' she sighed.

Odilie groaned, 'Not that. It's too sweet and virginal. I really want to wear sackcloth but Martha won't let me. Help me look my plainest, Grace. Dark blue doesn't suit me at all, so should I wear that?' She pointed at a shimmering dark dress that lay in a corner.

'Of course not. You must wear something that makes you look wonderful,' Grace said firmly as she rummaged about among the dresses. She pulled out a flounce of soft cream-coloured material with rosebuds embroidered all over it and announced, 'Now this is beautiful. Wear it.'

Odilie stood up and held the long straight gown in front of her slim body as she stared into her pier glass. 'Do you like it?' she asked and when Grace nodded, she turned and handed it to her friend. 'Then you must have it. It wouldn't do for a dinner party because it has long sleeves. There's a deep hem you could let down because you're taller than me. Take it and wear it to the Fair.'

Grace shook her head. 'Oh no, Odilie, I can't take it. I'd feel wrong – I'd feel like Cinderella wearing it. Anyway, I'm not going to the Fair.'

Odilie only laughed, but Martha was staring at Grace and suddenly asked, 'You're very white, my dear. What's the matter with you?'

'Nothing. I didn't sleep very well last night because after your note came I asked Hester about Bettymill and she said terrible things about my mother.'

'Of course – the note! I'm sorry, you must be longing to hear about your mother. What did Hester say?' asked Odilie and Grace shivered as she remembered.

'She said my mother was a whore . . .'

Odilie snapped angrily, 'What a horrible woman! Can't you complain to your father about the way she torments you?'

'I've told you, he doesn't listen and it would only make her worse. She'd wait till he went out and then get her revenge. It's odd that she didn't tell him about yesterday,

105

though . . .' Grace turned to Martha and asked desperately, 'Odilie said you knew my mother, Miss Rutherford. I want to know about her so much. Please tell me.'

Martha looked uncomfortable as if she wished she was miles away from the girls at that moment. 'I'm sorry I can't tell you very much, Gracie, but I assure you that Lucy wasn't a whore if that's what you're worried about. If there were any whores about, it wasn't her,' said Martha firmly, rising creakily to her feet and shaking a deluge of artificial roses out of her skirt. Though Odilie tried to stop her, she made to leave the room but added as a consolation for Grace, 'Don't let Hester bother you too much. She's never got over being your mother's servant.'

The girl among the dresses stared at her. 'A servant! Was she? I didn't know that!'

'She'd take care you didn't. Your mother brought her and Jessie as her servants when she came into town as a bride. Hester's father worked for your grandfather at Bettymill,' said Martha, pausing at the door.

Grace clasped both hands in an imploring gesture. 'Oh, tell me more. Tell me anything you can remember. Until yesterday I didn't even know about Bettymill. It's on the bank of the Tweed near Maxton, isn't it? Jessie used to take me there sometimes but I've not been back for a long, long time.'

Martha looked confused as if she'd said too much but her pity for the girl made her put off her departure long enough to say in a gentle voice, 'Your grandfather owned Bettymill. He was a prosperous man and your mother was his only child. He sent her to a fancy school for young ladies here in Lauriston because he wanted her to marry well and she was a credit to him, turned out very genteel and all that. She was quite a catch when your father met her.'

'And was he a catch, too?' asked Odilie sceptically.

Martha shook her head. 'Not so much. He was a poor laddie but he was clever as a box of weasels. Everybody knew he'd make his way in the world. He was awful ambitious.'

'If he was so ambitious, why did he marry Hester, his wife's maid?' asked Odilie in bemusement.

Martha shrugged. 'You've seen Hester – you should know why. She's aye been a roguish-looking woman and she was a lass for the men. She knew a thing or two.'

Grace's face was even whiter than it had been when she first arrived as she asked, 'Oh, please tell me what happened to my mother. She must have died very young.'

Martha was still at the door with her fingers on the handle. 'I think I can hear Canny calling on me,' she lied but her determination failed when she looked back at Lucy Allen's stricken daughter. 'Your mother was about twenty-two when she was – taken. Poor lassie. Now I must go because I've things to see to in the kitchen. Those maids can't be trusted on their own.'

Though Odilie ran over and tried to hold her back, Martha hurried out of the room and disappeared downstairs.

' "Taken" – that's a funny word to use but we'll not get any more out of her,' said Odilie coming back to where Grace stood among the tumbled gowns.

'I wonder why she's so strange about it. I'm beginning to think my mother must have killed herself or something and that's why people won't talk about it. If she did, I wish I knew why. She was so young and had so much to live for,' sighed Grace.

'I'm determined to find out the story though it'll take time,' said Odilie confidently. 'Now sit down and I'll tell you exactly what Martha and my father said last night about your mother, even though you know most of it already.'

Grace stayed at Havanah Court discussing the business of Lucy over and over again with Odilie all afternoon; she was still there at five o'clock when her friend began to dress for the Duke's dinner. At six she was standing in the hall, eyes round with wonder and admiration, when

Canny and his daughter mounted their carriage to ride up to Sloebank Castle.

When she was settled in her place and her skirt carefully folded around her by a solicitous Joe so that it would not crush, Odilie looked down at her friend on the doorstep and cried, 'But you mustn't walk all the way home, Grace. Come with us and we'll drop you at your door.'

The Elliots did not own a carriage and Grace felt tremendous pride as she rode along with the Rutherfords and saw how people came rushing to their windows to look at the equipage as it drove through the town.

She and Martha had prevailed on Odilie to dress in her most beautiful gown and she sat regally magnificent in cream satin with flounces of costly Brussels lace; a wreath of cream-coloured roses and ivy lay on her springing hair and a silken shawl patterned with Persian whorls in dark reds and purples was draped over her arms. She carried a fan of curled ostrich feathers and even though her father had wanted to deck her out in rubies and emeralds, the jewellery she and Grace had chosen was simple – a necklet of tiny seed pearls woven together into a broad choker that encircled her long neck and bracelets to match around both wrists on top of her white kid gloves.

'You look truly lovely, Odilie,' were Grace's parting words when the carriage stopped to let her out at Viewhill.

'Don't depress me,' said her friend.

Venturing into high society held no terrors for Canny Rutherford, nor for his daughter. He had the confidence of someone who long ago had taken the measure of many grandees and knew that, whether clad in fashionable clothes or rags, men were much the same all over the world. His money and mental adroitness gave him a security and an aplomb that allowed him to brush aside any social gaffes he might make. He knew he could buy and sell most of the people who looked down their snobbish noses at him anyway.

He had made sure however that his daughter was well schooled in the nuances of polite society. After he brought her back from Jamaica to join him, Odilie was sent to the most exclusive girls' school in London where she learned her lessons among the daughters of the aristocracy. After two years she pleaded to be allowed to return home but by then she could hold her own with anyone. She knew which pieces of cutlery and which wine glasses to use at dinner; she could make conversation upon any subject; she could play the harp, the piano and sing sweetly; she knew how to flirt with her fan and dance a stately measure. There was not a titled lady in all London who could comport herself with more confidence that Odilie Rutherford.

This paragon of a daughter now sat beside Canny with a set face and he squeezed her hand in reassurance.

'If you don't like him, I'll call it off,' he promised and meant what he said. Let Elliot and the money go hang, he thought, Odilie's the most important thing in the world.

She smiled but her lips were trembling as she whispered, 'It's not that so much. I'm nervous: are you sure he knows about my colour?' She was dreading the recoil that might show in the behaviour of the Duke or his friends when she was introduced, for she had witnessed such a reaction too often before. It was useless to console herself by saying that it did not matter, that it might be her way out of a distasteful marriage. Even though she loathed the man in advance, she would be personally wounded if the Duke was repelled by her colour.

Her eyes were seeking Canny's in entreaty and he assured her, 'He knows. Don't worry about it.'

He was almost bursting his skin with pride when their horses drew up at the portico of the Duke's mansion and a line of flunkeys ran forward to open the carriage door. Canny was so affected that tears glistened in his eyes as he stepped out first and held out a hand to assist his beautiful daughter to alight. Then he turned and proffered his arm so that he could lead her up the shallow steps to where their host was waiting.

James Aubrey Fox, second son of the penultimate 6th

Duke, had been scorned as a boy for his brutishness, stupidity and ponderousness. He enjoyed the ritual of receiving guests at his house because he relished their gratitude for being invited and basked in their compliments, for he had never expected to be in such an exalted position. Being an unloved son, he had grown up expecting nothing better than a life in the Army, a little hunting and the patronising hospitality of his brother and better-off relatives. Then his brother, who had succeeded their father at the age of nineteen, was drowned twenty-one years later and James, an officer in the Hussars, inherited the title and Sloebank Castle. Two years on he was still finding it difficult to believe his luck.

As he stood in the hall watching the dark girl in cream satin alight from her carriage, he made a futile effort to suck in his large belly. Far from being dismayed by her colour, he was excited by it. The dusky maiden was just what his jaded tastes required, for he'd had his fill of the bucolic blondes, brunettes and redheads available on his estate. He eyed Odilie as if she was a trophy, something that he had won in a game of Chance, and gave a vulpine smile that made her flesh cringe as his eyes ran from the top of her ivy-crowned head to the tip of her satin slippers.

His cheeks were flushed a deep shade of carmine and his lips were even redder for he had been drinking heavily and looked what he was – a middle-aged libertine who had tried every variety of dissipation and been satisfied by none of them. When he held out his hand towards her, it took all her schooling in manners not to draw back from him.

He did not notice Odilie's distaste and would not have credited it if he had, for after all – he was the Duke, wasn't he? She must admire him for his social position alone – everyone else did. All he was concerned about was his own reaction to the girl.

'I was right. She's a beauty. She could pass for an Italian any day. It won't be any trouble taking this one to bed. I'll have to get myself an apothecary's potion so that I can perform properly,' he thought, and squeezed her gloved hand tightly.

Odilie looked down at her feet as he took the shawl from her shoulders. In spite of her training the touch of his hand on her skin was almost too much to bear and her skin involuntarily flinched away from him. He noticed and smiled. So she was virginal – good. The more they fought, the more he was excited and the easier it was to do anything. He was beaming as he led her through the dark hall into a brilliantly lit drawing room with crackle-surfaced mirrors on its dark green walls. A group of fashionably dressed men and bejewelled women were clustered before a blazing fire for, in spite of the warmth of the summer night outside, fires were always necessary in a mansion where lingering chills and damp seemed to lurk perpetually in the passages and corridors.

The company fell silent and watched the approach of the Rutherfords with such open-mouthed curiosity that it was obvious they had been discussing Odilie and her father before they appeared. There was enough of Canny in the girl to make her draw back her shoulders and march proudly into their midst like a queen and she was gratified to see that the group parted deferentially in front of her. Led onwards by her host, she found herself beside a high-backed chair at the fireside. In it was sitting a very old crone whose eyebrows and mouth were heavily painted on to a mask of white lead. Although her hair was naturally grey, it was thickly powdered and dressed high in a style that had gone out of fashion thirty years before. She also wore an old-fashioned, diamond-shaped black patch stuck in the middle of one wizened cheek. She was eyeing the newcomer with undisguised curiosity as the Duke introduced them to each other. 'This is my aunt, Lady Augusta Morley,' he said, and the old woman twisted her wry mouth into a rictus of an insincere smile and raised a languid hand to Odilie. The little yellowed eyes in the painted face glinted maliciously beneath heavily wrinkled lids.

'I spent ten years in Ind-yah with my first husband – in Madras. Which part are you from?' she asked.

Odilie flushed slightly but kept her composure. 'I've never been to India, I'm afraid,' she said.

'Really . . .' drawled Lady Augusta and glanced round the company. 'Gel says she's never been to Ind-yah,' she told them and then laughed as if Odilie had either told an outrageous lie or made a joke. They laughed too, and then returned to their own conversations. Odilie felt her colour rising as Lady Augusta turned back and addressed a spot above the girl's head as if she was not there. 'I remember those half-caste gels, so lovely when they're young but it doesn't last long. How old is this one, I wonder – eighteen, nineteen? They get fat and much darker as the years go on. They end up black as coal in the end. And none of them can sing. They croak like crows – quite funny, really.'

She gave a witchlike cackle and someone behind Odilie laughed too, which encouraged Lady Augusta so she looked directly at the girl again and asked pointedly, 'You didn't say how old you are – and can you sing, my dear?'

'I'm eighteen and I leave singing to paid entertainers,' said Odilie boldly. In fact she could sing quite well but was not going to admit it to this horrible old woman.

'What did I tell you?' asked Lady Augusta of the company who, although they were pretending to be otherwise engrossed, were listening with unconcealed delight. Odilie glanced round at her father and saw that, like her, he burned with resentment. Their host stood with his back to the fireplace and a fatuous smile on his face. He did not have the courtesy to smooth the way for Odilie and she felt angry that he had presented her to the wicked old woman like a Christian being thrown to the lions. Her surge of anger made any nervousness or fear of rejection she might have still felt, disappear entirely. For the rest of the evening she was determined to adopt an attitude of bored indifference.

It was soon made obvious to the Rutherfords that if they imagined the dinner had ben laid on in Odilie's honour, they were mistaken. The other guests were all the Duke's friends or relations who cared little or nothing about her and it was even doubtful if they all knew that she had been suggested as a possible bride for their host.

Around a massive table in the dining room at Sloebank Castle sat a very mixed company. At the top of the table on her host's left, Lady Augusta held forth about her distinguished past to male sporting friends of the Duke who had come up to visit the Fair and follow that with some shooting. They were accompanied by a bevy of painted and brightly dressed women with cackling voices which became progressively more raucous as the night wore on.

In a company of twenty there were a few people of title – only a Sir This or Lady That with a Countess and a foreign Marquis thrown in for good measure but none of them were particularly distinguished and they all looked and sounded like the sort of people who would go any-where for a free bed and a hot dinner. Canny Rutherford took note of them and realised that he had met many people of similar sort in distant parts of the world.

He was proud that Odilie remained cool and self-contained as she was led to a seat on the right side of the Duke. When she looked at the place settings however, she realised that it was Lady Augusta and not she who was in the place of honour because the Duke's cutlery was laid out in reverse order with the wine glasses and knives ranked on his left. The host was left-handed. She remem-bered that Aunt Martha's word for someone who was sinister-handed was 'Foxy-pawed'. So left-handedness must be a Fox characteristic too – like the curse, thought Odilie with a faint smile.

The food, when it appeared after a long wait, was tepid which meant there had been a considerable trip from the kitchens. The menu was uninspiring and would not have been appetising even if served hot, so it was not difficult for Odilie to conform with the polite code of behaviour for young ladies and send most of her meal back untouched. She was not alone in that for many of the guests did the same although they made up their abstinence by drinking heavily. If the food was bad, the wine was of a very superior quality, for Sloebank possessed a famous cellar which had been laid down by a previous Duke and not yet drunk up in entirety by succeeding incumbents.

The Duke ate and drank with gusto and only every now and again would he suddenly remember the girl by his side and address a remark to her in much the same way as he would have tossed a scrap of meat to a pet dog. His comments were usually banal and easy to answer for he did not expect anything of moment to be said in reply to such things as, 'Fine weather . . . Hope it holds up for the Fair . . .' Not that he noticed her lack of communication because he was far more interested in drinking claret than in talking at any great length. It was the man on her left who told her about the Sloebank library. He asked her if she enjoyed reading and when she said she did, he went on, 'There used to be a splendid library here. The previous Duke collected it.'

'Used to be?' she asked with raised eyebrows. Their host, catching a snatch of their conversation, leaned over and said, 'My brother bought books. I'm selling them off.'

'That's a pity. Don't you share your brother's interests?' she asked him.

'Which ones? Don't worry my pretty, I'm not keen on boys if that's your meaning. Girls are more to my taste.' He laughed and put a freckled hand on her thigh, squeezing it so tight that she gave an involuntary gasp of pain.

After a second, she collected herself sufficiently to say, 'I meant, aren't you interested in books?'

'I sent the whole damned lot down to London. There was an awful fuss about the sale for some reason. People were buying like mad but it raised a good bit of money. They weren't doing any good up here, taking up space and gathering dust. Besides, nobody ever reads the things.'

Regretting the dispersed library Odilie stared around the dining room and noted how shabby everything was when she looked really hard. The gilding on most of

114

the pictures was flaking, the centrepieces lined along the middle of the table were tarnished, the curtains looked threadbare and the dessert china proved to be chipped when she ran her fingertip around the edge of her plate. The Duke either didn't care or he was more in need of money than even the locals imagined – he certainly was in need of taste.

She knew that by the rules of the game she should have been flirting with him by now but she deliberately desisted from doing so. They could go on standing on ceremony with each other for ever as far as she was concerned and as the night wore on her spirits sank. She saw him to be a boor and disliked him more and more. By the time the ladies rose and left the dining table, it had become a strain to talk to him.

When the party reassembled in the adjoining salon, there was a great deal of laughing and shouting by exuberant people who'd had a great deal to drink. Odilie stifled a yawn and looked curiously around. This room was hung with dusty tapestries of hunting scenes, and gaming tables, covered with cards and counters, were laid out around the two fireplaces, one at each end of the room. Lady Augusta led the rush to find a seat near the most comforting blaze. Her eyes glittered as she started to ruffle the cards with adroit sharper's hands while she called out to Canny Rutherford, 'You look like a gaming man to me. D'you fancy a hand of loo?'

He smiled cherubically. 'I was a gambling man once but my gaming days are over, my Lady. I stopped that long ago.'

She glared back at him, obviously disappointed for she had selected him as a likely bird for plucking but he did not give up his feathers easily. 'Tight pursed are you?' she asked rudely.

He smiled seraphically. 'Very tight pursed and it's a good thing I have been, I think.' His last remark was pointed and marked the end of the night's strained socialising as far as he and his daughter were concerned. His next move was to pull out his watch and say with a note of false surprise in his voice, 'How late it's growing! It's time we went home.' No one argued.

They left immediately and when the Duke took his leave of her, Odilie was given the unhappy impression that as far as he was concerned, she had scored a great success. As they rode back down the hill to Lauriston neither Canny nor Odilie dared to start talking about the subject that was uppermost in both of their minds. They wanted to retire to their beds and do a lot of private thinking first, for to talk without premeditation would have been like opening a basket of coiling snakes. They were both wrestling with the same problem, however, for they were wondering how Odilie could possibly become the wife of that particular Duke of Maudesley.

CHAPTER 5

Saturday 1 August

Both Odilie and her father endured wretched sleeplessness
that night but when dawn was about to break, they drifted
into dreamless slumbers that made them oversleep their
normal hours of rising.

Canny awoke liverish and in a grim mood. As he sat
up in bed and scowled at Joe who had wakened him, it
was possible to discern the iron in him which had made
it possible to survive and thrive in a lawless society. His
brows were lowered, his mouth thin and his blue eyes
half-hidden by dropped eyelids. He looked menacing and
Joe threw up his hands exclaiming, 'Lord a' mercy, what's
bothering you this morning?'

'It's Odilie. I can't do it to her,' Canny snapped, shoving his feet out of bed.

'It was a mad idea from the beginning,' said Joe unsympathetically. 'You went off too fast as usual. You should
have asked her if she wanted him.'

'Don't tell me what I did or didn't do! Send a messenger
and fetch that lawyer down here. Tell him it's urgent.
Then make me my coffee.'

Joe was impossible to deflate. 'You know what coffee
does to your liver. Miss Martha says you're not to have
it,' he told his employer.

Canny gave a roar like a wounded bull. 'I want my
coffee and I don't give a damn what Martha says! And I
want that lawyer here . . .' The last words were directed
at Joe's disappearing back.

Even before Canny had drunk his first cup of breakfast
coffee, a beverage he had become used to in the Indies
and which he imported for his own use, Grace was taking
a folded note from the hand of the boy who had carried

117

it from Havanah Court. 'Maister Rutherford's man said that I was to make sure the lawyer gets this at once,' the boy told her. 'He said Canny's in a wax, lowerin' like thunder.'

The girl nodded and ran with the message to her father, who was dressing for the office which opened on Saturday mornings. Because he was tying his neckcloth he tut-tutted irritably at the sight of the paper in her hand and told her to read it out to him.

' "Come AT ONCE. Do not delay. Important business" ' read Grace. 'The "at once" is underlined three times, Father.'

'Canny Rutherford!' said Elliot in a voice of disgust and started stamping about the little dressing room. 'What a damned man! Thinks I've no clients except himself. He and his daughter were up at Sloebank Castle for dinner last night, weren't they? This must have something to do with that business. I'll need to be quick and get it over with. Go and saddle the horse, girl.'

As Andrew Elliot was leaving the house he called over his shoulder to his daughter, 'Come down to town later and fetch the horse from Havanah Court stable. I'll leave her there and go straight to the office. Don't forget.'

He found Canny waiting for him, still clad in his white nightshirt, with a long Paisley wrapper around his shoulders and a red velvet nightcap on his head. In spite of two cups of coffee, he still looked thunderous and as soon as Elliot's head showed round the door, he called out impatiently, 'Come in, come in, what took you so long? I've decided to back out now. I can't marry my lassie to that man. I've seen too many of his kind – he's not good enough for her. You've got to get us out of it.'

Elliot closed the door carefully behind him and, as was his habit when he needed time to think, leaned his back against it for a few seconds before saying, 'The Duke's the same man as he was last Wednesday morning when you were so pleased to be claiming him as a future son-in-law. What's happened to change your mind?'

Canny stared bleakly across the room. 'He's a fool. If

118

he's not a drunk already, he soon will be. He's a lecher too or I'm vastly mistaken. He's greedy and stupid and insensitive and he'll never appreciate Odilie.'

'Who could?' asked Elliot, with only the faintest note of sarcasm in his voice.

Canny shot a sharp glance at him but went on regardless, 'I don't care about the money. I've plenty more where the ten thousand came from. What's been bothering me all night is what I'd have on my conscience if I were to do this to my girl. Her spirit would shrivel up if she was married to a man like that.'

Elliott pulled out a chair from the side of the table in the middle of the floor and sat down heavily in it. He sighed. 'You're a bit late thinking like this. You agreed to his first letter; you went to dinner at Sloebank; he showed her off to his friends. If he wants to go through with it, you'll find it hard to back out. Cool down: perhaps you're only overreacting, Mr Rutherford. You'd never met him before had you? What happened at the dinner? Did he insult you or something – has the girl been complaining?'

Canny shook his head. 'No, none of those things. He was cordial enough. It was just that I saw what sort of life Odilie would have with him. I could see that she disliked him too, though to do her justice she never said a word about it, but I noticed if he brushed against her, she recoiled as if he was a snake.'

Elliot clicked his tongue. 'My dear man, that's normal. She's virginal and probably terrified of men. Girls are often like that. It's rather appealing. I sometimes think they do it deliberately.'

Canny glared. 'My girl's not like that. You don't know Odilie if you even think it. No, I could tell that she didn't like him. He repelled her. Remember, I gave her my promise that I'd call it off if she felt she couldn't go through with it. So I want you to write to him and cancel our agreement today.'

Elliot gave a heavy shrug. 'On your own head be it, but I hope you realise what's likely to happen. He'll crucify you and all your family.' He said nothing about what was likely to happen to his own career but he was thinking about it with disquiet.

'It's only money. I've plenty,' said Canny.

The lawyer looked doleful. 'It's not just money, I wish it was. Who's going to marry your girl after all this? It'll be put about that the Duke turned her down because she's coloured or ill-mannered or sickly – they could say anything. No one'll believe that she was the one who did the rejecting. No one'll ever believe that she refused a Duke.'

'Odilie will easily find a husband. You've only to look at her to see that,' said her loving father.

'But what *kind* of a husband?' said Elliot in an insinuating tone. 'Certainly no man of rank and position will offer for her . . . the Duke'll see to that.'

Canny frowned but held to his decision. 'Don't try to change my mind. Just work out what we can do. You're a lawyer, you should know how to phrase it,' he said.

Elliot frowned. 'Mmm, perhaps we can say she's been taken ill. I know! We can say she's gone mad and you had to send her back to Jamaica. Thompson the surgeon's come to town from Edinburgh. I saw him arriving at the Cross Keys yesterday. He's an old friend of yours, isn't he? He'll give a medical opinion . . . He'll say anything you want.'

Canny gasped in protest. 'Odilie gone mad! I couldn't say that, of course not. There must be another way. Can't you think of something else?'

Elliot mused with his chin on his fist. 'We could say *you've* gone mad and need her at home – no, that wouldn't work because if she married him, she'd only be a mile and a half up the road. You could tell the Duke there's madness in your family and she's been advised not to have any children – but that mightn't put him off because of the size of the dowry.' He looked across at Canny and asked, 'Are you sure this is what you want to do? It's a tremendous chance for the girl and you know what those society marriages are like. They won't even need to see much of each other once the deed's done. They can maintain separate households if they like – no one will think anything about it.'

'I know all that and I can see the trouble with the excuses but I know how much she dislikes him and I gave her my promise,' said Odilie's father, who was weakening slightly.

Elliot pressed his advantage. 'As I've said before, you're far too indulgent. Sometimes parents have to be firm for a girl's own good. She might not be very enthusiastic at the moment but in the years to come she'll bless you for this. Did she say anything to you about calling it off last night? No? Then she might not be as against it as you imagine. Think of the advantages of contracting this wedding against the disadvantages of backing out – and I don't only mean financial. You ought to speak to Odilie about this.'

'She's not up yet and when we came home from Sloebank last night we were both so depressed we couldn't even mention it.'

'In that case, I'll go over to my office for an hour until you've had time to talk with her. Then I'll come back and we'll make up our minds what to do.'

Odilie was in her lace-edged wrapper and yawning when her father tapped on the door. He made no pretence about the object of his visit and came straight to the point. 'What did you think of him, my dear?' he asked.

She gazed at him and her caramel eyes were bleak. 'I disliked him, Father.'

'Do you want out of the marriage?'

'If such a thing is possible,' she said in a polite and measured tone.

'I'll speak to Elliot,' he told her and left, closing the door softly.

When the lawyer arrived back, Canny was dressed and waiting for him in the library. 'It's decided. We want to withdraw. Should I send him the money in orders or in cash?'

Elliot frowned. 'I've bad news, Mr Rutherford. When

I reached my office I found that there was a letter from Sloebank. The Duke wants to go ahead with the marriage and he's most enthusiastic.'

'So?' Canny raised his eyebrows. 'We write and tell him the arrangement's cancelled. I send the money and that's that.'

'It's not quite so easy, I'm afraid. He's very touchy. He'll be furious that we've waited for him to accept and then turned him down. It's a calculated insult to a man like him. Duels have been fought for less.'

'Odilie wants me to call it off,' persisted Canny.

In spite of his habitual restraint, Elliot was on the verge of sounding frantic. 'She can't appreciate the seriousness of this. Let me speak to her, please.'

Canny agreed but without enthusiasm. 'All right, speak to her but I want to know everything she says. If she's still upset, I'll call it off no matter what you say.'

When Odilie answered the summons to her father's library, only Elliot the lawyer was there. 'Sit down, my dear Miss Rutherford,' he said in a tone as smooth as butter. 'We've a great deal to discuss. I understand that you're reluctant to agree to this marriage.'

She sat looking solemn. 'I don't care for the man, if that's what you mean.'

The tall, grim-looking man and the dark girl with the proudly carried head stared at each other challengingly. 'What exactly do you not like about the Duke?' he asked.

She frowned. 'I don't like the way he looks for one thing, and he's much older than I am. Then I don't like his behaviour or his friends. He makes me feel uncomfortable.'

Elliot gave a thin smile. 'We can't all be an Adonis, unfortunately. As for his friends, when you're mistress of the Castle, it'll be up to you to invite the people who sit at your husband's table.'

The girl gave a shiver and, seeing it, Elliot tried a different tack. 'Your father has called me here to instruct me that if you want to withdraw from the contract, I must arrange that. But before I do so I must make sure that is really what you wish. You should first know that the Duke himself has repeated his offer – in most enthusiastic terms, I may add.'

She gave a little unsurprised nod and said, 'I only wish this whole thing had never started.'

'Perhaps – but it has. An offer has been made and accepted by your father, precipitately perhaps, but that's his way. Now because of your whim, we'll have to try to back out of it without too much pain being caused.' She opened her mouth to protest but he kept on talking in a musing way, 'we can't say you don't like him because he makes you feel uncomfortable, can we? Or that you don't like his friends!' He gave a little laugh at the absurdity of the idea as the girl stared at him without expression. Then he leaned forward and asked her, 'How would you feel if we said you've been taken ill? Your father's old school-friend who's a doctor in Edinburgh has come to town for the Fair. He'll testify that you're not in a fit state to marry. That would be a good way out.'

'But the Duke saw me last night and I was perfectly well then.'

'You could have developed some ailment that doesn't show. Something in the mind, perhaps?'

She stared at him in horror. 'I should go mad, you mean?'

Elliot leaned back. 'Your father's against the idea but I thought you might consider it a possibility.'

She stood up, very flustered. 'Certainly not! I'm not going to put myself through such a demeaning charade to save that man's face. This is ridiculous. Can't I just say I've changed my mind? People do that all the time.'

Elliot nodded. 'You're right, of course. If we said you'd gone mad or were even physically unstable you'd never find a decent husband though some man will still have you for your dowry no doubt.'

Odilie was pink-cheeked with anger. 'How dare you talk about me as if I was an animal to be sold! I have some choice in this. If I don't like the man I don't have to marry him. Tell him that! Tell him I don't like him enough to take him for my husband. Tell him he's not to my taste even though he is a Duke.'

Elliot took a notepad and pencil from his pocket with a sigh. 'All right, Miss Rutherford, that's what I'll tell him . . .' He wrote a few words. ' "Not to your taste". But I hope you're prepared for the consequences. Your poor father will suffer beyond his own imagining. How's he going to take leaving Havanah Court? He's so devoted to this house. Think of the work he's put into it . . . and he's not young any longer, the trouble could well kill him.'

Odilie's eyes were anxious as she stared at the man in front of her. 'What trouble? Why should Father leave his house? Surely it's only talk about what the Duke will do to him. He wouldn't be so petty.'

Elliot shut his notebook with a snap. 'It's not all talk, I'm afraid. I could tell you very sad stories about things that have happened to people who have annoyed the Duke in the most trivial ways – far beneath the scale of your rebuff. He's a vindictive man, I'm afraid, and has immense power. The gossip about this wedding is all over the countryside already and he'll be publicly affronted if you turn him down. It's beyond imagining what lengths he'll go to if you reject him but I know your father will be ruined, utterly ruined. So will you, come to that, but you're young – and you're the one who's making the decision.'

His eyes were cold and unsympathetic as he went on, 'Think about the consequences of this. Your position in this town will be impossible and your father will be broken – is that an incidental as far as you are concerned? The Duke will exact a terrible revenge. I'm telling you that the loss of your father's money will only be the start of it. You love your father, don't you?'

The girl nodded in a frightened way for she was only beginning to realise how tight was the corner into which she was being manoeuvred. Elliot pressed on, 'Then if you love your father and don't want to see him penniless, if you don't want to see him driven out of his home and deprived of his friends, if you don't want to see him ruined, perhaps even killed by the shame of it, start behaving in a realistic manner. I presume you know that your father started life in this town as a beggar – do you want him to die in the same condition because of you?'

She shuddered and sighed deeply. 'So what you're saying is that I haven't any choice really. All the talk about being able to back out was only a lie. That's what you're telling me.'

'Not a lie . . . it's only that events have overtaken us. You must look on the bright side, Miss Rutherford. You'll be a great lady,' the lawyer told her.

Odilie's face was bleak and she suddenly looked much older than her eighteen years. 'I'm caught in a trap,' she cried, and sank her head in her hands while her shoulders shook with silent weeping but Elliot's sympathies were not awakened.

'It'll be a very silken trap,' he told her.

When Canny Rutherford was called in and told by his grim-faced daughter that the agreement to marry was to stand, he took her hands in his, stared into her face and asked, 'Are you sure, Odilie? Really sure, I mean? It won't matter to me what I lose if you are against this.'

She stared back at him but her eyes were blank as she nodded her head. 'Yes, I'm sure, Father. It's too difficult to get out now so I've decided to go ahead with it. As Mr Elliot has reminded me, I'll be a Duchess after all and that's a great advantage. Don't worry about me, I can look after myself. I'm not your daughter for nothing.'

He embraced her and told her, 'You're a strong-willed girl, I know. Don't worry, I'll make sure you've a watertight marriage contract. You'll be richer than him from the beginning and you'll stay that way. He won't be able to waste your money.'

She smiled bleakly but the words that were in her mind were not uttered. 'Money isn't everything. What about love? Am I never to know what that feels like? Apparently not.'

A baby lay in its cradle in the sunshine while its mother

worked in her kitchen, fondly glancing out at her child every now and again with a rapturous smile on her face. The smile disappeared when she saw a gypsy girl come slinking through the garden gate and head up the path towards her door.

She pushed her head out of the open window and called with a fearful tremor in her voice, 'I don't want any pegs or horn spoons, thank you very much.'

Thomassin smiled and said sweetly, 'That's all right. I saw your baby and thought I'd put a blessing on it. Is it a boy or a girl, missus?' She spoke in the peculiar wheed-ling way that gypsies had and the young mother came out of the low-roofed thatched cottage, wiping her hands and preparing to pick up the precious child. The girl's flashing eyes intimidated her, however, for she was terri-fied of gypsies.

'It's a girl,' she whispered. She knew it was best not to antagonise these people for she was a country girl and had lived in Town Yetholm all her life.

Thomassin knelt down by the side of the cradle and smiled even more sweetly. 'She's a flower, a beauty. She'll break hearts and she'll marry money – lots of money. Look at her little hands.' She lifted one of the sleeping baby's tightly curled fists that lay like drifted pink petals on the white cover. Still smiling gently, she opened the perfect little fingers. The mother smiled too, half-flattered and hopeful that the gypsy meant no harm. But she was wrong, for before her horrified eyes Thomassin took a needle from the fold of her shawl and stabbed it into the baby's thumb. A scarlet pearl of blood welled up and the baby woke with a scream which the mother echoed when she sprang forward with both fists raised. Thomassin, still holding the baby's hand, put out an arm to fend her off. 'Stand back,' she ordered. 'Stand back, or I'll curse this child. I need some red stuff from it, that's all. I'll put a spell of good fortune on the bairn if I get what I want.'

Intimidated, the mother hesitated and while the baby screwed up its face and howled, Thomassin captured a few drops of its blood in a tiny phial of glass. Then she

126

dropped the little fist and ran away while the terrified mother hugged the equally terrified infant to her bosom and they both cried.

Rachel was in her dark and filthy bothy in Kirk Yetholm half a mile away when Thomassin came crashing in through the door carrying a full sack. 'I've got it all! I've got a goose quill, a church candlestick, a snake in a silken bag and a phial of baby's blood,' she gasped.

The old woman was almost hidden in the shadows by the fireside but her voice came out loud and clear. 'Go and pick a white rosebud and a red one and two leaves of white clover. When you've got them rinse them in fresh well-water. I'll dry the snake's head here by the fire. Leave the flowers at my cottage door and come back at midnight.'

Thomassin was disappointed. 'At midnight? So late? I want to give it to him soon.'

'At midnight,' said Rachel firmly. 'This can't be done in daylight or in a hurry. The potion won't be ready till Fair Day. I told you that already.'

It was after midday before Hester allowed Grace to leave Viewhill and fetch her father's horse.

'That's only an excuse,' she scolded. 'You're wanting to go down there to talk fancy with your friend. But make the best of it, she'd drop you when she's a Duchess.' It was not easy for Grace to maintain a meek attitude as she was harried through her work, but she managed to keep a curb on her tongue although something must have shown in her demeanour, there must have been a new look of defiance in her eye, for her step-mother was especially vicious and fault-finding that morning. It was only the fact that the grey mare had to be fetched and Hester herself was afraid of horses that gave Grace her eventual freedom.

Havanah Court looked deserted when she approached it and Joe Cannonball met her at the door. 'You've missed Miss Odilie, she's gone off over the bridge on her new horse. She's in a funny mood, like her father. She said to tell you to go after her.'

'What's happened?' asked Grace.

'It's that marriage of course but I'll let her tell you the story herself. Poor baby, she's low in spirits and could do with your company,' Joe told her.

Grace knew that her father was busy in his office and Hester was almost certainly asleep, for she claimed that hot days exhausted her though she slept just as heavily on cold afternoons as well. There was no reason why an hour or two could not be snatched to spend with Odilie. When Stevens saddled the grey for her, she did not head for home but kirtled up her skirts and turned the safe old mare off along the cobbles of Bridge Street towards where Joe Cannonball indicated Odilie had crossed the river. Grace was happy at being in the saddle and raised her head with a smile for people she passed on the roadway. The sun shone down and when she was riding she felt whole and healthy, an entirely different person, temporarily liberated from the constraints of her damaged leg and not the cripple she was when she had both feet on the ground.

It was just short of twenty minutes to three when she trotted up the approach to the Rennie Bridge. The toll-keeper knew her and waved her on without asking for any money but when she reached the other side, she paused at the cross roads: one road went south to Yetholm, the second led to Heiton and Jedburgh while the third headed west in the direction of Maxton – and Bettymill! A feeling of excitement rose in Grace's throat at the thought of going back there.

There was no sign of Odilie, no one to ask if she had passed that way and no indication of which road she had taken. On impulse Grace turned the head of the mare towards the west. If she met Odilie, good and well, but she had made up her mind to go to Bettymill.

The sun's blaze was dazzling; it was the hottest part of the afternoon and there were no other people walking on the dry and dusty road as it twisted along the bank of the

Tweed. On the far side of the river was the elegant spread of Havanah Court, embowered in its gorgeous gardens, but soon the road made a sharp turn to the left and headed for the confluence of the Tweed with the Teviot. Grace paused by the place where the waters mingled and watched the brown Teviot water surge into the blue-grey flow of the Tweed. The rivers seemed to rush at each other like old friends, laughing when they met, surging round in great swirls as if they were clasping arms. The sight of such exuberance made the girl's spirits lift – it was a beautiful day and she was free of her cares for a little while.

Happily she tapped her heel on the mare's flank and set her trotting towards the next bridge that raised its humped back across the Teviot. Grace had not been over this bridge for a long time and the keeper did not recognise her. With a curmudgeonly look on his face he held out a hand for her penny toll but she leaned down from the saddle and apologised, 'I'm sorry but I haven't any money.'

'In that case you'll not cross,' he said, jerking a finger at the bar behind him.

'You could collect my toll from my father,' she suggested, for now that she was on her way to Bettymill she was determined that nothing was going to stop her.

'And whae's your fayther then?' asked the toll-keeper suspiciously.

'He's Mr Elliot the lawyer.' The gate was swung open then, for Grace knew that Anrew Elliot was one of the turnpike trustees and no toll-keeper would dare to refuse his daughter the right to pass.

The road was prettier now because it ran along below ancient trees by the side of the field in which the Fair was to be held in two days' time. She could see that people were already erecting stalls and driving in stakes for horses to be hobbled. Grace loved the Fair and in her mind's eye she saw the empty field filled with crowds of people and animals, with stalls, sideshows and tents of every colour. She had visited the Fair every year for as

129

far back as she could remember and would hate to miss it, but she reminded herself briskly of her resolution to stay away this year, then had to scold herself not to indulge in self-pity. Her decision to miss the occasion still held good for she was more afraid of disappointment or disillusion than she was of going without entertainment while everyone else was enjoying themselves. If her resolution faltered she thought how she would feel if she saw the fair-haired young gallant with another girl – or if she met him and he did not recognise her! No, she told herself, it was far safer to stay away and go on dreaming.

The old horse that was carrying her so steadily along was tall, nearly seventeen hands high, and Grace's head bobbed above the hedgerows as she trotted on for about two miles. The countryside became strange to her as soon as she passed the Fair field but she vaguely remembered that the place she was seeking was set beside the river among a thicket of trees; she could recall her childish excitement when the carrier's cart left the main road and took a path leading under low branches. She wondered if she would recognise the turn-off corner again so each time they reached a path or a gate, she drew on the reins and sat in momentary confusion wondering if this was where she should strike into the woods. But none of the places woke her memory and eventually she went clip-clopping on up little hills and down the other side.

She was on the verge of giving up, convinced that she'd lost her bearings and that her memory had played her false, when she saw a grass-grown path leading off to her right. All at once there was no doubt in her mind – she'd reached the place. Old memories came flooding back. She remembered sitting on the carrier's cart with Jessie's arm about her; she remembered the gnarled oak tree that was the marking post; she remembered the mysterious green fairyland look of the pathway that snaked off in front of her.

The sun was still blazing and because she was bonnetless it was a blessed relief to turn off by the ancient oak tree whose branches hung low over the roadway. A grass-covered ride stretched ahead of her. All at once she was a child again and remembered it as being wide but was surprised to see how it had narrowed. The branches still reached down however and the ground was high with weeds. She realised from the luxuriance of the foliage that the path had been neglected and unused for a long time. A familiar smell assailed her, of greenery and damp moss, of wild flowers and a marsh-edged river – the smell of Bettymill.

The path stretched ahead like a green tunnel. The old cart ridges underfoot had almost disappeared in thick grass and tall spikes of meadowsweet which gave off a delicious, almost intoxicating scent as the mare brushed through them. Above Grace's head beech branches whispered and their leaves brushed against her face like caressing hands as she pushed through. In gaps between the trees, sunlight dappled the glades and lit up fading spikes of pink foxgloves and dying clusters of Scottish bluebells among curling fronds of pale green bracken. Bright pink campions dotted the banks and contrasted with the yellow stars of coltsfoot and the brilliant blue of cranesbill. The silence was like the hush inside a huge empty church and unhurried rabbits that bobbed slowly away at the sound of her approach seemed to move soundlessly. Some of them paused and stared up at the girl on the horse from round startled eyes but they were not really afraid because few people had passed that way for years.

The path led on for more than a mile, sometimes almost disappearing in the undergrowth but all the time heading deeper into woodland. Trees clustered closer and closer with the occasional young seedling almost blocking Grace's passage. She could see that there were berries, turning pale orange already, on the branches of the rowan trees. Soon they would be scarlet, the sign of autumn. The rose hips were colouring up too and clusters of tight green brambles like little rosettes covered the ends of trailing thorn branches that reached out to grab Grace's skirt as she brushed past them.

Her memory told her that the path to the mill was long

so she did not despair of reaching its end for she knew she was heading in the right direction. As she pushed through the undergrowth, however, she hoped that the mill might not be so overgrown that it would be missed, but suddenly a grey stone wall and a broken roof could be spied rising above a line of trees. She jumped down from the saddle and led the mare by the bridle towards the buildings. Surprisingly the path was clearer here and the grass was beaten down as if someone had pushed a way through quite recently. A little wooden bridge, rotting in places but still capable of bearing weight, crossed a stream that was channelled between two stone embankments. Grace stood on the bridge and saw that the trodden-down path led up to the front door of an old house.

She remembered it well but her heart sank at the sight of its dilapidation. The last time she'd been there it had been very different, but now the window glass was broken and the wood of the door was split and it swung open on one hinge. She tied her horse up in the shade beside a patch of tall grass that would give sweet grazing and walked towards it. Behind the house rose the old mill which was even more broken down, for an ash sapling was growing through a gaping hole in the roof and though the wooden waterwheel was still there, it was stained with green lichen and some of the spars were missing.

For a moment Grace wondered if she should turn and ride away again. She'd seen what she came to see and the dilapidation was heartbreaking. Besides, from the state of the path it looked as if someone else had been there not so long ago and perhaps whoever it was still lurked among the trees watching her.

But something drew her on. She had old ghosts to lay. Walking slowly she reached the front door of the house and pushed it fully open. When she had visited the house as a child, the room was warm and welcoming with a fire blazing up the chimney and coloured rugs on the floor. A table covered with food always stood in the middle of the floor. There had been a tall dresser in a corner with pretty plates on its shelves and a tall clock with a painted face had ticked away the time. She stepped into the dimness and blinked to accustom her eyes to the lack of light after the blazing sun outside. Then slowly, she gazed around.

The dresser was still there, dusty and hung with cobwebs but the pretty plates had all gone. The clock had vanished too but the old round table stood isolated in the middle of the floor. In the corners of the room piles of dead leaves and dried twigs had blown in over many winters. Yet, in spite of all that, the room did not look too desolate. Someone had been there recently, for the middle of the floor had been swept and a chipped plate stood on the table. Grace saw that there were crumbs on it and lifted them to her lips: they were not yet stale. Disquiet filled her and she looked questioningly around. A candle stump stood in a puddle of dried wax by the side of the hearth and a bundle of twigs was laid in the grate as if someone had been interrupted in the act of building a fire.

All at once she became painfully aware of the isolation of the place and knew that even if she tried to get away there was little chance of escaping an attacker. If she called out, no one would hear her. Her skin prickled with sensitivity as if someone was watching her but there was no place in the room where an unseen watcher could hide. Her disquiet made her so unsettled, however, that she decided against going upstairs and ran back outside, closing the door firmly behind her and tying a bit of string through the latch to keep it secure, although that would be no deterrent to a determined intruder.

In the open once more Grace felt safer and decided that she had been silly. Some innocent tramp was probably living in the empty house or perhaps a pedlar on his way to the Fair was using it as a temporary lodging. There's no reason to be afraid, she told herself and sat down to rest for a little before starting for home again. In the sunlit glade she felt warm and reassured so she lay down on the grass by the side of the mill lade which chattered through its course towards the river that could be seen glimmering silver through gaps in the trees.

She leaned on her elbow and looked down into the water of the lade which beckoned invitingly in the summer heat. Another memory wakened. Long ago she had bathed in that pool and she remembered standing naked in the water with someone – a woman – smiling down at her from the bank. On impulse she bent forward and took off her shoes and stockings, then dipped her thin white legs into the cool water. It gave her a delicious thrill as it surged around her legs and she kirtled up her skirt so as not to get it wet when she dropped off the bank and stood on the gravel bed of the little stream, staring down into the chattering water. Its flow was mesmeric and she was smiling as she watched it swirling around her calves. Though the day was hot, the water felt icy cold and stimulated the blood flow in her legs. She stared down at them – the right leg was white and strong-looking, a perfect leg, but the other was thin and wizened and seemed to belong to another person altogether. It was the leg of a cripple, of an imperfect girl. Balancing herself on the good leg, she moved the crippled one around gently in the water, holding it out and wriggling the toes as if trying to take some of the power of the rushing water into it. She wondered if the pulsing stream could make it whole and strong, could return it to what it had been when she paddled in the lade as a child, for her memory told her that she was not crippled then. She remembered running, jumping and splashing in the water. Her absorption was so complete that she did not see a woman walk up to the edge of the lade. Her reverie was broken, however, when a voice called softly from behind her, 'What's the matter with your leg, my dear? Have you hurt it?'

The tone was so friendly that Grace was not in the least frightened by the realisation that her suspicion was correct, unseen eyes had been watching her after all. She looked calmly up from her contemplation of her limbs in the water and said, 'I'm crippled. I've been like this for a long time.'

A tall thin woman dressed in black had come out from behind a thicket of little trees at the side of the house. Now she squatted down on the grassy verge beside the mill lade and she and Grace both turned their eyes down to the legs shining white in the clear water. 'It's the left one, isn't it? It doesn't look too bad to me. Exercises would help. Have you seen a doctor about it?' asked the stranger in a friendly and outright way.

Grace shook her head. 'No. It's been like this since I was small. My father and step-mother say that nothing can be done for it. I was sick in bed for a long time when I was seven years old and when I got up that leg didn't work like the other one any more. I just have to endure it.'

The stranger raised her head and stared at the girl. She wore no bonnet and Grace noticed that her hair was as dark as Odilie's but her skin was not dark and she had eyes of the palest blue like a spring sky. Those eyes were sympathetic when she asked, 'You've only a step-mother – no mother?'

Grace wriggled her toes in the cool water and sighed. 'She died long ago but she used to live here when she was a girl. That's why I've come today. I've only just found out that this mill was her home and I wanted to see it. It's lovely, isn't it?'

The woman stood up abruptly and the look on her face had changed. When she spoke her voice quavered as if she was having trouble breathing. 'What's your name, my dear?'

Grace looked up in surprise. 'Grace Elliot. My mother's name was Lucy Allen before she married.'

The woman looked down for a long moment and her voice was husky when she said, 'I knew Lucy Allen once.'

Excitedly Grace came splashing out of the water and limped over to her, exclaiming in delight, 'That's wonderful! How lucky that I met you. Tell me anything you can remember about her, please. I've never been able to find out much – my father won't talk about her at all and Martha Rutherford knows something but she's very odd

135

about it for some reason. No one else knows anything – or at least if they do, they won't say. Tell me about my mother – please.'

When the woman turned towards Grace her face looked strained and sad. 'I'm sorry to disappoint you but there's not much to tell, I'm afraid. She had a short life, had poor Lucy, and not a very happy one – at least it wasn't happy at the end although she was happy enough when she lived here as a girl.'

'Oh, but she was happy when she had me, wasn't she? I found a Bible that she'd written my name in and I could feel she was happy when she did that.'

'Yes, she was happy about you, very happy. She loved you dearly. It was so painful – you were only a bairn when she went away.'

Grace was surprised, 'went away? I thought she died.'

The woman gave herself a shake as if she had said something wrong. 'Of course, yes, she's dead. She's dead all right, but she had to go away first.'

'Tell me, oh, please tell me,' pleaded Grace but the stranger shook her head and said the same thing as everyone else. 'There's nothing much more to tell, at least I don't know anything. She went away first and then she died in London.'

The terrible finality of that statement made the day lose its glory for Grace. It seemed to her that a cloud crossed the sun and dark shadows crept into the glades between the trees. A chill swept over her and she shivered, raising a hand to her eyes, as she said brokenly, 'She went away. So she did not love me, either . . . no one has ever loved me.'

The strange woman saw the effect her words had on the girl and stepped quickly forward, saying in an urgent voice, 'Oh believe me, she loved you. She loved you very much.'

Grace shook her head. 'Why did she go away, then? It would have been bad enough if she died at home but to go away first – if she loved me, why did she leave me with a father who does not care about me – how could she?' Her head fell forward like a broken-stemmed flower as the dreams of her loving, caring mother rapidly disappeared.

The stranger put out a hand and gently took hold of the girl's chin, lifting her face up as she said, 'Lucy didn't want to go away, Grace. Please believe me. She was forced into it. She was brokenhearted to leave you. That's true, as true as I'm standing here now.'

Grace looked up with bewilderment in her blue eyes. 'How do you know?' she asked.

'I know because I saw her after she left Lauriston. She was bereft – no woman could have suffered more. She thought about you all the time, all the time.'

'You must have known her well,' said Grace, amazed. As she listened to the woman her face was beginning to look less stricken.

The answer was a vehement nod. 'I knew her very well. It is because of her that I came back here today. I wanted to find out if there was anyone still living in the mill but it looks as if it's been abandoned for years. It's a miracle that I found you here.' She took hold of Grace's hand as she spoke and the girl could feel that the hand holding hers was trembling and there were tears in the woman's eyes. After a little pause while they stared at each other wordlessly, the woman asked, 'Do you know what happened to Lucy's father, my dear?'

Grace shook her head. 'The last time I came here I was six or seven – before I took ill. Jessie, our maid, brought me. The old man who was my grandfather was here then. Jessie told me he'd died when I was sick and I haven't been back since – until today.'

Standing shoulder to shoulder they were almost the same height and together they stared around at the sad desolation. 'It used to be so busy here – with the wheel turning, the water falling and the millstones grinding away all the time, day and night. It was like constant music,' said the woman in a sad faraway voice.

Grace nodded. 'I remember that, too. It was exciting. But the old man was so sad and Jessie used to cry all the way home after we came to see him – I remember that, too.'

'Oh God – such sorrow!' sighed the woman. 'And Jessie – is Jessie still alive?'

'Oh no, she died about ten years ago too – while I was sick as well. When I got better Kelly our skivvy told me that Jessie had died of the fever. Did you know her too?'

'Yes, I knew Jessie very well. She used to live here in Bettymill too. There were five families living in the little houses at the back of the mill. How sad that they've all gone and the mill's not working any longer.' She sounded as if she was mourning.

Grace shook her head. 'But it wouldn't be worthwhile anyone staying here, would it? It's a ruin.'

The woman turned to look closely at the girl and her eyes became sharp again when she said, 'If both your mother and your grandfather are dead, my dear, this mill belongs to you.'

Grace was astonished. 'To me! It can't. No one's ever told me anything about that and my father's always saying that I've no dowry so I must do as I'm told.'

'Your father – is he well?' asked the woman guardedly.

'Oh yes, he's well and very busy. He's a lawyer in Lauriston, he's an important man.'

The answer was a nod and a small smile. 'I'm not surprised. And he married again, I expect.'

Grace looked downcast. 'Oh yes, it must have been shortly after my mother died – went away I mean – because I never remember a time when he wasn't married. He has three other children, too.' It was obvious from the girl's tone that this was not a happy subject for her.

'Whom did he marry?'

'He married Hester.'

The woman gave a wild peal of laughter that rang out eerily among the trees. 'Hester the maid! So he *married* the maid! Ha, ha, ha!'

'She came from here as well. Do you know her?' asked Grace in amazement.

'Oh yes, I knew her but not as well as I knew Lucy or

138

Jessie, not nearly as well.' The woman impulsively threw her arms round the surprised girl and hugged her close, crying, 'I'm so happy that I met you today. So happy, I can't tell you how much.' Then she held Grace away after a while and stared searchingly into her face as if she wanted to remember every feature. After a bit she said more soberly, 'You must be wondering about me. My name is Alice Archer. My man and I run a travelling freak show and we're coming to St James' Fair on Monday but I wanted to see this old place again. He brought me up on horseback this morning but went back down the road to settle the waggons for the night. He'll pick me up tomorrow. I hope you don't mind me wanting to see your mill and spending the night in it.'

'My mill!' Grace looked around at her new and unexpected possession. The revelation that Bettymill might belong to her made the whole place seem different. The house was not so ruined-looking, it was almost habitable, in fact. 'I could live here,' she thought in delight and her spirits soared. It seemed as if her whole world had started to change for the better and she smiled at the stranger by her side. 'Of course I don't mind. Stay here as long as you like. Or ride back to Lauriston on the pillion with me. The mare could carry us both easily. Come back to Viewhill and see Hester and my father.'

The woman threw back her head and laughed but again her merriment had a strange undertone to it. 'Oh no, that wouldn't do at all. I don't think I'd be very welcome at Viewhill. I was your mother's friend, not Hester's. Anyway, my husband'll come looking for me tomorrow morning and he'd be worried if I wasn't here – he's always half-expecting me to disappear, I'm afraid. Don't worry about me. I've seen what I came for – much, much more than I came for, in fact. Before you go though there's one thing I want to do. Sit down on that stone and let me look at your leg. I'm a sort of a healer – I do a lot of it with the freak show folk and I might be able to help you make that leg better.'

Grace sat and watched with fascination as Alice's

strong capable hands rubbed and kneaded the wasted muscle of her leg. The woman's touch seemed to send heat down into the girl's bones as she worked. Now and then she instructed, 'Bend your toes up – now down. Twist your foot to the side, bend your knee.' After about twenty minutes, she sat back on the grass and looked up to tell Grace, 'Your leg's not as bad as it looks. The muscle's wasted, that's all. If you could do exercises every day and bathe it in a herbal potion that I make it would improve a lot.'

'It would be wonderful to be able to walk without such a limp. I've always felt different from other girls and Hester says no one will every marry me because of my leg – and because I don't have a dowry, of course,' Grace sighed.

Alice frowned. 'No dowry? But of course you've a dowry! You've this mill for one thing and your grand-father was a rich man. He owned a lot of other property as well. He'd have left it all to you because there wasn't anyone else and he was careful about things like that. He'd have made a will, I know that.' She stood up with her hands on her hips and a determined look on her face, then she said, 'I tell you what, come to see me at the Fair and I'll try to find out what's happened to your grandfather's property. And I'll make up a potion for your leg and give it to you at the same time. Promise me you'll come. It's very important. We own Archer's Freak Show and you'll find it easily because Jem always gets a good site in the middle of the field. Come on Monday evening because that will give me time to make my enquiries.'

Grace found that she trusted this strange woman but she was still very puzzled. 'But how do you know all this? Who are you?'

The woman patted her gently on the cheek as she said, 'My dear, I lived here when I was a girl like you. Your mother and I were close. She was a very trusting girl, and now I see that she was silly in a way because she believed what people told her. She never thought them

140

capable of lying so she got her heart broken. That's why she had to die. I'm sorry.'

Tears filled Grace's eyes. 'My mother died of a broken heart! Oh, how terrible. There's one thing I've been frightened of – tell me, she didn't kill herself, did she? I couldn't bear to think of her doing that.'

A bleak look crossed Alice's face. 'Kill herself? Oh, no. She was more a victim of other people than a victim of herself. Don't grieve for her too much. She couldn't have gone on as she was. But I know she'd want you to be happy and to have what's yours by right so remember to come and see me at the Fair. *Do not forget.*'

The last words were said with fierce vehemence and there were tears in the woman's eyes. Seeing them Grace thought, 'This woman must have been very fond of my mother.' So she held out her hand and promised, 'I'll come. We'll meet again on Monday.'

As if drawn by some force which they were unable to resist, they stepped closer and clasped each other in a warm embrace. Alice's hands cradled Grace's head on her shoulder and tears ran down her cheeks as she said through her sobs, 'You're a lovely girl. Your mother would be so proud of you . . .' Then she pushed at Grace's shoulder and said, 'It's growing late and you mustn't travel the roads in the dark. You'd better go home now, my dear.'

She held the grey mare while Grace climbed into the saddle and they stood looking at each other for a few minutes, not knowing what to say, until Alice raised a hand and gave a little wave. Then Grace urged her horse forward into the leafy lane. Her crippled leg felt sore but her heart was light and her mind was full of a host of new thoughts and impressions – the strange encounter had given her much to think about.

Before Bettymill disappeared from view, she turned in her saddle and took a last look at the place which might belong to her – *might*, she stressed to herself, for she had endured too harsh an upbringing to expect things to turn out well. The solitary black figure in the middle of the clearing had one hand raised in farewell. Grace waved back and called out, 'I'll see you at the Fair.'

When the fretwork of tree branches swung back behind the grey horse and the last sounds of Grace's departure disappeared, a deep stillness fell over the huddle of old buildings in the wood. Then, very slowly, the woman in the black dress stopped waving and dropped her arms by her sides, letting her head slump forward. For a long time she stood still with huge tears running down her cheeks like rain. She looked like a statue representing sorrow.

It seemed that her tears came from an unquenchable well for they flowed on relentlessly, but after a long time she brought her clenched fists up to her mouth and bit viciously into the knuckles. It did not bother her that she drew blood for she welcomed the physical pain and her tears mingled with blood on her hands at the same time as the gasping sobs made her shoulders heave. She stood with her hands against her mouth till she managed to control her emotion and examine the damage she had inflicted on herself. Then, careless of pain, she wiped her bleeding knuckles on the side of her skirt and walked slowly back towards the mill house. At the door she untied the string with which Grace had secured it and stepped inside.

In the dim room she looked around longingly. Her eyes rested on the empty fireplace, the dirty windows and the dust-covered shelves of the dresser. Walking warily as if she was acutely sensorily awakened, she crossed the floor and opened a little door in the righthand wall which revealed a flight of rickety wooden stairs leading to the first floor. Bending her head, for she was tall, she entered the doorway and disappeared upstairs. Soon her footsteps were going from room to room, stumbling up and down on the uneven floors till eventually she re-emerged from the doorway carrying a frayed wicker basket and her flat straw hat. Placing the hat on her head she went back outside, tied the door up again and walked over the grassy sward to pick up a long stave that leaned against the mill house. Beside it was an overgrown rose bush, thickly covered with small pink flowers and she broke some of them off before holding the little nosegay up to her face and inhaling its sweet scent. Then she stuck the roses into the brim of her hat and prepared to leave, but before she went there was one more thing she had to do. Positioning herself in front of the house, she stood very still and stared fixedly at it for a long time as if branding its image into her brain. After that she turned slightly and stared at the old mill: she seemed to be trying to take in every detail of the thick undergrowth, the broken roof, the lichen-stained waterwheel, the grey slates of the roof, the rioting bushes with their enchanting flowers. There were no more tears and no weakness in her now, for her eyes were dry and burning with determination.

When she had looked her fill, she took the stave in one hand and lifted up her basket, which had nothing in it except a few bits of broken china. Without a backward glance she strode off up the shady lane towards the main road. At the first clearing, where Grace had paused and where the path took a turn to the right, Alice hesitated. She wanted to look back, but with an effort restrained herself and stood very still facing forward for a few moments before striding on with her face hard and con-trolled.

When she reached the main road she did not hesitate again but headed away from Lauriston in the direction of Maxton village. Alice was a tall, erect woman with a striking figure and she marched along with long regular strides, staring straight ahead and oblivious to other people she passed on the way, and she met many for the roads leading to Lauriston were thronged with itinerants making for the Roxburgh field. There were traders, ped-lars, quacks, merchants, cottagers with flax for sale and others driving a few cattle or geese that they hoped might find a buyer. All were eager to camp near the Fair field so that they could be out early on Monday morning and secure a good pitch for themselves. One or two of them knew Alice from other fairs and greeted her by name but she only acknowledged their greetings with a swift word and kept striding on, never pausing to gossip with them. They looked surprised because her eyes kept staring straight ahead like the eyes of a woman following an irresistible lure.

It was dark when she passed through Maxton, never looking to right or left, but she knew she had almost reached her destination. Half a mile farther on, she noticed a secret sign scratched on a stone by the side of the road next to a deep wooded gully through which the road wound. She crossed a stream at the bottom by a small bridge and then turned off the road on to a path that led into the heart of the gully. She guessed by the sign that it was here that Jem's waggons were parked and she was right, for before her as she trod up the path she could see the glimmer of their cooking fires. Her approach was heralded by the fierce barking of dogs but she calmed them by calling out as she walked, 'It's only Alice, it's Alice . . .'

The carts of the freak show were lined up behind a stockade of bushes and people were moving about among them. The draught-horses were grazing by the side of a burn and a motley pack of dogs could be heard scavenging about in the undergrowth, sending up game. Sometimes a rabbit took a chance and shot out in a bolt for freedom but it was unerringly pursued by one of the dogs, which caught its quarry and despatched it with a vicious snap of terrible teeth.

The arrival of Alice was hailed by people hunkering down beside their flickering fires and she waved in acknowledgement of their calls but hurried on towards her own caravan. Its door stood open and a set of movable wooden steps led up to the interior. She laid her basket on the first step and called out softly, 'Jem! Are you in there, Jem?'

Immediately there was a startled clatter from within and the bulk of Jem appeared. He was wearing a collarless white shirt with the sleeves rolled up to his elbows and a scarf knotted around his neck. He grinned at the sight of her and cried, 'Alice, I'm glad you're back but why didn't

144

you stay there till tomorrow, lass?' He stuck out a hand and half-pulled her up the steps into the dimness of their caravan. Still holding his hand she sat down heavily on the bunk by the far wall and her tears began to flow anew, flooding from her like a torrent.

Jem's florid face looked stricken. The sight of tears always unmanned him. He knelt down beside her, reaching out to enclose her in his arms and saying, 'Oh, don't take on like that, Alice. What's the matter? Nobody's hurt you, have they? If they have tell me who they are and I'll MURDER them . . .'

She shook her head and sobbed even more agonisingly as she reassured him, 'No, no Jem, it's nothing like that. I shouldn't have gone there. It was stupid of me. But if I hadn't I wouldn't have met her – thank God I did!'

This ambiguity confused him and he asked her, 'But what's the trouble then? When I left you this morning, you said you'd sleep the night there. You weren't disturbed by anyone, were you? I wish you'd tell me. I know something's up. Did you meet someone who scared you?'

'No, I met a young girl at the mill but she didn't scare me, far from it. There's nothing to fear from her.' She gave another sob and clutched him to her as if she needed his strength.

He hugged her close groaning, 'Oh Alice, I don't care what this trouble is all about, just tell me. You've been acting funny for days. I'll look after you no matter what it is. You should know that by now.' Her tear-washed face was turned to his as he went on brokenly, 'I wish I'd made you stay in Carlisle. Something tells me you shouldn't have come here. You're in danger. I'll send Long Tom back there with you now if you like.'

She looked sadly at him, 'I can't go back. Not now. I've things to do here. I used to live in this part of the world, you know that, don't you Jem?'

He nodded. 'Yes, you said you lived at that old mill.'

She went on, 'But I'm afraid in case someone I used to know when I was a girl recognises me. That's all.'

145

'Would it matter if you were recognised?' he asked slowly.

She nodded, 'Yes, it would matter if I was seen by the wrong people. I'd be in trouble – a lot of trouble.'

'With the law?' asked Jem cautiously and Alice nodded again. He hugged her close and there was relief in his voice when he told her, 'The law – is that all! Who cares about the law? You'll be safe enough with me. I'll not let anybody near you. I'll not let you out of my sight. Is that why you dyed your hair, my dove?'

For the first time that night she gave a small smile. 'Yes, that's why. I'm sorry. I know you don't like it but I'll wash it out when we get away from here.'

'But why do you want to stay? I'd be better pleased if you went back to Carlisle now. I'll be worrying about you the whole time,' he told her.

'No, I can't go back. I've something to do now since I met the girl. I'm safe enough with you to look after me. And anyway, I'm a different woman in every way to what I was when I lived here. I'd be hard to recognise, I think.' She put both arms round his waist and wept against his chest as if she was mourning her lost youth and he crooned gently over her as if she was a baby. In a time she was calmer and wiped her eyes as she gazed at him saying, 'You amaze me, Jem. Don't you want to know why I'm in trouble with the law?'

'No, I don't care,' was the reply. 'I don't want to know anything about it. Whatever you did I'm sure you didn't deserve the punishment you've had. I don't care what it was. It won't make any difference to the way I feel about you.' He held her close till she relaxed in his arms and when he felt her head droop, he said, 'I'll look after you, Alice.'

She smiled at him and said in a voice of great earnestness. 'I'll tell you the whole story one day. I promise you I will.'

'Only when you're ready but stay with me Alice, that's all I want,' he entreated her.

She kissed him in confirmation of this and then stood

146

up to take off her heavy shoes. When she was barefoot, she stared into a scrap of looking-glass on the wall as she tidied her hair. Then she put on a large apron that was hanging behind the caravan door and when she was dressed in her workaday wear, she turned back to the watching man and said in a new brisk tone, 'Now tell me, what's been going on since I left? How's poor Billy?'

'He's worse than ever, shouting and raving ever since we got here, terribly excited. You'll have to give him a draught or he'll kill somebody.'

She nodded. 'All right. I'll make one straight away.'

Jem stood still with a frown on his face. 'I'm worried about Billy. He's getting too strong. I'll have to ask around at the Fair to find if there's any of his people there. If the old woman's still alive she'll want to know about him because she was fond of him and he was never wild with her.'

'Why did she give him to you then if she was so fond of him?' asked Alice.

'She knew she couldn't keep him. She'd not been well and she was growing old. He'd have ended up on a gibbet sure as death if she'd kept him.'

Alice sighed. 'It's so sad. Poor Billy. The Vikings used to keep men like him. They used them as warriors and sent them out of the longboats first because they were so strong and hadn't any fear. They called them berserkers.'

Jem was interested, 'Did they now! You know such odd things, Alice. But there's no longboats any more for the likes of Billy now. They wouldn't even take him in the Army when the war was on. It's a worry what's going to happen to him when I can't go on mastering him and I'm like the old woman, I'm not getting any younger either and no one else can cope with Billy when he's wild. I'll have to ask his people what's to be done.'

Alice stared at him. 'But you're as strong as an ox, Jem! You can carry four men on your back and still walk upright as a tree. You don't feel ill, do you?'

'No, nothing like that but I'm over fifty years old,' he reminded her. 'I can't stay like I am forever. I'm luckier

147

than most but I'll have to grow old one of these days. How do you fancy living with an old man who likes his porter and his pipe – just you and me together.'

She laughed. 'I'd love it but I don't think it's going to happen for a long time. Now, where's my box of herbs? I'll have to fix a strong draught for Billy if he's as wild as you say.'

When she and Jem emerged from the caravan half an hour later, the shadows of night had gathered like velvet beneath the trees and the flames of the cooking fires were leaping up in bright orange streamers towards the dark vault of the sky. Jem and Alice made a tall and handsome couple as they walked slowly from group to group, talking to first one grotesque or misshapen creature and then another.

As they gathered together in the firelight of their night camp, the exhibits from Jem's freak show looked like figures out of a vision of Hell. Some were tiny and hunched: others immensely tall, angular and skinny. A young and pretty-faced woman had a long, luxuriant black beard that flowed over her chest in magnificent ripples. Meg the dwarf sat by the fire suckling a baby and regarding it with love as it clung to her little breast. Alice bent down to look at the child and told its mother, 'She's growing up awful bonny, Meg. You're making a grand job of her.'

Meg looked up anxiously. 'She's going to be normal-sized, isn't she Alice? She's not going to be a dwarf like me and him over there?' She jerked a thumb across to where a wizened little man called Hans was turning a spit handle over the fire. He was even smaller than Meg, barely three feet tall, and he also had an immense head, a broad barrel chest and doll-like legs that did not look strong enough to bear the weight of the top half of his body.

Alice reassured the tiny woman. 'Don't worry. I think your baby'll be normal because it's the right size now for its age. Jem told me that he got you from a woman who kept babies in boxes to stunt them and Hans was raised by somebody that put knot grass, dwarf elder and daisy root in his food when he was a child so that he wouldn't grow. That means the smallness of both of you is artificial, it's not something that'll be passed on.'

The bearded woman who was listening, raised her voice and called to the dwarf Hans, 'D'ye hear that, you little bastard! If you hadn't been so greedy and eaten everything that was given to you, you might be as big as Jem today. Ha, ha, ha!'

Her vengeful cackle rang out amongst the trees and the dwarf turned an angry face towards her, spitting out, 'And how did you get that thicket on your face? It's a good thing you've not got a bairn or it'd be born with a moustache and Jem'd have another freak to show off to the crowds.' Soon they were all quarrelling, shouting and swearing at each other. It was the normal way for them to spend their evenings.

Alice and Jem's attempts at pacification were interrupted by an extremely tall, thin man who stepped into the circle of light and told Jem, 'One of the bears is sick. I'm worried in case it's going to die. Maybe Alice could have a look at it.'

They followed him to the edge of the clearing where a cage with metal bars on the sides stood. Three dark figures were huddled in one corner. As he approached the cage, the tall man made coaxing noises and called out, 'Come out for a locust nut, come and get it, come on, come on . . .' He held out his hand and two of the figures lifted their heads. Alice felt a chill of distaste at the sight of them, for their faces were pink-skinned and human-looking but their bodies were covered with coarse brown hair. She knew that their grotesque appearance was because they all had their faces and necks shaved in order to appear human when they were paraded before the credulous public dressed up as women and billed as the Pig-Faced Ladies. The bears had been trained to dance a lumbering quadrille which Alice hated to watch because the animals' tragic eyes haunted her. She was sure that all

149

of them – and particularly the biggest one called George – loathed the demeaning fate that was forced on him.

When they heard their keeper approaching their cage, two of them came ambling over towards the door snuffling eagerly and Long Tom, who with the aid of stilts and high-heeled shoes doubled as the Tallest Man in the World, said, 'Here's Jenny. She's always the first. And Willy's fine too but it's big George that worries me. He's so poorly that he can hardly rise.'

He opened the door of the cage and stepped in beside the animals, gesturing to Alice and Jem to follow. Gathering up her skirt to keep it clear of the stinking straw, she did so, swallowing down the nausea she felt at the rank smell of the animals. Two loomed over their keeper looking for titbits and he gave them what they wanted as he pushed past towards the third bear which lay in a pathetic huddle in a far corner. The animal's yellow eyes were tragic and pleading in its grotesque face.

'Take a look at him. Any idea what's wrong with him, Alice?' asked Tom, kneeling down beside the panting bear.

Alice gazed into the animal's shaven face and noted the gathering glaze in his eyes. She sighed, 'I think he's dying, Tom.'

'Can't you do something? He's my best bear. He's the best dancer of the lot.' Tom like everybody else in the show had great faith in Alice's curative powers and her knowledge of herbal medicines.

'Try giving him some brandy. That's all I can think of,' she said. She had little hope that anything would cure the poor animal's broken heart but at least liquor would help it to die in peace.

Alice breathed a deep sigh when she stepped out of the stinking cage where the bear lay dying. In the open camp site, the smell of woodsmoke was sweet to her senses. Jem stood beside her at the cage door and she told him sadly, 'That bear'll not see the morning, poor thing.'

When she walked away, Jem shook his head and said quietly to Long Tom, 'Get a couple of men to dig a grave for George and don't let Alice see you burying him. You know how things like that upset her.'

Tom had travelled with Jem for many years, first in the boxing booth and then in the freak show, and he remembered how the big man had first met Alice, lost her again and spent years searching before he found her. He remembered travelling from town to town, asking everyone if they'd seen her and he knew how tenderly his old friend took care of his woman, how he considered her wishes in everything and how much he dreaded Alice disappearing again like a dream. For some unexplained reason Alice was prey to strange, engulfing melancholies and Jem did everything he could to avert them.

After he had given his orders, Jem ran to catch up with Alice whose dark outline could be seen heading towards the furthest caravan of the group. This vehicle was deliberately situated in the most remote part of the gulley and as she approached it, Alice heard the familiar thuds and strange animal grunting noises emanating from it. She knew the sounds showed that Billy was fretting, fretting, fretting. The noise was not worrying a tangle-haired girl, the daughter of Long Tom, who perched on the caravan steps with a piece of tatting in her hands. She was working very fast and concentrating totally on the work in progress. Jem caught up with Alice just as she reached the girl and asked, 'How's Billy now?'

The girl didn't look up from her flying fingers and said with an expressive shrug, 'Oh, just the same. I put his food in and left him to it. He's finished. I heard him smashing the plate a little while ago.'

With a grin Jem thudded his huge fist on the closed door and shouted, 'Billy, hey Billy. It's Jem, Billy!' The sounds from inside ceased and after a few seconds, Jem turned the key on the outside of the door and slowly pushed it open. Inside was pitch dark. Still talking soothingly, Jem stepped into the blackness but his muscles were tense and his fists were half-up. He called out as he went, 'Where are you, Billy? I'll light your lamp – if you've not broken it that is.'

Alice and the girl watching by the door saw the glimmer of a scratch of flint on tinder and soon a faint gleam of light appeared inside. They leaned forward to see more clearly and could just make out Jem standing with a lamp held above his head. On the floor on the far side of the caravan, a thickset and muscular young man was squatting surrounded by broken bits of china. It had only been one plate but he'd fragmented it.

When the lamplight shone on Billy's face he smiled and at first sight he looked almost normal, for he had a mop of curling dark hair and a boyish, fresh-coloured face. He was wearing buckskin breeches and a shirt that had once been white but was so no longer because he'd wiped his hands on it after his meal. When he smiled, he showed stubby ridged teeth and his eyes glinted merrily. If it was not for those eyes, he would have looked like a splendid specimen of young manhood but they gave him away because they were the eyes of a madman. Jem walked on into the caravan asking softly, 'How's Billy, then?'

The answer was a crooning murmur and Billy stood up holding his arms out. He liked Jem. When he was standing erect he revealed his impressive height and the staggering width of his shoulders. He came ambling over towards Jem and said, 'Hello Jem. Take Billy for a walk. Billy wants to go out.'

Jem had a calming effect on Billy. He patted his arm and said, 'That's good. You must be feeling better. But it's dark and we can't go out walking now. I'll take you tomorrow. Look, I've brought Alice with me to give you some medicine that'll make you sleep like a babby. You'll take it, won't you Billy, a sleep's what you need.'

When he saw that Billy was acquiescent, Jem turned his head back towards the door and whispered, 'You can come in. It's all right. He's calm.'

She stepped through the door and stood close to her man. Billy lifted his head and sniffed because like an animal he could smell her fear but Jem took her hand

and said, 'It's all right, give Billy his medicine and then I'll sit with him for a bit. He gets lonely shut up here in his waggon, don't you Billy? But when we get to the Fair you'll get out. I promise.'

Alice was carrying a tin mug in her hand and she silently handed it over. It contained the potion she'd concocted and Billy obediently swilled all of it down without pausing for breath. Then he wiped his mouth with his hand and smiled at her. She smiled back but nervously, for she never knew when Billy was going to turn awkward. Tonight he was genial enough but when he was having one of his blacknesses she found him terrifying; fits swept over his poor brain like thunderstorms across a summer sky and when he was in the grip of them he was hideously violent, breaking everything within sight. Only Jem could cope with him then. Alice shifted closer and remembered what he had said earlier about the time when he could no longer master Billy by superior strength. What will happen when that day comes, she wondered? She knew that Jem was right. He was growing older and Billy was growing stronger. In a couple of months the young man would be twenty and in the full strength of his manhood. Already he well deserved the title of his billing in the freak show, for Billy was the Strongest Man in the World who bent iron bars and split planks of wood with one blow of his fist.

As Alice clung to Jem's arm she wondered what would happen when Billy wanted a woman. So far he had been strangely innocent sexually but that could not last much longer. What would happen when he had a need for sex? The potions she concocted for him contained ingredients that stifled desire and they worked well for the moment but she doubted if they would continue to be effective for much longer. Billy in search of a woman would be able to burst through any door and Alice made a mental note to tell Jem that Long Tom's girl must stop acting as Billy's watcher or something terrible could happen.

Jem sensed Alice's nervousness and patted her hand when Billy handed back his mug. 'Go back to our caravan,

Alice, and I'll sit here with Billy for a little while,' he said and settled himself down on a wooden bench by the door. Billy came shambling over and sat beside him. 'We'll have a chat,' said Jem companionably.

As Alice stood in the doorway she heard him saying, 'That's right. Sit near me, Billy and I'll tell you about the place we're going to on Monday. It's called St James' Fair. There'll be lots of people and hundreds of horses. You like horses, don't you? If you're good you can go out and have a look at them . . .'

Billy was excited and bounced on his seat, the muscles of his upper arms and thighs rippling beneath his clothes when he moved.

'Billy likes horses,' he said in a childish voice.

'Course you do and you like Jem too, don't you? Sit down quiet again and I'll tell you about the Fair.' With one hand Jem pulled Billy back down on to the bench where he sat staring all the while at Jem who was talking in a soft, reassuring voice. 'The Fair's held in a big field facing a castle. It's been there every year for a long, long time and people come from all over the place. We'll make a lot of money and Billy'll have two whole roast chickens to himself for supper and as much ale as he wants to drink. So you'll behave well, won't you Billy, when all the people come to see you?'

Billy nodded. 'Billy'll be good,' he promised.

'You'll bend the bars and bite the nails in half but you won't try to run away. Last time you did that you frightened all the ladies and a man wanted to shoot you. I had the devil of a job stopping him, Billy.'

Billy threw back his head and laughed as if the memory of the occasion was funny, though Jem remembered it very differently. 'Billy won't run away,' he said gleefully.

'That's right,' advised Jem. 'You'll have to wear your leg-chains for the show but the new ones are extra strong. It'd take two elephants to break them. Just do your tricks Billy and everybody'll clap and cheer you and pay lots of money to see you.'

Billy threw back his head again and gave a huge guffaw,

exposing his strong throat with muscles like hawsers up each side of his neck. When he was in a good temper, as he was at that moment, he looked like a big strong farm boy, a simple-minded plough laddie who could be relied on to carry out any heavy task that defeated the other men.

Jem stayed with him for an hour. Before he left, Alice's potion was beginning to work and Billy was yawning, lying down fully-clothed on the floor ready for a sleep. Jem draped a blanket over his body and stood looking down at him with pity in his eyes. 'Poor Billy,' he thought. 'I'm fond of you. I wouldn't like to see you with someone who'd beat you or keep you under with cruelty. You're not a bad lad. You don't mean to hurt – you just don't know your own strength.'

When he got back to his caravan, Alice was sitting alone in the circle of lamplight. She looked up when he entered and said, 'You're good to Billy. You like looking after people, don't you Jem?'

He laughed. 'I suppose I do.'

'Was it because you wanted to look after me that you searched for me for so long?' she asked.

'I don't think it was that. You haunted me and I looked for you for six years before I found you in London.'

'I'm glad you did. I was nearly at the end. But why did you want to find me? We'd hardly spoken,' she asked.

Jem's face was solemn. 'I just knew I had to find you. There was something about you – something lost – and I knew you thought I'd been responsible for McKay dying and I couldn't stomach that because I'd nothing to do with it. I wanted to tell you that.'

'I didn't know who to blame, I was so angry,' said Alice, shuddering as she remembered the first time she'd seen Jem. 'I'd been cheated and deceived by so many people by that time, I didn't know who to trust. Poor McKay trusted people and he died because of it.'

Jem sighed. 'That toff who was running McKay killed him right enough because he matched him against a man twice his size and then bet against him. He wanted him

155

to lose and he couldn't care less if McKay took a beating. When he was knocked out like that I was mad because I knew what was going on. McKay was only a youngster. He shouldn't have died.'

Alice's face was grim as she remembered the inn near Northampton where they'd all foregathered eight years ago for a boxing match. She was with a young man called John McKay who'd been her man since she left Scotland. She'd let him pick her up on the road because a woman couldn't travel without money or a man to protect her and she had neither so she was grateful when she met him. McKay was like Billy in a way, strong and simple-minded but he was also gentle and kind. He'd felt sorry for Alice and taken care of her.

McKay was a barefist boxer who was matched one day in a big bout organised by a group of gambling gentlemen against a lumbering and villainous-looking man who was said to be failing in his powers. When Alice saw him, however, she was afraid because he looked as if he had been drugged and when it came to the fight, he literally pounded her lover to pieces before her eyes. The blood flowed and McKay slumped on to the ground unconscious before a shrieking crowd who were too busy exchanging money to bother about him. Only the big man in charge of the ring seemed concerned. He held back McKay's opponent and picked up the unconscious body as if it had been that of a doll. The big man who acted as the referee was Jem.

Now when she looked at him sitting beside her she remembered running behind him as he carried McKay slung over his shoulder up the inn stairs to a bedroom on the first floor. When a doctor arrived he pronounced McKay dead and told Alice that he would probably have died of his injuries anyway but the journey upstairs with his head hanging down caused the final trauma that killed him. She went raving down into the bar parlour and attacked Jem, pounding his chest with her fists and shrieking, 'You killed him, you bastard! You did it deliberately!' Someone quietened her down in the end and the innkeeper's wife gave her a bed for the night. Early next morning she headed for London and a life on the streets. What followed was a period in her life that she preferred to forget.

Six years later, when she was being kept by a vicious and loose-living young buck in Chelsea, she met Jem again on the street in Covent Garden. He'd recognised her from the other side of the carriageway and hailed her, running across beneath the hooves of cantering horses to grab her arm. To her surprise he said that he'd been looking for her ever since that night in Northampton. They joined forces and she'd been with him ever since but she knew he was unsure of her. Nothing she said would reassure him. He did not know if she stayed with him because it suited her or because she loved him. As she watched him sitting in the lamplight beside her, she realised that the answer was love.

'Do you realise we've been together for more than two years?' she asked in a gentle voice.

'I know. I was thinking about that this morning. It's time we got ourselves properly spliced, Alice.'

Her face went sad in the candlelight. 'Not yet, Jem. I don't know if I can but if it's possible there's nothing I'd want more.'

'What's to stop us? I'm a widower and if you were married when you were young your man's either dead or he's found another wife by now,' said Jem, but she shook her head and told him, 'I'll make enquiries in Lauriston. I promise you I will.'

He sighed. 'You're a mystery, Alice. You always hold something back. Maybe one day you'll tell me the lot.'

'I promise I will – one day,' she said solemnly and leaned across to kiss him.

CHAPTER 6

Sunday 2 August.

At half an hour after midnight a light glittered in the window of Rachel Faa's cottage in Kirk Yetholm. In the bare room inside, Thomassin knelt beside the old woman watching a small clay crucible which steamed slowly by the side of the fire. Rachel was staring into the flames with dilated pupils and muttering strange incantations, a long stream of incomprehensible words and Thomassin knew better than to interrupt or distract her but after a bit she paused and turned to the girl with some instructions. 'Draw a six-pointed star on that paper over there. Use the goose quill to do it,' she ordered.

Thomassin went over to the table where a thick yellow tallow candle was burning in the church candlestick that she had stolen from Linton Kirk. Its flame flickered feebly in the draught that came beneath the ill-fitting door making weird shadows dance in the corners of the room. Her heart was thudding as she lifted the quill which she was about to dip into a pot of dark liquid that stood beside it when Rachel stopped her in time. 'No, no, that's toad's bile! Use the bairn's ratti I told you to bring,' she instructed.

The girl brought the phial of baby's blood out of her pocket and used that to make the star. Then she held the paper up to contemplate her handiwork in the dim light. She was disappointed when Rachel did not even glance at what she had so laboriously done – for Thomassin could not write – but only reached out for the paper and with more strange words, ceremoniously floated it on top of the logs of the fire where it slowly shrivelled and burnt up before their eyes.

'Are you sure this'll work?' Thomassin asked doubtfully. She was surprised at how harsh her voice sounded. Her throat felt dry and tight when she spoke.

Rachel laughed, a low and cunning chuckle. 'It'll work. You'll be rommed by next week.' She put the point of a poker into the crucible and drew out the limp headless body of the snake which she also threw into the fire where it hissed and crackled horribly. A sickening smell filled the room as it burned up. The snake's head lay on the hearthstone beside her and she lifted it gingerly and dropped it into a large mortar. Then, kneeling on the floor, she proceeded to pound it into a pulp. When she was satisfied, she poured the liquid from the crucible on top of the mess.

Thomassin felt bile rise up inside her at the rank smell of the preparation. Suddenly she was afraid for Jesse. 'Gare, gare,' she whispered, warning old Rachel to take care. 'I don't want my Jesse to be made into a mullo.'

'Don't worry, he's my grandson. He won't be a dead man. He'll be like a cooroboshno when you get him.'

Cooroboshno meant fighting-cock in their language and Thomassin smiled at the idea. 'As long as you're sure,' she said. She wanted him so badly she'd try anything.

'I'm sure. I could make him a mullo if I wanted to but Jesse's my own kaulo ratti, my own family. I'll do him no harm.' Rachel was pouring the contents of a horn mug into the mortar now and the smell as even worse than before. 'Give me the flowers,' she instructed and when they were passed over, she tore them into tiny pieces and dropped them also into the mixture.

'This is a gentle potion. Not like some,' she told the girl as she worked.

Thomassin nodded for she knew of Rachel's expertise and had heard tales of expeditions to graveyards for digging up recently interred bodies to provide the ingredients for the old woman's more discreditable potions. The gypsies knew better than to annoy Rachel in any way and the girl's eyes were glittering in the firelight as she said in admiration, 'You're yokki, Rachel.'

The compliment pleased the old woman who smiled

back and said, 'Watch what I'm doing and one day you may be clever too.' Thomassin knew that she had been granted a great honour by being allowed to be present while the love potion was being brewed, for usually Rachel worked in secret and guarded her recipes jealously.

'How will I give it to him?' Thomassin asked when the potion was nearly ready, for it still smelt strange and she doubted if Jesse could be persuaded to taste any of it.

'He'll only need panch drops, that's all,' said Rachel, holding up five fingers. 'No more or you'll harm him. I'll mix it with tatti pani and you can give him some of that in his ale.' There was a bottle of brandy, which Thomassin had been instructed to provide, on the table and she gestured to the girl to pass it over. Into a little bottle she measured the precious five drops from a silver spoon and then poured a small measure of brandy on top of them. Shaking it up vigorously, she cried, 'There's your love potion then, girl!' And as she passed it over she added, 'Give it to him tomorrow and use it wisely. Take care of him when you get him because he's a good man.'

'I will, I will, thank you Rachel,' cried Thomassin in such open delight that the old woman laughed and raised the brandy bottle to her lips to take a long swig. Then she toasted the girl, 'Aukko tu pros!' she cried and lifted the bottle to her mouth again. It was obvious that the leftover brandy was part of her fee.

It was one in the morning when Thomassin slipped out of Rachel's cottage with the tightly-stoppered flask tied in the corner of her shawl. As she walked along among the shadows of Tinkler's Row heading for her own home, she heard the footsteps of a group of men who were coming back from their night's poaching. Stepping back against the wall of one of the houses she watched them and her heart leapt when she saw Jesse in the middle of a crowd of his friends who were laughing and punching each other on the shoulders.

Thomassin clutched her love potion eagerly at the sight of him and wished that she could administer it straight away but Rachel had warned her that it had to lie for twenty-four hours before it could be used. She drew back deeper in the shadows because she did not want him to see her, but she had not taken into account the fact that Jesse was one of the sharpest-eyed in a race of sharp-eyed people. He had seen her right enough and was surprised that she was out so late for the women of their community usually retired to bed when the sun set and rose with the dawn.

For a moment Jesse considered walking across to where she stood and flushing her out like a rabbit from a covert but he decided against it because he knew that it would be dangerous to be alone with Thomassin on a moonlit night. They were both young and she was a striking-looking girl who made no secret of the fact that she was hungry for him. It would be hard to resist her. The last thing he wanted was to be a married man in Kirk Yetholm with a crowd of children so the best thing to do was stay away. He walked on past, pretending to be unaware of how hot with passion were the glittering eyes that she fixed on him.

On Sunday morning, the Elliots were preparing to go to church. This was always a nerve-straining occasion because the three younger children hated church-going and squealed, cried and fought against Grace when she tried to chivvy them through breakfast. Eventually, as the bells pealed out over the town, the family could be seen emerging from their front door and heading down the street. The black-clad lawyer led the procession with his flame-haired wife on his arm. As usual Hester was flamboyantly dressed with a rakishly tilted hat shading her slanting, knowing eyes and a dress of shiny green satin straining over her prominent bust. Behind her straggled her three children – ten year old Edward, a sullen and callous boy who enjoyed teasing and cruelly ill-treating his pets, Effie, aged eight, a sly-looking girl who resembled her mother in colouring and baby Amelia, the indulged pet who could do no wrong. At the end of the line, limping rapidly to keep up, came Grace.

161

In church the family filed with piously lowered heads into their pew and sat down with pretend humility to endure two hours of tedium. At the head of the line sat Elliot, then came Edward, followed by Effie, Hester and Amelia. Grace was at the end nearest the wall and silently enduring the kicks and fidgets of the little girl whom it was her duty to keep quiet. Every now and again the child made a particularly loud rustle with her stiffly-starched petticoats and Hester craned forward to glare along the line – not at Amelia, of course, but at the longsuffering Grace.

During prayers, the crippled girl folded her hands and leant her head upon the pew edge. She wondered what words the other members of her family were sending up as she began to compose her own thoughts into appropriate form. It proved impossible, however, to achieve a sufficiently humble frame of mind for her head was in a spin. Her whole world had been turned upside down during the past few days and her brain was swirling with strange ideas. The most overwhelming of them were her memories of the previous day when she had met the strange woman at Bettymill, the woman who hinted at things so bewildering that they made Grace feel giddy.

Normally when she tried to pray she either felt deep despair at the unlikelihood of any answer being sent to her or anger at what seemed like the indifference of God. Today her outlook had changed: her leg still hurt but already she imagined that the treatment Alice had given it had made it stronger. Her attitude of mind seemed to have changed, too, because she was able to contemplate her future with more confidence that she had ever felt before.

She started to plan out her day – first of all she must go down to Havanah Court and tell Odilie about her adventure at Bettymill and then, as soon as she had a chance, she was determined to broach the subject of the ownership of the mill with her father. What was even better was that she could look forward to the exciting prospect of meeting the kind dark-haired woman again at

162

the Fair tomorrow and finding out more about her unknown mother. As far as the Fair was concerned, though, there was still one black cloud on the horizon, but she decided that she simply would not think about the young man with the bonny hair. Because of Alice Archer she had to go to the Fair now but if she did meet him, she'd walk straight on by rather than embarrass him into recognising her.

She was rudely awakened from her reverie by Hester reaching over and jabbing into Grace's ribs to alert her to the fact that Amelia had fallen on to the floor with a loud crash and was sitting sobbing among the hassocks.

'Look after the child, can't you?' hissed Hester. 'What do you think you're here for?'

Grace's eyes moved sideways and stared without blinking into the face of her hated step-mother. 'Look after her yourself, Hester. She's your daughter,' she whispered with the slightly imperious inflection in her voice that people used towards wayward servants. It was her first real rebellion.

The Sunday midday meal at Viewhill was usually a fraught affair with Kelly flustering about and Grace being bullied by Hester but today the tone was more muted. Grace's act of defiance had in some way quelled her step-mother though from time to time she realised that Hester, on the verge of giving her a slap or making a cruel remark, was restrained by a look from her father. Then the girl realised that she was being treated carefully and decided the reason must be Andrew Elliot's need for her to act as an intermediary with Odilie.

After they had eaten, she boldly took off her apron and announced that she was going to pay a call at Havanah Court. No objections were raised although there was still a considerable amount of work to be done in the kitchen.

She found Odilie and Martha in the boudoir surrounded as usual by pretty fripperies. Odilie, whose face wore an unusually sombre expression, seemed to have lost some of her enchanting sparkle and Grace's first concern was for her friend. 'How did things go at Sloebank Castle?'

she asked, taking Odilie's hand, 'I've been longing to know. I hope he was better than you imagined.'

Odilie shook her head. 'He was dreadful. I can't bear to talk about it.' Grace knew that she was being warned to keep her curiosity for later when they were alone and with a smile Odilie held out a hat towards her and said, 'Look, Grace, I'm trimming this for Aunt Martha to wear at the Fair. She wants to go in that old straw bonnet of hers but I'm determined she'll have something new. Have you got a pretty hat for tomorrow?'

Grace sank into a chair with a gasp of relief for her leg was still aching. 'To tell you the truth Odilie, I didn't think I was going to need a hat. I wasn't going to the Fair, you see.'

'Not going! But you're coming with me. I'm determined to go with my friend like any ordinary girl! Is it Hester that's stopping you? I'll have a word with your father about that.' Odilie looked genuinely disappointed.

Grace put up a placatory hand. 'No, no, don't worry. I've changed my mind. Or at least I've had it changed for me. The strangest thing happened yesterday and I've been longing to talk to you about it.' When she leaned forward in the chair her face was vibrant with excitement and both Odilie and Martha were struck by the change in her. The diffidence and fear had gone – she looked confident and beautiful.

Odilie laid down Martha's hat and said, 'Oh, do tell us. You look as if it was something marvellous.'

Grace nodded. 'It was. I took the grey mare out to look for you, Odilie, because Joe said you'd ridden over the bridge. I hope you don't mind but I didn't search for very long – I went to Bettymill instead and met a remarkable woman there.'

Martha and Odilie looked at each other in surprise. 'At Bettymill you met a woman? It's a ruin now, isn't it? Who was she?' asked Martha who knew most of the people in the district and was always curious about their doings.

'She said her name was Alice Archer,' Grace told her.

'Never heard of her. She's probably one of those vagrants. They camp down in every field or broken-down bothy for miles around before the Fair. Some of them would cut your throat for a farthing. You shouldn't have been wandering about on your own like that.'

Martha looked disapproving and that look deepened when Grace nodded and said, 'Yes, she was one of the Fair people. She said her husband ran a freak show.'

Martha gasped in horror. 'Freaks! They're the worst kind. They steal wee bairns and grow them up in boxes so that they're stunted; they buy calves with two heads and weans wi' no legs. Keep away from her!'

Grace did not react because she'd heard all the stories about freak show people before. 'No, no, she was a very nice woman. She rubbed my leg and said it isn't as bad as it looks. She actually helped it, I think.'

Martha leaned forward and asked earnestly, 'She didn't ask you for any money, did she?'

'Of course not. Anyway I didn't have any. She never mentioned money except for one very odd thing – she told me that I've a dowry I don't know about. She said Bettymill belongs to me and perhaps other things as well. She knew an awful lot about me and my family.'

Martha looked sideways at Odilie and then asked, 'Are you sure she wasn't one of those fortune-teller wifies? They can spin a story like nothing you've ever heard but they're really only telling you what you want to hear.'

Grace's air of happiness was undimmed. 'No, she wasn't a fortune-teller, I'm sure of that. She was very respectable looking, lady-like I'd say. She told me that she knew my mother when she was young.'

Martha's hands went very still on her lap and she sounded apprehensive as she asked, 'What else did she say?'

Grace stared into the old woman's eyes. 'She said my mother didn't die here. She said she died in London – not from childbirth but from a broken heart. Apparently she didn't want to leave me and grieved sorely. Is all that true?'

There was neither confirmation nor denial from Martha

whose eyes were round in consternation. 'Anything else? Did she say anything else?' she demanded.

Grace shook her head, 'No. Is what she said true? Please tell me.'

'I don't know about London but I know Lucy went away and I'm sure she had a broken heart. Poor soul,' Martha's voice was full of pity. Then she rallied and said, 'But who was this Alice person? I've never heard of her. What did she look like?'

Grace's eyes went abstracted as she summoned up a mind picture of Alice. 'She was as black-haired as you, Odilie, and tall and thin with a sort of sad face. Her eyes were very pale blue and shadowed, as if they'd been bruised. She looked tired. She had a cleft in her chin . . .' The girl laid her finger on her chin and felt a cleft there too. 'It was a little like mine but much deeper. The thing I remember most about her were her hands. They were long and capable and her fingers were very strong.'

'Black-haired, was she? What did she speak like?' asked Martha cautiously.

'She sounded like a lady. But you must tell me – why did my mother have to go away?'

The old woman looked harried. 'How can I tell you the reasons? Things like that are private. Who can tell what goes on in other people's houses? I'll tell you one thing though – when Lucy married Andrew Elliot folk in Lauriston said she'd regret it. He was aye scheming and untrustworthy. I'm sorry to talk about your father like that but it's true. She was very different – open and free and generous – too generous, too trusting.'

Grace nodded. 'Yes, Alice Archer said the same thing. But didn't people wonder when my mother went away?'

'Oh aye, they wondered right enough. They talked about nothing else for a long time. But let me warn you, lassie, dinna let on to your father you know about this. He doesnae like it to be hashed over. About six months after she left, he gave out that Lucy was dead and then it all quietened down. By the time your grandfather died folk had found something else to talk about.'

166

Grace nodded. There were so many questions running through her head about this mysterious business that she did not know which to ask first but Odilie took the initiative for her and asked, 'But what's all this about a dowry? What do you think of that, Aunt Martha?'

Martha pursed up her mouth. 'How can I say? I'll tell you one thing though, Lucy's daughter shouldn't be treated like a pauper the way you are, Grace. Lucy was a lassie with money and that's why Andrew Elliot married her, folk said. Not that she wouldn't have found a husband quick enough for she was very bonny. But once he'd got his hands on her property, he treated her badly. There was a lot of talk about him and the maid . . . folk didn't blame Lucy.'

The girls chorused together, 'The maid – you mean Hester? They didn't blame Lucy for what? For going away?'

'Hester right enough,' nodded Martha. 'But for God's sake don't let on I told you.' She didn't vouchsafe an answer to the second question.

'But what about Grace's dowry? If she has one what should she do?' Odilie was very practical as far as money was concerned for she had inherited her father's business acumen.

Martha pursed up her mouth. 'Your father's not a poor man, Grace. He has property all over the district – houses and farms and I'm sure some of them are places that belonged to Davie Allen though I don't know how you'd find out which. The rents alone must come to a tidy bit of money.'

'I'll ask Father to do a bit of snooping. He loves that kind of thing,' cried Odilie, who was glad of a diversion from the troubles that were plaguing her mind.

'I don't think he'll have much success,' said Grace. 'My father's very close about money. He likes to save. Even Hester has a hard time prising money out of his pocket. I know she steals his purse every now and again and helps herself and she's always grumbling because he won't keep a carriage or hire more maids except poor Kelly who's little better than useless. When she complains he says that he's making sure the children will be well off when he's dead – but he doesn't mean me.'

Odilie jumped to her feet and cried out, 'Enough of this. I sense a mystery here! Thank heavens you met that odd woman, even if she was from the freak show! I'm going to put my father on to the problem of your dowry, Grace but now, no more gloomy talk. Try on this hat. You'd look beautiful in it.'

Playfully she stood on tiptoe and popped a large-brimmed straw hat on to Grace's head and with a flourish draped a pink ostrich feather around its crown. Odilie's hands could make things of beauty out of all sorts of objects. She stood back with a smile on her face and regarded her friend. 'I'm right, you're a beauty. Now you must add this as the finishing touch.'

Over Grace's shoulders she draped a pink silk shawl with tiny golden metal acorns weighing down each corner. The colour gave a glow to Grace's cheeks and she looked transformed. At the sight of her Martha gave a stifled gasp. 'Oh my, but you look like your mother,' she said. She could not have said anything that pleased the girl more,

'Do I, do I really? That's wonderful!' Grace cried, and clutched the pink shawl to her shoulders.

'Yes, you're beautiful. You'll wear that to the Fair and break all hearts. This is to be your lucky year, Grace Elliot,' pronounced Odilie.

'All right I'll wear it, but keep it here so that Hester doesn't see it or she'll make me feel foolish,' said Grace. 'I'll dress myself properly when I call for you tomorrow, Odilie.'

When Grace left Odilie searched out her aunt and found her in the stillroom counting jars of pickled peaches made from the bounty of Canny's conservatory. She closed the door and leaned against it saying. 'Now you can't get away. You've got to clear up this mystery for me.'

'What mystery?' asked Martha in a blandly innocent tone.

'You know well enough. The mystery of Grace's mother. I can read you like a book and I know there's a lot more that you didn't say this afternoon, isn't there?'

'What of it? There's some things that are best not talked about – things that happened, mistakes people made, they shouldn't be dredged up.'

'You talk about everyone else, so why not Lucy Allen?'

The old woman paused in her work and stared bleakly at the girl. 'Don't underestimate me. I talk about little things easily enough but not big things. This is best forgotten. I'm proud of the folk in Lauriston that they've kept it from Grace for so long. It shows that they've got hearts. If you've any heart you'd better leave it alone too, Odilie. I'm warning you.'

Odilie was instantly sobered. 'But Aunt Martha, I'm not asking for myself. I'm doing this for Grace. She's been so sad and lonely and now she's found out about her mother, it's given her a sort of identity. You saw how different she was today. If there's something awful in the story don't you think she should be warned by people who love her in case it's sprung on her by an outsider. What a shock that would be!'

Martha shook her head. 'I've thought about all that too, Odilie. If it helps you I can say that what happened was a tragedy and Lucy certainly didn't want to leave her bairn. She took on something terrible. I'll never forget hearing her weeping . . . go away, Odilie, and don't ask any more. I've no intention of taking bellows to cold ashes and I think it's a sore pity that a loose-tongued Fair woman met Grace at Bettymill. Some folk don't know when to hold their tongues.'

Sunday was just another working day for the freak show. Long Tom had buried George, the dead bear, in the chilly light of dawn so that when Alice rose there was no trace of it except a mound of freshly turned earth in a distant corner of the camp. Alice deliberately did not ask about

George and Jem took care to steer the conversation well away from the bears, but the death had cast a gloom over the freak show and its people tacitly sunk their differences of the previous night as they stood together beside the breakfast fire with their arms clasped around their chests and their legs shivering in the chill of the mist that drifted along the Tweed valley.

Spirits brightened, however, when the sun rose, promising another brilliant day, and the dogs began rustling about in the undergrowth looking for rabbits. As usual Jem went from caravan to cart speaking to his people. To his relief he found that because of Alice's potion, Billy had spent a peaceful night. When Jem unlocked his door he was still sleeping but the sound woke him and he sat up from the floor rubbing his eyes. He was smiling and in a good mood so Jem gently chivvied him and led him down to the stream where Billy stripped off and washed himself. He stood in the water, white-skinned and muscled like Hercules. He had a magnificent physique and if it had not been for the terrible confusion of his mind, he would have been a prime example of young manhood. Jem often thought that Billy was a mistake on the part of God who had missed out something vital when creating the lad.

Because they were within a short distance of the field where the Fair was to be held, they decided to spend another night in the same camping place and use Sunday as a time of preparation so that everything would be ready to move at dawn on Monday morning. Jem wanted to be one of the first on the field so that he could pick a good site.

All morning he walked about among his people, giving orders, advising on how posters should be displayed, advertising signs re-painted or costumes repaired. Each sideshow attraction kept most of their own earnings but paid a share to Jem for looking after them and he was a good protector who organised the quarrelsome and acid-souled freaks with infinite tact and patience, shepherding them from fair to fair and mediating in their disputes which were frequently violent and occasionally bloody.

Only Billy, who was incapable of handling his own affairs or making any decisions for himself, had no control over his own destiny. He belonged completely to Jem as if he was a dog or a horse.

As he watched the boy bathing, Jem reflected that it was coincidental Billy had come into his possession at a St James' Fair twelve years earlier, handed over at the age of eight by an old gypsy woman called Rachel, who was beginning to despair of controlling him when he was engulfed by one of his terrible destructive rages. She did not trust any of her own people to treat Billy well so, unusually, she chose Jem as his protector because she recognised the gentleness of the big man's soul. Originally Jem had hoped to train Billy as a boxer but his unrestrained violence made that impossible, for he would go on beating his opponent until the man died. By the time Billy reached puberty it was found that he could only safely be displayed before the public in chains and so Jem trained him to perform terrifying feats of strength which the chains accentuated in a way. When he was only fourteen years old, Jem started displaying him in a sideshow as a challenger to the Strongest Man in the World, an aged prize fighter who was also in the entourage. The two of them arm wrestled and bent iron bars in competition with each other until they reached the stage when Billy always won. Then the old fighter retired and Billy took the stage alone after that.

Jem was sitting watching his protégé when a young lad came into their camping lot and looked around for the boss. 'Are you Mr Archer?' he asked Jem and when the answer was affirmative, he went on, 'Your brother's circus is in a field up the road and he sent me down to tell you that he'd like to see you.'

When Billy was settled back in his caravan, Jem went in search of Alice. 'Simon's in a field a bit along the road. I haven't seen him and Bella for years. Let's take a walk over and have a word with them.'

Alice smiled. 'How many relations have you got? You seem to claim one in every circus or side show we come across all over the country.'

'Well, yes, there were ten in my family and they're all in the travelling trade. We're always glad to see each other.'

Jem was beaming at the prospect of a family reunion and Alice squeezed his enormous hand as she said sadly, 'What a pity you've no sons yourself.'

He shrugged. 'No matter. Simon's got three and my other brothers have at least twenty among them. My family are the people in this show – and as much trouble if you ask me,' he said, looking over his shoulder at the busy encampment where fortunately all was peaceful at the moment. She took his arm while they walked behind the messenger through the gulley and about half a mile up the road to the field where Simon's circus was camped.

His entourage was much bigger than Jem's for at least forty caravans and carts were scattered over the field and people were running here and there with buckets and bales of hay for the string of horses that fidgeted, neighed or lashed ineffectual kicks at each other in a line of pickets by the riverside.

'Simon always has grand horses. He's a great eye for an animal,' said Jem in an admiring voice as they neared this display of horseflesh. He and Alice were walking along looking at the greys and bays, the chestnuts and the piebalds when a huge roar came from behind them and a man as big as Jem, but younger, came running towards them.

This was Simon, who, clapping his brother on the shoulder, bellowed out, 'It's good to see you! I heard your lot was camped near here so I thought I'd get in touch. Oh, but it's grand to see you again.' Then he looked at Alice and stuck out a hand. 'Pleased to meet you, too, ma'am. We heard there was a lady travelling with Jem.'

'This is my Alice,' announced Jem with pride as Simon bent gallantly over Alice's hand, for like his brother he appreciated the style of the tall, dignified-looking woman who had taken up with Jem.

Then he grabbed them both by the arms and said, 'My van's over there. Bella's inside. Come on and I'll give you a glass of negus. How's trade? What are you hauling around these days? Have you still got that killer of a laddie – the one called Billy? You should get rid of him before he does someone in.'

When she saw them coming Bella bounced down the caravan steps, a tiny, taut-muscled bundle of energy. She was bursting with delight at seeing Jem and with curiosity to meet Alice. Soon they were all seated in comfortable places in the caravan with full glasses of brandy and water into their hands and the brothers were talking ten to the dozen about people Alice had never heard of before.

She looked around and noted how sparkling and immaculate the caravan was with brightly painted china displayed on every shelf and in every nook. It was obvious that like most travelling women Bella had a strict routine. Prior to any move she always took down her treasures and packed them carefully. On arriving at the next stop, even if it was only overnight, the china was brought out first and put on show even before a cooking fire was lit.

'It's not like you to come so far north, Jem. You usually stop at Appleby or Carlisle, don't you?' Bella was asking.

'Alice wanted to visit St James' Fair,' was the reply, which made Bella look curiously at the stranger whom she held in a certain awe because of her air of ladylike remoteness.

Bella's smile, the same smile that illumined her face when she went stepping proudly along the rope above the heads of her audience, was in brilliant place but her brain was actively speculating, for she had heard stories of how Jem searched the country for Alice after their first meeting. She doesn't look all that special, thought Bella, not spectacular enough to awaken such devotion in a man. 'Have you got people up here, Alice?' she asked, wanting to know more about the strange, silent woman that her husband's brother had picked up on his travels.

Alice shook her head. 'Not really, but I used to live here when I was a girl so I wanted to see it again. I'll go and look out some old acquaintances in the town tomorrow because I've just found out that I've a bit of unfinished business here.'

Bella knew better than quiz any more for Alice's face had a reserved look about it so she switched her attention to the brothers who were catching up on travellers' gossip.

'How's Bartle?' asked Jem, enquiring about their eldest brother.

'The same as ever, drinking like a lord and blaspheming fit to bust but he can make a horse work better than anyone I've ever seen. He's still got his old charger Gibraltar. It's thirty years old now! He's off to America to give a show but some of the fight's gone out of him. His missus died last year and she was a sore loss to him,' said Simon.

Bella chipped in, 'We've had a loss as well. We're short of a trick rider. Wouldn't you believe it but just before we got here our El Diavolo had a fall and broke his leg. In bits it is and he won't be in the saddle tomorrow or for many days after that. A doctor looked at him in Blackshiels and said he might never walk again.'

'Poor devil,' said Jem. 'And poor you – before the biggest event of the year. Maybe you'll pick up somebody at the field – there's always lots of young hopefuls hanging about.'

Simon snorted. 'It'd take more than a young hopeful to replace him. He's suffering a lot, too. I hate to hear the groans of him.' He was as soft-hearted as his brother.

Jem glanced across at Alice and suggested, 'Do you think you might be able to help?' Then he explained to Simon and Bella, 'Alice is good with cures and potions. She keeps Billy quiet and I don't have an ache or a pain that she can't soothe away.'

Bella looked hopefully at Alice who smiled and said, 'I don't know if I can do anything but I'll try if you want. Where is he?'

'Next door. I'll just tell him you're coming,' said Simon disappearing out of the caravan door. In a few minutes

174

he was back gesturing to Alice and saying, 'Come on, it's a good thing you're here because the poor devil's groaning in agony. It'll be Christian work to help him.'

Alice soon saw that the caravan inhabited by El Diavolo and his blowsy wife was very different from Bella's immaculate home, for it was as dirty as ever and littered with cast-off clothes and bits of saddlery. The sick man was lying on his tumbled bed with the same dirty covers and the same line of empty bottles beside him. He was unshaven and his eyes were glittering with fever but he exerted himself to be courteous to the newcomers and called out in his Irish tongue, 'Come in, come in, make yourselves at home. Take a chair, take a chair.'

He adopted gentlemanly airs and claimed to have been a captain of dragoons in the Peninsular War, but in fact he had been an ordinary rough rider in Lord Ancrum's Regiment of Horse. After being wounded he became disillusioned with military life and simply disappeared from the barracks one night. Then he stowed away on a ship and found himself back in England where he changed his name to a Spanish one in honour of his war service and, through his talent as a rider, found himself a place in a circus troop. He was a genius on a horse because he was totally fearless and his acts of gymnastic daring made crowds gasp in admiration for he could stand on his head in the saddle while the horse went full tilt beneath him or stand on one leg with a glass of wine balanced on his head. He could also jump in the saddle with a skipping rope while his horse galloped around the ring but his most spectacular achievement, and the one he kept for the climax of his act, was when he came bursting into the ring standing with a foot in the saddle of two galloping horses.

By the time of the accident he'd been with Simon for several years but increasing fondness for the bottle had made him unreliable, and even before the accident it was becoming obvious that this rough rider would soon have to be replaced. Now fate had taken a hand.

When Alice asked the laid-low hero how he felt, he

groaned and put the palm of his hand against his fore-head. 'It's in there. It's as if all the devils in Hell are prodding at me brains with their toasting forks. If I move the pain grabs me like a dragon's tooth.'

'You should lay off the bottle then,' said Bella unfeel-ingly, 'She means how's your leg?'

'Me leg's smashed to smithereens,' groaned El Diavolo as Alice bent over him and gently uncovered the limb which Dr Thompson had swathed in bandages and tied to a broom-handle to keep it straight. When her fingers moved down the swollen purple thigh the patient gave a sickening yell and cried out, 'Don't touch it, oh God in heaven missus, don't touch it!'

Her face was concerned as she turned to Simon and said, 'I think he needs something to take the heat out of that leg. I'll go back to our camp and make up a medicine for him. I won't be long.'

'God bless you, God bless you,' sobbed the patient and dropped his hand down at the side of the bed to feel for the neck of another bottle, but seeing this Alice adroitly moved it out of his reach.

'You'd better stay off that or you'll be seeing things crawling out of the walls soon,' she told him firmly. As Simon watched her in operation, his eyes were full of admiration. This is a good woman our Jem's found, he thought.

When she returned to the circus an hour later, she brought lotions, poultices and a jug of herbal medicine for El Diavolo to drink. 'He won't like the taste,' she told Bella, 'but you must tell his wife to force him to take it and keep the brandy away from him. It looks as though his leg's going to take a long time to mend. He won't be able to stand on it for at least a month and he must lie still or it won't heal. I'll make up more poultices and bring them to the Fair tomorrow and give them to you there.'

The circus owners were very grateful and Simon laughed as he told Jem, 'Well, well, old man. Your Alice is a wonderful woman. She couldn't produce a trick rider as well as a poultice, could she?'

They spent a happy day together but with nightfall the time came for Jem and Alice to return to their own encampment. On their walk back, they linked arms and laughed about the things they had seen and heard while over their heads the moon swam up out of its nest of clouds and glowed down on them like a friendly protector. The night was full of the scent of honeysuckle; white owls flitted ghost-like above the hedgerows and plump hedgehogs waddled grunting and complaining out of their path.

When they reached their own glade, they were relieved to see that the freak show caravans were quiet and the fires safely damped down. Even Billy's caravan was silent and dark and Jem sighed a deep breath of satisfaction as he gazed about his domain.

'On nights like this I know why I enjoy travelling, Alice. I forget all the misery of long slogs through mud and rain and I realise that I'll never be able to settle down with a churchwarden pipe.'

'I didn't ever seriously think you would,' she laughed gently and slipped her arm around his waist in an affectionate gesture.

By the time they went to bed the moon looked huge in the sky, swimming in an opalescent sky netted in silver skeins of clouds. Alice arose and opened the caravan door so that she could watch it from where she lay in bed and there was wonder in her gaze as she turned to whisper to Jem beside her, 'Look at that moon. It's a magic moon. It's a moon for casting spells.'

He raised his head and gazed at it. 'If there's a moon like that tomorrow night, there'll be plenty of bairns made among the young folk at the Fair,' he told her as he reached out to hold her to him.

'St James' Fair is famous for making bairns,' said Alice in a faraway, sad voice. Then she sank her head on his shoulder and slipped a loving arm around his neck.

*

The windows of Havanah Court were glowing with the light of massive banks of candles. They shone out across the River Tweed that flowed at the foot of Canny's garden. A convivial party was going on in the house and the host sat proudly at the top of his dinner table knowing that his dining room put the one at Sloebank to shame. His mirrors and pictures sparkled richly on walls painted an attractive shade of pale apple green beneath a plaster-embossed ceiling encrusted with medallions painted in pink, white and cerulean blue. His furniture, which had been made to his special order in the local workshop of James Mein, another of Canny's boyhood friends, glea-med like glass because it was lovingly polished every day with lemon-scented oil. His silver was brightly burnished and his plates were of eggshell-thin porcelain imported from China where they had been specially painted by artists in Canton with his own device – a full-rigged ship and a palm tree enclosed in a wreath of tropical flowers. Canny felt prodigious pride as he surveyed this domain and luxuriated in the way the carpets felt silken through the thin soles of his evening slippers.

The guests around his table were not constrained by ceremony but leaned their elbows on the stiffly starched cloth and shouted remarks at each other in happy ani-mation as they relished a good meal. It would have been considered scandalous to send anything back to Canny's kitchen uneaten as more sophisticated guests had done at the Duke's table. A beaming Joe Cannonball and his army of flunkeys were running to and fro bearing aloft silver platters of steaming capons in fragrant sauce, roast veal with oranges, gaping-mouthed fish that had been specially sent up from Berwick in boxes filled with ice, and paper-thin slices of pork stuffed with forcemeat and set in quiver-ing aspic. Joe was grinning more broadly than the hap-piest guest because there was nothing he enjoyed so much as a party.

Most of the guests at the gathering were people the host had known all his life. In place of honour was his oldest friend, Wattie Thompson, now Professor Walter

Thompson of Edinburgh University, who was peacocking it over a brace of rich farmers and prosperous local businessmen with their plump and cheerful wives. Martha was there too, quite at ease and shyness forgotten now that she was among old friends. Her lace cap was still pinned askew on to her grey hair and her cheeks were flushed by her brother's magnificent claret. Best of all, his daughter Odilie sat facing him at the other end of the table. He could see her over banks of flowers and the glittering standards of burning candlesticks and he looked at her with love noting how beautiful she was in the candlelight that sparked flashes of colour into her hair and gave a satiny sheen to her skin. Tonight she was gloriously gowned in a dress of the same deep pink colour as a geranium and pearls were looped through her hair. Canny was happy to see that she was looking more cheerful than she had been since the Duke's dinner party and that she was talking animatedly to a young man called Playfair whom Thompson had brought along to the party.

'He's staying in the Cross Keys too and the place's so full that the food's like swill. I thought if I brought him here, you'd give him a good meal,' Thompson had explained to Canny when he introduced the extra guest.

Odilie had taken to the young man, who was obviously dazzled by her and Canny wished he could hear what they were saying to each other. In fact the conversation between Odilie and William Playfair that so intrigued her father was very innocent. When Playfair told the glowing girl that he had been commissioned to draw up the plans for the Duke's new mansion, she seemed to shrink in her seat and some of the animation left her, so he wished he had not mentioned the Duke's name for he knew very well that she was the girl who was on the verge of marrying his patron. Gossip had it that the betrothal was to be announced officially on the day after Fair Monday but till then it was a secret – a Lauriston secret – which of course was no secret at all for every guest in the room looked at Odilie with open and frank speculation that night. However, when Odilie sobered at the mention of the Duke, Playfair thought that he had committed a breach of etiquette by referring even obliquely to her intended husband and tried to make up for it by animated conversation in the hope of bringing brightness back to the lovely girl. He leaned forward in his chair and told her, 'I want to build the finest mansion in Britain up there at Sloebank. My head's so full of it that I was up most of last night making drawings. I'm producing new ideas all the time. It'll be a miracle, a place of delight like the palace of a Mughal Emperor. I want people to stand and look at it in wonder like they do when they see that Indian palace near Delhi some rajah built for his wife. I saw engravings of it in a book . . .'

She smiled at that and a delicious dimple appeared in her right cheek. 'What a huge task you've set yourself,' she said. 'Does your patron know what you're doing?'

'Not yet. I'm not doing it for him anyway . . .' he said. He didn't dare continue and say the other words that were on the tip of his tongue . . . 'I'm doing it for you,' but his eyes said it for him.

The moon that enchanted Jem and Alice was not regarded with the same favour by eight mounted men who came slipping like wraiths down the dark lanes from Kirk Yetholm. Each of them rode one horse and led another by a short halter rope as they trotted along the grass verges at the sides of the road in order to muffle the sound of their horses' hooves, which otherwise would ring out through the still night on the stones of the sun-dried road surface. They took this precaution even when there was no habitation visible for miles because the habit of seeking secrecy and invisibility was ingrained in gypsies.

Shortly after eleven struck on the town clock, they reached the end of the Rennie Bridge and headed up the north bank of the Tweed, passing a darkened grain mill by the roadside and looking across the water at the windows of Havanah Court which were still glowing with light because Canny Rutherford was giving his pre-Fair dinner party.

180

Gib Faa, leader of the line, stared across at the gleaming windows of the sprawling mansion with interest but without envy. He knew that it belonged to a fellow who'd made a fortune in pirate waters and he respected the man's enterprise but did not envy his settled life in retirement. Gib's idea of the perfect existence was to be on the road all the time until he died and he would have loathed passing his days sitting in grand rooms filled with fancy furniture and remembering an adventurous past. When Havanah Court disappeared over his right shoulder, he turned his leonine head back towards the west and heard Abel, his son, who was riding behind him, muttering, 'I wish that glim would go doon. It's as light as day. It's not good to be seen.'

But the moon was not going to disappear for hours yet and Gib had to make a decision. Should the gypsies risk crossing the River Teviot in moonlight or wait until it was pitch dark? He raised his arm and his band drew up in a line, one after the other, in the lee of a hedge on the approach to the Teviot Bridge.

'Pandlo mengro!' exclaimed Gib, pointing ahead and indicating that the toll-gate was locked against them. His horse arched its neck and mouthed on its bit as he turned to look back at his companions. His eye rested on Jesse who was riding third in the line. The young man sat with a hand on his knee and an impassive look on his face. Pointing back at the closed toll-gate Gib asked, 'What do we do, then? What do you think, Jesse? Will we wait till the choon goes down and it's dark. It irks me that the rajahs can close us off from our fords.'

'We should fight them for it,' said the angry voice of Abel who was riding second horse. Abel was rash and always too ready for a battle which was why his father had passed him over as his successor, and Abel was aware of the fact that his father preferred Jesse so his jealousy of his cousin was fierce. Recently it had grown worse because of his unrequited passion for Thomassin who had eyes for no man except Jesse.

As Abel turned and stared with dislike at his cousin,

181

Jesse leaned forward in his saddle and said in a low voice, 'There's no point in a chingaro. Fighting'll do us no good. It'd be the staripen if they caught us.'

Abel's voice was full of scorn as he hissed, 'And scared of the staripen, are you?'

Jesse retorted, 'Yes, and so should you be. Have you heard of the convict hulks, Abel? Do you want to spend your life chained up like a stinking rat? I don't. It's not clever to let them pen you up for the sake of a fight which you're sure to lose.'

His anger ran as high as anyone else's, however, when he contemplated the injustice that had been inflicted on local people when the fords which they had used from time immemorial were closed. This had been happening over the last few years with the aim of driving travellers on to the turnpike roads and toll-bridges which were the monopoly of local landowners who had discovered them to be a good way of raising money. Now a local by-law had been passed decreeing prosecution for anyone found using the old crossing places on the Border rivers where there were toll-bridges. Those who still used the fords were fined, or, in the case of persistent offenders, they could be sent away to the Antipodes in a convict ship. This piece of legislation blatantly enacted by the moneyed folk was a standing invitation to the gypsies to flout it but Gib and Jesse knew that they had to use caution and guile. The most popular fords were guarded and if they were caught trying to cross by them, it would be the dreaded staripen, the prison, for them.

Gib nodded. 'You're right, lad. We'll wait for darkness. Pass the word down that we'll hide on the river bank. I wish we'd brought the jakkalors though. Look at the merryfeet up there.' He pointed upstream at a grassy bank where rabbits were hopping about gaily in the moonlight, blissfully unconscious of how lucky they were that the gypsies had not brought their dogs: the lurchers would have made swift work of them.

Jesse laughed. 'We've enough trouble without dogs. It's

going to take us all our time to get these horses across the ford without the Duke's bailiffs having a deek at us.'

Abel found it impossible to stay out of the discussion and pushed his way up beside his father to whisper hoarsely, 'Damn their eyes for closing the fords. We've aye crossed freely here but now they want their bars. Why don't we jump the gate and defy them? If I could get my hands on that Duke I'd glib him right enough.' He put his hand on a pistol that hung from his side as he spoke.

'Calm down, Abel. If you go talking about glibbing the Duke your body'll be hanging on a gibbet quick enough. Put that pistol away and see you don't use it,' warned Gib.

The angry man hissed derisively, 'You're as bad as the rajahs. You're letting us down. Your father, my grandfather, wouldn't have stood for this. You're getting soft. We've all got a Yetholm jagger in our belts tonight, why don't we use them? Have you one, Jesse Bailey?'

When the dark-haired young man looked over at Abel his eyes were flashing with scorn. 'Act sensible, Abel. Don't play the fool. There's no point giving them an excuse to hang us one by one. It was my brother last time, it could be you tomorrow. If I've a jagger on me I'm not saying and I'll only use it if I have to. Otherwise it stays sheathed and so should yours if you've any sense.'

Abel only snorted. 'A pol-engro, that's what you are. When a man learns reading and writing, he loses his guts. Instead of sitting with your head in books you should be bedding Thomassin. What's wrong with you anyway – are you a chavi in breeches?'

'You know damned well I'm no chavi,' said Jesse.

His temper was rising because of Abel's goading, however, and Gib saw that his fists were clenching on the reins so he put out an arm and pushed Abel back into his saddle ordering as he did so, 'Keep quiet or you'll waken the toll-keeper. There's no point in all this useless talk. I'm the leader and I say we go up the river and lie low till the glim goes down. Come on.'

They followed a path up the grassy bank and found a

183

convenient place where they could wait under the branches of a circle of sheltering trees. Gib took care that Abel was left behind with one group of men while he led Jesse and two others farther up the river. Then they loosened their horses' heads and sat silently in their saddles till they seemed to merge into the landscape. They were so still that the nocturnal animals started coming out and playing around their horses' hooves. Hedgehogs waddled by; a hare sat up and brushed its whiskers with its paws; dozens of rabbits flopped foolishly about; a badger winked its eyes at Jesse from its set at the tree roots and hunting owls flitted among the branches giving an occasional bloodcurdling screech as a kill was made.

Jesse sat with his head lowered as if asleep but he was pondering his usual problem. How was he going to find enough money to leave Kirk Yetholm? The argument with Abel had only stiffened his resolve to go. He put his hand up to his neck and stroked his throat thinking that if he stayed, there would be a rope around it sooner or later, either because of his own impetuosity but more likely because of someone else's. If he could pick up some money at the Fair, he thought, he'd give half of it to Thomassin to assuage her for the disappointment of not marrying him and go away with the rest. Twenty pounds in his pocket would be enough to carry him a long way – perhaps to London where the feuds of the Yetholm gypsies which so ruled his life at home would be forgotten and the obligations expected of him by people like Gib would be left behind.

He knew that although he had never pretended to love Thomassin it was expected by both their families and by the girl herself that they would marry. If he refused to do so, yet another feud would begin. Blood would flow, new hatreds would be born. He sighed and looked over at the proud figure of his uncle whose white head shimmered as if it was surrounded by a halo in the moonlight. Jesse felt deep admiration for Gib who had been like a father to him since his real father died in a brawl with rival gypsies from Alnwick but he realised with a feeling of sadness that he did not want to grow old like Gib. He did not want to pass his life dealing and dickering, cheating and choring. Daily he grew more tired of it, tired of always being on the wrong side of the law, always in danger of apprehension and often for something that he had not done. The fact that he was so obviously a gypsy was a mark of culpability in itself.

He longed to get away and see the places he'd read about in the minister's books. He wanted to experience another kind of life, to escape from Kirk Yetholm and the destiny that was marked out for him there. He knew better than talk about this to anyone – he'd never even mentioned it to the old minister who had died deeply mourned a couple of years ago, but it was a cherished secret that he carried inside his head.

CHAPTER 7

Monday, 3 August.

It was not until four o'clock in the morning that the moon began to sink down towards the black outline of the hills and the stars shone brighter, spangling the dark purple sky like diamonds. There was no need to pass a signal among the gypsy men for as soon as Gib raised his head, they stiffened, sat up straighter and lifted their reins in readiness to move. One by one after their leader, they rode out of their waiting place and headed for the river. Gib and Jesse made a proud sight, like an aged knight and his squire, as they rode side by side. They were the same height and sat their mounts with the same elegant mastery. Like the steeds of knights of old, too, their horses paced majestically over the mist-silvered grass leaving ghostly hoofmarks on the sward behind them. The whole tableau was uncannily silent, for even the horses seemed to be as aware as the men of the need for stealth.

In pairs they crossed a short strip of field towards the entrance to the old ford. It was one that was known to few people and its entry point was marked by a dip like a notch in a stick in the river bank. The horses slipped down the declivity on their haunches, their hooves slithering in the mud. The river was not high because there had been a long stretch of fine weather so there was no fear of being swept away as long as they kept to the line of the ford, and each man was told in a whisper by Gib to head for a special marker, a big stone shaped like a bull's head that jutted out of the bank on the other side.

'Remember, head for the bull rock and avoid the middle pool. Keep to the same side as the fir tree,' he hissed as he sat on the bank watching while each rider drove and pulled his charges into the water. The horses were nervous of the swiftly-flowing stream and lowered their heads to sniff the water as its coldness chilled their legs. They walked gingerly through its flow, lifting their hooves fastidiously and breathing heavily through distended nostrils. One or two of them tried to take a drink but their heads were hauled up and they were not permitted to linger, for the crossing had to be made as quickly as possible. The riders were used to crossing water and knew not to look down into the flow but to sit upright and keep their eyes fixed on the exit point. One after the other they entered the water. When each crossing was complete, the next rider went in.

In a short time they were all across and Gib followed last. When he climbed the bank on the far side he waved his arm again and the men clustered around following him into a cluster of scrubby trees that sprouted out of the base of the mound which was surmounted by the ruins of the ancient castle. In a way that was almost miraculous they seemed to disappear, for they had ways for making themselves appear invisible that were not known to other people.

Later, when the horses were unsaddled and dawn was about to break, the still silence along the river was broken by the sound of a man singing. His song was one of defiance and it went soaring up through the night sky like a challenge to anyone who was listening.

Can you rokra Romany?
Can you play the bosh?
Can you jaladry the staripen?
Can you chin the cost?

He was informing the bailiffs that the gypsies had outwitted them, had reached the other side of the river by the old routes. But if any bailiffs heard the song, they did nothing about it.

By the time the sun was fully risen above its eastern bed of pink and lavender clouds, the gypsies had been sleeping on the grass beside their horses for only a few hours. They lay like dead men with their heads on their rolled-up coats while their horses grazed around them; they had no fear of being trodden on because they knew that no good horse will ever stand on a human body if it can possibly avoid doing so.

Jesse Bailey lay on his front with his face turned towards the earth and his jet black hair tumbling over his neck. As the sun rose, his grey horse nuzzled his cheek and woke him up. Jesse grunted and slowly opened his eyes. The horse had its muzzle close to his face and was breathing softly on to him. He put up a hand to push it away but he smiled as he did so.

Wide awake now, he rolled over on to his back and stared into the vast bowl of sky above his head. The world looked brand new and smelt sweet, as if it had just been created. He was the first to waken and everything around him was totally silent. His spirits rose and he was filled with optimism. 'I'll do it, boy, I'll find a way,' he told the horse, remembering his thoughts of the previous night.

With the horse's head still down beside him, he crouched on all fours and then slowly rose to his feet, stretching his back and raising his arms above his head as he did so then, very quietly, he tiptoed over the bodies of the other men and walked up to the point of the ridge with the horse ambling along behind him like a friend. Tumbled stones, some of them carved with the Norman dog's tooth pattern or studded with worn old corbels from the ancient castle, were piled around him like a giant's play bricks. He climbed on to a fallen arch stone and perched there like a sentinel, staring out over the panorama. Above his head the sun swam up higher, changing the colour of the sky from pinkish grey to pale blue and birds began singing in a glorious chorus from the massed trees along the banks of the two rivers.

As he watched, a heron went swinging along the surface of the water beneath him. It moved with long, slow wing strokes staring sharp-eyed into the deep brown pools of the Teviot where trout and salmon lingered. He felt companionship with the bird for it was poaching as he himself often did. On his other side spread the expanse of meadow that had once been a town and would come to life again today. He wondered if there were ghosts watching the preparations for the return of life to their haunting place.

Jesse raised his head and stared across the Tweed. The carpenters had completed their wooden footbridge on time and it stretched its yellow newness over the eastern twist of the Tweed. Crowds were crossing it already and from his eyrie, Jesse could see the first movements on the roads. Singly and in groups people were converging on St James' Fair like ants; advancing from all directions in their hundreds, intent on a good day.

Meanwhile, in the big house of Sloebank, yawning maids straggled down from the attics to the cavernous basement kitchens where full daylight never penetrated. They rubbed their eyes and grumbled to each other for the house was full of demanding guests and there was much to be done. In his vast bedroom, His Grace the Duke of Maudesley was totally unconscious, lying on his back with his mouth open and snoring like a pig in his pagoda-like curtained bed. He dreamed of cockfighting and the vividness of his imaginings made him wake with an erection. Pity he'd not taken a girl to bed with him the night before but it didn't matter, he'd probably not be able to keep it up anyway – hadn't been able to for months. He lay among his pillows puzzling about his inconvenient impotence and remembering the days when he had been as rampant as a stallion. Something would have to be done about it . . . His thoughts ran on and he remembered it was Fair Day. The proceedings began at noon and when everything was well launched he would take his party over to see the attractions.

The blackamoor he was going to marry must be invited to join him – she was a beauty, thank God, so it was not going to be too much of a sacrifice. He'd have to ask her old villain of a father as well but what did it matter? He'd think about the fortune, mentally count the old man's gold. James Aubrey Fox contemplated Odilie in memory

189

and felt deep satisfaction. She was a delightful little thing but he'd have to do something about his impotence before he bedded her. Then he remembered how he could solve his problem. The gypsies would be over on the field today. He'd send to the old woman who made up potions. She'd fix him up – she'd done it before.

Thomassin rose early and pulled aside the tattered sacking that covered the window of her one-room home and stared out at the sky. Good, it promised to be fine so the first condition for casting Rachel's spell was fulfilled. She stepped barefoot out on to the dewy grass and gazed into the sky. Clutching her hands together like someone praying she slowly whispered the magic word 'Temon'. Then, for a second time she said it, more confidently this time – 'Temon'. After that she paused for a few seconds, cocking her head as if to listen for an answer but the only sounds were of cocks crowing somewhere on the other side of the village. With a laugh the girl threw back her head and shouted it out, 'TEMON'! A dog began barking in the cottage next door and in the distance she heard a baby starting to cry. She stood defiantly on the grass, brushing her tangled hair back from her face with both hands while optimism flooded into her. She was positive that the spell was going to work and that before nightfall a man was going to fall desperately in love with her. That man would be Jesse Bailey.

In Havanah Court Canny Rutherford turned heavily between Melrose-made linen sheets in his bed with the dark green velvet curtains that shut out the creeping light of day. His mind was going over and over the same old track and once again he asked himself if he was doing the right thing by his girl. Was an exalted title enough to make up for marrying a man she did not love?

When he was young, he told himself, folk didn't think of love as a prerequisite for marriage. Parents picked a husband or wife for their children because of suitability – looking for someone from the right background or with property that would augment theirs. He'd been lucky because by the time he'd seen the girl who became his wife he was rich enough not to worry about dowries or parental approval so her parents received him well. They were Creoles with French names, whose complacency had been shaken by the news of revolution coming from France where members of their family were losing their heads at the guillotine. To marry their daughter to an Englishman – and it had been impossible for Canny to make them appreciate the difference between a Scotsman and an Englishman – seemed ideal.

Jacqueline became his bride within three months and brought a sugar plantation with a lovely house in the middle of it with her as a dowry. Best of all, she fell in love with him – a strange and unexpected burst of affection for a couple with twenty years between their ages. How devastated he had been when she died after only six years of happiness! Was it possible for Odilie to develop a similar passion for the bridegroom her father had so expensively procured for her? When Canny remembered the slack-mouthed Duke he doubted it.

In her pretty room with its curtains of rose-patterned chintz at the other end of the broad corridor the object of Canny's concern was dreaming of her birthplace. She was back beneath rustling palm trees with sand so white and soft that it felt like silk between her toes. Then she was sitting in the old garden swing being pushed to and fro by her nursemaid big Elma, whose dear coal-black face was sweating beneath the brightly coloured turban that she wore wound rakishly around her head. The swing stopped and Odilie turned round to see that Elma was smiling and holding out a cascade of grapes. Odilie took one and put it into her mouth. The grape was soft and juicy but the taste, instead of being sweet, was sour and acrid. She woke up feeling sick with her mouth filled by bile.

In a third bedroom on the same landing, Martha Rutherford was also dreaming. She had taken a long time to fall asleep the night before for her mind had been too full of what Grace had said about the woman she'd met in the old mill. Who was she, Martha wondered. How did she know about Grace's mother? What had happened to poor Lucy anyway? Martha had not thought about that sad affair for years until Grace brought it all back but now she was haunted by the memory of Lucy being led away from her husband's house by two law officers. Her glorious hair had been wild and uncombed and her face swollen with weeping. Martha had been walking down the street at the time and could not avoid seeing how Lucy stumbled along like someone on the verge of madness. That scene had begun haunting her dreams again and she worried about what chance a girl like Lucy would have had in the cruel world without money or protection. What sort of death was visited on her? Martha was sure that she could not have survived very long. Like a cage bird turned free, she would be pounced upon by the first crow that came along. When Martha eventually woke she felt deathly tired and deeply depressed. In spite of the glory of the morning, a sense of foreboding filled her.

The sense of dread that assailed Martha was not shared that bright morning by the crowd of people massing over in the middle of Jedburgh. Ten miles from Roxburgh field, this old town clustered around the majestic ruins of another crumbling abbey and there had been unprecedented activity in the streets since early morning. By seven o'clock dozens of people were assembled in the cobbled square alongside the abbey gate to watch Jake Turnbull, Provost of Jedburgh, preparing to lead his cavalcade off to St James' Fair. Jake was a florid-faced burgher who had been born in Jedburgh and thought there was no place on God's earth to equal it.

At half-past eight o'clock precisely, wearing a black bonnet with a red and white checked headband and an impressive golden chain of office around his neck, Turnbull mounted his charger in the square under the eyes of a gaggle of impressed folk who cheered when he settled his plump buttocks in the saddle. Then with a flourish of his whip, he stood up in his stirrups and yelled out in a hoarse voice, 'Jeddart's here! To Lauriston, lads!'

The townsfolk gave another ragged cheer and Turnbull's retinue of twelve stout men, all well-primed with drink already although it was so early, lined up behind him. They looked like reivers about to make a raid on an ancestral enemy because they had the faces of warriors – craggy noses, lantern jaws and beetling brows. All they lacked were the steel bonnets that their ancestors wore when they went raiding but their grim expressions made it obvious that they were spoiling for a fight.

'Jeddarts here! We'll show 'em,' cried Turnbull again to the gawping crowd on the cobbles of the square.

'That's right, Jake, you show those fancy folk in Lauriston that Jedburgh's the best toon. They're nothing but lackeys for that Duke. Jedburgh's a free man's place,' shouted a bent old fellow who leaned on his stick in the front rank of bystanders. In his time, before rheumatics crippled him, he had often ridden in the cavalcade to St James' Fair and had many memories of enjoyable fights with the men of Lauriston, for the two towns were at daggers drawn over the Fair and had been in that hostile state of mind for more than three centuries.

When Roxburgh town disappeared, its privileges and revenues were transferred by the king to the nearest royal burgh which was Jedburgh, because at that time Lauriston had not been awarded royal burgh status. Since then it had been an annual pleasure for the Town Council of Jedburgh to ride ostentatiously over and parade themselves through Lauriston's streets before going to the big field and, with great ceremony, calling the burley for the opening of St James' Fair.

Jedburgh not only enjoyed the right to open and police the annual event but, what was worse, it took one third of the considerable revenues from the Fair as well. The other two thirds went to the Duke of Maudesley and nothing went to Lauriston. That was the real bone of contention.

As Provost Turnbull and his men headed out of Jedburgh, more men came clattering out of the narrow vennels along the High Street and joined on to the end of his cavalcade. When the procession reached the town boundary, the Provost stopped and took off his chain of office which he slipped into a bag tied round his waist because there was no point in tempting highway robbery till he got to his destination. Then he'd put it on again to dazzle the Lauriston folk.

He took a swig from his brandy flask, checked that his saddlebags were full of stones for throwing back at the rabble that would be waiting for him in the rival town and, feeling as important as the Duke of Wellington, victor of Waterloo, gave an upward lift of his arm and signalled to his army to move.

On their travels they passed a waggon full of bonny laughing lassies and waved cheerfully to them not knowing they were the contingent from Wauchope's farm at Morebattle. On that farm, as on many others that day, the animals had been fed early in the morning and the workers given permission to go fairing. Mary Scott had bribed a young ploughboy, who was not worried about how he smelt, with a silver sixpenny piece to feed the pigs for her and she spent the morning curling her hair with a pair of crimping tongs and titivating herself. When she heard wheels rumble up to the cottage door, as a final touch she drenched her carefully folded white neckerchief with Aunt Lily's lavender water before running out. She was the last to climb aboard the big dray cart that was to carry all Mr Wauchope's workers to the Fair. 'Heavens take us a', what's the reek?' asked the old man who was driving the massive pair of bay horses yoked between the shafts, and everyone, including Mary, laughed. Good humour prevailed.

At Fairhope, deep in the Cheviot Hills, there had been hustle and bustle since dawn. Tom and Adam had their work finished by the time sunlight suffused the sky and when they returned home from the hill, Catherine and Leeb had all the eggs collected and the hens fed; the pony groomed and contentedly tucking into a net of hay and the kettle singing on the hearth beside a slowly heaving pot of porridge.

Two metal irons were heating at the side of the fireplace and Catherine was using them to press her men's trousers with great thumping thuds. The heat of the iron on the damp cloth which she laid on the trousers positioned on the kitchen table sent clouds of steam rising up around her. When Tom pushed open the door and saw her at this work he cried out, 'Aw woman, couldn't you have let us have oor breakfast afore you started wi' the pressing?'

She didn't even look up but went on thudding away with the iron, switching one for the other as soon as it lost its heat. 'No I couldn't. I'm wanting you two to look smart and no' let me doon. And I'm wanting oot o' here in plenty of time to meet Mary. We've to be at the bridge by twelve o'clock, mind. You can eat your porridge standing up for once,' she scolded.

Tom stared at the clock on their mantelpiece and exclaimed, 'But it's early yet!' though he knew there was no use trying to argue with Catherine when she was in a fever to get started. Her urgency transferred itself to the men and after a hurried breakfast, while Leeb bustled about tidying up the cottage and getting everything ready for their return at night, Adam and Tom took turns to wash in the water trough at the front door. Then they went into the parlour to dress in their best, freshly-pressed clothes.

When they emerged Catherine regarded them with satisfaction, proud to lay claim to such handsome fellows. Father and son stood tall in the kitchen, hair brushed and faces shining as she walked around them, scrutinising their outfits with a critical eye. It was always said among country folk that shepherds were more smartly dressed than other working folk for they were the aristocrats among farm servants, and she was determined that the Scott men would not let the calling down. Their plaid trousers fitted well and their dark coloured jackets were carefully brushed and buttoned up over pristine white, stiffly starched shirts with high tied cravats. Tom wore his black bonnet with the heron's feather – it was by way of being his trademark – but Adam was as usual bareheaded.

After close scrutiny Catherine declared herself satisfied and said, 'That tailor's done a good job for you this year though he was slow. We'll maybe gie him another order. Aren't you wearing a bonnet like your father, Adam?'

The young man shook his head. 'No, Mam. It's going to be a fine day. I'm no' needing a bonnet.'

His little sister giggled and said, 'He's wanting to show off his bonny heid o' hair, that's why he'll no' put on a bonnet. The lassies all like his hair and they'll notice him more if he's not got it covered.'

Catherine scolded, 'Dinna tease your brother, Leeb. Away you go and dress yourself now and don't take long about it.' She'd seen her son's face flush at the jibes of his little sister. Maybe there was something up. Her maternal senses were alert though he had said nothing about any girl.

Before nine o'clock they were on their way, sitting two by two in the cart behind their fat pony who was none too keen to leave its stable and haul the family all the way to the Fair.

Catherine sat proudly beside Tom whom she regarded as the finest-looking man of his age in the whole Border-land. They made a handsome couple for she was tall and well-made too and looked as prosperous as any farmer's wife in a striped bombazine dress with a white fichu draped across her breast. On her head was her feathered bonnet that only came out of its striped bandbox for special occasions. Pinned in the front of her bodice was her greatest treasure, a brooch in the shape of a loveknot that Tom had given her when they married.

She reached out and patted her husband's arm. 'D'ye mind the day we met?' she asked with a sidelong smile.

He nodded, smiling back as he cracked the whip over the pony's back to absolutely no effect for it maintained the same plodding step. 'I mind fine. We met at the Fair twenty-five years ago to the day. You didnae think I'd forgotten, did you?'

'Oh, aye the Fair's the place for lovers,' said his wife happily.

'Tell us the story, tell us the story!' chanted Leeb who'd heard the account of this meeting many times before but never tired of it. It was difficult for her to sit still but she knew she'd be scolded by her mother if she fidgeted for she was all decked up in starched white cotton with four frilled underskirts that made her dress stick out so far that her brother on the other half of the seat hardly dared move for fear of crushing her. A broad blue sash was tied round her waist and her fair hair beneath a little chip straw bonnet was tied up with more rosettes of the same ribbon.

Catherine never needed much encouragement to launch into her story. 'I was at the Fair wi' other lassies from the Makerstoun big house where I was working when I saw this braw-lookin' lad all on his ain. My word, but you looked grand, Tom. You took my eye at once. I said to my friend that I was going to speak to you and she dared me. So when I got the chance I tripped up right at your feet – didn't I? I fell flat. You bent doon and picked me up off the ground. I mind it was a rainy Fair that year and the path was covered wi' mud. I got my dress all clairty but it didn't matter. I got you, didn't I?'

He laughed fondly. 'You got me right enough. We were married by the time the Fair came around again. I was pleased you fell doon because I'd been following you about all day but I was too scared to speak to you.'

She punched his arm lightly and they smiled with love at each other. In spite of his impressive appearance, Tom Scott was a shy man and it took a great deal to break down his reserve. Every year, however, when they went to the Fair, he temporarily lost his inhibitions and became thoroughly frivolous. The children laughed about their father's fairings because though it was Tom who drove them there, Catherine was invariably at the reins for the return journey with Tom asleep at her side. The Fair was the one day of the year when he let himself go and she made no attempt to stop him. He was allowed to go off with his shepherd friends and spend the day in the ale tent. Not till evening did he rejoin his family and by then he was always happily drunk.

When their cart jolted over the brow of the last hill, the town could be seen clustering cosily around the truncated tower of its abbey on the far bank of the Tweed and Catherine took the opportunity to deliver her annual injunction to her husband. 'Now Tom,' she scolded, 'I don't want you going off and getting fu' like you did last year.'

'I'll not,' he promised but both of them knew that her warning was only a formality and his promise was the same. He always had a few drinks more than he should at the Fair and she would have worried if he came back sober, because that would mean he had not enjoyed himself.

They skirted the edge of the Rennie Bridge and joined the end of a long line of carts, traps, carriages and gigs that trailed slowly along the road by the river. Crowds of people were lined up by the verges waiting for friends and relatives for this was a well-known meeting place.

At the approach to the Teviot toll-bridge, a group of girls were giggling together beneath the big trees. Even from a distance Catherine's sharp eyes could pick out her daughter and she cried, 'Oh there she is! There's my bonny Mary! My word, hasn't she grown? What a pretty dress, it must have cost a bit! Oh dear, she's a woman now, she'll soon be getting married.' Her voice quavered because it hurt her to think that Mary was growing up and changing while away from her mother. Catherine hated to miss any of the precious days of her children's lives.

Mary had been waiting beneath the trees for about half an hour. As she watched eagerly for the fat pony and the Scotts' old brown-coloured cart, she saw from the tail of her eye that Jockie Armstrong was hanging about on the other side of the road. She did not acknowledge him and kept on talking animatedly with her friends but she was very conscious of his unwavering stare. It made her feel angry and self-conscious, like a rabbit being hypnotised by a stoat. At last she glanced along the road and saw her family's cart coming into view in the slowly moving line. All thoughts of anything else were forgotten and she ran forward, smiling with delight and holding up the skirt of her new sprigged cotton dress in both hands. 'Oh Ma, oh Pa, oh Adam, oh, Leeb!' she called as she ran and her brother leaped down from his seat to help her in beside her little sister who was so pleased to see her that she forgot her fear of crushing her dress and squeezed up close. 'What's the funny smell, Mary?' she asked.

Catherine's heart was full but all she said was, 'You're looking well, lass.' Voluble protestations of affection or love would have embarrassed them all, for that was not their style but the day was perfect now that they were all together. Turning in her seat the mother surveyed her daughter with a sharp eye and saw that she still had a maidenly look. So nothing untoward had happened yet. Mary was the perfect lady in her new gown though a give-away triangle of tanned skin on her face showed this was no genteel housemaid but a girl who worked in the fields with a cotton square tied around her head and knotted on her chin. The triangle marked the part of her face that was exposed in all weathers.

Mary was enthusing, 'I'm grand. I like Morebattle Mains. It's a good place.' She leaned forward to kiss her mother's cheek beneath the feathered hat.

'You're not ready to take a maid's place yet?' asked the mother cautiously. She herself had worked in a big house and had the snobbishness of an indoor servant about girls who worked on the land.

'Oh no, Mother, I like field work,' said Mary firmly. Catherine sighed and accepted that Mary was happier working outdoors than slaving in somebody's kitchen. Anyway the girl was in the care of Sandy and Lily – good, kind people who could be relied on. She'd have a word with them at the Fair and glean all she could about

Mary's private affairs. Most of all she wanted to know if her lassie had a beau.

Chattering happily to each other they waited to pay their toll and cross over the bridge into the field where the Fair was to be held. They were in good time for it was still only twenty-five minutes to twelve. Not till noon would the festivities officially commence.

The crowd at the toll-gate was happy but impatient. The slowness of the snaking line made them grumble as they waited to hand their coppers to the fat toll-keeper and his wife who stood with aprons held out before them to catch the money thrown in their direction.

'Sixpence a cart load,' the toll-wife was calling out as the Scotts reached her. Tom felt in his jacket pocket and handed some coins to Catherine, who carefully counted out the sum in half-pennies and farthings.

'It's a scandal asking folk to pay good money to cross the river,' she scolded as she bent forward to throw her money but the toll-keepers paid no heed. They were used to hearing this complaint.

Thwarted of a reaction Catherine turned to her children and loudly announced, 'It's these toffs and their turnpike trusts that're doing this. When your father and I came to the Fair as young folk, we crossed at the fords for nothing. Now they've closed them to force folk on to the bridges.' She raised her voice so that the other carts around about could hear and several people shouted their agreement back to her. An old man called, 'Nothing's free now. They'll soon be making us pay for the air we breathe.'

Catherine turned to her husband. 'Do you hear what that old man said, Tom? We'll soon have to pay for breathing.'

'Take care, wife,' was his reply. 'You shouldn't be talking sedition in a crowd like this. You don't know who's listening.'

His admonition sobered Catherine who folded her hands in her lap, assuming the expression of a well-behaved woman who knew her place in life but her thoughts were still rebellious.

In Lauriston the Cross Keys Hotel that overlooked the square was crowded. Every chamber was full and the proprietor and his wife rushed around chivvying their servants and placating customers who all wanted food at the same time. Before breakfast was over patrons were already cramming into the first-floor windows to watch for the arrival of the cavalcade from Jedburgh.

William Playfair went for a walk after eating his breakfast and, on his return, was wandering along the Horse Market when he heard a sudden roar of voices and the sound of galloping horses. He had walked right into the middle of a mêlée. A rabble of boys and young men burst out of Roxburgh Street with their arms full of missiles – rotted fruit and vegetables, eggs, stones, clods of earth and horse droppings which they had been saving up for days for this moment. At the same time, Jake Turnbull, with his Jedburgh provost's chain glinting again on his chest, appeared at the opening into Bridge Street on the opposite side of the square and the mob set upon him, pelting him and his followers with ordure.

The attack was not unexpected. With a whoop like a battle cry and the defiant yell of 'Jeddarts here!' Jake's followers, who had been eagerly anticipating this opportunity, spurred their horses and dived into the middle of the mob, lashing out with riding whips and canes as they went. Bodies were sent flying; the air was loud with curses and imprecations and the watchers in the windows held their sides in glee. A good skirmish between Lauriston's hooligans and Jedburgh's dignitaries was an essential part of the Fair Day festivities.

Playfair took one horrified look at the grappling, swearing hooligans and the furious Jedburgh men on the prancing horses and beat a retreat, going round the back of the hostelry to enter by a rear door. On the stairs he encountered Professor Thompson who cried out in glee, 'A grand fight's going on down there. Did you see it? Happens every year. It's Jedburgh's substitute for a war against the English. They're a wild lot over there still – descendants of the reivers, you see.'

201

Playfair nodded. 'Is that it? I thought it was best to keep away. I don't want to get my head broken.'

'Sensible fellow,' cried Thompson. 'Are you going to the Fair?'

The young architect nodded. 'Yes, sir. I stayed on in town so that I could go over and buy myself a new horse because people tell me it's the best place to find one.'

The Professor tended to pomposity for he was an important man and knew it. 'You'll only find a good horse if you're careful. Know much about horseflesh, do you?'

Playfair laughed. 'Not a lot, I'm afraid. I buy a horse if I like the look of it.'

'Thought as much! You'd better come along with me. You'll get stung badly by the rogues of gypsies at the Fair if you've not someone to watch out for you. I've a good eye for a horse and they won't dare take advantage of me. When I pick a horse I look for the same qualities that make a well-bred man . . . style and depth of chest, good bone and a proud carriage, an open eye and an alert expression. You can always tell good breeding.'

Playfair said nothing but reflected that Thompson's description could not be applied to his patron the Duke though they did summon up the girl with the glowing copper skin who had danced in his dreams since the dinner party at Havanah Court.

By this time Thompson was ushering him back downstairs again and saying, 'That's settled then, you'll join us. We'll be leaving in an hour. A couple of my students have come down from Edinburgh and I'm showing them around the Fair.'

Sideshows and freak shows; two circuses and wild animal displays; Indian slack rope walkers and musical bands made up of superannuated soldiers wearing faded uniforms; troops of pedlars, gypsies and sharp-eyed dealers in every commodity that country people need; the people who came up from England to buy the cottagers' bundles of dried flax, honeycombs and home-woven linen; hundreds of horses and beer tents; medicine sellers and two tents where importunate couples could contract an irregular marriage for such liaisons were legal in Scotland, were all already on the field when the contingent from Jedburgh finally arrived, red-faced with outrage and splashed with mud or worse.

Jem's freak show had been in a good place since mid-morning for the waggons had filed out of their camping place before six o'clock. After their arrival at Roxburgh field, everyone in the show except Alice and Billy had been busy driving pegs into the ground, heaving up planks of wood to make a platform and draping sheets of coloured canvas around the walls of a makeshift stage. Even the dwarves hurried about, for each had an allotted task and in time their concentrated efforts achieved a magical, garish, flag be-draped world for the enticement of the credulous.

Jem gazed up at the bright blue sky and thanked the gods for providing a good day. In fact the temperature was still rising steadily and it was almost too hot for comfort. He noted as he wiped his sweating brow with his hand that far away on the western horizon a cluster of deep purple clouds were gathering like a threatening army. There was thunder on the way but with luck it would hold off until tomorrow when he would be on his way south again. He was anxious to hurry Alice out of Lauriston for the discovery that she was wanted by law officers in the town worried him. He was not concerned about what she'd done to earn the law's disapproval, that didn't matter a straw to him. He'd protect her no matter what it was.

Usually she took a share in erecting their stalls but this time he'd told her to stay hidden for he was afraid of what would happen if she showed her face in the open. The harried look in her eyes perturbed him and so he gave her the commission of watching Billy who could not be trusted out of captivity because of the strange agitation that still gripped him.

At a quarter to twelve everything was ready for business and Jem went back to his caravan for a wash and a drink of ale. With a big shady hat on her head, Alice was sitting in the shadow of the overhanging roof and she had allowed Billy out of captivity to sit with her. The lad looked peaceful and Jem guessed that she had been dosing him with one of her potions because a half-empty pewter pint pot sat between them. He sank down beside Alice and said, 'We're all ready. They'll be calling the Fair in a little while. Do you want to go up on to the hill with me and hear them call the burley?'

She shook her head but Billy nodded vigorously. 'Yes, yes,' he said excitedly.

Jem grinned. 'All right, Billy. I'll take you up. You stay here, Alice, and watch our things because there's a lot of thieving hands about. I'll be back soon.'

She sat with her chin in her hands watching the big man lead off the shambling lad who held on to his hand as if Jem was his father. When he was being good, Billy behaved as if he was a little boy instead of a man who stood nearly six feet tall and weighed more than his protector. For herself she was deeply agitated by the familiar scenes around her. If she turned her head she could see the chimney pots of the town that she had once known so well and her heart hammered in her chest with the pain of her memories. Nerves fluttered in her stomach and made her feel breathless while the calves of her legs were quivering with weakness. The effort it would take to stand up and walk about seemed almost beyond her. And she was afraid, for when anyone passed by, she lowered her face so that her hatbrim cast a wide shadow over her features but her eyes were sharp and watchful.

She sat very still, quivering but alert, until the sound of singing came wafting down from the small hill where Jem and Billy had gone. Then she turned and gazed across the field towards the source of the sound and saw hundreds of people massed around a circle of tall trees that crowned the hill's summit. She stood up and shaded her eyes with one hand as she listened intently. Eventually she heard the clang of a ringing handbell that seemed to be trying to drown out the toll of the town clock that

204

wafted in competition across the river. Together they were striking midday. 'One, two, three, four, five, six, seven, eight, nine, ten, eleven, TWELVE!' they rang and when the last stroke boomed out, the handbell began clanging again and a stentorian voice started shouting. It was Jake Turnbull announcing the opening of the ancient Fair. The crowd hushed and all eyes were fixed on him as he called, 'Oh yea, Oh yea, Oh yea . . . As representative of the royal burgh of Jedburgh, of the King and of His Grace the Duke of Maudesley, I declare that this fair dedicated to St James is OPEN.' Then the crowd cheered and threw their bonnets in the air, happy because, after six centuries of continuity, an ancient tradition was being faithfully carried on.

When the midday bell rang, the Scotts were still fretting in a queue snaking towards the field gate. They heard the Jedburgh Provost calling the Fair and leaned forward in their seats with eagerness and frustration showing on all their faces for on the other side of the hedge, the fun was starting and they were missing it.

'We should have started earlier,' said Catherine to her husband who soothingly shook his head and told her, 'Calm down, calm down, wife. We'll get there in time.' The sound of the ringing bell was followed by a wild burst of cheering that made all the horses near them bucket around and even the Scotts' phlegmatic pony gave a little jump when the din broke out, scuttling sideways as if threatening to bolt, something that it had never done in its life. It was greatly flattered when Adam descended from his seat in the cart and led it by the bridle through the gateway that opened into the Fair field. Rolling its eyes, it mouthed and jiggled on its bit pretending that it was an Arabian racehorse.

A gang of boys were waiting at the Maxton end of the green spit of land between the rivers and as each equipage came through the gate, a boy ran forward offering to take charge of it and mind it for the day if the owner paid him a penny. When a deal was done with the tousle-headed laddie who took the Scott pony, he swiftly unbuckled its harness, upended the shafts of the cart and tied the rope of the pony's halter to a stake ready driven in the ground. By this time the pony had quietened down and reverted to its normal lethargic self so when the bale of hay, which had been brought from Fairhope for it, was shoved under its nose, it started to tear into its food happily and was quite prepared to pass a slothful afternoon under the trees. The only effort required of it was to flick its tail now and again in an effort to drive away the clustering flies that the hot spell had made so troublesome. When she dismounted from the cart Catherine cautioned the boy to take good care of their equipage and the precious hamper of food inside it. Then the Scott family were ready for the delights of the Fair.

They instinctively drew closer together as they walked into the densest part of the throng for it suddenly seemed that they needed each other's protection. After the isolation and supreme silence of their day to day lives, the suffocating closeness and din of crowds of people affected them with the same shocking impact as a huge wave of ice cold water. They felt overwhelmed, submerged, terrified by the concourse of humanity and all of them except Mary, who had become more used to other people by this time, staggered slightly with shock as an earsplitting volume of noise engulfed them. Little Leeb was the worst affected. Her face became strained and she put her hands over her ears. Catherine noticed that even her proud and reserved husband assumed a vulnerable expression that made her heart turn over with love for him. Tom was deeply conscious of his position as head of the family and was determined not to show how intimidated he felt. He drew himself up, stood tall and straight and gazed around with eyes that tried to appear indifferent but were really as innocent and wondering as those of his youngest daughter. Catherine saw him widen his shoulders and tenderly took his arm as they stood shoulder to shoulder surveying the throngs of people.

If they had not been so overwhelmed they would have noticed that all around them clustered families who were

206

equally abashed by the cosmopolitan glories of the Fair –
husbands, wives and bairns from farms touns and hill
cottages were all trying valiantly to pretend that the
excitement was not more than they could cope with, pretending that it did not intimidate them more than it
enticed them. The fathers lowered their brows over puzzled eyes in an effort to appear formidable but their
slightly dropped jaws showed their uncertainty. Conscious
of their familial responsibilities they herded their women
and children close and gazed over their heads in search
of known faces. When they spied another man they recognised, a profound sense of relief could be heard in the
tones of their voices as they called out greetings. All of
them were plums ripe for plucking by the shysters, crooks
and fakers who hung around the fairground.

Tom Scott did not have to stand alone for long because
he was well-known in the district and was quickly spotted
by friends. One after the other came up and clapped his
shoulder, so that his confidence grew and in a short time
he had recovered most of his poise. This confidence was
passed on to his family who also began to feel brave
enough to face the delights of the day. Catherine and
Mary, with a protesting Leeb in tow, went off to look for
Lily and have a good gossip on a grass bank. Tom's fellow
shepherds prevailed on him to go with them to the ale
tent and his wife allowed him to accompany them without
protest and only a meaningful warning look which he
acknowledged with a smile. Adam drifted along behind
his father, glad that he was tall enough to see over the
heads of most of the other people in the ground. He was
looking for a girl with yellow hair.

It did not take long for Catherine to track down Lily
and they settled down for a good gossip. Mary sat with
them for a little while but she'd heard all her aunt's stories
already and soon began to feel bored. Besides, she knew
she was out of place because her mother and aunt could
not really get into meaningful discussions of illnesses,
difficult births and possible adulteries until she left.

After a while a giggling trio of girls came past where

she sat and waved to her. One of them was the bold Elsie and Mary jumped up so eagerly to wave back that her mother looked over and said, 'Do you want to go with those lassies, Mary? All right, go on, have a good time but mind and come back to where we left the cart at four o'clock.' The four o'clock meeting was a ritual with the family. They always foregathered at that time to eat the carefully prepared meal Catherine brought from home. It was part of their day at the Fair.

'I'll be there at four, Mam,' she promised and ran over the grass to join her friends. Under the watching eyes of the older women, they linked arms and strolled away acting very casual.

Lily nudged her sister-in-law in the ribs as she watched them go and said, 'Look, Catherine, look over there. D'ye see that big lad following the lassies? That's Jockie Armstrong, the blacksmith's laddie. He's going to be your son-in-law.'

Catherine stared in surprise and saw that, like a bee after a pot of honey, a lad was strolling behind the girls, pretending none too successfully to be indifferent as Mary flounced along with her friends. It was the done thing for a girl to toss her curls and bend her head towards the heads of her friends like a bunch of flowers in spring. She must not let on that she knew she was being followed.

There were other lads tailing on as well as Armstrong but they were not as persistent as he was and they needed courage, so one by one they dropped off and disappeared into the open flaps of ale tents when they reached them. Though they acted as if they did not know nor care what was going on behind them, the girls were very conscious of the dropping off of their swains and first one girl and then another would cast a furtive glance over her shoulder to see if she was still being followed. Her disappointment was obvious if she saw that she wasn't. Though they pretended the boys were beneath their notice, each girl had already picked out the lad she fancied best and when he dived into the beer tent, her face reflected secret chagrin. The next time the boy turned up he'd be given a little

208

more encouragement. That's what we come to the Fair for after all, isn't it, the girls asked themselves silently. Mary however did not look back and did not see that the eyes of the women staring after her were full of love and a sort of wistful envy that showed they remembered what it felt like to be as young and optimistic as she was that day.

Adam Scott was left behind by his family at last and he smiled when he saw his father heading for the ale tent. In a couple of hours, he knew, the silent Tom would be singing ballads and revealing a jokey, happily silly side to his character that stayed hidden for all the other days of the year. By four o'clock – the Scott mealtime – he would be as frolicsome as a circus clown and it would be necessary to go and haul him out of the ale tent.

Before he struck out on his own in his search for the limping girl, Adam was suddenly smitten by a feeling of pity for Leeb. She was too old to want to play with the other little bairns who clustered round their mothers' feet, and too young to be given free rein to wander through the fairground crowds alone. On an impulse he turned back to where she sat dolefully beside her mother and held out a hand to her saying, 'Come on, Leeb. Leave Mam with Aunt Lily for a wee while. I'll take you to see the stalls.'

She jumped up beaming and took his hand which she grasped tightly as they walked up and down the broad pathways between the tents and sideshows. There they gazed at all the attractions and watched the other equally starstruck visitors. Adam waited patiently while Leeb lingered before displays of brightly painted bits of pottery; lengths of cloth or garlands of pretty ribbons and he bought her a scrap of lace, then gave her an extra penny so that she could buy something from a stall displaying multi-coloured confectionery that ranged from jaw-breaking black toffee to bright pink and green marchpane.

While he watched Leeb debate whether toffee would last longer than sugar boilings, he fingered the coins in his pocket and planned what else he would buy. There was nothing he needed really but it was customary to take a remembrance home from every Fair. He decided to see everything there was on offer before he made his decision.

As he and Leeb walked around he was conscious of groups of girls flirting their way past him. Some cast him enticing glances and a few smiled in invitation. When this happened Leeb giggled and nudged him and he smiled back but did nothing to pursue the girls' invitations. There was only one girl he was seeking and all the time his eyes were ranging everywhere for her. Surely she'd come to the Fair? Doubt crept in because he'd dreamed so much about her all year that he was now beginning to wonder if she had only been a figment of his imagination. He blinked in an effort to summon up the vision that had seemed much clearer when he thought of her in the isolation of the hills but it did not come.

Now his memory of her was being overlaid by the other girls that were all around him – there were girls with dark hair, girls with red hair, tall girls and short girls, bold girls and shy girls. They were everywhere but she was not among them and he thought that if he did come across her soon he'd have forgotten what she looked like. He feared he might not recognise her but then he remembered there was one thing that would give her away and that was the touching way she limped. It had made his heart turn over for her.

When Leeb had toured the sideshows to her full satisfaction and was beginning to tire in the heat, he took her back to where their mother still sat deep in conversation. The child ran to her, displaying her new treasures and cuddled up beside Catherine with her head in her mother's lap. Soon she would be fast asleep.

Catherine smiled up at her son. 'Thanks, laddie. That was kind of you. Off you go now and have a good time yourself. Keep an eye on your father in that ale tent and mind about four o'clock . . .' Her world would stop if the Scotts did not all gather together at the right time for their meal.

Adam nodded and promised her, 'I'll be there, Mam,'

before turning on his heel to hurry off in the direction of the footbridge. That was where he had met the lame girl last year so she must have come over from the town. She'd probably use the bridge again. Patience was part of his nature and he did not care if he had to wait all day. She'd appear on the bridge some time during the day, he was sure of it.

CHAPTER 8

The cheering of the crowd hailing the crying of the Fair came booming over the river like a distant thunderclap as Grace pushed open the creaking iron gate of her home and set out for Havanah Court. She was in a hurry because she thought that Odilie would be impatiently waiting for her there.

When Joe Cannonball opened the door to her, he had a letter in his hand and a puzzled look on his face. 'Where's Miss Odilie?' asked Grace and Joe frowned. 'Upstairs, but she says she isn't.'

'What do you mean? Is she in or isn't she?'

'She's in all right but I've to send this letter back and to say she was out when it came.'

'Back where to?'

'To Sloebank . . . She don't want to go to the Fair with the Duke and his party. You'd better hurry Miss Grace, she's cooking something up.'

Odilie was looking extremely cheerful but surprisingly was still running about in her nightgown and wrapper with Scamp at her heels when Grace entered the bedroom. As usual there were dresses of all colours piled on the bed and Grace lifted the edge of a frilled skirt as she said, 'Is this the one you're wearing today? It's such a pretty shade of green. You'll look wonderful in it.'

Odilie laughed. 'I've been trying to make up my mind what I should wear all morning but a letter's just come from the Duke asking me to join his party this afternoon and that finally made up my mind for me.'

Grace's face fell. She was relying on Odilie's company at the Fair and, in spite of her original misgivings about going fairing, she had been looking forward to their outing. She needed her friend's support.

Odilie saw her disappointment and laughed. 'Don't

212

worry, I'm not going with him. I told Joe to say that I'd already left when the letter came. I'll come back later, hear about it from him then and join the Duke's party after that. I'm not going to miss visiting the Fair with you and seeing your mystery woman.'

'She told me not to look for her till evening,' said Grace but Odilie swept that aside. 'We'll perhaps see her anyway.'

Grace laughed and told her friend, 'All right, but hurry and get dressed or your father'll hear about the Duke's letter and stop you.'

Odilie threw out her arms. 'I *am* hurrying! I'm waiting for my dress coming over from the outfitter in the square.' She giggled as she saw the puzzlement of her friend.

'The outfitter – over in the square?' asked Grace in puzzlement because Odilie had enough dresses to fit out a dress shop on her own and anyway they were nearly all sent up from London costumières.

Odilie chuckled. 'Don't look so amazed. We're going in disguise, Gracie. We're going to be a pair of bondagers. You can forget all those . . .' Her outflung hand pointed at the disregarded lovely gowns. 'I've sent a maid out for some working dresses and aprons. Nobody's going to recognise us dressed like that, are they?'

Grace's mouth went round in surprise. 'Oh Odilie, you can't! What if you're caught?'

'Who's going to catch us? We'll keep among the thick of the crowds and no one will notice us. It'll be such fun, like going to a masquerade.'

At that moment Martha came bustling in and asked her niece, 'Haven't you made your mind up yet? The Fair's going to be over by the time you get there. Your father's gone off already.'

'Thank heavens for that,' said Odilie. 'Come on, Aunt Martha, I need your help. Have you any of those old sunbonnets that Father hates to see you wearing – the big ones stretched over bamboo?'

Martha looked guilty. 'Aye, maybe I've still got a few left. Your father says they're not proper wear for ladies but I like them because they keep the sun off my head when I'm in the garden on hot days.'

'Lend one to me, please. And have you another for Grace?'

'What for? You've dozen of lovely hats – real hats, not cotton poke bonnets.'

'I want to wear a poke bonnet today.' Odilie's voice was coaxing and Martha laughed as if she was being teased.

'Och lassie, only poor women wear cotton pokes. That's why they're called "uglis". The lassies off farms and bond-agers wear them because they're cheap.'

Odilie swung around gleefully. 'That's exactly why I want one. Please, Aunt Martha. Grace and I are going to the fairground for a couple of hours disguised as farmgirls. Those big hats will shade our faces and we won't be recognised. Please lend them to us.' She folded her hands in a beseeching way like a child and Martha gasped when she realised that this was serious.

'Oh Odilie, I cannae do that. What'll your father say? What if somebody that kens you sees you got up like a bondager? What if . . .'

'What if my betrothed the Duke hears about it, you mean? Maybe he'll decide he doesn't want to marry me after all. Wouldn't that be fortunate for me! Now be kind to us, Aunt Martha. Go and get the bonnets. I've sent one of the maids out to buy me a working dress – maybe you can find an apron for Grace and a couple of your old neckerchiefs. I know you never throw anything out and it'll be best if they're old and faded because we don't want to look fancy. We'll go to the Fair and be ordinary. No one will know who I am. I don't want them pointing me out and talking about my dowry and who I'm going to marry. I want to know what it feels like to be an ordinary girl out for the day with her friend. It might be my last chance to do something like this.'

Grace was still looking doubtful but only on Odilie's behalf because the idea of slipping through the crowds unnoticed appealed to her own self-effacing nature. 'Your father'll be so angry if he hears about this and my father will blame me for going along with you,' she protested.

Odilie's mind was made up. 'If you won't come with me, I'll go alone but it could be such fun if we were together and it'll only be for a little while. It's just a jape. I promise I'll not keep it up for long. Please dress up like a farmgirl and come with me.'

Her voice was wheedling but just when Grace was on the point of yielding, another thought struck her and she sobered instantly. 'What if *I'm* recognised? Most folk know me, far more than know you,' she said flatly.

'If you dressed plainly . . .' protested Odilie. Once she got a plan into her mind, she was almost impossible to deflect.

Grace shook her head again. 'But Odilie, think about it. I'm always dressed plainly. I wouldn't look any different. And I *would* be recognised because of my bad leg. I limp, remember, and I can't hide that.'

Odilie's face showed remorse at having overlooked this but she had become so used to Grace that she scarcely noticed her friend's disability and privately thought that Grace was too conscious of what was only a minor flaw. She could walk almost as well as everyone else, when she was not thinking about how awkward she must appear to others.

'But you'd only be noticed if you were walking to the Fair, wouldn't you? In the ground itself there's such a big crowd that there's hardly room to move. No one will see how you walk. I've Papa's telescope here. Look through it – there's hundreds of people in the field already, aren't there? There's hardly enough space for people to move, far less limp.'

Grace's eyesight was good and she needed no telescope. She gazed out of the window and saw that what her friend said was true. The field was already black with people, swarming about among the brightly coloured tents like busy ants. Two plainly dressed girls would certainly escape attention in that throng.

'All right. I'd be safe enough on the field but how do

I get there without somebody recognising me? They all know me and when they see me, they'll recognise you as well,' she protested more weakly.

Odilie had the answer to that. 'I know, we'll take a horse from Stevens and ride over. We'll cross the toll bridge and come back down the Yetholm Road as if we've arrived from that direction. No one'll notice your limp if you're riding. I'll get one of the old ponies from our stable and you can sit on the pillion behind me. Say you'll do it, Grace. It'll be such an adventure. It's a chance to be like other people for a little while. We'll be away from our families and all our responsibilities. Come on, keep me company. No one'll find out. We'll be back here and ready to go out all dressed up in our finery before they even know we've been away. Martha won't tell, will you Martha?'

'I'm not having anything to do with this,' said Martha firmly but of course, in the end, she was won round and persuaded to produce two old-fashioned and faded sunbonnets with big brims stiffened with canes which were bending with age.

When the girls put them on, the bonnet brims flopped forlornly around their faces and Odilie laughed. 'This is as good as a mask any day. No one'll be able to see me, far less recognise me.' Grace put on the ugli bonnet with a sigh and looked sadly at the lovely feather-trimmed creations lying around Odilie's bedroom. She'd far rather have worn the pretty hat her friend had trimmed for her.

While they were trying on the bonnets a curious maid came up the stairs carrying a large parcel which was unwrapped to reveal a selection of cheap flower-patterned cotton gowns with round necks and long tight sleeves. 'These won't do,' said Odilie, lifting them up disdainfully. 'I couldn't kirtle the skirts up enough to ride a horse. I'll have to sit astride because no working lassie would own a side saddle. Go back and get me one of those full skirts that farmwomen wear – and a pair of big boots. I want to look the part.'

Grace, who was to ride pillion, was dressed first in a

washed-out gown of blue belonging to Martha and the floppy bonnet. Odilie laughed aloud when she saw her. 'You're quite the thing, a perfect country lassie. Keep your head down and you'll be safe.' Then the maid returned and while her aunt tutted in horrified disapproval, Odilie dressed herself up as a bondager. It was difficult to restrain her for she wanted to stick bits of straw in her hair and dirty her face but they managed to persuade her that even the poorest girl would want to look her best on Fair Day. So in time she stood in the middle of the carpet wearing a voluminous black and yellow striped skirt, a patterned blouse with a pair of heavy black boots on her feet in place of her usual satin slippers, and the ugli bonnet on her head. Even Scamp had trouble recognising her and sniffed suspiciously at her booted feet.

By now Grace was beginning to enjoy herself and joined in the masquerade with enthusiasm. Giggling she tied the strings of Odilie's large apron at the back and then, arm in arm, they ran downstairs and crossed the garden to the stables. Stevens' face showed outright astonishment when he realised that the farm servant girl who came tramping over the yard in her enormous boots turned out to be Miss Odilie and he was far from pleased when she said that instead of riding on her lovely new mare, she wanted him to saddle up the heavy-footed old pony that was used by the servants for doing errands around the town. 'And use the oldest saddlery, nothing fancy. I'm in disguise,' she ordered.

'You can't ride that pony, Miss. I've been grooming your chestnut mare all morning so that you can show her off today,' protested the groom.

Odilie waved a hand. 'Don't worry, I'll take the mare later. Keep her ready. This is just a game – I'm pretending to be a girl up from the country for the day. Don't tell anyone about it, especially don't tell Father.'

Stevens grumbled. 'Farm lassies walk, Miss, they don't have ponies – even message ponies – to ride.'

Nothing would put Odilie off, however. By now she

had climbed on to the top of the stone mounting block in the corner of the yard and her face was glowing with mischief as she called over from her perch, 'Of course they do. At least this one does. She's a girl with a kind employer, a soft-hearted old man living away in the country some place. He's lent her his carthorse.'

Laughing she hoisted herself into the saddle with her skirts kirtled up almost to her knees and her legs in the coarse boots boldly showing. 'Come on Grace, get up behind me,' she cried, half-turning in the saddle and patting the horse's broad back with one hand. Grace threw the last of her misgivings away and climbed on to the mounting block too. When she was safely seated with her arms round Odilie's waist, she started to laugh and they clattered away over the cobbles while Stevens ran a hand through his hair and groaned aloud, 'Oh my God I hope her feyther doesn't hear about this.'

William Playfair was an equable fellow and Professor Thompson's officiousness did not irritate him as he was ushered into a waiting gig and seated alongside two well-dressed young fellows who were medical students from Edinburgh. At the front door of the hotel a few bruised and battered survivors of the fight were nursing their wounds but the Professor obviously considered them beneath his notice for he literally stepped over them as he told his friends, 'Pay no attention to them, lads. Off we go!'

Soon they were bowling along in the direction of the Tweed Bridge and Playfair, staring out at the people on the road, noticed ahead on the road two giggling girls, one riding pillion behind the other. They were dressed in cheap clothes and cotton sunbonnets and were mounted on a heavy-legged horse that ambled along at a leisurely pace. The girls did not seem to mind their lack of speed and were clinging together with much laughter as the gig rolled past them. When they were level Playfair started in surprise and gazed at the girl nearest to him . . . he felt sure he knew her – but I must be mistaken, he thought, it can't be her, of course not! What would the Duke's rich fiancée be doing going to the Fair dressed as a working girl on what was little better than a carthorse? Don't be silly, you're fantasising, he told himself.

By the time Grace and Odilie reached the Fair field they were enjoying themselves thoroughly and had entered into their parts with enthusiasm. They were delighted when people walking on the road greeted them as equals and young men ran along beside their horse making remarks which they flirtatiously parried. It was easy to be carefree when you were acting a part, Grace realised.

The pony's bridle was grabbed by a boy when they rode into the field and he ran alongside them calling up to Odilie, 'I'll look after your horse all day for a penny, lass.'

She put on a country voice and answered doubtfully, 'That's an awful lot of money. I'm only a poor bondager.'

'A penny's not a lot,' said the boy in a surprised voice.

'It's too much for me,' she said in what sounded like an overdone rural accent to Grace but the boy was taken in and conceded, 'All right, I'll take a half-penny.' He looked at Odilie's heavy boots as he spoke. Any lassie who couldn't afford a pair of proper shoes for Fair Day must be in dire straits, he thought. As he held the pony while the girls dismounted he asked in a sympathetic way, 'Have you come from far?'

'From Earlston,' said Odilie at a venture.

The boy grinned and told her, 'That's a fair bit. I'll give your pony a bite of hay from this cart here. They're shepherding folk down from the hills and they've plenty to spare. Their pownie's fat enough already.' He was an obliging boy and the Scotts' pony did indeed have plenty of feeding.

Odilie was delighted at having pulled off her first bit of deception and when they walked off across the field she held on to Grace's arm and whispered, 'He believed me, he really believed me!' They were both beaming with pleasure as the press of people opened up and swallowed them like a sea.

The excited girls held hands to prevent being separated in the crowd which was dense in the middle of the field. Men and women, boys and girls, infants, dogs, pick-pockets, young and old, halt and nimble were all packed together, sweating under the brilliant sun, cooling themselves with waved hatbrims, wiping their brows, chattering, eyeing each other, greeting old friends and making new ones.

'What'll we do first?' asked Odilie, gazing around with enthusiasm. The crowd did not intimidate her for she was used to the throng and bustle of West Indian markets. Clinging close together they were carried along like twigs on a stream by the crowd, following a path that led uphill to the place where the gypsies were camped and when Odilie saw a big brightly painted sign before her advertising fortune-telling, she cried, 'I know, let's have our fortunes told. Aunt Martha told me that there's one old woman who comes here every year and has a wonderful gift for reading the future. Her name's Fatima or something and she told my father that he'd make a fortune when he was just a boy. If she knew that she must be very clever. Let's go and find her.'

Where the crowd was thickest, that was where you found the gypsies. The women, children and old men had arrived by foot or on carts at the field well before midday, meekly joining the queue waiting to file through the entrance gate. Like everyone else, they had paid their toll money for the Teviot Bridge but the men watched from the ruins of the castle and when the crowd was at its thickest they came clattering down with their horses from their hideaway and pushed into the jostling crowd without being noticed by officialdom.

Jesse Bailey rode bareback with his booted legs swinging and his capable brown hands lying lightly on the withers of his grey stallion Barbary. He was a master at the art of making a horse look good but his skill was not needed with this mount, which was truly magnificent. He had bought the horse as a colt – then a puny, sickly creature – and reared it with tenderness till it grew into the magnificent Barbary. The horse had a small Arab head and wide dark eyes held erect on a high curving neck. It was short-coupled, well-muscled and with a coat like polished steel. The flowing mane and tail made a fine contrast with the dark grey coat because they were the colour of buttermilk.

Many people came to the Fair with the express purpose of buying a horse and they turned and stared when they saw Jesse's mount. It was well-known that every horse any gypsy displayed was for sale and even before they were through the entrance gate Jesse received shouted offers for Barbary but he only waved a hand and called out, 'Come and see us when we settle in. We camp under the big copper beech at the top corner. Ask for Jesse Bailey or Gib Faa . . . We've all the best horses and we're sure to be able to suit you.'

He had no intention whatever of selling Barbary. The horse and he were so much in tune that they seemed to think and move through the same brain, the same impulses. The young gypsy had never owned a mount of such quality and it would take a mound of golden guineas to tempt him to part with the grey. But the horse was like a lure to greedy fish – once a purchaser was interested, no matter whether they were in search of a spirited steeplechaser or a quiet hack for a nervous lady, Jesse would be able to offer them something suitable from the other horses of the string. Gypsies always had the perfect horse to offer – often the same one for any purchaser. Silver tongues and polished horsemanship made all their geese look and behave like swans.

The place where Gib always set up business during the Fair was in the shade of a circle of beech trees, where there was plenty of cover for the hottest day or when the rain pelted down as it had done on many Fair Days in the past. This site had already been reserved by the Kirk Yetholm women, who looked so fierce that no encroaching parties dared to camp beside them. The gypsies regarded their outing to the Fair as a communal enterprise and hoped that enough money would be made there to keep them all for the rest of the year. They lived communally, pooling anything they earned; even what was stolen by any member of their community – and there would be much stealing during the Fair – was handed over to Gib to be distributed among them all.

'Sore simensar si men,' they whispered to each other in Romany, meaning, 'We are all related. All is one and one is all . . .'

When the cavalcade headed by Gib could be seen approaching across the field, a big raw-boned woman called Reck stood up and called out, 'They're coming, they're coming!' She pointed down to the lower ground where the crowd could be seen swaying like an eddy in water because of the passage of riders. 'There's Gib, there's Jesse,' cried another old crone and the dogs began to bark as other women came rushing forward to watch. The most excited was Thomassin and it was on Jesse Bailey that her glittering eyes rested.

When the horses reached the gypsy encampment, Jesse jumped down from the back of his horse and handed the reins of Barbary and the horse he had been leading to a young lad who came running forward to help.

'How did it go?' asked the boy.

'Kushto – good,' was the reply. At that moment Thomassin came up behind Jesse and slid a slow hand up his spine so that in spite of himself he shivered as he slowly turned his head to look at her.

'I've kept food for you,' she said, smiling.

He nodded. 'Thank you, Thomassin. I'll come in a minute. I want to speak to Gib first.'

The white-haired man was also surrounded by women and looked like a lion with his lionesses. Babies played around his feet as he stood among his family and a lean greyhound lovingly rubbed its head against his knee. When Jesse went up to him he was speaking rapid Romany to old Rachel who stood close to him, her sharp and piercing black eyes searching his face as they talked.

The younger man did not have a chance to join in because their conversation was unexpectedly interrupted by the approach of a party of gentlemanly-looking men. At the sight of the visitors, Gib and Rachel switched from Romany and started talking Border Doric.

Gypsies had the power to unerringly pick out which member of any group was the most important and Gib's eyes went instantly to a well-dressed gentleman in a high hat and a jacket of good quality with golden buttons – a detail that did not escape his sharp eyes. This fellow was being sorely pestered by a gypsy child who hung on to his coat-tails and whined for money in such a piteous way that he was obviously convinced she was in danger of starving. When he gave her a coin, she took it quickly but did not stop her begging. She wanted more and the man tried to shake her off, saying, 'Go away. Go away. Don't be greedy. I've already given you threepence.'

Rachel stepped forward and said in the wheedling voice that gypsy women adopted for all dealings with giorgios, 'Let the gentleman alone, Esther. Be off with you, you little devil, be off . . .' then she added in a hectoring tone, 'Mang, pal, mang!' The old man and his companions nodded in approval, thinking that the child was being reprimanded in two languages but in actual fact the gypsy words meant 'Beg on friend!' so Esther kept up her whining and successfully dodged Rachel's swinging hand. Eventually, in desperation, the man in the high hat gave her another few coins and only then did she quieten.

While this tableau was going on no one noticed how two country girls drew back as if afraid. The shorter of them was intent on pulling her friend out of the sight of the well-dressed men and they slipped to the back of the crowd but did not go away for they wanted to watch what was going on.

When Esther had been given more money and was satisfied, Gib nodded to the strangers and asked their business. His tone was brusque because he left the demeaning business of buttering up strangers to the women.

The smartly-dressed gentleman asked, 'Are you Gilbert Faa?'

The answer was a nod. 'That I am.'

The other man introduced himself. 'I'm Professor Walter Thompson from Edinburgh. I've brought with me a young architect fellow who's looking for a good horse and someone directed us to you. Have you anything that'd suit my friend?' With an outstretched hand Thompson indicated a young man in his group who stepped forward smiling.

Gib scratched his head and looked at Jesse. 'Your bay's up to this gentleman's weight, isn't it?' he asked. Jesse nodded. Like Gib he did not smile or try to ingratiate himself with the customers. He was too much imbued with dignity. 'Just throw your leg over its back and let them see it going through its paces then,' Gib told him before turning to young Playfair and adding, 'It's a good horse, sir. It can go at a canter for twenty miles without pausing and it jumps like a cat, though I don't suppose you'll have much call for jumping in Edinburgh. Do you hunt, sir?'

Playfair was shaking his head as Jesse vaulted neatly on to the bare back of one of the horses in the string. Then he leaned forward, took the rope lead of its halter from the attendant boy, turned it around and cantered off to a cleared area of field where other gypsies were putting horses for sale through their paces. Everyone made a way for him and he rode his mount on by the power of his thighs and calves, driving it forward, making it bend and twist, canter and trot to command.

Professor Thompson, Playfair and the two students from Edinburgh watched spellbound until Jesse had finished and reined up the panting horse. Then Thompson turned to Gib and asked, 'Is that young man a relative of yours?'

'He's my nephew,' said the older gypsy. 'His mother was my sister but both she and his father are dead so he's my son now.'

224

'Ask him if he'd like to come to Edinburgh with me,' said the Professor.

Gib cast him a baleful glance out of his watchful hawk's eyes and said bleakly, 'It's the horse I'm selling, sir, not the rider.'

'Don't misunderstand me. I'm Professor of Anatomy at Edinburgh University and quite frankly I don't think I've ever seen such a fine specimen of humanity as your nephew in my entire career. The bodies I get to show my students are usually undernourished or diseased and it would be a great chance to show them such a perfectly muscled man. I've never seen anyone like him myself. Take a look at that, boys, he's a wonderful specimen . . .' The last remark was addressed to his students who nodded eagerly.

Gib laughed. 'I hope you're not suggesting that our Jesse should be made into a cadavar before his time, your honour.'

Thompson laughed too. 'Of course not. I'd just want him to pose for my students, to show off his physique to them. Ask him to take off his shirt, would you?'

Gib, straight-faced, shouted across, 'This gentleman wants a closer look at you, Jesse.'

The young man slid off the horse's back and ran a hand down its legs as he called over to Thompson, 'Come and see then. He's very quiet and a fine-limbed horse, your honour.'

'It's not the horse's limbs that's interesting him. It's yours,' said Gib who was obviously enjoying himself. 'He wants you to take your shirt off, he wants a look at your chest.'

Jesse stepped back as if he'd been jabbed with a dagger. 'Dammit no,' he said sharply and added in an angry aside to his uncle, 'I'll chin his curlo first.'

Gib guffawed and translated for the Professor. 'My nephew's shy. He says he'd cut your throat rather than bare his chest for you.'

The old man threw up his hands. 'But he doesn't under-stand. Nobody ever understands. My interest is purely professional. He's just a bundle of muscles and sinews as far as I'm concerned. Tell him that.'

The message was conveyed to Jesse who shook his head even more vehemently. There was no way he was going to agree to the strange request. At length the Professor sighed and said, 'Ah well, if he won't, he won't, but it's a pity because I'd have paid him ten sovereigns to come to Edinburgh for a day and sit in front of my anatomy class. His musculature is magnificent.'

'Musculature?' Jesse and Gib looked suspiciously at each other and the young man shook his head vigorously. He could put ten sovereigns to good use but he wasn't prepared to undertake the Professor's demeaning commission to get them.

As he turned angrily away, Thomassin came up behind him with a pewter pot in her hand and pressed it on him. 'You must be dry, Jesse. Drink this ale,' she said. Without thinking, he raised the pot to his lips and swigged some of the contents down while she watched with a strange smile on her face.

When Professor Thompson and his little entourage walked away the crowd around the horses was disrupted by the arrival of an older man linking arms with a young giant who seemed immoderately excited by the sight of the horses and pushed through among the watching people to get at them. His companion tried to soothe him by saying softly, 'Steady on Billy, just wait a bit.'

Jesse was standing with Gib and Thomassin, all resplendent in scarlet and green and with her mother's jewellery, when the pair approached and Jem asked, 'Can this lad clap your horse, mister? He's fond of horses.' Gib looked at Billy and a frown appeared on his brow. He opened his mouth to say something but Jem forestalled him by asking, 'Are you the Kirk Yetholm folk?' When the answer was affirmative, he went on, 'Is the old woman called Rachel still alive? She was one of your people.'

It was Thomassin who answered, 'Yes, she's eighty-four but she's still alive. Who wants her?'

Jem indicated the enraptured Billy who was laying his

226

face against the grey stallion's neck and nuzzling his nose into its skin. 'This lad would like to see her and I think she'd like to see him. He's her grandson – or great grandson maybe, I was never quite sure which.'

The faces that turned towards Billy were astounded and Gib stepped forward exclaiming, 'It's the lad, it's our Billy, you've grown into a big man, haven't you? You were just a chal when I saw you last.'

Billy looked up from his worship of the horse and said, 'Yes, I'm big and I'm strong.'

'You look strong. What's he been feeding you on – nails?' asked Gib with a laugh and turned back to Jem to say with a smile, 'He's Rachel's great-grandson in fact and she told us she'd given him to the boxing booth man. That's you, I guess. My word, but you've done a good job. We thought he'd be dead by now – one way or another.'

Jem back smiled a little ruefully. 'It's not always been easy to cope with him but he's a good lad at heart. It's just that he doesn't know his own strength or when to stop once he get's started. I brought him over to ask what Rachel thinks we should do with him now that he's grown because I'm not going to be able to cope with him much longer. I'm getting on in years and it takes strength . . .'

Gib took a step back as if Jem had handed him a red-hot poker. 'Away man, you look in good shape. You're still fit. You can keep him a bit longer, we don't mind,' he said in a magnanimous tone.

Jesse stepped up beside Billy who was paying no attention to the conversation concerning him and laid an arm around the big lad's neck, hugging his head into his chest as he said, 'Hey, Billy, d'ye remember me? I'm Jesse. We used to play together.' When he looked back at Jem and Gib there was a strangely stricken look in his eyes but he laughed and said, 'He's not much younger than me. I remember him as a bairn, he played rough even then. I've still got a scar on my leg where he bit me. Aw, poor Billy . . .' He turned back to the smiling giant and told him, 'I'm glad you're still alive. We thought you were dead, Billy.' Then he hugged the giant again.

When they embraced, Billy clapped Jesse on the back and laughed uproariously. 'Billy's not dead. Billy's fine,' he roared.

Watching the two of them, Jem was forcibly struck by the family likeness between them. Billy was bigger and bulkier than Jesse but he had the same curling dark hair and the same well-muscled body, although his movements were uncoordinated and his face was like a blank slate compared to Jesse's. His eyes were clouded and confused where Jesse's were alive and dancing. In a gesture of friendship Jesse handed Billy his pot of ale and said 'Take some . . .'

When the two men stood apart, Billy's eye fell on Thomassin who was standing beside Gib and he went suddenly quiet with his face taking on a troubled look. Like someone trying to touch a delicate flower, he put out a tentative hand towards her but she stepped quickly away from him. It was obvious that he scared her. Jem saw the disappointed look on Billy's face and told the girl, 'Don't worry, he's all right. He won't hurt you. He's only trying to be friendly. Take his hand.'

Reassured she put out her thin, dark-skinned hand and held Billy's enormous fist. He looked down at their clasped hands and smiled, a pitiful grimace like the smile of an ape. 'You're pretty,' he mumbled and flushed scarlet. She stepped back again as if he'd struck her.

Gib saw her confusion and said to Jem, 'Old Rachel's over in her tent telling fortunes. Thomassin here'll take you there. Rachel'll be glad to see Billy again. She was right fond of him.'

Thomassin, who had wrenched her hand from Billy's grasp, said hurriedly, 'Yes, come on, I'll show you where she is. You'll have to be quick because there's a crowd of people waiting to be dukkered by her.'

Rachel's tent was made of dark green material like stained velvet and swags of tarnished gilt and tassels were looped above the entrance. It was a bell-shaped tent and from the centre pole flew a flag with the symbols of a dragon with a forked tail inside a six-pointed golden star painted on it. Propped up at the tent door was a long, green-painted wooden board with a carved top like a big tombstone. On it was written in cursive flowing black and gold letters like those that were painted along the sides of carts and coaches. *Madame Fatima, Clairvoyant, Possessor of Mystic Powers, Consulted by Members of Royalty and the Nobility*.

When Thomassin shoved her head through the half-open tent flap, Rachel was leaning over a table listening to something being told to her by a tall, neatly-dressed man who looked like a superior servant. The man was saying, 'My master wants the strongest potion you can make – he's getting married, you see.'

Rachel's obsidian eyes searched the face in front of her. 'I hope your master's a rich man. The strongest is expensive,' she said.

'He's rich. It must be the best. How much?'

'Fifty guineas – and you can add five for yourself when you bring me the fee.' Rachel knew perfectly well that her client was the Duke's manservant although he had not told her his master's name.

'That's a lot of money. You're sure it will work?' he asked.

Rachel cackled. 'It works – never fails. He'll be like a frisky colt for his wedding day but it'll take time to prepare. I have to find the right ingredients and that's not easy.' The man shivered because he was afraid of her. 'He has time. The wedding won't be till the end of the year, probably.' He rose to go as if anxious to get away but Rachel put a restraining hand on his arm. 'Tell him it's genuine magic,' she said in a baleful voice.

'He'll want to know what's in it.'

She shook her head. 'That knowledge is not for sale. Just tell him the things that go into it are not easy to come by – not even for a Duke. There'll be no bargaining, either. Fifty guineas, that's the price.'

Hurriedly the man pushed past Thomassin and gave an audible sigh of relief when he found himself in the open air again. When he had disappeared into the crowd, the girl came farther into the tent and said, 'Rachel, d'ye remember Billy? The man you gave him to is here and he's brought the lad to see you.'

The old gypsy stood up from her stool and clasped her hands together, making her dozens of bangles rattle and clink as she stepped forward. In her haste she knocked over her little table and playing cards were scattered all over the grass at her feet but she ignored them as she cried out, 'Billy, my Billy! Bring him in, Thomassin.'

The girl looked up at the low tent roof above her head. 'I think it'd be best if you come out. He's grown into a big lad.'

'Take him round the back then,' said Rachel, 'and tell that crowd out there I'll be starting again in half an hour. I must see Billy first.'

When Thomassin went out to summon Billy and Jem round the back of Rachel's tent, a line of women were patiently waiting to consult Madame Fatima. Among them were Odilie, Grace and Mary Scott.

'You'll have to wait,' Thomassin told them. 'Madame Fatima must stop to build up her powers again, but don't go away ladies, she'll be ready for you again in half an hour or maybe less . . . Just wait here on the grass.' She spoke in the wheedling tone that was quite different from her normal speaking voice. As she spoke she ran her eye over the clients and thought them a poor-looking crew with nothing worth stealing on them.

Mary Scott, next in line in front of Odilie and Grace heaved a sigh. 'Och, what a pity. I was so looking forward to having my fortune told.'

Her friend Elsie turned and said, 'You still can. It's too hot to go stravaging around, so let's wait. We'll sit here for a bit and maybe some of those lads that are hanging about'll go to the ale tent and bring us a drink. Give one of them the eye.'

Mary looked shocked. With disquiet she remembered Elsie's account of her revels of the previous year, the aching head that lasted for three days. Mary herself did not like ale much and homemade nettle beer was strong enough for her but she dared not say so to Elsie for fear of being thought a killjoy. So she contented herself with saying, 'Oh Elsie, you're terrible!' and sank down on the grass, taking off her bonnet for the heat was indeed tremendous. She hoped that her face was not scarlet. The scent of the lavender water that Aunt Lily had given her seemed to be stronger than ever for when she moved, it wafted up around her in a sickening wave. She flapped the ends of her white neckerchief in a futile attempt to make it go away.

Elsie, with a loud laugh, leaned over and nudged Mary in the ribs. 'If you won't I will,' she said, and crooked a finger at a pair of young men who were watching the waiting girls from the other side of the pathway. There was no need to repeat the summons. They came over smartly and were soon engaged in the thrust and parry of flirtatious conversation with Elsie who was a past mistress at the art. She told them that she thought one of them was her cousin though of course he wasn't. 'He's a fine-looking fellow like you are, that's why I got confused,' said Elsie, flapping her eyelashes.

Mary said nothing and stared down at the grass wishing she was back with her mother but the second young man sat boldly down beside her and asked, 'Have you any cousins that look like me, lass?' She shook her head, acutely conscious of the lowering presence of Jockie Armstrong who of course was still in view, having doggedly tailed her up the hill. Now he was lounging beneath a tree a short distance away and it seemed to Mary that his eyes were boring into her.

Odilie and Grace, sitting next to Mary, were safe from flirtatious attentions because they looked so shabby. They watched the tableau with amusement and smiled when Mary, in an attempt to escape the attentions of her suitor, turned to them and tried to start a conversation. She'd do anything to show Jockie that she was not encouraging the young man beside her.

'Where have you come from?' was her first question.

She saw their working clothes and thought with pity that they must be very poor indeed not to be able to afford proper dresses for Fair Day.

For a second Odilie was confused for she'd forgotten what she'd told the boy who took her horse. But Grace remembered and she leaned forward to say, 'We're from Earlston.'

Thankfully Mary knew no one there. 'My word, that's a fair bit away!' she said.

'Not too far,' said Odilie. 'We rode over. I was lent a horse.'

'That's lucky, it's a long walk,' said Mary. 'I'm from Morebattle and we came on our farmer's dray. I'm a bondager too. Have you a good place?'

She was looking at Odilie when she asked the question. 'Oh yes, very good,' said Odilie, who had no wish to become involved in anything other than generalities about her make-believe work. She changed the subject by saying, 'I like your dress.'

Mary fingered the cotton of her skirt. 'Aye, it's a pretty colour. Aunt Lily and I made it ourselves.' She leaned forward. 'You don't think I smell funny, do you?'

Grace and Odilie leaned forward too and sniffed. 'You smell of lavender flowers. It's a nice smell,' said Odilie.

'That's fine. It's my aunt's perfume. I poured most of the bottle on before I left home and I think I've used too much. It's fair making my head swim.'

By this time Elsie had persuaded the swains to fetch beer and she pressed a mug into Mary's hands saying, 'Drink that up, it'll cool you down.' Mary obediently drank it and Elsie took the empty pot, handed it to the young men and said, 'We'll just have another, thank you.'

'Oh no, ' protested Mary but she might have saved her breath. No one listened to her.

Meanwhile, at the back of the fortune-telling tent, Rachel was weeping and clasping her arms around Billy. She was so much shorter than him that she could only hug him round the waist while he stood with his head bent and a puzzled expression on his face, staring down at the top of her head. Eventually she stopped crying and rubbed her eyes with swollen and arthritic knuckles as she told him, 'Oh but I'm pleased to see you, Billy. Are you being a good chal then? Are you doing everything this man tells you?'

'Yes,' muttered Billy in confusion. Then some memory seemed to waken in him, he gave a groan and tried to hug Rachel. Whatever stirred in his brain made him very sad and tears welled up in his eyes.

Fearful in case he hurt the frail old woman Jem stepped forward but Rachel put out a hand out to stop him. 'He'll do me no harm. I can tell,' she said, and let the young giant crush her closer.

When Billy relinquished his hold of the old woman, Jem said to him, 'Now, sit down here on the grass and we'll talk to your Granny for a bit. She'll sit beside you if you like.'

Rachel held Billy's hand and pulled him down on to the ground beside her as she told Jem, 'You've looked after him well. I knew I could trust you.'

'It's that I've come about. He's nearly too much for me now and there's no one else in my show that I could trust with him. Long Tom would be cruel to him if I wasn't watching and Alice is terrified of him though she won't admit it. When I get too old to manage him or if anything happens to me, what's to be done with Billy?'

Rachel groaned. 'I've lived too long. I'm having to face problems I hoped never to see. There's no one in our community who could cope with Billy. Gib's as old as you and he was never a patient man, especially when he's had a drink. There's only young Jesse but he's not much older than Billy. He has the makings of a fine man but to ask him to take on Billy would be like putting a shackle on his leg . . . You've brothers in the travelling trade, haven't you? Maybe one of them could take him when you're ready to give him up?'

Jem frowned. 'There's Simon. He's here today with his circus. I could ask him but I doubt if his wife will let him take Billy . . . she's got daughters you see. I've thought about this a lot. There are plenty of freak shows that would take him on but I don't want to see him bullied or ill-treated. I'm as fond of him as you are. I'll think about it a bit more and you think, too. Before the Fair's over, we'll have to come to some decision.'

When the time came to take their leave it was with difficulty that Jem persuaded Billy to go back to the freak show with him for he wanted to stay among the gypsies: he felt at home there. Rachel had to promise that he could come back that night when his show was over before he agreed to go peacefully. As they were walking away, Billy hung on Jem's hand and stared at Thomassin who was sitting at little way off watching all that went on. 'What's your name?' Billy suddenly asked her.

She raised her head and looked at him with her slanting eyes. 'I'm called Thomassin,' she said.

'My word you're braw. I love you,' said Billy.

The interlude seemed to have done Madame Fatima a power of good because she whipped through the waiting queue at a terrific rate when she returned. And the clients were satisfied for each one re-emerged from the tent looking dazzled, bright-eyed and optimistic. Soon it was the turn of Elsie and Mary who went in together giggling and clinging to each other like a pair of children. Mary felt strange because three mugs of ale had been forced on her and that combined with the heat was making her head swim. When she and Elsie disappeared through the tent flap, Odilie saw that the two men who had been buying the girls' drinks nudged each other in anticipation.

Inside the tent Rachel held Elsie's work-chapped hand and reeled off the usual anodyne formula – a happy marriage, several children not all of who whom would grow to adulthood, a long but hard life, trouble in store but you'll overcome it. When she took Mary's hand she looked obliquely and with more genuine interest at the girl. 'This is an important day for you and for all your family. You're at a crossroads in your life. You can take the right road or the wrong one. Take care . . . for if you take the right road you'll live a long and happy life and end it in prosperity with your children's children all around you. But be careful because you're at the decision point now.'

The portentous note in her voice frightened the girl who drew her hand back and whispered, 'How will I know which road to take?'

Rachel shrugged. 'You must think. You come from a loving family. Think about them.'

Mary looked shaken when she came out and the change in her was noticed by both Odilie and Grace as they stood up and filed one after the other through the door of Madame Fatima's tent.

Rachel looked at Grace's hand first. 'In this hand I see sorrow and tears, many tears both from you and about you but don't worry because most of them are shed already and you're about to step into sunlight. You'll blossom soon. Don't be afraid. Someone from the past is about to come back to you, it is someone who has been thinking about you a great deal. But you have enemies, too. Another person is trying to defeat you but with help you'll win through in the end.'

Grace leaned forward, her face alight, and asked, 'Do you see anything else in my hand?'

'Oh yes, I see money, plenty of money. It's the cause of much of your trouble – most of it, in fact. You can have it or you can lose it. You must show determination. And I see love.'

'Love?' queried the girl in a whisper.

Rachel laid down the hand and nodded. 'Yes, love. Don't worry, it's there and it's waiting for you – very near.'

She was tiring now and longing for a rest but another girl still sat at the back of the tent waiting her turn. When she was done, when she was satisfied with the old stories, Rachel could look forward to tying up the tent door and lying down for an hour or two to think about the problem of Billy. She gestured peremptorily to Odilie who stepped forward and slipped on to the stool that Grace vacated.

'Cross my palm with silver, lassie,' said Rachel shortly as she did to each customer.

The shabbily dressed bondager slipped a silver shilling on to the old woman's hand and as her fingers closed around the proffered fingers, Rachel noticed with surprise that this girls hand was as soft as velvet. She had never wielded a scrubbing brush or a hay fork; she had never laboured in the fields although she was dressed as if she did. The gypsy's interest was wakened and she stared sharply into Odilie's face, noting the dark skin and strangely coloured eyes.

'This could be a gypsy lassie,' she thought and decided to try a bit of Romany on her. 'Been dukkered before, chavi?' she asked but Odilie looked blank and Rachel had to repeat the question in ordinary Scots. 'Have you had your fortune told before, my girl?'

The bondager shook her head making the big sunbonnet flap around her face and Rachel wished she would take it off so that it was possible to get a better look at her. With a feeling of interest, she bent her old head over Odilie's hand and then gave an involuntary gasp of surprise at what she saw there.

'What's wrong?' asked the girl with a scared note in her voice.

'Oh, nothing's wrong. Far from it. I see a great future for you. Not what a working girl from a farm can expect. I see you in a place where the sun shines all the time and you're very happy there but your life takes you to many other places as well – across the black water. I see mountains and oceans, cities and vast plains. My word but you're going to wander, my lass, though it'll be from choice. And you'll never want for anything. You've been born under a lucky star.'

Odilie nodded and nervously licked her lips as she asked, 'What about marriage? Who will I marry?'

Rachel frowned and looked at the hand again. 'There's trouble about marriage. You do marry but it looks very confused – perhaps you promise yourself to one man and marry another . . . I can't make it out exactly. You have

236

a great love all your life but I can't tell if that's the one you marry or not. It's very confusing. You're very bold and headstrong. You're going to be a great lady. I can see that.'

She laid down the hand in a gesture of dismissal but Odilie was not satisfied. She hurriedly reached into her skirt pocket and produced another shilling which she laid on the table between them. 'Tell me about the man I marry. Describe him for me,' she said in the tone of one accustomed to giving orders.

Rachel raised her eyebrows and lifted the shilling, biting it between her gaping teeth to test it before she said, 'All right, let me see your hand again then. You're a hard one to fathom. I haven't had such a difficult hand for many years.'

Intently she stared at Odilie's palm, tracing the lines with her fingertip before she said, 'You'll be carried away by love. It causes trouble – terrible trouble. After that you marry. The one thing I can see about the man is that he's bango-wasted.' She deliberately used a Romany expression because she was still not convinced that Odilie did not secretly understand the language.

The girl's eyes were enormous as she stared into the old woman's face and asked, 'Bango-wasted? What's that?'

Rachel leaned back in her chair and sighed. 'All right, he's left-handed, that's what it means.'

'Oh no,' groaned the girl as she rose to her feet. 'Surely you've made a mistake.'

'No mistake, it's there in your hand but I don't know what you're worried about. It'll be a great love,' said Rachel and pointed to the door telling them it was time to go.

When they were standing together in the open air again Odilie's eyes were flashing and she raged to Grace, 'Well, that was good money wasted! What an old fraud. Aunt Martha's right, she only tells you what you want to hear. She must have recognised me, that's what all that stuff about bango-wasted was about because everybody knows the Duke's left-handed. How could I have a great love for that horrible porpoise?'

Grace shook her head. 'Well, I thought she was good. I hope what she said was true as far as I'm concerned. It sounded fine to me and so did yours. Remember what she said about you having a great love and travelling so far, never wanting for anything and being bold?'

'If she recognised me, she could have guessed all that. She's a fraud, Gracie. I wish we'd never gone near her.' All Odilie could think of was the gypsy's prediction that she was to marry a left-handed man. It was as if the final seal had been set on her marriage contract. She'd really have to marry the Duke after all.

After Jem went away to show Billy the horses, Alice dressed herself in her finest gown, put on a deep-brimmed bonnet that hid her face and hurried of through the crowds in the fairground in the direction of the wooden bridge over the river. She walked quickly with her head down and looked directly at no one in her way for she was afraid of being recognised.

When she stepped down from the bridge on the town bank, she glanced up at the forbidding façade of Viewhill House and the sight of it made her shudder. Then she lowered her head again and hurried on, climbing the steep little path that led to Roxburgh Street. She walked quickly down it and when she reached the square she hesitated for a minute before starting to walk slowly around its perimeter, staring into shop windows and scrutinising the plates on the doors. The shops were busy because many visitors from out of town were stocking up on things they needed to last them for the rest of the year – clothes, shoes, ironmongery and chinaware. St James' Fair brought a good measure of prosperity to the tradespeople of Lauriston even if they did not get a share of its revenue.

At last Alice came to a halt in front of the big grocery shop and peered through its window, seeing hams, all neatly tied up in white muslin, hanging above the counter; an array of cheeses in colours ranging from almost white to deepest orange; ice floe sugar cones and tins of tea with japanned designs painted on them; racks of dark bottles of port and wine lined up behind the servers at the counters. The bottles were lying on their sides in lines of racks one above the other, like a sleeping army.

When she pushed open the door a brass bell above her head rang sharply making her jump but she walked on up to the counter where Mr. Burns was serving a voluble lady who could not make up her mind between gunpowder tea or the black variety. Burns stood smiling patiently for he was used to this sort of vacillation and would wait an hour if necessary to make a sale. Alice sat down on the chair that was provided for waiting customers and kept her head lowered, breathing in the delicious smells that flavoured the whole place – spices and sugar, cheese and China tea. The effect was mouth-watering. Eventually she was brought out of her reverie by a voice above her head asking, 'Can I be of service to you, madam?' Tom Burns was leaning forward on his white marble counter and smiling at her.

Flustered she rose to her feet and said, 'I want some sugared lemon peel please and a piece of cheese.'

Tom, with a masterly flourish, indicated the cheeses of which he was rightly proud. 'Take your pick. Which would you like? Taste them first . . . try this one, it's very flavoursome.'

He passed a morsel of cheese over and she nibbled it. 'Very nice,' she agreed, 'I'll take a piece, about that size . . .' With outspread fingers she indicated what she wanted and it was quickly cut of by the cheese wire to her specifications.

Tom wrapped it up and then added a stiff curl of yellow lemon peel in another paper packet. When her parcel was handed across to her, Alice asked in a casual voice that cost her considerable effort, 'I was wondering if Mr. Anstruther, the old lawyer who used to have his office next door, is still alive?'

Burns shot a look at her and said, 'You must have been away a long time. He died a good ten years ago. But his

239

widow's still living there in the flat above.' He noted that the stranger was behaving oddly, keeping her head down under the enormous bonnet as if she was afraid to look him in the eye. He leaned slightly closer in an effort to get a better view of her but she stepped back to prevent him succeeding in his ploy. That's queer, he thought and something niggled in the back of his mind. Although he could not see her clearly, he felt that he recognised her. Perhaps it was the voice.

'Don't I know you, madam?' he asked. People who returned from afar for the Fair were usually happy to be recognised but this woman hurriedly grabbed her purchases and laid the exact money on the counter top. 'I don't think so. I've never been here before,' she said.

In that case, how do you know about Mr. Anstruther, thought Tom Burns, but he did not have the chance to ask because she literally fled from the shop as if devils were chasing her.

The doorway alongside Burns' shop had a brass knocker that gleamed in the sun and Alice thudded it down hard. After what seemed an unconscionable time the door was opened by a pert-looking little maidservant who asked, 'Yes'm?'

'Is Mrs. Anstruther at home?' asked Alice.

'She's always at home,' was the reply.

'I'm an old friend, perhaps I could come in and see her.'

'Who'll I say?' asked the maid.

'Say it's someone from the past who wants to give her a pleasant surprise.'

'Oh, all right, come in. She's upstairs. But I should warn you she might not know you, she's wandering a bit in her mind. She sometimes doesn't remember things,' said the maid, holding open the door.

The first-floor drawing room was packed with furniture and a huddled little figure wrapped in shawls was seated in a chair beside the window overlooking the square. The maid announced Alice, 'A lady to see you, mum,' and the figure turned its head revealing a tiny white face with a skin so wrinkled that it barely looked human.

There were tears in Alice's eyes when she walked across the floor and bent down beside the chair. 'Mrs. Anstruther, I've come to see you,' she said and took one of the tiny wrinkled hands in hers.

The old lady stared into the face so close to hers for a few seconds. Then a smile of incredible sweetness lit up her eyes and she said, 'Oh, Lucy, it's you. I'm so pleased to see you.'

Alice put a finger on the old woman's lips as if to silence her and looked back at the curious maid who was shamed into closing the door and going away. When they were alone, she took off her bonnet and kissed Mrs. Anstruther on the cheek. The old lady responded in a sweet, fluting voice and asked, 'Where have you been, Lucy? It seems such a long time since you came to see me. George'll be glad to know you're back. He often talks about you.' Then she gave herself a shake and said, 'I'm a silly old woman, what am I saying? I'm wandering again. Of course poor George is dead. I keep forgetting that.'

Alice eyes were glossy with unshed tears as she held her old friend's hands. 'Oh, Mrs. Anstruther, I've been far away and no one must know that I'm back. You won't tell anyone, will you?'

Tired, faded eyes stared into her face and then there was a deep sigh. 'I'd forgotten that, Lucy. Of course I'll not tell. I'm nearly ninety you know and it's difficult to remember things sometimes.'

'I came to ask you some questions. I knew I could trust you. Maybe you can tell me what happened to my father?' whispered Alice in a low voice.

'Your father? Davie Allen. Such a good man. Poor Davie, he didn't want to live after you went away and they told him you were dead. He was found dead in his bed one morning but I don't remember what year. My George was very upset when they came and told him about Davie. I remember that he came up here from the office, sat down in that chair over there and wept like a bairn.'

Alice dropped her head into her hands like a broken woman and sobbed, 'It was all my fault – one mistake, that was all, just one mistake and then this terrible thing happened. I'm haunted by it.'

'George said you didn't do it,' whispered Mrs. Anstruther, patting the heaving shoulder.

'I didn't do what they said I did but I made a mistake nonetheless. And, oh God, I've paid for it. I can't tell you how I paid for it. I'm paying for it still.'

'Don't grieve, my dear. You were young and innocent. They used you . . .'

Alice lifted her head. 'Yes they did, didn't they. What happened to my father's property after he died?'

'There was a lot of trouble about that. George was very worried. He died not long after your father – within weeks, in fact – yes, the very same year. Andrew Elliot took over his practice.'

'My husband took it over?'

'Yes, he paid me some money and closed George's office. All the clients went to him. His place is on the other side of the square. Look, that's his window over there. I didn't know what else to do – there was no one to advise me, you see.'

Mrs. Anstruther stared vaguely around her room as if she'd forgotten where she was and it was obvious that her mind had been taken over by a temporary blackness so Alice sat quietly holding her hand and they were silent together till the maid pushed open the door, carrying a tray of tea things.

'She likes a cup of tea about this time,' she explained, setting it down on a table by the old lady.

Alice looked up at the girl. 'Who looks after her?'

'I do. Elliot the lawyer pays my wages. She has lots of visitors mostly old ladies like herself. They come and take tea with her.'

Mrs. Anstruther was nodding her head and saying,

242

'I'm very well really, thank you. You mustn't worry about me, Lucy.'

'I'm not Lucy. My name's Alice,' said the stranger, smiling at the maid and adding in an aside, 'I can see she gets a little confused.'

'She does, but sometimes she's bright as a button,' said the girl, who was obviously kindly. 'It's worse when she's tired, though. When you've had your tea perhaps you should go and I'll tuck her up for a wee sleep.'

Alice left a short time later and went hurrying across the square with her deep bonnet on her lowered head. Mrs. Anstruther's maid watched her from the window and when her employer was asleep, she slipped downstairs for a few rashers of ham for the old lady's supper. She was stopped in the shop by Tom Burns who asked, 'Who was the woman that came in here and asked about the Anstruthers earlier on?'

'I don't know,' said the girl. 'She told me her name was Alice but my lady called her Lucy and she's not often wrong about things like that.'

'Dammit, of course,' cried Burns, slapping one fist onto the palm of his hand. 'I thought I knew her and I'm not often wrong about faces. It's Lucy Allen! By God, who'd have thought she'd come back. Poor soul, I hope Elliot doesn't see her.'

CHAPTER 9

After Odilie and Grace left Madame Fatima's tent they almost ran into the group led by Professor Thompson. He was complaining to his students, 'They always misunderstand, don't they? You'd think he'd be flattered to be told he has a magnificent physique but oh no, he takes offence. Silly young man.'

His companions nodded as he went on, 'I hope you paid good attention to him, boys. I tell you he's the finest specimen of manhood I've ever seen. It's because of the way they breed them. Gypsies only rear the best. Weaklings are killed at birth – deliberately culled.'

One of the students laughed and said, 'You're not suggesting we should do the same are you, Professor?'

Thompson made a humphing sound. 'Pity we can't. It'd save us doctors a lot of trouble but the Kirk wouldn't stand for it at all . . .' He paused for a moment and then continued, 'What a pity he won't come to Edinburgh – those shoulders and those muscles were magnificent.'

'There's no spare fat on him – I wonder what he eats?' said the other student, a little wistfully because he was running to portliness himself.

'Hedgehogs,' snapped Thompson. 'They eat hedgehogs and rabbits, badgers and foxes too – and any chickens they can steal. There'll not be a hen left in a run round here by tomorrow night.'

'It's not a diet that we could really recommend to the burghers of Edinburgh, is it?' said the first student in a cheeky way and he was quelled by a stern glance. They were all so engrossed in their medical speculations that they did not notice when they almost bumped into a girl dressed as a bondager who dodged smartly out of their way. Young Playfair, however, feeling rather bored and left out, did see her and his eyes opened wide. He was about to reach out a hand and stop her when she darted away from him and disappeared into the crowd. 'I'm sure that was Miss Rutherford. I thought I saw her earlier as well,' he said excitedly to the Professor, but the older man was not listening, for he was too intent on moaning to his students about the failure of the young gypsy to take him up on his offer of posing for the anatomy class.

When she watched Thompson's broad back disappearing down the hill Odilie felt safer and, dragging Grace along, she pushed deeper into the throng where she could get a better view of the horses. A dark-haired young gypsy was grooming a grey stallion which was by far the most impressive horse on view and Odilie's discerning eye told her that the horse had a lot of Arab in its breeding. As if it knew that it was the object of much interest, it was preening itself with nostrils flared wide showing the pink membrane inside and dark eyes flashing with a light that showed great spirit. She sighed in appreciation at the sight of the beautiful beast and as she watched, a man pushed his way through the crowd to ask if the stallion was for sale.

'Money couldn't buy him,' was the proud reply and the gypsy ran a loving hand down his horse's face, lingering gently on the velvet muzzle and letting it nuzzle his palm with its lips. Finding no titbit there, it raised its head and touched his face as if it was kissing him.

Gib saw that the grey horse had captured the crowd's attention and announced loudly, 'If you want to see this horse in action, there's going to be a jumping contest later on. We'll challenge any other horse to outjump ours. Put your bets on with me.'

Then, for the entertainment and enticement of the onlookers, Jesse swung the horse round and jumped on to its bare back. He looked like a centaur rising above the press of people and with her eyes shining, Odilie whispered to Grace, 'Just look at that, aren't they magnificent?'

She made as if to push farther forward, right to the edge of the crowd but Grace held her back, whispering,

'This is the gypsy men's place, Odilie. We shouldn't be here.'

'Why not? I want to see that horse. Come on, it's broad daylight and no one's going to hurt us.'

'But you know what they say about the gypsies. They steal and murder. If they find out who you are, you'll disappear and your father'll have to pay a ransom to get you back,' said Grace, who was visibly apprehensive.

Odilie laughed. 'And that would be an adventure, wouldn't it? I might not want to come back.' Overriding Grace's scruples, she pulled her friend onwards and pushed her way through the ranks of men who were watching Jesse and his horse. Then, without a by-your-leave, Odilie stepped into the middle of the clearing and bent down to run a hand along the horse's fetlock. When she raised her bonneted head, her voice was solemn. 'This is a very fine horse indeed. How old is he?'

A laugh came from above her head but the sunlight was so bright in her eyes that she found it hard to see the man clearly. 'Do you know many horses, then? Have a care that he doesn't bite you. He doesn't like strangers,' came a teasing voice.

'Oh, he won't do that,' said Odilie confidently as she held a hand up to the horse's muzzle. 'How old is he?' she repeated.

Jesse told her, 'He's not four yet.'

'He's got Arab blood, hasn't he? Did you breed him yourself?' she asked next.

There was a hint of respect in his voice when he answered her questions. 'Yes, he's Arab and I bought him at Appleby Fair as a yearling. He's got Eclipse breeding.'

'He's beautiful, quite beautiful.' Odilie sighed and gently rubbed the horse's ears. Jesse was surprised at how trustingly Barbary lowered his head towards her.

'You must have a price for him in spite of what you told that man. What is it?' she said suddenly.

Jesse looked down at her again and grinned broadly, his smile good-humoured. 'How much can you afford?'

he asked in a way that showed he thought it would not be very much.

She laughed back, looking down at her cotton dress and heavy boots. At that moment she remembered Grace's warning about the dangers of revealing her true identity in the middle of the gypsy camp. 'I was only wondering,' she said. For some reason she felt excited: her heart was beating fast and she did not know why.

'He's not for sale. I wouldn't part with him for a hundred guineas – but if you like horses there's plenty of others almost as good as this – almost. Go and have a look at them,' he told her as he turned his horse, leapt back on him and rode away.

As if they were iron filings drawn by a magnet, the crowd flowed off behind him leaving Odilie, full of strange emotions, on the hillock with Grace pulling at her sleeve and saying, 'Come on – let's get out of here. I don't like the way those women are watching us.'

Behind the girls a hostile crowd of women were approaching, led by Thomassin, who had watched the exchange between Odilie and Jesse. Her olive-skinned face was incandescent with anger and she seemed on the verge of violence. She rushed up and one hand reached out for Odilie's shoulder, grabbing her from the back. The fingers were vice-like on the soft flesh.

'Leave my man alone,' she hissed.

Odilie turned around and in spite of herself, her heart leaped in fright when she saw the expression on the gypsy girl's face. She controlled herself, however, and looked impassively back, shrugging the hand off her shoulder. Her eyes were flashing too as she said flatly, 'I wasn't doing anything to your man. It was his horse that interested me, not him.'

When Thomassin looked into the stranger's face and saw the colour of her skin, she spoke some words in a language that neither Grace nor Odilie understood. They looked blankly at the gypsy girl, who leaned forward aggressively and repeated her words. When they still looked uncomprehending, she hissed like a threatening snake, 'Don't pretend you can't understand me. I'm asking if you're a Romany. You must be with skin that colour. Where are you from? Are you one of the Lochmaben lot or did you come up from Alnwick with the Earl of Hell? You'd better get out of here before my people see you or there'll be trouble.'

'I'm not a Romany,' protested Odilie, trying to conceal the tremor of fright which threatened to reveal itself in her voice. She heard Grace beside her draw in a sharp breath and they both knew that if they were mistaken for members of a rival gypsy gang, they could be in real danger, for it was common knowledge that the Romany families from different parts of the country hated each other with an implacable loathing. Nearly every year St James' Fair ended with terrible fighting and killings in perpetuation of ancient feuds between the gypsies. It was a rare year when none of their blood flowed.

Something held Thomassin back, however, for she contented herself with giving the other girl a sharp push in the chest and spitting out, 'Get away from here and keep your eyes off my man. You'd better not try to cast your glamourie on him.'

'What did you say?' asked Odilie in a trembling voice.

Thomassin stepped very close to her and whispered, 'I said, don't cast the glamourie on him. You know what that means well enough. If you do I'll kill you.' With her eyes fixed on Odilie's face she flicked up the hem of her skirt and revealed the hilt of a dagger stuck into the top of her boot.

That was enough for Grace, who grabbed Odilie's hand and together they took to their heels, running as fast as her limp would allow over the uneven ground. When they reached the safety of the crowds around the stalls on the flat ground, they came to a panting stop and Odilie gave a wry laugh. 'Don't say it, Grace! I know we shouldn't have gone up there at all – what with that horrible old fortune-teller and then the virago with the knife. As if I wanted her demon lover!' Now that she was safe she felt bold again and announced, 'But I'm not ready to go home yet. What will we do now?'

'Mrs Archer said not to come till the evening but we could go and see if we can find the freak show,' suggested Grace.

By this time the hands of the town clock had reached ten minutes to four and while the girls were searching for Jem's stand, Adam Scott was still standing at the end of the footbridge, scrutinising the face of every girl who passed him. Gradually he was giving up hope, for although plenty of pretty girls had paid their penny to cross the river, and many of them had smiled at him, the girl with the limp was not among them. By late afternoon, the stream of new arrivals had become a trickle. Most people who wanted to come to the Fair were already on the field. If she was going fairing, the chances were that the girl he sought was somewhere among the throng behind him.

He turned and gazed across the crowd. There were upwards of two thousand people in the field, he calculated, and that meant he had little chance of coming across her by accident. With a shrug of resignation and disappointment, Adam lifted his crook from the grass and walked off in the direction of his family's pony cart. The position of the sun told him it was almost four and his mother would be laying out their meal.

Although he looked assured and self-sufficient as he strode along, Adam was feeling intensely lonely. The stalls around him were laden with brightly coloured goods for one lover to buy for another and happy young couples were purchasing fairings for each other. He walked along deaf to the blandishments of profusely sweating sideshow buskers who were bawling out their attractions. More couples were giggling in front of the stalls, holding on to each other's arms, sometimes surreptitiously stealing kisses from each other, for the sun and the ale had swept away all inhibitions even among the most reticent people. The sight of so much happy abandon made Adam feel even more alone. As he watched the happy faces around him, it seemed to him that he must be the only young man without a girl on his arm and he wished he was back in his lonely hills.

When he came to the opening of the ale tent he lingered, wondering if his father was inside. He shoved his head in but could not pick out anyone he recognised in the shouting, reeling, red-faced crowd. Tom had probably gone back to the cart already.

On his way there too Adam had to walk across a flat stretch of land adjacent to the river. To his surprise he saw that a dense crowd was gathered and as he walked towards them, more and more people appeared to be running in the same direction. Something interesting must be going on, he thought, and veered off his path a little to see what it was. When he reached the edge of the crowd he saw that the attraction was a cleared arena in which two brushwood fences had been erected. This was the exercise yard for horses that were for sale and where would-be purchasers could trot or canter around and pop the horses over the fences if they had the courage.

Gypsies as usual were out in force where there were horses and they had all gathered together by the side of the arena, eyes flashing and fists brandishing money at each other. They were spitting into their palms and slapping hands together. What's going on, wondered Adam leaning on his crook. His attention was particularly drawn to a gypsy with a proud head of white hair who seemed to be a leader and who stood at the entrance to the ring with his shirt unbuttoned at the neck and sleeves rolled up to his elbows. He had a dashing look which was enhanced by the fact that he was carrying a bag of money and men were running up to him proffering coins which he slipped into the bag. That's it, thought the young shepherd, they're laying bets. But what on? The excitement was infectious and Adam could not drag himself away.

Then the big gypsy bawled out, 'We'll start soon now. There's three contenders today for the jumping contest and the prize'll be ten bars – ten pounds, that is. Take

250

your pick and lay your wagers, gentlemen. I'll hold the money.' Behind him, a trio of mounted men were waiting and he turned to them to shout, 'Bring out your horses, lads, and let the rajahs see them.'

In answer to this summons the three horses and their riders broke through the crowd at the arena entrance. First out was a huge black horse with mean, white-rimmed eyes; then came a piebald. Of all colourings for a horse, gypsies like piebalds best. The last horse was a beautiful dapple grey that pranced lightly on its feet with its head lowered in a way that made it look like a dragon breathing fire. All the horses were well-caparisoned but the grey was once again the best because it was wearing a magnificent bridle embellished with glittering bosses of silver along the brow-band and a curving silver bit that made it open its mouth and chew the air in a manner that added to its dragon-like appearance.

The rider was equally eye-catching for he sat impassive but with wrists flexed as if all the power in his body was concentrated in his hands while the muscles of his fore-arms rose and fell in a pulsing motion beneath his matt brown skin.

The crowd's levity changed to rapt attention as the men on the horses, each with a sharp turn of his body, made their mounts head one after another for the first fence. In a line they all soared easily over it while the spectators sighed 'AAAAH' admiringly at each leap – for there is no more elegant sight than a good rider on a smoothly jumping horse.

After such a tantalising display the horses left the ring again while the presiding gypsy cried out, 'That's the contestants then. Have you all decided on your fancy? Lay your money with Gib Faa.'

By this time Adam's interest had been well and truly captured. Though it was now past four o'clock he decided that his mother wouldn't mind if he was a little late for tea. This he wanted to see.

The sideshow Odilie and Grace were seeking was not

251

difficult to find. *Archer's Freaks – Wonders of the World* declared a huge banner that hung along its front, and an enormously tall man wearing a high stovepipe hat and playing a fiddle stood on the platform beside a tiny dwarf who was banging a drum almost as big as himself.

The girls paused at their feet and Grace called up to the fiddler, 'Are you Mr Archer?' She hoped that this was not the husband of her friend Alice for he had a crabbed and mournful face and, because of his stilts and excessively high hat, he looked about eight feet tall.

Still playing he shook his head and jerked his head backwards. 'He's in there,' he said, and as if in answer to a summons, the curtains parted and a burly man with a broken nose poked his head out. He was looking very worried. 'Are you Mr Archer?' asked Grace again.

The man emerged on to the platform. 'I am. Who wants me?' he said. 'Have you come about Alice?' She nodded and his face lightened as he asked, 'Where is she? She didn't say she was going away.'

The girl looked up at him with large blue eyes and said, 'I don't know. Isn't she here? I met her on Saturday at Bettymill and she told me to come and see her at the Fair today.'

Jem's eyes were suspicious as he stared at the girl. He remembered Alice's tearful return from the old mill and her account of meeting someone there. The last thing he wanted was for her to be upset again. 'She's gone out. I don't know where she is but she'll be back later I expect. Who will I say came looking for her?'

'Say it's Grace Elliot and tell her I'll come back in the evening. Goodbye,' she said in a dejected voice and wandered off into the crowd with her friend.

Odilie took her arm comfortingly. 'You're disappointed, aren't you? But don't worry. She did say to come in the evening, remember? My father's sure to be searching high and low for me by now. It's time I was going home. Come with me and I'll dress you up properly so's you can look really grand when you come back to see your friend Alice.' She pulled gently on Grace's arm and they headed off towards the wooden bridge. Grace allowed herself to be towed along for suddenly she felt very sad and very tired. With a pang she remembered how she'd dreamed of meeting the young man who'd helped her last year. That was just another of her useless fancies, she thought dispiritedly. She was not to know it but she stared at the crowds of lovers all around in the same way as Adam was also doing, and with the same bereft feelings. Everyone has a lover except me, she thought.

They climbed the steps to the bridge with Grace clinging to the rail for support. When Odilie was on the level she turned for a last look across the fairground and it was then that her eye caught sight of the jumping horses. She exclaimed with renewed excitement, 'Oh, I must watch that. Come on, let's go back for just a few more minutes. If you're tired we can sit on the bank and watch the jumping. That grey horse I admired so much is there.'

'What about your father? You said he'd be searching for you by now,' protested Grace but Odilie was not to be gainsaid.

'It's only for a few minutes. I must see the grey horse jumping,' she pleaded. 'Come on, dear Grace, come with me please.' She looked so entreating that it was impossible not to do what she wanted.

They did not have long to wait because the jumping contest was about to begin and excitement was running high.

The first horse into the field was the piebald ridden by a grim-faced man who rode with his shoulders hunched high as he cantered into the enclosure. The crowd knew him and went quiet. His name was Alfie Fleckie and he was a gypsy from the village of Gordon, a man of about forty who had spent years in the Army during the war with the French. Fleckie had been a troublemaker in his youth and if the authorities thought they were rid of him forever when he took the King's Shilling, they were wrong for Alfie survived the fighting to come home again and spend his nest-egg of sixty pounds on the mare he was riding. She was his pride and joy although her temperament was almost as evil as his own. Fleckie was determined to win the contest and this determination was clear to see in the set of his thin shoulders as he cantered around the ring. He cleared both fences easily and then rode off to give the other contestants a try.

He was followed by a very dark-skinned gypsy called Charlie Horner, who came from Lochmaben, another gypsy town on the western side of Scotland. Horner was also well-known because he was infamous for having survived a sentence of transportation to Australia for sheep-stealing. Like Fleckie he returned home after ten years to take up his old career of thieving as if nothing had happened. The day he appeared in the jumping ring was his sixtieth birthday but he was as fit and lean as a man half his age and an expert horseman who had the power of almost lifting mounts over stiff obstacles. For five consecutive years since his return from Botany Bay, Horner had taken the gypsy jumping prize and he was determined to continue doing so.

As Fleckie had done, Horner cleared both the fences and also left the ring to be followed in by Jesse Bailey on his grey horse Barbary. When they entered a rustle swept the crowd, for Jesse was well-known locally. He sat down firmly in his saddle as he circled the field and when he gathered the horse beneath him, he bent forward to whisper something to it. Then they plunged forward in a canter and as they reached the first fence Barbary changed his stride, stood back on his haunches like a cat and reared up high into the air. The man on his back raised himself till he was standing straight upright in the stirrups and together they flowed high over the pole as if they were turned into liquid. Barbary landed with all four feet close together and Jesse spread both arms along his neck with a broad smile on his face. They'd cleared the obstacle by a good foot and a half.

While the crowd was cheering, Odilie turned to Grace with her eyes gleaming in excitement. 'I could do that. I could do that with my little mare. She could out-jump the lot of them, I'm sure of it!'

Grace, who was sitting on the grass rubbing her leg, sighed, 'Oh Odilie, haven't you had enough adventure for one day?'

'No, listen Grace, I'm serious. I'd like to jump,' said Odilie and before Grace could stop her, she stood on tiptoe and shouted out to the gypsy who was in charge of proceedings, 'Can anybody enter a horse?'

He laughed. 'Anybody with an animal good enough!' he called back and an old man beside the girls added, 'But I've been coming here for sixty years and I've never seen this won by anybody except a gypsy.'

The girls faced each other without speaking while Grace shook her head vehemently but Odilie paid no heed to the warning. She held up a hand and told her friend, 'Wait here for me. I won't be long. Go over and tell that big gypsy that I want to enter, too. Go and do it now, Grace. I'll be back in fifteen minutes.' Then she turned and ran off towards the line of trees where her horse was tied up.

Grace stared after her in consternation but, rising obediently to her feet, she limped tiredly through the crowd to the front and pulled at the gypsy's sleeve. 'My friend would like to enter a horse, please,' she said.

He looked down at her in astonishment. 'Where is it?' he asked.

'It'll be here directly. It's being fetched in about fifteen minutes. Can you wait till then?'

Gib laughed good-naturedly. 'All right. We'll hold off for a bit.' He did not mind a slight delay because it gave more time for people to lay bets and for the excitement to rise. He threw back his head and yelled to the crowd, 'We're to have another entry so the jumping will start again in fifteen minutes.'

Adam Scott was about to leave the crowd when he heard this announcement but as he turned to go he noticed that the girl who had spoken to the big gypsy was walking away – and she limped! He stared at her very hard and then his face lightened. He was wearing his broadest smile as he pushed his way through the close-

255

packed ranks of people to reach her and when he did, he put a hand on her shoulder from behind to stop her walking away. Beneath his fingers he felt her jump with surprise. She turned quickly round and stared at him. 'I've been looking for you everywhere,' he said.

She gazed back at him and he saw that her eyes were the same colour as the sky above their heads. As he looked into them a feeling of complete and utter happiness flooded through him in a surge of delightful warmth.

'Oh, it's you!' she said in a wondering voice that showed how pleased she was to see him. Then recovering herself, she spoke more formally and remarked primly, 'It's nice to see you again.'

He looked into her face beneath the floppy bonnet and cast all pretence aside as he told her, 'I was afraid you weren't at the Fair this year. I was so disappointed because I thought you'd gone away and got yourself married or something.'

'Oh no, nothing like that,' she said in a soft voice. He was surprised but pleased as well to see that she was so poorly dressed and wearing such a shabby bonnet. Last year she'd been more ladylike but he did not mind if she turned out to be just a poor country girl, because that gave a shepherd a better chance with her.

Smiling he proffered his arm and told her, 'You look tired. Will you lean on me?'

It seemed to Grace as if the world around her was singing as she took his arm. She smiled at him and said, 'My friend's gone back to town. She's on some scheme . . . I've to wait here till she returns.'

'In that case I'll wait with you. I've been looking for you all day and I've only just found you so I'm not going to lose you again now,' he told her. It was amazing how they slipped into easy conversation, as if their acquaintance had only been interrupted by a few moments and not by a year. They were delighted with each other. He thought she was even prettier than he remembered and she was thrilled by him because he was all she had

256

imagined and more. Neither of them were entirely sure that they were not in fact asleep and dreaming.

'Let's sit down here and wait for Odilie,' she said, sinking on to the grass. He settled by her side and took her hand. It felt so right to be held like that by him. In wonder they stared at each other and the loneliness of them both was completely vanquished.

Meanwhile Canny's daughter was running at full tilt through the press of people, dodging this way and that to avoid collisions, brushing past family groups, swerving round gossipers standing in her path. She grabbed the bridle of her pony from the boy who was watching it and climbed inelegantly aboard, not caring that her skirt was kirtled up around her knees as she pushed her feet into the stirrups. Then she went cantering out of the fairground and back up the road to Lauriston.

In the stableyard of Havanah Court, the boys sitting idly on upturned buckets in the sunshine looked up in astonishment when their mistress came clattering into the yard on the puffing old pony. 'Where's Stevens?' she called imperiously.

They looked shiftily at each other because they knew that in the absence of his employers, the head groom had slipped over the footbridge to see what was going on and cast a professional eye over the gypsy horses.

Odilie groaned, 'I should have guessed – he's gone to the Fair, hasn't he? But you lot can do it. Get my new mare ready. I'm taking her over there now – and hurry up, hurry, hurry!' She slipped off the pony and stood harrying them while the boys ran about, bringing the suede side saddle out of the harness room and giving the chestnut mare's coat a final polish with a silk cloth as Stevens always did before they put on her tackle. Odilie took one look at the saddle and cried, 'Not that! Get me a cross saddle. I'll ride astride!' In a few minutes her pretty little mare was standing fully accoutred on the cobbles and Odilie, adjusting her recalcitrant bonnet, prepared to mount.

At this point one of the older boys protested, 'But Miss Odilie, you cannae ride such a bonny mare dressed like that. You should go in and put on your habit. Your father'll be fair mad if he sees you . . .'

Odilie gathered up the reins and urged her mare forward. 'I haven't time to change. I'm in a hurry. The jumping contest's about to start. I don't want to miss it.'

Then she clattered off again leaving an astounded group of boys staring after her.

The gypsy jumping contest was famous and when the word went round that it was about to start again with an unknown outsider taking part, the other attractions lost their customers and the show people put up boards saying that business would start again in an hour for they too wanted to see the fun.

When Odilie rode up to the ringside, people were pressed close together elbowing each other in search of a good place. Grace saw her arrive and stood up to wave, gesturing that she had spoken to Gib. Odilie waved back and rode directly at the gypsy, forcing her horse through the people. When she was near him she cried out, 'Who jumps first?'

He looked up and she saw a spark of admiration in his eyes which she guessed was for her horse. Trust a gypsy to see the mare's quality first, she thought. She did not realise that she herself looked wild and farouche enough to engender admiration as well. Her stomach was churning with a mixture of emotions – exhilaration, the thrill of danger and the challenge of competition. Gib laughed at her obvious impetuosity. 'Want to make a bet, miss?' he asked.

'All right, I will,' she said, and thrust a hand into her skirt pocket. To his surprise she brought out a golden guinea and proffered it to him.

'Who'll you bet this on?' he wanted to know.

'On myself of course,' said Odilie.

'On yourself?' Gib was genuinely astonished this time.

'Yes, on myself. What odds will you give me?' she demanded.

'Let's get this straight, you can't jump. Women don't jump,' he spluttered.

'Don't be silly,' Odilie told him. 'You've been waiting for the fourth contender, haven't you? Well, that's me. My mare's a fine jumper and so am I. We can do as well as any of those men.'

'Go away miss, you'll get your pretty neck broken,' groaned Gib.

'That's my problem, not yours. I want to jump,' snapped the girl.

In desperation he turned to the other contestants who were waiting impatiently behind him. 'Let's get on with it. We've waited long enough,' snapped Fleckie.

'But this girl says she wants to jump,' said Gib.

'Let her. She'll not last long,' was Fleckie's shouted reply as he rode his horse into the ring at a hard canter.

A rustle swept the crowd because the fences were raised to well over five feet for this second round. Fleckie seemed to have lost his concentration because his horse's hooves tipped the first pole as it leaped and the wooden bar went flying. His supporters groaned, for that meant he was out of the contest. When he realised what had happened, he took a short cane out of his boot and started laying viciously into his horse till his son ran forward and stopped him – not because he was being cruel but because, if he broke the animal's skin, its potential sale price would fall.

Horner entered next and, warned by Fleckie's fate, was very careful, cantering round the ring slowly, eyeing the fences and judging exactly where his horse should leave the ground. Then he rode up at what seemed like a slow pace, gave a touch of the spurs at just the right moment – and cleared them both. The crowd howled delightedly.

Gib's hands were full of money as people laid even more bets and all the while Jesse sat staring straight ahead, seemingly unaware of what went on. His face looked as if it was made of marble, like a pagan statue, with dark ringlets of hair falling in clusters down the back of his neck. Every woman in the crowd was acutely conscious of him.

The crowd was very silent when he came in to jump and again he cleared both fences. He was followed by a neat chestnut that came cantering into the ring with a girl riding astride on its back. She had taken off the blinding sunbonnet and curls of hair flew around her face. Though she was as dark as any gypsy and very poorly dressed, everyone could see that her mare was magnificent and must have cost a good deal of money. The saddlery was top quality as well and the crowd nudged each other in amazement asking, 'D'ye think she's stolen it?'

At the back of the crowd Grace stood up to watch with a face drained of colour. She hung on to Adam Scott's arm, not realising how her fingers were biting into his flesh and gasped, 'Oh, Odilie! I hope she doesn't hurt herself. She's so reckless.' Adam put his hand over hers and tried to calm her but he could feel how she was trembling as she leaned on him.

'Don't look. I'll tell you when it's over,' he whispered. Like Grace, the crowd held its breath while Odilie cantered around the enclosure. She sat well down in the saddle, head high and back as straight as a lady going hunting. 'Go on lass, show them!' came a jocular voice from the audience.

Bending and weaving like a reed in the wind, she headed slowly for the first fence, eyes gazing fearlessly ahead at the obstacle. The mare gathered herself at just the right place, leaped upwards as if it had been propelled from a gun and landed with forelegs extended on the other side. Odilie was still bolt upright and secure in the saddle with her whip unused in her hand. She did exactly the same at the second fence.

The crowd howled in excitement and Adam yelled out, 'She's over them both!'

Grace gave a huge gulp as she opened her eyes and hopped excitedly up and down calling, 'Hooray, well done, hooray!' Even the other contestants raised their fists in congratulation.

'Put the pole up to six feet,' called someone in the crowd and Gib gave the orders for this to be done but said that this time only one fence need be jumped. Then he walked over and asked the girl, 'Are you going to try? It's a big fence.'

She was quite calm. 'Of course I'll try,' she said.

'The lady will go first,' Gib called out to the crowd and once more Odilie entered the ring but this time she decided on a different tactic. Instead of taking a long slow run she set off at a flat-out gallop that sent clumps of earth flying in every direction from her horse's hooves. She and the mare looked like a bundle of gutta-percha as they bounced up in the air, hovered for a moment above the pole – and landed safely on the other side.

'She's done it again, the lassie's jumped clear,' people in the crowd yelled in disbelief and thumped each other on the back as she rode out of the ring. When Horner followed her he sent the fence flying. It was Jesse's turn last and the silence was total as he cantered in. Not a leaf stirred in the sultry air and all that could be heard was the drumming of hooves on the hard ground. He circled the enclosure twice, staring at the fence all the while, and then he gathered his horse – but just at the moment when its hooves should have left the earth, a shot rang out from somewhere among the watchers. All eyes turned to where a swirl of cordite smoke could be seen drifting towards the sky. Someone in the press of people had let off a pistol and the noise made Barbary swerve in terror and bump into the fence. With a terrible crash the pole fell down.

'The lassie's won! The lassie's won!' called out a voice and Horner ran into the ring with his arms in the air.

'You bastard, you did it, you did that!' cried Gib, running in after him and taking the exulting man by his shirt-front. Soon there was a mêlée of fighting gypsies in the middle of the field and Odilie's victory was forgotten as a battle raged around her.

She was looking about with rising panic and wondering how to get away when the gypsy on the grey stallion pushed his way through to her and said, 'You'd better get out of here. Follow me.'

When they emerged on the outside of the enclosure, he turned in his saddle to say to her, 'Well done. You'd probably have won anyway because that's a grasni shantu you've got there.' When she did not react to the Romany expression he added, 'A fine mare, as we say.' He looked in frank admiration at both the girl and her mount. She proudly lifted her chin to meet his glance and in the second that their eyes met, it seemed to both of them that another shot had been fired. Odilie gasped and blinked her eyes as an explosion of light lit up the air around her and Jesse too looked shaken as if he had experienced a shock. Blinking he raised his hand to brush the hair back from his eyes for when the girl's stare met his a strange flash of light had dazzled him. He looked around in surprise but no one else seemed aware of it.

The man and the woman sat gazing fixedly at each other in silence while their horses panted and fidgeted beneath them. They found that they were breathless too and felt as if they had received an earth-shattering shock. The entrancement between them was broken, however, when a man pushed his way through the throng to reach them. He clapped a hand on the shoulder of Jesse's stallion and announced loudly, 'I'm Simon Archer from the Circus Royale and I'm looking for a stunt rider. You were both magnificent – you'd make a wonderful pair in the ring. I'll hire both of you to give a display tonight if you like.'

The mounted gypsy looked down at Simon as if he could not understand what was being said. 'What?' he asked in a bemused way.

Odilie looked at Jesse first and then back at the show-man before shaking her head. 'Sorry, no,' she said. Both men thought that she looked incredibly beautiful with tightly curling tendrils of dark hair clustering around her face and sticking to her cheeks. The heat was oppressive and she raised a bare forearm to wipe her glistening forehead as she gathered up the reins in preparation for riding away.

'Wait,' said Jesse Bailey in a hoarse voice. He ignored Simon completely.

She dropped her reins and looked at him.

'Wait. You bet Gib that you'd win. You'll have to collect your prize – ten bars.' Even to Jesse his own voice sounded strange.

The girl smiled and said, 'That's right. I forgot but it doesn't matter. I don't want the money.'

'Money doesn't matter? Don't be silly.' Jesse sounded angry as if she was belittling the contest.

'I don't want it. I only wanted to win,' she said, picking up the reins again and driving both heels into her mare's flanks.

Simon, standing there, shivered because the physical attraction between them was palpable. He could almost smell it. He looked up at the man again and put a hand on his knee, shaking it this time to secure Jesse's attention as he repeated, 'Listen, I mean it. Come to my ring tonight at seven o'clock. And bring the girl. I'll pay you well if you give that jumping display again. The crowd will love it.'

Jesse looked down with a bemused expression. 'You'd better run after her and ask her yourself. I don't know her,' he said and at that moment, Simon heard someone come up behind him and turned to see the furious face of a young gypsy woman who was staring at the back of the disappearing girl on the chestnut horse with fierce and burning hatred.

'Go away. You heard what he said, he doesn't know her,' she snapped but Archer was having none of it. This is only some sort of affair of the heart, he surmised, and decided to persist. Turning to Jesse again he asked, 'But she's a Romany, isn't she? She's black enough.'

The answer was a shake of the head. 'I don't think so, she can't speak the lingo anyway. I've never seen her before today.' While Jesse spoke Thomassin was standing with a hand on his boot toe as if making a claim to him.

Odilie had only gone a few yards through the crowd, who were all trying to reach up and shake her hand in congratulation and patting her horse, when a furious-looking Professor Thompson pushed his way towards her. He shook an admonishing finger and scolded, 'Miss Rutherford, what have you been thinking of! Your father will be scandalised when he hears about this. My God, you could have broken your neck, girl.'

Odilie flushed scarlet and gathered up her reins hurriedly. There was no use pretending she didn't know him for they'd dined at the same table the previous evening. 'Professor Thompson, my father doesn't know – don't tell him, please. I'm going home now,' she said.

'I should think so too. Home you go at once,' said the outraged Professor and stood with his hands on his hips until Odilie rode out of sight.

Jesse Bailey broke away from Thomassin and Simon Archer and rode up to the Professor's party, leaning down to the first of them, who happened to be young Playfair, to ask, 'Who's that girl? Do you know her name?'

The architect looked up and smiled as he replied, 'Yes, as a matter of fact I do, although I can hardly believe it myself. She's Odilie Rutherford. Her father's a rich merchant and they live in that big house by the river called Havanah Court.'

Jesse sat back in his saddle with an astonished look on his face. 'God in heaven, no wonder she didn't want the money,' he gasped.

Catherine Scott was worried. At the stroke of four o'clock she had a checked cloth spread on the grass in the shade cast by their up-ended pony cart and was directing Leeb and Lily in laying out brown crusted loaves of home baked bread, cheese made from sheep's milk and an enormous game pie. A bottle of buttermilk and another of cold tea provided liquid refreshment – but nobody came to partake of the feast.

It was not unusual for Tom or Sandy to be missing from the family meal for they always remained in the ale tent until fished out, but Mary and Adam had never missed the rendezvous before and their mother hoped that nothing bad had befallen them. She stood up in an anxious way and stared across the field but could not catch a glimpse of either of her missing children. 'Where's Adam and where's Mary?' she fretted.

'Don't take on,' said Lily tolerantly. 'They're both old enough to look after themselves. Maybe they've met up wi' some lads and lasses.' She was right.

At four o'clock, Mary, quite unconscious of the time, was wandering to and fro like someone lost among the bewildering array of stalls with Elsie and the two strangers. Her head was swimming and she found it difficult to focus her eyes because of the beer that was still being pressed on her. By now she had only one wish, to lie down and have a sleep for the heat was oppressive. The young man she was with saw her stifle a yawn and took her elbow, steering her away from the loudly laughing Elsie. 'Come and sit down in the shade,' he said and directed her to a quiet place beneath some willows on the river bank.

Mary hesitated but he was smiling so pleasantly that she gave in and soon they were sitting side by side watching the water flow by. Scattered around them were other couples lying close together in the grass. Mary tried not to notice what they were doing. She yawned again and he patted the grass by his side. 'Lie down and have a nap. I'll guard you,' he suggested. Because she was scandalised by the goings on of the others, she wouldn't lie down though she leaned her back against the bole of a tree but soon, in spite of herself, a strange numbness overtook her and she felt her head nodding . . . 'Oh my God, it must be four o'clock and my mother'll be looking for me. She'd not be happy if she could see me now,' was her last thought before sleep overtook her.

Adam's mother would have been equally astonished and disturbed if she could have seen how engrossed her son was with a girl in a bondager's bonnet. He was gazing into her face, smiling in an entranced way and he was talking more than he had ever talked before. The words flowed out of him because he found it amazingly easy to tell this girl things that he had held inside his head for years. For him the passing of the significant hour of four o'clock had simply been forgotten.

As he walked away from the jumping ring with blue-eyed Grace by his side, he felt immediately proud and resolute for he had come to a momentous decision – this was the girl for him. All his ancestors down through the ages had been obstinate fellows and once Adam made up his mind about something he was impossible to shift. The realisation that he wanted to stay with Grace forever was enough and once it came into his head, he did not question it. He knew that if he missed this opportunity, he would regret it forever.

For her part Grace walked beside him with a smiling, serene face but inside she was churning with a mixture of emotions. She felt exhilarated, but calm too – daring, but safe – deliciously thrilled but nervous. Every fibre of her body tingled with awareness of Adam's proximity, for she found him even more handsome than he was in her dreams and she looked at his tanned face with open admiration. She wished she was bold enough to put up a finger and trace it around his firm mouth. By the way he was watching her she knew that he was equally aware of her and for the first time in her life she felt strong and powerful as she smiled sweetly at him, gazing full into his face as she did so.

They walked along talking as if they had known each other all their lives. He told her about his life in the hills and because their minds were full of the jumping contest she told him about Odilie, who had been born in Jamaica and brought to Lauriston by her father, Canny Rutherford the rich merchant. She confided in Adam how angry Odilie was because of the plan to marry her to the Duke.

'But that's a good match for a merchant's daughter, surely?' he asked in amazement.

'She doesn't think so. It's her father and my father who are pushing her into it,' said Grace.

He paused and stared at her. 'What's your father got to do with it?' he asked.

'Because he's the town lawyer. He's Odilie's father's legal adviser. He wants this marriage to go through because if it's called off the Duke'll be furious and take it out on him,' she explained.

Adam's brow furrowed. 'But why are you dressed like a working girl if you're the lawyer's daughter? Why the ugli?' He looked at her bonnet as he spoke and then down at her boots. 'And only farm lassies wear those . . .' He pointed at her feet.

She laughed. 'Oh, all this is Odilie's idea. She said we should dress up like poor lassies so's we could hide in the crowd and not be recognised. It's been fun, really. I've enjoyed it though I thought I wouldn't.'

Adam was looking disappointed. 'Your father's the lawyer! But I thought you were off a farm like me. Now it turns out you're a lady and I'm only a shepherd. Your father won't let me marry you.'

The words hung in the air between them and she took his hand. 'What did you say?' she asked softly.

'I said your father won't think I'm good enough to marry you,' said Adam.

'Why shouldn't I marry you?' she asked him.

'Because you're above me socially,' he told her but she shook her head.

'That's nonsense. I am a working lassie. I work as a servant in my father's house. I'm not rich – I haven't any dowry. No one except Odilie gives a fig for me. My mother was my father's first wife and now she's dead I'm not important.'

'You're important to me,' said Adam, squeezing her hand tightly.

As they stood close together she looked up and whispered to him, 'Say that again. Say what you did about marrying me.'

He nodded. 'I want to marry you, Grace. I've been dreaming about you all year and now that I've found you my dreams have come true. I don't care if you are the lawyer's daughter. Let's go and see your father right away. I'm not going back home to Fairhope till I know we can be married.'

Her eyes were glistening. 'I've never been so happy in my whole life,' she told him.

'Does that mean you'll marry me?'

'Guess,' she teased. 'Just look at me and guess.' Then she leaned forward and boldly kissed him on the mouth. The world stood still for them both as they clung together, not caring that people around them were nudging each other and laughing but it was all right to kiss in the open at St James' Fair.

When they stood apart again, a clock began chiming over the river. In a daze Adam counted the strokes – one, two, three, four, five. 'It's five o'clock! My mother'll be distracted,' he cried, seizing Grace's hand. 'Come on, we'll have to go and have our tea.'

Mary did not have so pleasant an awakening. She came back to consciousness because someone was lying heavily on top of her and grappling with her clothes. She tried to sit up but found that the young man who said he would guard her was wrestling her to the ground. 'Lie still, you silly bitch,' he grunted as he tried to pull away the neckerchief she wore crossed over her breasts.

Mary screamed. 'Let me up! Leave me alone,' she started to shout.

He put one hand over her mouth and said through gritted teeth, 'Stop struggling or I'll smother you and throw you in the river.'

She could tell by the staring look in his eyes that he was serious and she started to cry, trying to bite the palm of his hand at the same time. She felt her teeth bite into the flesh but his other hand came swinging over and crashed into the side of her head, half-stunning her.

'Lie still, I tell you! You've been asking for it all day,' he snarled, tearing at her petticoat. Mary sobbed and heaved around but she knew it was useless. He was too big and strong for her. This must be what the gypsy woman foresaw, she thought. I took the wrong road when I came here with this man.

She had almost given up hope and was ceasing to struggle when she felt the weight suddenly lift off her and heard strange scuffling noises. She opened her eyes in time to see Jockie Armstrong drawing back his arm to hit her assailant in the face. The stranger went down on his knees with the force of the blow and then scuttled away like an ape with Jockie running after him. Still crying, Mary stood up rearranging her tattered finery and brushing grass and twigs out of her skirt. She felt bitterly ashamed of herself for being found in such a compromising situation but when Jockie came back he put an arm around her and seemed to think no less of her for it.

'I heard you yell, Mary,' he said, 'and when I saw what he was trying to do, I let him have it. He'll not try it on again with another lassie in a hurry.'

There was blood on his cheek but a pleased smile on his face as he spoke. To her he looked like a knight in armour. 'Oh Jockie,' she gasped and threw herself into his arms. 'Thank God you were there.'

'Of course I was here. I've been following you about a' day,' said the phlegmatic Jockie.

Then five o'clock struck and it was Mary's turn to gasp, 'Oh, my mother'll be worried about me. Come on and have some tea with us. My family will be awful pleased to meet you.'

There was nothing Professor Thompson liked better than possessing information about someone that they did not know themselves. Although Odilie had asked him not to tell her father about her exploits in the jumping ring, it was impossible for him to keep the secret. This was really something he had over old Canny and Wattie was like a little boy again as he rushed across the grass towards the place he had last seen his old friend. After all, he told himself, it was best that Canny got the news from a friend and was warned in advance before the town was abuzz with the story.

At every Fair the current Duke always hosted a party in an enormous pavilion erected on a prime site by the side of the river. People of importance were ceremoniously invited to partake of his Grace's hospitality and this year an invitation had been extended to Mr William Rutherford who turned up accompanied by his black footman to be plied with excellent chilled champagne.

When the Duke enquired into the whereabouts of Odilie, Canny put on a concerned face and said that she would join them shortly for she had been suffering from a headache brought on by the extreme heat of the day. Then as soon as he could, he whispered to Joe to go back to Havanah Court and fetch the missing girl.

Time crept by and champagne flowed. The heat outside built up but the green shade inside the tent was cool and comfortable. As they sipped at their glasses, people chatted about the weather and predicted thunder. Canny's anxiety, though not disappearing, was softened. Joe would be back soon bringing Odilie with him, he told himself.

He had just accepted a fifth glass of wine when Wattie Thompson popped up by his side with a knowing look on his face.

'Canny,' he whispered, looking at his old friend through his professorial glasses. 'Canny, where's your lassie?'

Canny gazed casually around as if Odilie had been merely mislaid somewhere in the crowd. 'She's coming, Wattie. She's coming, of course,' he said affably.

His assumption of ease and lack of anxiety deceived the Professor. 'So you know about her being at the jumping then?' he asked in tones of amazement.

Odilie's father's poise slipped. 'Jumping? What jumping?'

Thompson beamed. 'I've just seen your lassie all dressed up like a bondager over at the horse jumping,' he said, lowering his voice and looking around shiftily as he spoke.

Canny heaved a sigh of relief. If that was all he didn't really care. 'Of course, I should have guessed she'd go

270

there. She's mad on horses. Joe'll find her because he'll look beside the horses first. He knows her as well as I do.' He took another swig of champagne and beamed happily at Thompson but a restraining hand was laid on his arm.

'He'll not find her there now – I sent her home. But by God, Canny, you shouldn't let her take such chances. Even though she's a fine horsewoman she could have broken her neck jumping out there against those cut-throats of gypsies. She gave a great display though, I'll say that for her. The crowd loved it.'

Canny gaped at him. 'Broken her neck? How? The crowd loved it – what crowd?'

Thompson was thoroughly enjoying himself. 'Man, don't you know! Your girl won the jumping contest. She beat that good-looking gypsy laddie, the one to whom I offered ten pounds to come to Edinburgh for my anatomy class. What a physical specimen! But that's another matter altogether.'

Canny shook his head to clear the ringing from his ears. 'She did what?' He still couldn't believe what he was hearing. At that moment Joe entered the tent looking solemn and shaking his head. Canny reeled and the bearer of the astonishing news was gratified by the way his tidings had been received for he liked causing a sensation, especially back home in Lauriston. He bent nearer to Canny's ear and whispered urgently, 'Listen to what I'm saying. Your girl won the gypsy jumping contest. She cleared nearly six foot on a chestnut mare and she was all dressed up as a bondager so I didn't recognise her at first but it was her right enough. The gypsies are as mad as wasps about it – especially the women.'

Thompson stood back smiling, remembering the look on the face of the girl in the red shawl as she gazed after Odilie Rutherford. But now he found he was speaking to an empty space for his schoolfriend was bustling towards the tent flap without so much as a goodbye.

When Odilie reached home she only had time to hand over her horse to the waiting grooms and hurry across

271

the courtyard to the house before her father appeared with Joe driving their gig at a furious pace. Canny's face was scarlet and he was puffing like a grampus so she looked extremely guilty when she saw him advancing towards her.

'Papa, sit down. Don't get so excited, it's not good for you,' she cried.

'Not good for me! You'll be the death of me! Thompson's in the Duke's tent talking about you winning some jumping contest and you're here cool as a cucumber telling me not to get excited. I can't believe what I'm hearing.'

She folded her hands in a beseeching attitude and looked over her father's shoulder at Joe, whom she could see was vastly amused by what had happened. 'Yes, I admit it. I did win the jumping. I'm sorry, I didn't think you'd mind. It was all on impulse. I knew the mare could do it. But no one knew who I am. Look how I'm dressed.' She held out the striped working skirt with one hand.

'My God, does that make it better? Thompson knew you quick enough and his tongue's wagging already,' cried her father.

Odilie tried soothing him. 'But he's the only one. Surely if you ask him to keep quiet, he will. I'm sorry, Papa. I promise that for the rest of the Fair I'll be such a lady that you'll hardly know me. I promise I won't let you down from this minute on.'

She walked up and put her arms around his neck, kissing him on the cheek. Canny visibly melted and his thunderous expression became more benign. 'Oh Odilie, why don't you *think* first before you do things? I'm afraid you've taken after me in that respect. Oh heavens bless us, how are we going to stop this whole town hearing about all your doings before nightfall?'

She stepped back a little from him with her eyes dancing. 'But I won, Papa, didn't I? You should have seen that contest – you'd have been so proud. The mare jumped like a bird. What a feeling it was – I thought I was flying.' Her voice was ecstatic.

272

'Thompson did say you put on a great display,' agreed Canny, who was unable to conceal the pride in his voice.

And Joe chimed in from behind him, 'Everyone's talkin' about it. Miss Odilie was a sensation.'

Then Canny remembered that he at least must continue to reprimand her, so he shot a quelling glance at Joe and told his daughter sternly, 'But it wasn't *ladylike*, Odilie.'

She went on mollifying him. 'Who cares about being a lady when she can be a Duchess and do what she likes – that's what you said, anyway. Besides, I think I won quite a lot of money, about thirty pounds! I didn't take it, though. The gypsies'll drink it tonight no doubt.'

Then she burst out laughing and her father knew he was beaten but he still sounded concerned when he asked, 'And where's young Grace Elliot? She was with you at the Fair, wasn't she? Her father probably hasn't heard about all this yet but he'll be furious with her when he does.'

Odilie put her hands to her mouth and gasped, 'Oh poor Grace! She mustn't get into trouble because of me. But she's all right, Father. I left her with a fine-looking young fellow.'

'You left her with a man? Who?'

'I don't know his name but he looked respectable enough.'

'Odilie, this gets worse and worse. Let's hope nothing happens to the poor lassie,' groaned her father.

At this point Joe Cannonball drew a letter from the pocket in the skirt of his linen coat and brandished it at Odilie with a broad grin on his face. 'This letter came for you when you were out, Baby,' he lied.

She took it from him, feigning surprise, and read it. Then she explained to her father, 'The Duke's invited me to join his party at the Fair. What a pity. They'll all have gone home by now.'

Canny shook his head. 'Oh no, he and his party were in the big tent when I left ten minutes ago. You'd better dress yourself properly and get across there directly.'

Odilie sobered. All at once it seemed that the glory had

gone out of the sun. Her day of mischief, her day of being someone else, was over.

In the field the Fair was still going on at full pitch. Adam Scott who was walking with Grace towards the lines of horses, looked up at the sky and frowned because instead of being bright blue and cloudless, the expanse above his head was slowly turning a deep shade of brownish purple like chased bronze. The sun still beamed down relentlessly but without its previous happy shimmer; it now held a gleam like the reflection from a shield of war, threatening and full of foreboding.

'I think it's going to thunder soon,' he told his girl and as if to confirm his words, far away could be heard a muffled peal of thunder like the drumroll of an advancing army. Grace, who did not like thunderstorms, looked scared but Adam told her, 'Don't worry, it won't come yet. It's only threatening. It might not arrive till tomorrow but it's on its way.'

He took her hand and said, 'Come on, my family will be wondering where I've got to.'

Grace had been limping along but now she said, 'Wait,' and sat down on the grass to unlace the heavy boots and draw them off her white feet. 'They hurt me,' she explained. 'It was Odilie's idea to wear them. It's easier to walk barefoot – and cooler too in this heat.'

Adam sat beside her and put a hand on her bare left foot as he said, 'There's not much wrong with it, is there? But I think your limp's very appealing. It's what made me want to take care of you for the rest of our lives.'

She looked up at him with the eyes of love. 'It's strange but I don't care about my limp any more since I met you. A healer woman I met at Bettyhill yesterday said it could be cured. She told me to meet her here at the Fair. Perhaps you'll come with me after we've been to see your family, Adam.'

He nodded. 'Yes, of course I will. But don't worry about a cure – you're perfect as you are.' Then he added, 'Isn't this amazing? It feels as if we've known each other

274

for ever. I want you to start at the beginning and tell me all about your life, Grace.'

Her confidence in him was complete and she allowed pent-up words to flow out of her in a rush. He nodded as he listened and she could tell he understood.

She started with, 'I can only vaguely remember my mother. Her name was Lucy Allen and she went away for some reason. When I think of her I feel that she's a friend like Odilie, not a mother really. In my memory she's just a girl, pretty and gentle, soft to the touch and always kissing me. Then she disappeared. That bit's black in my memory.'

There was a short pause as she remembered that unhappy time and then, with a sad look on her face, she continued, 'My father must have married Hester quite soon after my mother went away. I really hate her. I know you shouldn't hate people but she's so cruel. She made me believe that people were whispering about me and I thought it was because of my leg . . . the woman in Bettymill knew all about me. There's so many questions that I've thought of since I met her and I want to ask her. I must see her again.'

He nodded. 'You will, don't worry. I'll take you to find her but you mustn't be disappointed or sad whatever she tells you because it sounds like a very unhappy story and none of it could have been your fault.'

Grace shook her head. 'I won't be sad, I only want to know. It's awful not knowing.'

He stared into her eyes. 'I understand. We'll go and look for the woman but let's go to see my mother first.' When he led her across the grass she left her heavy boots behind beneath the trees.

Catherine Scott was fretting as she bustled about around her pony cart. A tarpaulin had been stretched from the back flap and was supported on a pair of poles making a shelter from the sun for the family. Tom and Sandy had been fetched out of the ale tent by Lily and they were a very subdued pair sitting eating slices of game pie. Leeb was there of course and so was Mary, flush-

275

faced and flustered-looking in the company of the brawny young man who was introduced as Jockie Armstrong. But where was Adam?

'I saw our Adam in the crowd at the jumping and he had a lassie with him,' Mary told her mother.

'Good for him,' said Tom, reaching out for another slice of pie. 'I met a lassie here once too, d'ye remember, Catherine?'

'I remember well enough,' she said, pushing his hand away from the pie. 'You've had your share of that. I'm keeping it for Adam. Oh, where is he?'

Mary, still blushing, created a diversion by saying, 'Ma, Jockie here has asked me to marry him.'

Catherine looked up from her task of covering up the precious pie. 'And will you, Mary?'

The girl glanced at her awkward swain who was shuffling about in the background. 'I might. He's awful persistent. He'll no' go away and he's aye there when I need him.'

'That's a good reason to marry somebody,' said Catherine approvingly, but she could not give her full attention to the betrothal because of her worry about Adam. Mary's news seemed to have fallen flat as her mother looked out across the field again and groaned, 'Oh, where's Adam do you think?'

'Och, cut into the pie and gie' us all another piece,' said her brother Sandy. 'The laddie'll turn up when he's ready. If he's courting he'll not be wanting any pie.'

The situation was saved when, 'Here's Adam coming now,' called little Leeb staring out from under the tarpaulin flap. 'And he's got a lassie with him!'

Grace was shy but that, plus her limp, endeared her to Adam's family who all had tender hearts. They fussed around, making sure she sat in a shady place and pushed food on to her plate. Then they sat back and tried not to show that they were scrutinising her while she flushed under their concerted stare.

'Grace is from Lauriston. Her father's Mr Elliott, the lawyer,' said Adam by way of introduction. His family

276

nodded in unison, much impressed. 'We're getting married,' was his next announcement.

His mother gasped, 'Not you too!' astounded that her family could achieve two engagements at one Fair. Then she added, 'So soon? At least Mary knew her lad before today. But you've only just met, haven't you?'

'We first met last year and I went looking for her this year again,' said her son and Catherine was slightly mollified, for that seemed suitably lover-like to her. She smiled at Grace and said, 'I hope you know it's a hard life in the hills, lassie. And it's lonely. Have you enough inside yourself for that?'

Grace passed the test by not looking confused at the question. Only those with enough inside themselves knew what was being asked. 'I think so,' she said softly, 'and anyway I love Adam.'

First his mother and then his aunt and sisters kissed her while his father, uncle and future brother-in-law wrung Adam's hand. They were all romantics and the deal was done as far as they were concerned. Two marriages had been arranged.

CHAPTER 10

As she bustled about with all her family around her, Catherine became calmer and more able to appreciate all that had happened. She looked at her dear Mary, fluttering and flirtatious, though she pretended not to be impressed by the dogged determination of her suitor Jockie. That big lad was good and true, decided Catherine, and he'd marry Mary right enough and prove to be a good provider: she could see that. In relief, she turned to her daughter and grasped her in a fond embrace that made up for her earlier distraction.

Then she let her attention turn to Adam. His lassie looked awfully delicate and his mother hoped that a life in the hills would improve her strength and bring some colour to her cheeks. Catherine furrowed her brow. There was something she remembered hearing about the Lauriston lawyer's family – what was it? Lily, her sister-in-law, would know because she loved gossip and could trace the genealogies of most local families back for at least four generations. Yes, Lily would have all the information on the Elliots but Catherine would have to wait till Adam and the lassie were out of the way before she could ask.

'Maybe we should be making our road home soon,' she mused as she looked out at the crowds of people still filling the fairground. It was best to go before the rush began and people all headed for the exit at the same time. Besides she always wanted to be away before the Yetholm knives were drawn and the drunks began fighting.

'Oh no, not yet,' cried her children in unison and Tom looked up to agree with them.

'Not yet, Catherine. That thunder's far away. It's only a warning. The weather'll not break till tomorrow.'

'You mean you've not had long enough in the ale tent,'

278

scolded his wife but she respected his wishes as well as his weather lore.

Now it was Mary's turn to speak. 'Jockie'll see me back to Morebattle so don't let the dray wait for me,' she told her Aunt Lily and Uncle Sandy. 'He's brought his own gig.'

The family all looked at the silent Jockie Armstrong with respect. To be driving his own gig at his age was a big recommendation for him as a husband for Mary.

Then Adam stood up. 'If you're going home don't worry about me. I'll hitch a ride on some cart going back to Hownam later tonight. Grace and I have things to do – we've got to speak to her father and we've to see some friend she has at the freak show,' he said, taking Grace by the hand.

His mother cried out, 'But lassie, you've nothing on your feet! When the dew falls, you'll catch your death.'

Grace looked down and wriggled her bare toes in the grass. 'It feels lovely and it's not a bit cold. I like going barefoot,' she said. Then, as if this was a signal between them, she and Adam rose to their feet and after taking their farewells, went off together in the direction of the main concourse.

They headed for the broad walk that stretched down towards the river from where the gypsies camped. At one end of it stood a pair of official tents used by the Provost of Jedburgh and his companions who had the administration and policing of the Fair as their responsibility, while at the other end, surrounded by a roped-off enclosure, was the impressive tent set aside for the Duke.

The lovers walked past the Duke's tent and along a line of attractions for children – coconut shies and canvas-backed open stalls where balls could be thrown at the heads of Frenchmen mounted on poles. Then they reached the animal and freak shows where the noise and the array of horrors chilled the blood though even the most gullible knew that many of the bizarre exhibits were only tricks. In the middle of the row they found the largest show of all, a curtained platform surmounted by a banner with *Archer's Freaks – Wonders of the World* emblazoned along it.

The very tall man with the long mournful face was still playing his fiddle on the platform and the tiny dwarf was still banging his drum.

'Is Mr or Mrs Archer about?' called out Grace and the dwarf nodded, pointing over his shoulder with the drumstick. Grace and Adam walked in the direction he had indicated and found themselves in a hidden encampment behind the platform. From the dark caravans, dwarves glowered at them and a miniature woman cuddled a baby protectively. Grace's sensitive soul ached for the people who were on show because her own lameness gave her some inkling of how isolated and cheated they must feel. She was sorrowful-faced by the time they reached the last caravan of all and a big dog on guard at its door stood up growling threateningly at their approach. But its noise was heard and a voice called its name. A hand pulled its chain back when the hidden watcher saw who they were. Jem emerged from the caravan door and beckoned them up the steps.

Billy, his shirt sweat-stained, sat on a stool in the farthest corner of the caravan with his hands hanging down between his knees. His head was lolling and his shoulders drooped as if he was asleep but his eyes revealed wakefulness because the whites could be seen glistening between slits of eyelids as he stared blankly at the light. As Grace and Adam entered, Alice was standing in the space in the middle of the floor but when she saw strangers in the doorway, she drew back into the shadows. Jem however raised his hand and told her, 'It's all right Alice, it's your friends. It's the girl who was here looking for you earlier.'

The woman turned quickly on her heel with her face suddenly vibrant and alive, blazing with energy and emotion as if a light had been lit behind it. She rushed towards Grace with her hands extended, crying out, 'Oh, I'm so glad it's you, my dear. I wondered if you'd come. I'm so pleased to see you. Look Jem, this is the girl I met at Bettymill. Come in and sit down, my dear. Come in, come in, I want to look at you.' She sounded as if she was greeting a long lost relative and Grace looked flustered and surprised as she found herself being pulled through the painted doorway into the big green caravan.

Before she could settle down, however, she was startled by a strange gulping sound. Alice saw her disquiet and said reassuringly, 'Don't worry. It's only Billy, he's crying. Something's upset him today.' She turned and said to the huddled figure in the corner, 'Hush Billy. Nothing's wrong. Being shut up in this heat has been too much for you.'

Jem pushed his way down the caravan and took Billy's hand. He raised him to his feet and led off the sobbing figure. They listened to the sorrowful sounds receding as the shambling lad was taken out into the evening air and Alice called out after them, 'Let him sit outside for a while, Jem. It'll be like a furnace in his own caravan. I'll give him another potion before the show starts.'

Then she went over to a little barrel in the corner from which she drew two mugs of beer and carried them out to Billy and Jem, who downed them in a trice. Billy wiped his mouth with the back of his hand and smiled waveringly at her.

'You liked that, didn't you?' she asked and he nodded. 'I liked it,' he said. When Billy was calmer he could speak properly, as well as understand what was being said to him.

Jem and Alice nodded to each other and Jem put a shackle round Billy's ankle before locking its other end to the caravan wheel. Meanwhile Alice was bustling back into the caravan, bringing out bread and cheese and filling mugs of beer for Adam and Grace. Though they had no appetite after their gargantuan tea with the Scotts, they ate and drank politely rather than hurt her feelings.

Before they could settle down to talk to each other, however, another figure loomed up by the caravan door. It was Professor Thompson, who pointed at Billy and without any formal greeting asked Jem, 'I've been wondering how you keep that one under control. What's the secret? D'ye have to dope him much?'

'My woman – Alice, my wife – gives him potions and rubs things into his skin. We wouldn't be able to keep him quiet without that. He'd tear the place apart,' was the reply. Jem recognised the man who was speaking to him.

The Professor went up to Billy and spoke in a coaxing voice as if he was addressing a dog. 'Come on lad, let me see you,' he said.

Obediently Billy rose and stood erect but he didn't like strangers and his eyes were reddened and his lips working, twisting and contorting as if he was trying to say something and the words would not come out.

Jem took pity on him and explained, 'This is Professor Thompson, an old friend of mine and of yours, Billy. He knew you when you were a little lad. He knew your great-granny.'

Billy gave a groan and a sound like 'Granny', came from his mouth. Then he started to cry again.

'He's just seen her and he's upset. But he'll forget soon. He doesn't remember anything for more than a couple of hours,' explained Jem to the Professor, who nodded vigorously with an interested expression on his face as he looked searchingly at Billy.

When he'd gazed his fill he turned to his companions who were standing well back from the wild man and gestured, 'Look at his shoulders. Look at his biceps – what a specimen! With that body he must be related to the fellow who won the jumping. If he'd been born with even an ounce of sense he'd have been a world champion prize fighter, but his cranium is completely empty.' He then turned to Alice and asked, 'What did you say you give him?'

To Grace's surprise Alice replied in a pert Cockney voice not unlike Jem's, 'I give 'im ground ivy in 'is beer every morning and if 'e's bad 'e gets poppy paste. I make it into an ointment and rub it on 'im – 'ere.' She indicated the inside of her elbow.

'Can't do any harm I suppose,' mused the Professor, 'but watch him. I didn't expect him to grow so big when Jem took him on. He must weigh upwards of fifteen stone now.'

'Sixteen!' said Jem proudly. 'He once upset his caravan just by throwing himself at the walls.'

'My God, poor creature,' said the Professor. 'Tell you what! When he dies, Jem, I'll give you a hundred pounds if you bring me the body.'

Jem's face was sombre. 'I'll be a sad man that day. I'm fond of him.' He made a soothing sound to Billy, who sat back down again looking confused.

'Something'll have to happen soon. He's not going to get any quieter,' said the Professor in a brisk way as he departed, calling back over his shoulder, 'Remember – a hundred pounds for the body.'

While the shadows of the evening lengthened outside, Grace and Adam sat eating the food that Alice pressed on them. Then, when Jem and the young man began discussing shepherding, Grace felt Alice's hand reach out and grasp hers in the semi-darkness. How strange that I should feel such sympathy with this woman, she thought. It's as if there's a bond between us.

Alice leaned forward and asked, 'Can I have another look at your leg, my dear?' They stepped further into the dim interior and all of a sudden, as if she could not help herself, Alice threw her arms around the girl and hugged her close. 'Oh my dear, you're so lovely. Just the way I hoped you'd be. I'm so happy for you,' she said with a sob in her voice.

'Have you any children?' asked Grace and Alice's face went bleak.

'No, no – I had a baby but I lost it. In fact I lost two,' she said in a stumbling way.

'I'm sorry,' apologised Grace but Alice only said, 'Don't worry. It was bad at the time but it's long ago now.'

'You said you'd tell me about my mother,' whispered Grace. The subject had hung unmentioned between them

283

since she first sat down but now she felt that Alice wanted to talk and the mention of her leg was only a pretext.

'What do you want to know?' Alice's hands were still holding Grace's.

'Where did you meet her?' The lamps were coming on in the caravans all around them and it seemed they were alone in a secret little dark place that encouraged confidences.

Alice frowned. 'I first met her here in this countryside at Bettymill, but I got to know her best in London.'

'When was that?'

'About twelve years ago.'

Grace nodded. 'When I was six. That's when I thought she'd died. But why did she go away?'

Alice's eyes were dark and haunted as she stared out into the gathering evening and Grace sat forward attentively awaiting her reply. 'She went away because she had to – she hadn't any choice. She was sent away but she grieved sore at having to leave you. Every time she saw a child the same age as you her whole body ached . . . the pain was awful.' Alice's voice was eloquent with suffering.

Grace's expression grew harrowed but she persisted. 'If she loved me so much why didn't she take me with her?'

'Your father wouldn't let her do that.' Alice's tone became hard.

'You know my father too? I can't understand why he wanted to keep me because he's never cared about me. I've only been a nuisance to him.'

'But *she* cared for you so he kept you. It was to punish her. Besides, she couldn't take you where she was going.'

Grace furrowed her brow. 'Where was that? Did she leave him for another man?'

'Oh, no. She went away alone. She didn't know what lay before her and it was just as well. After that she began to see life through new eyes. That was when she changed.'

Jem half-turned on the step and was gazing in at Alice with a worried look on his face while she was speaking. She looked over at him from time to time as if she was telling him something as well as Grace. Both he and Adam were listening intently to what was being said between the women.

'Tell me about Lucy. Tell me everything you remember,' pleaded the girl.

'She was a wilful, spoiled lassie when she was young. Her father doted on her because her mother died when she was wee and there was only the two of them. She had a lot of yellow hair that she was very proud of, a bit conceited I suppose but that didn't last long. She liked singing and dancing and enjoying herself too . . . that didn't last, either. She used to believe what people told her. That was the first thing to change.'

Alice's tone was bleak and Grace shivered as she listened. Then she asked in a trembling voice, 'When did she die? What did she die of?'

Alice looked at Jem and asked, 'When did she die? I can't really say.'

Jem's rough voice sounded low and consoling as he spoke to his wife. 'I don't think she died, Alice.'

She looked across at him with her eyes glistening and said, 'Oh, she died all right, Jem. That girl died.'

Grace put a hand up to her eyes and gave a sob. 'I wish she hadn't. I wish I'd known her and could remember her better.'

Alice threw her arms around the girl. 'Don't cry, don't cry. She'd be so proud if she could see you now and this young lad with you. She'd bless you both.'

Adam stood up and came into the caravan to hold the weeping Grace's hand as he said to Alice, 'We're getting married, Mrs Archer.'

'I thought you might be. I hope you're very happy. Where will you live?'

He told her. 'We'll start at Fairhope above Hownam in the Cheviots. My father's a shepherd there and we've an empty cottage on the place but one day I hope to buy a wee hill farm of my own. That'll be a while yet though.'

Alice looked at Grace with her eyes shining. 'Maybe not so long. Isn't it lucky I met you at this time! When's the wedding? Don't wait, do it now – life's short, you know.'

'We're going to tell my father tonight,' said the girl.

Alice laughed. 'That'll be a shock to him. Ask him about your dowry when you're at it.'

Grace shook her head. 'Oh, I've no dowry. I told you that before but I think he'll be glad to be rid of me.'

'I wouldn't be too sure. You ask about your dowry anyway. Your mother's father was a rich man and you're her only child. Ask what happened to her fortune. But if you want advice from me, get married before you tell him. There's a marriage tent pitched down at the bottom of the field. Go there and get wed before you tell Elliot. It'll be legal enough. Jem and I were thinking of doing it ourselves, weren't we Jem?'

The young couple stared and Grace asked, 'But aren't you married already?'

'We're a couple of old sinners but we're married in our minds though not officially. We've been meaning to do it for a long time. Maybe we'll manage it one day. Jem wants to, don't you, old man?'

'I do that,' he said fervently.

Grace and Adam looked at each other with love in their eyes and he was the first to speak. 'I'm ready. Let's go down to the marriage tent and get wed,' he said to her.

She gently took his hand. 'Oh, I want to – but it's only right that we tell my father before we do, and your people too. I could see how close you are to them. They'll feel hurt if you got married without letting them know. We shouldn't rush into it like two runaways.'

Alice seemed inexplicably agitated. 'I've been thinking – don't worry about telling your father. Get married first and tell him afterwards. Go and do it, Grace.'

Jem was surprised at her vehemence. 'Hold hard, Alice! You're telling them to rush into something you'd want to think about first yourself. The lass must tell her father. How old are you anyway, Grace?'

'I'm eighteen,' said the girl.

'That's legal up here. She can be married without her father's approval,' said Alice urgently.

'Who's to say he won't give it?' asked Jem, puzzled.

'You don't know Andrew Elliot like I do . . .' said Alice and as soon as she'd spoken, her voice fell and the words died away. They were all looking at her in astonishment and she followed her outburst up by saying weakly, 'Oh, perhaps I'm being too impetuous. It's just so romantic . . . Yes, go and tell your father Grace, but if there's any trouble come back here to me and I'll see what I can do.'

'What you can do?' repeated Jem in amazement gazing at her, but she avoided his eye.

'Remember to come back and tell me if he's difficult,' she repeated urgently.

Grace stood up, full of resolution and excitement. 'All right, I'll come back,' she promised, 'but there's such a lot to do. I want to find Odilie and tell her too because she's my dearest friend and if I do get married today I want her to be there. She'll be so surprised. This is like a dream. And I'll have to dress myself properly. I can't get married like this . . .' She looked down at her working clothes and bare feet.

'I don't mind having a barefoot bride but if you want to be dressed fancy that's all right with me too. Let's hurry before the marrying man gets too drunk to remember what to say!' laughed Adam.

When the young couple hurried off into the gathering darkness, Jem and Alice stood at the door of their caravan watching them go. As they turned the corner and disappeared she shivered and he put an arm around her, hugging her close to him. 'I'm sorry you're upset Alice. But what's going on? I've not seen you so agitated for ages. What are you afraid of?'

She looked at him and said slowly, 'I'm afraid of Andrew Elliot, Jem. He's up to no good with that girl because of the property that was left to her. Oh Jem, I'm so frightened. This is not turning out the way I thought it would. There's still so much that I haven't done and I'm afraid to do it.'

He shook his head. Some of the puzzle was falling into place for him but he had not yet worked out all the unanswered questions. 'Don't be afraid. You're the bravest woman I know. And you've only to tell me when you want help. Just say the word, Alice, and I'll be there.'

'I have to do this by myself but I'll tell you the whole tale when it's finished,' she promised him solemnly.

There were noisy drunks filling the field and evening was drawing in when Adam and Grace found themselves outside the marrying tent. Adam peered inside and saw a tall man with a face like an ape and very long arms, dressed in a rusty black suit and a dirty cravat, sitting on a rickety chair with a bottle of porter on the grass near his foot. Three collie dogs lay beside him and empty bottles and bunches of wilting summer flowers, relics of other weddings that had taken place during the long day, were scattered around his feet. When he saw Adam peering in he looked up blearily and brightened at the sight of another amorous couple. 'Come in, come in. Are you for a wedding? Just haud on a whilie till I find a couple of folk for witnesses . . .'

He got up and reeled towards the tent door but Adam put out a hand to stop him. 'Yes, we're wanting to marry but not yet. We'll come back in an hour – exactly an hour – and I want to be sure that you'll be here then and that you'll be sober.'

'Patie Mudie'll be here. I'm ready and willing to marry folk till midnight. I'm not so sure about the sober, though, but that doesnae matter, it's no' me that's taking a wife, it's no' me that'll wake up sorry in the morning. Patie Mudie's my name and dinna forget it. I'm the best marrier in the district. I marry folk in the toll-house at the end of Coldstream Bridge and I've joined some real nobs thegither. There's another man who's trying to do the marrying here today, but he's not as good as Patie – or as cheap.' He laid a finger along his bulbous nose and peered bibulously at the young couple.

'How much will it cost?' asked Adam. The question of money had not occurred to him before.

'Five pounds?' ventured Mudie.

Grace and Adam were obviously disappointed. 'I haven't got so much money,' whispered Adam to his would-be bride.

Patie Mudie heard him. 'A pound then,' he offered, looking at the bride's costume and doing a rapid calculation about how much he was likely to squeeze out of them. He'd marry a beggar couple for a florin and this girl was obviously just a farmservant but the laddie was dressed like a shepherd and he could rise to a pound surely. The calculation was correct.

'I'll pay a pound,' said Adam with relief in his voice. 'And you're sure it's legal? We'll be married for true when you've done with us?'

'As true as death and as legal as a lawyer's will, you can be sure of that. It's all right, dinna worry. I ken my Scots law and I dinna pretend to be a meenister or onything daft like that,' was the promise.

Outside, lamps were sparking into light all over the showground, filling it with wonder and romance. The field that was once a town was becoming a place of fantasy. Grace's eyes shone in the lamplight when the couple stood in bedazzlement at Patie Mudie's tent door, staring at each other in happiness and delight. Every now and again a distant drumroll of thunder could still be heard as if the approaching storm was reminding everyone that it was on its way and could strike when it chose.

She broke the spell by gently touching Adam's arm and telling him, 'Come with me and I'll show you which house is my home. Then I'll go to Havanah Court to tell Odilie what's happened before going home to break it to my father. You go back and tell your people while I'm at Odilie's and meet me again at Viewhill. We'll face Father and Hester together. I'll need you with me when I do that.'

She put her arms around him and kissed him on the lips. The sweetness of the embrace made them both breathless with delight and desire. 'I love you so much,' she sighed, but when he tried to kiss her again, she pushed him firmly away. 'Not now. Come on, we've so much to do. We mustn't let ourselves be side-tracked – no matter how much we want to.'

The footbridge was groaning and creaking beneath the weight of crowds of people returning home from the Fair. Pushing across it were tired adults carrying sleeping or querulous children, all exhausted by enjoyment; there were staggering drunks who every now and again broke into bursts of song; there were old people straggling in groups and gossiping among themselves about the scenes they had witnessed that day; there were lovers with arms amorously entwined; there were traders with empty baskets on their arms and pockets swinging full of coins, for this had been a good day for them thanks to the clemency of the kindly weather.

Holding Adam's hand, Grace limped along in the middle of the press of people, jostled from every side, but happier than she had ever been before. She did not feel tired any longer and her leg did not hurt for she was buoyed up with an almost uncontainable energy and excitement. When they reached the far bank, she pointed up at a grim grey fortress of a house that reared above her head. 'That's Viewhill,' she told him. 'Be at the gate in three-quarters of an hour. Now back you go and tell your family. I hope that they've not set off for home already. I want them to come to our wedding.' They kissed once more with passion and then they parted.

Havanah Court was blazing with light when Grace turned in at the tall gate-posts. For a second it seemed as if Joe did not recognise her when he first answered the door but he took a second look and exclaimed in astonishment, 'Oh, it's you, Miss Grace! Don't you look fine! But you're in trouble, Miss, your father's been down here twice tonight looking for you.'

She put up a hand to stop him and said, 'No, no, I don't care about him. Let me in. I must see Miss Odilie. Where is she?' Her tone was quite different from that normally used by the shy and humble Grace and Joe stood back with respect as she swept inside.

'Well, I can tell you one thing that's happened at the Fair today. Miss Grace's sure had a revelation of some sort,' he announced in the servants' hall when he went downstairs.

Odilie was lying on her pretty bed with its flower-embroidered curtains when Grace rushed into her bedroom. She looked as if she had been crying but Odilie never cried, thought Grace, she was probably only tired. Excitedly the visitor limped across the silken carpet and plumped down on to the soft coverlet beside her friend.

'Odilie, listen. I'm getting married.'

Her friend sat up like a jack in the box. 'To that fine lad with the golden hair? That's quick work.'

'Quicker than you think. We're going to do it in the marrying tent in the fairground in an hour. You must dress yourself and come with me as my best maid.'

Any sadness that Odilie had been feeling disappeared and she swung her feet to the ground, groping for her slippers with her toes. 'What're you going to wear? I know, there's that dress with the rosebuds that you liked – and the big hat with the feather round it that I trimmed for you. That's what you'll wear.'

She was across the floor and rummaging in her cupboard like a frantic squirrel, throwing out pieces of finery that draped themselves over the furniture like wraiths. 'Here's the dress. You'll look beautiful in it! I'll wear my pink – I have to do you justice. Ring the bell and we'll send one of the maids for Aunt Martha. She won't want to miss this either.'

'No, no, just you. I don't want too many people. Besides, I've not told my father yet. I'm going home now to do that and then I'll go back to the fairground to meet Adam – that's his name – Adam Scott. Will you join us at Patie Mudie's marrying tent at nine o'clock exactly?'

Odilie paused in her rummaging and nodded agreement. 'All right. So he's called Adam. That's a good manly name and he looked nice, too. Put on the dress and take the hat with you – and those pink slippers, your feet are the same size as mine, aren't they? Oh, I'm going to miss you Grace when you're married. Where does this Adam Scott live, anyway?'

Grace laughed. 'I don't know really. It's called Fairhope and it's in the Cheviots some place. He says the nearest neighbour is four miles away. His father and mother have one cottage on the place but there's another next door that's not used. We're to have it.' Her face was shining and she did not seem at all worried about the prospect of living in such isolation.

Odilie sobered and ran across to her friend to hug her close. 'My dearest Grace, I'm so happy for you. It's so romantic. You're really in love. You're lucky, so lucky. God bless you.' Then the tearful look came into her eyes again but she brushed the drops away with determination.

Wearing the rosebud-dotted gown and carrying the pretty hat, Grace ran out of Havanah Court and went flying up the road. She glanced up at the town clock as she crossed the square and her heart began beating fast – there was less than half an hour left. I must hurry, hurry, hurry. I mustn't be late for my own wedding, she told herself.

CHAPTER 11

I've been entranced – something strange has happened to me, thought Odilie Rutherford as she looked at her reflection in the long pier glass after an excited Grace left. She'd felt melancholy and light-headed all evening and even Grace's magnificent news only lifted her spirits for a little while. Her malaise had begun when, like an obedient daughter, she'd returned to the fairground with her father in answer to the Duke's summons but, to her great relief, they discovered that by the time they got there the ducal party had left and gone back to Sloebank. The big tent was deserted except for servants and so, with her arm through Canny's, Odilie walked home again.

On the way she saw the young gypsy man again. They met face to face and he recognised her right enough, for her stared at her almost hungrily as if his eyes could not see enough and she knew he'd noticed how she was now wearing a fine gown and an expensive bonnet. Then he smiled in a sort of sad way and passed her by without speaking. In the solitude of her bedroom she went over the details of their fleeting second encounter in her mind – over and over and over . . .

Dressed in her geranium pink gown to go to Grace's wedding, she turned slowly in front of the mirror and stared at her reflection. Even to herself she looked like a stranger. Her dark face had lost its pertness and now looked vulnerable and yearning as it stared back at her from the shining surface of the glass. Her slim figure was silhouetted by the glittering light of dozens of candles in the brackets on the walls of her room and their flames flickered and danced like wraiths. It seemed to her that some dark and handsome stranger was about to walk out of the shadows and stand beside her. She closed her eyes and imagined him, dark-haired and daring. Then she opened them wide and said aloud, 'Go away, go away. I don't want to think about you, I don't want to dream about you.' The gypsy girl's words about 'casting the glamourie' came into her mind – what did it mean? Had the glamourie been cast even before the words were spoken? Yes, that's what's wrong – I've been enchanted, Odilie told herself.

Wrapping a long shawl around her shoulders she left her bedroom but was only half-way down the stairs when Joe opened the front door to admit Grace's father. Andrew Elliot strode in looking unusually dishevelled, for he was normally very fastidiously dressed, and as he glanced up the stairs towards her, Odilie could see unguarded dislike in his eyes. He hid this quickly however and smiled his cold professional grimace.

'Good evening, Miss Rutherford. Are you going to the entertainment at the Castle?' he asked.

'No, not tonight. I cried off. I'm taking a walk over to the fairground again,' she said lightly, because something warned her not to mention Grace's hastily arranged marriage.

'Alone? At this time? Your father's a very liberal parent.' Elliot bared his teeth but he was not really smiling.

'I won't be out for long and I won't be alone, for I'm meeting Grace there. I'm only going out to take the air. Besides, my father trusts me,' she said imperiously and swept on down the stairs, brushing quickly past him before he could question her any further.

He put out a hand to halt her. 'Grace will not be there, I'm afraid,' he told her in a less cordial tone of voice.

'Why not?' she asked, afraid that he would see how disturbed his statement had made her.

'Because she's been taken unwell. I've ordered her to stay at home.' His voice was smooth as cream.

'In that case I'll go to Viewhill and see her there,' cried Odilie angrily, and flew out through the door before he could detain her. Her heart was pounding as she hesitated in the garden, wondering if Elliot had been bluffing. From where she stood she could see the second wave of fairgoers queuing at the bridge as they headed back to the field for the rest of the evening's entertainment and could hear the distant blare of musical instruments playing catchy tunes. Reflections of brightly coloured flares were already beginning to spangle the water of the river. It was a warm night, a perfect end for the Fair, and she did not really believe that on such a wonderful night for lovers the new Grace would knuckle down to her father again. Even if Elliot believed that his daughter was staying at home there was no certainty he was right. The best thing to do, Odilie decided, was to go across to the fairground and keep the rendezvous that Grace had made with her. She started to run. It was five minutes to nine.

She reached Patie Mudie's marriage tent at five past nine and found a small crowd of people waiting there. 'Have I missed it? Is the wedding over?' she gasped, her eyes searching around for her friend.

Catherine Scott, who had a sleepy-eyed little Leeb hanging on to her hand, looked at the girl in the lovely coloured gown and asked, 'Are you looking for Grace Elliott and my Adam?'

Odilie nodded. 'Yes, I'm her friend. She said to be here at nine o'clock.'

'I'm Adam's mother and he told us the same thing,' said Catherine, 'but neither of them are here yet.'

By her side her husband was rocking gently to and fro on his feet with a beatific grin on his face. 'My laddie's getting merrit,' he was murmuring to anyone who passed. Mary, who recognised Odilie from the fortune-teller's queue and was embarrassed by the memory, stood in the background clinging to the arm of her faithful Jockie who was beaming with pride at having won her at last.

Aunt Lily had gone home reluctantly because Uncle Sandy had been carried back from the ale tent at half-past seven too drunk to stand up, far less understand that a marriage was being arranged. 'Just wait till I get you home. I'll box your ears for you,' she scolded as she guided him out of the fairground towards the cart which conveyed them back to Morebattle.

After a pause during which time the waiting party all stared around, eyeing everybody that passed nearby, a disappointed Catherine spoke again. 'What's happened? Do you think they've changed their minds?' she asked nobody in particular.

Odilie shook her head. 'I'm sure they haven't. Something's gone wrong. I saw Grace's father before I left home and he was acting very strange. If they don't come soon I'll go across to her home and find out why she's not here.'

Catherine lowered her voice slightly. 'Her father's Elliot the lawyer, isn't he? The one with the office in the square?'

Odilie nodded. 'Yes, he is.'

Catherine said in a worried voice, 'That's what my sister-in-law said. He's the one whose wife killed her bairn, isn't he?'

Odilie's heart seemed to freeze when she heard this. 'Killed a baby? When?'

'Oh, Lily said it's a while ago now – about ten years, maybe more. I can mind something about it myself but not much. Apparently it caused a great stushie in the town. Lily thinks the woman that did the murder must have been the mother of this lassie Grace . . . I'm fair worried about it. I'm sure Adam doesn't know.'

Odilie's throat was dry and she murmured, 'Grace doesn't know anything about it, either. I'm sure there's some mistake.'

'Lily's not often wrong,' said Catherine doubtfully while her eyes ranged over the people in the fairground but there was still no sign of her son or of the girl he had so precipitately decided to marry.

They waited, with hope slowly dying, for another half an hour but by that time they all knew that neither Grace nor Adam was coming. Catherine and Tom Scott tried to hide their confusion but they were secretly sure that their laddie had been led astray by a girl from a strange background who'd had second thoughts. 'We'll have to go home. Leeb's fair wabbit and it's a long way to go,' Catherine told Mary. 'If Adam does come, tell him we couldn't wait any longer.'

Mary nodded and embraced her family one after the other and promised, 'I'll tell him. Jockie and I'll wait here till he comes. I like the lassie Mam, I'm sure she'll be a good wife for him. You go away home now and dinna worry about it.'

Odilie, listening to this exchange, nodded and said, 'I'll wait too. Don't worry – we'll find out what's happened and as soon as I know the answer, I'll send a messenger up to Fairhope to tell you.'

She watched with pity as the dejected Scotts reharnessed their pony in the darkness under the trees. Because Tom was unable to do much and stood swaying on his feet, she disregarded her beautiful gown and helped Jockie and Catherine to coax the fat animal between the shafts. Mary was carrying the sleeping Leeb and when her mother had climbed aboard, she passed up the child and asked anxiously, 'Do you want me to come with you? Are you sure you'll be all right, Mam?'

Catherine shook her head. 'In the twenty-five years I've been married to your father, we've never missed a Fair and in all that time I've always been the one to drive home. I'll be fine but I'm worried about Adam. That Elliot's a hard man. Lily says he's not got a good name in the town.'

'We'll go and find him now,' said Jockie, who rarely uttered but when he did, it was with decision.

His calm confidence soothed the women and Catherine helped her husband into his seat saying, 'Settle down there now, Tom, and go to sleep. We've a long drive ahead of us.' They drove off with Leeb lying along the back bench beneath a blanket with her fair hair flowing out. She looked like a sleeping angel.

When they had disappeared, Jockie turned to the two girls and said grimly, 'Right! Now we'll go and find them. I'm good in a fight.' He held up his right hand and the muscle in his upper arm bulged ominously. Mary coloured again, remembering the other fight he had been in that day on her behalf.

'Thank you,' said Odilie. 'I hope it won't come to that but I'd appreciate your help anyway. Let's go to Grace's home first . . .'

There were still crowds on the bridge and the riverside footpaths but they took little notice of the fashionably dressed girl with her two companions who hurried up the lane to Viewhill.

When they reached it the place looked bleak and the only sign that it was inhabited was a single candle burning in the window of the stairway. They stood at the garden gate and debated what to do and while they were talking, there was a rustle in the shrubbery out of which Adam suddenly appeared. There was a bruise on his cheek and his normally neat appearance was completely gone for the shoulder of his jacket was torn open revealing the white stiffening material on the inside and his hair was tousled. 'Thank God you've come. I couldn't leave here . . .' he said.

Mary gasped and put her hands over her mouth while Odilie asked, 'What on earth's happened? Where's Grace?'

He pointed bleakly at the house. 'In there. She wanted to speak to her father alone first and so she went in but she never came out again. I waited for about twenty minutes like she told me and then I knocked on the door. A man came out – it was her father I suppose – and hit me with a stick. I kicked at the door and made a terrible fuss and he sent somebody for the law officers. They threatened to lock me up if I didn't go away. They wouldn't listen to anything I said.'

Odilie nodded. 'He's an important man in the town and they won't go against him. But he won't dare threaten me. I'll knock on the door. When I saw him earlier tonight I said I was going to meet Grace – that must have been after he shut her up. One of you stay watching the front door and someone else go round to the back.'

When the others hid themselves, she boldly climbed

the steps and rattled the knocker. After a little time a rustling noise could be heard behind the door and Hester's voice asked sharply, 'Who is it? What do you want at this time of night?'

'I want to see Grace,' called Odilie.

'Who?' The voice sounded incredulous as if no such person as Grace existed.

'I want to see *Miss Grace Elliot*. It's Odilie Rutherford, her friend.'

'She's not here. Go away.'

'Where is she?' Odilie rattled the knocker again.

'She's not here. Go away.'

'She is here. Tell her Odilie's come to see her.'

When it replied, the voice sounded louder as if the speaker's face was pressed up against the keyhole. 'You go away, Miss Rutherford. You shouldn't be out knocking on folk's doors at this time of the night. She doesn't want to see you.'

Odilie banged the knocker, heavily this time and cried, 'If she doesn't want to see me let her tell me that herself,' but there was no reply. Then in despair she jumped off the steps and stood back on the gravel that crunched beneath her feet as she called up at the unlit windows, 'Grace, Grace, where are you, Grace?'

By this time lights were going on in the houses all around and faces could be seen at the neighbours' windows, but still Odilie called, 'Grace, shout if you can hear me!'

Then she paused and listened. Somewhere far away she heard a voice. It was calling, 'Adam – Adam – Adam.'

Just at that moment the door opened and a red-haired woman with a furious face stood in the opening. 'I don't care if you are going to be the next Duchess. Get off our property or I'll call the law out again. We've had enough trouble here for one night. Go away this minute.' Then she slammed the door shut and they heard the sound of bolts being driven fiercely home.

There was nothing Odilie could do now but retreat, though, as she ran back to the gate, she felt exhilarated.

'At least we know Grace is there and that she's being held against her will,' she told the others. 'Now we've got to work out how to free her! You stay here watching the place and I'll go and tell my father.'

Adam chimed in, 'Mary and Jockie, you watch the house. I'm going back to the fairground to fetch that woman from the freak show. She told Grace she'd help if there was any trouble and I've a feeling she knows a lot more about this than she lets on. I'll be back as quick as I can.'

Meanwhile Odilie was running at full tilt down Roxburgh Street with her skirts held high. She was burning with indignation on Grace's behalf but was also surprised at how much she was enjoying herself.

Her father was sitting alone in his library and it was obvious he was infinitely relieved to see her as he stood up saying, 'I've been worried about you, it's getting so late. You look as if you've been in a scuffle, my dear. What's happened? You haven't been involved in this awful business with Grace, have you?'

She nodded, gasping, 'Yes, yes I have. It's terrible, Father. What are we going to do?'

Canny looked concerned but shook his head. 'There's nothing we can do, is there? Her father's been here telling me about the business and now he's gone off to find Wattie Thompson to sign the committal certificate.'

Odilie gasped, 'What certificate? What are you talking about? Elliot's locked Grace up because she wants to get married. She's old enough to do that without any certificate, isn't she?'

'Oh my lass, you don't know the half of it. Poor Grace.' Canny walked towards his daughter with a very sad look on his face. 'Elliot's just been telling me about the girl. He's gone over to the Cross Keys to ask Thompson to do something about her. I know you're fond of Grace but don't you worry, my dear, Thompson'll give the very best advice.'

Odilie's elation disappeared and she looked terrified. 'Advice? What sort of advice? Grace wants to marry a shepherd called Adam Scott. I've met him. He's a very decent young man. Don't listen to her father, Papa – what's he been saying?'

'I know this'll be a shock to you my dear, but Grace is unstable. I don't usually talk like this about people but Elliot's been telling me how Grace isn't like other girls – she's rather strange. It's inherited, apparently.' He shrugged his shoulders. 'It's been a lifelong sorrow for her family. That's why she's been so carefully guarded,' he added.

'Are you talking about her limp? What's that got to do with this? It's not even a very bad limp. She's just been told it's bad,' said Odilie defiantly.

'Oh, no, I'm not talking about her limp. I wish I were,' her father assured her. 'It's her state of mind, her nerves – her *imagination* that's the trouble. Elliot says her mother was the same, a very exciteable person. That's why she killed her baby. It was crying apparently and she went over to the cradle and strangled it, just like that. Hester was there and gave evidence at the trial. Elliot's first wife didn't know she'd done it, poor thing. Even when they showed her the body she denied she was responsible. Said it wasn't her, carried on something terrible.'

Seeing his daughter's horrified eyes, he shook his head sadly and added, 'And Grace's grandfather, old Davie Allen, was the same. They were an unstable family and when Grace had a brainstorm tonight, her father said he's been expecting something of the sort for a long time. It's heredity.'

Odilie was unconvinced. 'My God, Father, he's spun you a pack of lies. Grace is no more likely to have a brainstorm than you or me. She went home to tell him she was being married – and he's kept her prisoner in the house. I know, I've just come from there and I heard her calling out. You must believe me, you simply must, and we've got to stop Elliot in whatever plan he's hatching.'

Canny took a turn in the room and there was a worried look on his face. 'Why should he want to certify his own daughter just because she wants to get married?' he asked.

301

'I don't know but it could have something to do with property – Grace told me she's just learned from someone that Davie Allen left her all his property when he died. Her grandfather was rich, wasn't he?'

Canny nodded, 'So they say. Yes, that could be right – and Elliot's damned greedy. But I'm not convinced, Odilie. Just in case though, let's go over to the Cross Keys and stop Thompson before he does something drastic without checking up for himself. Maybe Elliot's right, maybe the girl has gone mad but at least she should be judged so by someone else before she's confined.'

They were just in time.

When Odilie went rushing up the stairs to Professor Thompson's room with her father puffing behind her, the doctor was in the very act of dipping his pen in the inkpot to sign a commital order for Grace Elliot.

'Don't, don't!' cried Odilie, bursting in with both hands upheld. 'Go and see her first. Don't sign it without seeing her.'

Thompson looked up from the paper with an astonished look on his face. 'But I've listened to her father and questioned him thoroughly. I know him well. Why should I not believe what he tells me? It sounds as if the girl is raving mad and dangerous. She is violent and she's broken up half of their home.'

Canny was behind his daughter in the doorway now and he pushed into the room. 'My daughter thinks that Grace is being held on a pretext, Wattie, and I admit that perhaps she's got a point.'

Elliot looked angry and dangerous as he stared at the new arrivals. 'My daughter has gone mad! It's a great grief to me. Do I have to put up with this nonsense as well at such a time?' he asked, glaring at Odilie and then at Canny whom he told, 'Your daughter's a troublemaker and far too spoiled. I told you long ago you should take a firm hand with her. She's been messing you around and now she's started on me and my family. Tell her to stay out of this.'

Canny sat down heavily on a chair beside Thompson

and said to Elliot, 'When we were wondering how to get Odilie out of her marriage contract it was you who told me to say she'd gone mad, wasn't it? Have you taken your own advice when dealing with a rebellious daughter?'

Elliot snapped, 'Of course not. Grace has had a brainstorm. She's a danger to my family. She needs to be confined in a bedlam.'

'All Grace has done is tell her father she's getting married,' interrupted Odilie staring at the bemused Professor.

Elliot was furious and spat at the accusing girl, 'That's very far from all. She's been going around poisoning people's minds. That's why you don't believe me. She's been saying that Hester and I are cruel to her – I'm sure she's told you that, Miss Rutherford – but it's a pack of lies. Tonight she came home in a state of hysteria and announced she wants to get married to some unknown she met at the Fair. Who in their right mind decides to marry a stranger they've known for about half an hour? And she's demanding a dowry. That's the key to the whole thing, I suspect. Some fortune-teller she met at the Fair told her she was a rich heiress and I suspect the would-be bridegroom thinks he's going to transform his life with her money.'

'Has she any money?' asked Canny.

'A little, not much. A broken-down property left to her by her grandfather. It wouldn't fetch fifty pounds at auction. She gets it when she marries. The trouble is that her mind's gone the same way her mother's did. What can I do, Thompson? You must know of a good place where I can send her before she hurts herself or someone else.'

He was standing at the side of the fireplace facing Canny and Professor Thompson, leaning forward as if trying to persuade them to his point of view. Their faces showed that they were divided in their opinions and then Odilie made her last effort. 'If there's any doubt, you *must* go and see Grace yourself, Professor Thompson. That's the only way you'll be sure you're doing the right thing. It's a girl's whole life you're signing away if you don't.'

*

There was something wrong with Billy. Instead of falling greedily on to his food as he usually did, he pushed his supper plate aside when Alice carried it to him.

'Eat it, Billy,' she said gently. 'It's good mutton stew and you've to go out to do your turn in half an hour. You'll have to be strong for that.'

But Billy only put up his hand and pushed the proferred plate away again. His head was sunk on his chest and when Alice bent down to look at him more closely, she saw that tears were trickling down his cheeks.

'Oh Billy, what's wrong? Are you sick? Stand up and let me look at you.' She put out a hand to help him up from where he was sitting on a bundle of blankets by the side of the caravan. He rose with a jangling of chains and pointed to his right leg, the one that bore the manacle with which Jem had tied him to the caravan wheel.

Alice knelt and examined his ankle and bare foot. A trickle of blood was running over the top of the arch and where the manacle was locked around his ankle there was a huge patch of raw and bleeding flesh.

'Oh Billy, that must hurt. How did it happen? It wasn't like that earlier. What have you been doing?' she cried in sympathy. When she lifted his hands there were stains of dried blood on the tips of his fingers and beneath his fingernails. 'You've been scratching yourself, Billy. You've been tearing away at yourself. Were you trying to get the manacle off? You know you mustn't do that.'

Billy groaned and gave a convulsive sob and when she looked up she saw he was staring out at the crowds of people going up and down the pathway between the stalls. 'Aw poor Billy, poor Billy,' he moaned.

Alice's heart ached for him. 'Poor Billy,' she agreed, 'Do you want to see what's going on out there? Do you want to walk about the Fair for a bit? I'll ask Jem what he thinks. You've been a good boy today. He might let you out again later. But first let me dress that sore place for you.'

As she worked over him, rubbing a yellow paste on to the wound and covering it with a thin bandage, he made

304

happy noises and rubbed the top of her head with his huge hand. He could have broken her neck with one movement but she could always tell when his mood was good and tonight, as far as Billy was capable of loving anything or anybody, he loved her.

Jem was busy on the platform, his battered face lit up from beneath by rows of candles behind curved metal shades. He was yelling out the attractions of his side-shows. 'Come and see the Bearded Lady – Come and see the World's Smallest Married Couple with their baby – Come and see the Tallest Man,' he bawled, drowning out rival buskers on either side who were bruiting abroad the attractions of contortionists, performing dogs and a team of dancing ladies from Arabia who, it was rumoured, bared their navels when they performed.

Alice stood behind the curtain and whispered, 'Jem, Jem . . .' so when he finished his spiel, he nodded to tell Long Tom to take over from him.

Alice told him, 'Billy's awful sad. He's been scratching himself again and he only does that when he's unhappy. He wants to see the sideshows, I think. Oh, he's just a bairn really. After he's done his turn perhaps you can let Tom take him up and down for half an hour? It would quieten him.'

'If you think it's safe enough. Bring him out now and he can do his act, then he can go out for a bit before he performs again,' agreed Jem.

When Adam Scott, breathless from his headlong dash from Viewhill, arrived at the freak show, the crowds were thick around it and a press of people were listening to Jem doing his spiel . . . 'Billy the Strongest Man in the World will now perform for you, ladies and gentlemen. You will witness Feats of Strength that will make you gasp. Ten men can stand on Billy's chest but he brushes them off like Flies. He can Straighten out Horseshoes and pull a Laden Cart across the stage with his Teeth. Pay your shilling and come to see Billy, the Modern Hercules!'

Jem's eye could not be caught because he was staring out over the heads of the crowd as he shouted and though

Adam tried to push his way to the back of the stall to where he knew Alice's caravan stood, his way was barred by a grim-looking Long Tom who shoved him off in the direction of the queue of people paying their money to see Billy.

Adam handed over a coin and found himself inside the enclosure staring up at a stage on which stood a half-naked black-haired man dressed as Hercules with a mangy tiger skin draped half-across his chest. Chains hung around him and there was a thick manacle around one ankle that also bore a blood-stained bandage. Jem, wearing a top hat, appeared on the stage beside him and bellowed, 'Billy will now bite a chain in half . . .' Billy obliged. 'And straighten out three horseshoes . . .' Billy obliged again, pulling the horseshoes as if they were made of rubber. While Jem was yelling out Billy's next amazing achievement, Adam pushed his way to the end of the gaping row in which he stood and found himself against the back of the tent. He then dropped to his knees and crawled under the edge of the canvas.

Alice was walking towards her caravan carrying a bucket of water from the river when she felt a hand on her arm and a voice said urgently, 'Mrs Archer, I've been looking for you! It's about Grace – something bad has happened to her. Her father's shut her up. He won't let me see her.'

Alice stopped dead. Her face was stricken as she stared at Adam. 'He's shut her up? He's not hurt her, has he? Where is she?'

'In their house in Roxburgh Street.'

'He would.' Alice's tone was bitter. 'Wait till I put this water in the caravan and I'll come with you.' He followed her over the grass to where Long Tom was now sitting on the steps of Billy's van.

'Tommy, when Billy comes off the stage you've to take care of him. Take him for a little walk so's he can see the sideshows. Tell Jem I've gone off with Adam to see Grace – he'll understand. I'll be back soon,' she ordered.

Tom reluctantly agreed. 'Oh, all right, I'll do it if you give Billy a potion first.'

Alice snapped, made irritable with urgency, 'He doesn't need another potion! He had one an hour ago. If I give him any more he won't be able to work later. Just dress him in case he catches cold. He won't be any trouble. I'm going now – tell Jem I'll be back soon.'

Then she ran towards her own caravan but was only inside for a few minutes before she re-emerged and said urgently to Adam, 'Let's be off. There's no time to lose.'

Together they slipped into the darkness at the back of the stalls and disappeared.

Long Tom watched Alice go with disquiet because he was mortally scared of Billy, and when a burst of applause signalled the end of the strong man's act he visibly quailed. The curtain at the back of the stage parted and Billy in his tiger skin appeared and Tom jumped up, going towards the strong man and saying, 'Fine Bill, fine, you did well tonight.' Then he added in a coaxing voice, 'Would you like a drink?'

From the tailpocket of his coat he brought out a squat black bottle and drew out the cork with his teeth. The smell of whisky was strong as he put the bottle to his own lips and swallowed a large mouthful. Then he wiped his mouth on his sleeve and passed the bottle over to Billy who sniffed at it curiously.

'Taste it. It'll put you in a good mood. Go on, try some. It's a man's drink, Billy,' said Tom.

The massive creature opposite him raised the bottle to his mouth and swallowed. Then he coughed, spluttering as if he was drowning. 'Ugh,' he exclaimed, throwing the bottle on to the ground.

Tom dived after it. 'You silly fool, that's good whisky . . . Damme me, you've drunk the lot. No wonder you coughed!' He sat back on his heels and grinned at Billy who laughed back and slapped a huge hand on to his knee. Tom's fear of Billy was beginning to lessen and he said, 'Come on then lad, let's get you dressed. A singlet and pants, I think, and a jacket. Where's your jacket, Billy?'

But Billy wasn't listening because he was fiddling with the bandage on his ankle which had been displaced by the manacle. He tore at the dressing with his fingers and made little moaning noises. Blood was marking the bandages. 'What's that? Have you hurt yourself? Oh I see Alice has put a cover on it. Leave it alone. Don't scratch it, you're making it bleed. Oh damme, I'll have to take off this manacle to get your pants on. Stand up Billy while I do it.'

He removed the manacle and when it was off Billy stretched out his foot gratefully. Tom tried to put it on again afterwards, but the young giant made threatening noises and the tall man sat back saying soothingly, 'Oh all right, if you don't want it – as long as you behave . . .' Then he took Billy by the arm and they walked sedately out into the fairground from the back of the freak show platform. Jem, on the stage, waved a hand to them and told the crowd, 'There goes Billy, the Strongest Man in the World. He's off for a little constitutional before he does his amazing act for you again. He can bend iron bars, bite nails in half, smash a cart-wheel into kindling with one blow of his fist. You'll have to come back and see Billy perform, ladies and gentlemen!'

Billy looked back over his shoulder laughing as if he understood what was being said but Jem knew he didn't really for when he started his act, all that had to be done was point him at the various things that he was to demolish and whisper, 'Kill it, Billy, kill it!' The problem was making him stop. Only Jem was able to put an end to his orgy of destruction.

But he was quiet as he walked out with Tom because the thrills of the Fair entranced him. Eyes shining, he stopped in front of every stall, sometimes reaching out to try to take a particularly colourful exhibit. Many of the stall-keepers knew him because they travelled the same fairs as the freak show, and without protest handed over a twist of toffee or a square of coconut tablet. One gave him a couple of coloured balls and told him to throw them at the French heads on the poles at the back of the shies but Tom knew better than allow him to try because Billy's throwing had a tendency to become violent and Tom feared that he might knock the whole stall down in his enthusiasm.

Billy looked benignly at couples linking arms as they walked along; he smiled at children and tried to pat wandering dogs on the head and all the time he pulled Tom in the direction of the gypsy camp.

'Would you like to look at the circus, Billy?' his escort asked in an effort to create a diversion when he saw the enormous canvas spread of Simon's establishment off to his right but Billy shook his head and pointed in front of him. He was being surprisingly singleminded. 'There's lots of horses in the circus,' coaxed Tom. 'You like horses. Jem's brother runs the circus. He'd like to see you. Come and see Jem's brother, Billy.'

Little by little he drew his charge across to the circus enclosure where Bella, in her dress of spangles, was limbering up at the back of the tent. Her face registered disquiet when she saw Tom approaching with the lumbering Billy on his arm.

'My God, what's that?' she asked. 'He's grown to a helluva size. Is he safe enough?'

Tom nodded. 'He's good tonight. He wants to see the horses. Just let him have a look round for a wee while and then I'll take him back to do his turn.'

Bella grinned and said, 'If you say he's all right, in you go. We've landed lucky in our hunt for a trick rider. Simon's over there with a young gypsy who's offered to do a turn in place of El Diavolo tonight. I don't know if he'll be much good but we're lucky to get anybody.'

The interior of the circus tent was dim because it was not yet time for the next show, when all the lamps would be blazing and the public admitted to sit on the rough benches around the ring. Somewhere in the background a band was tuning up – first one instrument and then another played a snatch of music. A troop of young tumblers, the children of Bella and Simon, were rolling over and over in the ring, jumping up and down and scissoring their legs energetically. There was an overpowering smell of horse droppings and lamp oil.

Tom held Billy's arm as they stumbled forward in the half-dark. Ahead of them they saw Simon's back as he stood looking up at a dark-haired young man seated on a horse in the middle of the ring. The horse was broad-backed and barrel-bellied and instead of a saddle it wore a broad surcingle around its middle. Its head was held in one position by fixed reins leading from the bridle to its belly belt.

Billy sank down on a bench with Tom beside him as Simon stepped back and cracked his whip. At that signal the horse began circling the ring. The acrobats jumped clear as it started to canter, head down, round and round and round. The man on its back sat easily with his legs dangling, then, as Simon called out an order, he crouched up on the horse's back and stood with both arms held out at his sides. The horse's pace became a gallop and the rider stood erect smiling, calling over, 'It's easy. I used to do this sort of thing when I was a laddie.'

'Can you jump through hoops up there?' called back Simon.

'Not really. What I'm best at is showing off a horse, making it perform. Loosen its bridle and I'll show you.'

Simon ran forward, stopped the horse and unlatched the reins. Then the rider sat down on the horse's back and started to ride it forward, making it bend and curve, rear up and kick out with its back legs. When the display was over Simon shouted, 'Well ridden, lad. You'll do almost as well as El Diavolo!'

Billy stood up in his place to give a strangled kind of cheer. They all turned and smiled at him and the rider raised his hand, calling out, 'Thanks Billy!' The young giant glowed with pride and was so happy that he allowed himself to be led back to the freak show without any more complaints.

Tom's mistake was to relax and forget his fear. He

310

had been drinking whisky all evening and was swaying unsteadily on his feet but he knew that it was almost time for Billy's next performance and he had to get him out of his ordinary clothes and into the tiger skin again. When he knelt down at the giant's feet to remove his shoes, Billy bent slowly as if watching what he was doing. When the shackle was about to be replaced, with a sweet smile on his face, Billy joined both hands together so that the knuckles made a weapon like a mace head. Then he brought his joined hands sharply down on to the kneeling Tom's bent head.

Without a sound, without knowing what had happened to him, the tall man slumped forward and Billy looked with surprise at his own clenched hands. He knelt and said in the same sort of coaxing voice that Tom had only seconds before been using to him, 'Poor Tom, poor Tom' but the huddled form lay completely still. With a shrug of indifference the huge young man stepped over the body and ran out into the darkness. Despite his bulk it was uncanny how the shadows swallowed him up as if he was a wraith.

When he was clear of the sideshows, he paused like an animal to sniff the air. Then stealthily and silently he made his way towards the most thickly wooded part of the field. Simple as he was, he knew that he must keep clear of people if he was to enjoy his new-won freedom so when anyone came near, Billy veered away. In quiet, hidden places, lovers were lying together and Billy dodged them indifferently. Once, stumbling upon an oblivious pair, he jumped clean over them in an enormous vaulting leap. The girl opened her eyes and screamed as his shadow darkened the star-filled sky above her but the man on top only grunted, thinking that she was effusively grateful, and kept on at his work. She later told him she must have been completely transported to have imagined such a thing as a jumping devil.

At last Billy found himself a solitary hiding place on the highest elevation above the gypsy camp and hunkered down to gaze around. The Fair with all its lights and noise was spread out at his feet like a world in miniature. In the middle, and most brightly lit, was the circus tent where people were flocking in for the last show. As strains of music went drifting up to him, he smiled, beating his hands in time gently on his knees. Greedily his eyes ranged around the panorama. He did not know where he was, he could not remember the name of the town at which he was looking but it represented freedom, though he was not aware of that as a concept. All he knew was that like an escaped animal, he must avoid recapture.

Lauriston entranced him. Pinpoints of illumination sparkled all over its dark mass. Candles shone in windows and blazing lamps drove away the shadows at street corners. Along the parapet of the Rennie Bridge, tall braziers cast their reflections down on to the smooth waters of the Tweed. The most gloriously lit building in the town was Havanah Court, illuminated by Canny in honour of his daughter's coming betrothal which, he hoped, would be officially announced the following day although most of the townspeople had heard about it already. Billy's eyes ranged over the town, up the snaking length of Roxburgh Street towards Sloebank Castle, which also glittered with hundreds of lights in the middle of its black, tree-filled park. He smiled silently to himself, relishing his first taste of freedom.

CHAPTER 12

The layout of the Elliot home was obviously familiar to Mrs Archer, Adam noticed when they arrived at Viewhill House. He and Jockie were all in favour of storming the door in order to rescue Grace, but the older woman counselled caution. 'Wait,' she said holding them back. 'I must work this out. The stable's empty and the horse is away so that means her father is not at home. If I can get inside I could free Grace before he gets back. Believe me, that's the only way we'll get Grace out of his clutches because Hester will never open the door to us. Then I'll wait in there for him to return. I want to surprise him.'

'But you'll never manage to get in, it's like a prison,' groaned Adam, looking at the immense iron-studded door and barred windows.

In the moonlight he saw that she was smiling at him, however, 'Oh yes I will,' she said. 'That's one of the things I learned during a misspent youth. I know a way. Mary can come and help me. You stay here and warn us if Elliot comes back.'

She took Adam's sister by the arm and led her towards the kitchen area where, in the semi-basement, she clambered up on to the sill of a low window. Hanging on to the pitted and corroded bars she scrutinised them carefully and then whispered to herself, 'Good, they've not been replaced. What matters now is whether I've changed too much. I wonder if I can still get through.'

Bending her head she looked in at the glass and saw that the frame behind the bars was half-lowered and there was a marble shelf running beneath the window with a few brown earthenware bowls full of milk and cream standing on it.

'I'll have to step carefully or I'll get a milk bath,' Alice said to Mary and then started trying to squeeze sideways between the bars. 'Oh dear, I used to be able to get through so easily,' she groaned to the watching girl. Then she tried again but the gap was just too narrow and she said dispiritedly, 'I was afraid of this. I'm fatter than I used to be. There's nothing for it – I'll have to take my clothes off. Don't let the men come round the corner Mary, but stay and help me. Hold my clothes and when I get inside slip them to me through the bars – and be careful, there's something in my skirt pocket that I don't want to lose. I'll probably need it in there.'

The moonlight shone brightly while Alice slipped out of her long skirt and cotton blouse. Then she bundled up her shawl and laid her shoes neatly side by side. Like Mary herself she wore no underclothes, not even a shift. They were unnecessary luxuries for poor women. After a few seconds she stood naked in the half-darkness, narrow-waisted and full-breasted, still lithe and beautiful, like an ageing nymph. Once more she climbed on to the sill and with a huge effort that made it seem she was in danger of breaking her ribs, she finally succeeded in squeezing her white body between the bars. She paused for a moment on the other side to catch her breath, then stuck an arm out for her clothes and whispered, 'I've done it! Now tell the boys to wait and not to worry. Grace will be out very shortly.'

Mary passed in Alice's clothes, noting how heavy was the weight of the bulky shape in the skirt pocket. She watched through the dim glass till Alice's shape could be seen slipping ghostlike out of the kitchen and everything returned to silence and waiting.

Inside the house it was very still and dark. Though it was years since she'd been there, Alice was surprised at how much she remembered. With one hand reaching out she felt her way around the kitchen and her fingers told her that the paint was still peeling from the walls. Elliot, she thought, was as loath as ever to spend money where the expense would not show and a rush of anger rose in her as she thought that Grace had been doomed by an

314

unloving father to spend her life in those dingy surroundings.

Very quietly she opened the kitchen door and crept up the uncarpeted stairs to the main hall where the decoration was more ambitious. Huge gilt-framed pictures hung on the walls, the floor was white marble and a bust of a Roman emperor perched on a tall plinth in one corner. The effect was so intimidating and chilly that the hall looked like the interior of an ancient temple.

The light of the moon coming through the glass panes of a semi-circular fanlight above the front door showed Alice the way up the stairs and she tiptoed stealthily, pausing to listen intently every time she took a step. When she reached the first-floor landing, she headed unerringly for the door of the principal bedroom and turned its handle very softly. As she had hoped, there was only one figure lying in the middle of the big bed. Hester, her hair flowing out over the pillow, was snoring loudly and Alice stepped silently across the carpet to pause by the bed, looking down reflectively for a few seconds before she put out a hand and shook the sleeping woman by her hunched-up shoulder.

Hester shrugged off the hand and murmured, 'What time is it? Have they taken her away?'

Alice did not speak but shook the shoulder again till Hester opened her eyes, half-turned her head and brushed back the tangles of hair with one hand. When she saw that the intruder was a woman she gasped, 'Who the devil are you? What do you want?'

'You've not changed much, Hester. You're still a sluga-bed,' said Alice in a cold voice.

'Who are you?' asked Hester in a voice that trembled slightly.

'Look harder. Don't you know me?' Alice's voice was bleak.

Hester clutched the sheet up to her face and made a gobbling noise. 'You're not a ghost, are you? He said you were dead . . .'

315

'He hoped I was dead. Bigamy's still a crime, isn't it? Where's my daughter?'

Hester pointed above her head with a trembling hand. 'She's up there. I'll give you the key. Just go away, Lucy, go away.'

'Get up,' said Alice grimly. 'I don't trust you. Come upstairs and let my girl out of there. You've been wickedly cruel as well as a liar and a perjurer. You should be made to suffer but I haven't the time now. Just get up and don't force me into anything.' Her voice was cold and Hester saw that she was drawing a long-barrelled pistol out of her skirt pocket as she spoke. Any thoughts the red-haired woman had of attacking the intruder disappeared and she swiftly rose from the bed, running ahead of Alice into the hall and up a narrow flight of stairs to the attic. In her imprisonment Grace heard the approaching thud of feet and started hammering on the door with her fists, shouting, 'Let me out, let me out!'

While Alice jabbed her in the back with the barrel of the gun, Hester unlocked the door, flinging it wide and Grace came charging through, hair wild and fists flying, no longer her meek and mild self. She looked like a raging fury as she knocked Hester back against the wall and was about to attack Alice too when she realised who it was standing behind her step-mother.

'Mrs Archer! What are you doing here?' she gasped.

Alice had no time to waste on explanations. 'Get out of here at once. Adam's in the garden waiting for you. Just get away as fast as you can. I'll wait till your father comes back and then I'll join you at Mudie's tent.' While she spoke she was pushing the girl towards the stairs. Grace did as she was told. Without a backward glance she flew down both flights and disappeared through the front door. When it slammed behind her Alice let out a long sigh of pent-up breath. Part of her mission had been accomplished.

Silence took over the house again and she brandished the pistol at Hester, smiling and saying, 'Now we wait for our husband! Go back to bed, Hester.'

Their vigil was not protracted for soon the door slammed and a voice called out, 'Hester, where are you?'

Alice nodded to the terrified woman in the bedroom who croaked out, 'Up here. In bed.'

His footsteps could be heard hurrying upstairs and as he opened the door he was saying, 'Get up, get yourself dressed. That damned Rutherford's bringing Thompson here to look at Grace. They didn't believe me – that daughter of his stuck her meddling nose in.'

On the threshold he stared across at the bed and said, 'Don't you ever get tired of lying there? Where's the candle, where's the tinder?'

There were sounds of him searching round in the darkness but he stopped when a voice came from a distant corner. 'There's no need of candles,' it said.

Elliot whipped round and stared at a dark figure sitting half-hidden in a chair by the chest of drawers. 'Who are you?' he demanded.

'It's Lucy. It's your wife,' croaked Hester from the bed.

He did not seem surprised. 'I heard a rumour you'd been seen in the town. Burns the grocer was talking about it. What a fool you are, Lucy. When they catch you, they'll hang you.'

The half-hidden woman stood up and walked slowly towards him with a silver filigreed pistol hanging from her hand. When she was close to him she levelled the gun and he heard a click as she pulled back the trigger. 'It's loaded,' she said.

He felt beads of sweat break out on his brow and held out both hands towards her. 'Come, come, Lucy. Don't be silly. I won't give you away. I'd be happy if you just vanished, after all . . .'

'After all you're a bigamist and you knew I was still alive when you married her.' Alice waved the gun at the terrified Hester.

'No, I didn't,' he protested.

'You did because I wrote to you asking you to send my daughter to me. But you didn't, did you, because my father was dead by that time and you were helping yourself to Grace's property. You committed bigamy as well as theft and you knew it.'

Elliot backed away with his eyes fixed on the gun and said soothingly, 'You're not going to shoot me, Lucy. That would only make things more difficult for you.'

'Why shouldn't I shoot you? You as good as murdered me. Lucy Allen's dead right enough and it was you who killed her. You deserve to die for that and for what you've done to our daughter. Even if they hang me it doesn't really matter providing I get revenge.'

His tone changed to pleading. 'I'll do anything you want, anything. Go away and I promise not to say you've been here.'

'She made me let the girl out,' squeaked Hester from behind him but they both ignored her as they gazed at each other over the menacing pistol.

Alice indicated the chair she had vacated and said to Elliot, 'Sit there! I want to ask you some questions. First, who killed my baby? Was it you or was it her?'

'It was her,' he said, quickly nodding at Hester who gave a cry of protest.

'But it was your idea, wasn't it?' Hester nodded vigorously at this. 'You worked it all out so that I'd be judged mad or wicked – and either way you'd get rid of me. You must have been very disappointed when I didn't hang but I suppose banishment was almost as good. It took me away forever and it let you get your thieving hands on my property.'

'Yes,' he agreed, recovering some of his nerve. 'Banishment from Scotland for the whole of your natural life – and a hanging if you ever came back.'

Alice sighed. 'And you haven't a scrap of remorse because I was banished for something I didn't do.'

He snapped back, 'You'd been unfaithful! You'd taken a lover and become pregnant by him. That child who died wasn't mine.'

Her voice rose in anger. 'How dare you! You'd not been in my bed for three years before I took a lover. You were in *her* bed – and in the beds of others too if my suspicions are right. You treated me cruelly. You made it obvious that you'd only married me for my property.'

'So then you fell in love . . . But he didn't stand by you, did he? He soon disappeared when the scandal broke. You've not been much good at choosing men, Lucy,' he sneered.

She shook her head, 'Lucy wasn't, but I'm better, much better. But that's all past. What did you do with my father's property? Have you still got a copy of his will, the one you took from Mr Anstruther's office?'

'Do you think I'd show it to you if I had?' he sneered.

'Then it's a good thing that old Mr Anstruther privately kept a copy. His widow gave it to me yesterday. You didn't know that, did you? Not everyone was entirely convinced by you. When you told my father I was dead he left everything to Grace and she inherits on the day she marries or when she reaches the age of twenty-five. What were you planning to do – poison her, perhaps?'

The guilty man was silent as he stared at her and she gestured to him to rise to his feet as she said, 'Now we'll go and look for the deeds of my father's properties. I'm sure you still keep them in the same hiding place. You come too, Hester.'

For a moment it was obvious that Elliot considered refusing to accompany her but the set look on her face changed his mind. He knew she would shoot him as soon as look at him if he did not do as he was told.

She ushered them downstairs in front of her and into the library where she ordered Hester, 'Lift the carpet by the window – there's a loose board beneath it. Take it up and you'll see a metal box. Bring it to me.'

When this was done, Alice told Elliot, 'Now give me your watch keys. I'll open it.'

He handed them over very reluctantly but before the box was opened a great thundering came at the front door and Canny Rutherford's voice could be heard shouting, 'Let us in, Elliot!'

Alice told Hester, 'Let them in. I'd like them to see this.'

When the new arrivals Canny and Professor Thompson, appeared in the doorway, she was tucking a bundle of papers into the neck of her dress. She smiled and told them, 'You're just in time. We've been having a discussion about the past and my husband's confessed his sins . . . perhaps he'll tell you, too.'

She brushed past the astonished men and said, 'He'll feed you a pack of lies when I've gone but don't believe a word he says.' Still clutching the pistol, she strode through the bleak hall like a queen and out through the front door which she left swinging open behind her. The darkness swallowed her up.

The first Jem knew of Billy's disappearance was when he announced his act to an expectant crowd . . . 'Billy, the Strongest Man in the World, will terrify you all with his strength; this young giant has the strength of a team of six horses! Give a cheer for him, ladies and gentlemen!' With a flourish, he threw a hand out towards the painted backcloth draped behind him but nothing happened. A sinister silence hung over the empty stage.

Jem stepped forward and lifted the corner of the cloth. His face registered surprise when he saw that there was no one to be seen in the area behind him.

Damn! he thought and then muttered, 'Where's Billy?' A sickening feeling of panic rose in him as the next words that came into his mind were, 'And worse, *where's Alice?*'

Flustered, he turned to his audience and roared, 'Billy's not able to appear tonight, folks, but don't worry, I'll give you your money back.'

The dwarf called Hans was standing at the side of the stage and Jem thrust the leather money bag at him. 'Pay them,' he ordered and jumping off the stage, ran to his own caravan. It was forbiddingly dark and empty. One look was enough to tell him that Alice was not there. In a panic he headed for Billy's waggon. It was dark there too but Long Tom's daughter was sitting on the steps with her chin in her hands staring at nothing.

'Where's your father?' asked Jem.

'Dunno. He took Billy for a walk and he's not come back yet. I'm waiting to give the big one his supper when he's finished his act.'

'Have you looked inside?' asked Jem.

The girl shrugged. 'Why should I? There's no noise and no light in there.'

Urgently Jem pushed her aside and raced up the steps, throwing open the door. In the half darkness he saw that Long Tom was spreadeagled face down on the floor with Billy's chains in a tumbled heap beside his hand.

Cold water wiped over the tall man's white face revived him and in a little while he was able to sit up, rub his neck and groan, 'It was that brute Billy. He could have broken my neck. He pole-axed me.'

'But where's Alice? She was with him,' Jem asked anxiously. The loss of Billy was bad enough but to lose Alice was worse, especially now he knew that she was in trouble with the law.

'She went off earlier. She told me to tell you that some lass called Grace's getting married. She was so excited you'd have thought she was the bride herself. Oh, my head hurts!' groaned Tom again.

Jem stood up with a look of confusion on his face. 'Alice went to a wedding? And how was Billy then? You must have had some idea that he was going to attack you. Was he excited? Did he fight you?'

Tom was able to stagger to his feet by this time. 'Not a bit, he was quiet as a lamb. I never thought for a minute . . . I even gave him a drink of whisky from my bottle.'

Jem put both hands up to his head and shouted, 'You gave him whisky! That's the worst thing you could do. How much did he drink? He'll go mad. Oh, my God, he'll kill somebody. We've got to find him – and I need to find my Alice. Close the show and send everybody out to look for Billy. I'll go after Alice.'

The fairground was still packed full of people but the crowd now was made up of adults, many of them helplessly drunk and others looking for trouble. This was the time when respectable folk with their families stayed at home and the fights started. The squad of men from Jedburgh, whose duty it was to keep law and order, patrolled up and down wearing their distinguishing black bonnets with red and white rosettes, and carrying heavy cudgels in their hands.

Even these patrols kept well away from the area that the gypsies claimed as their own. It was left to them to do their own policing. In past years men had been murdered among the Romany people but the body was lifted and taken away by his tribe with nothing being done by the authorities to follow up the killing. The gypsies themselves never forgot those slayings, however, and ancient blood feuds ran high among them.

The Kirk Yetholm people had two main enemies among their own race. The families who came from Lochmaben were generally hated but the greatest loathing was reserved for the Romanies from Alnwick who were led by a man known as the Earl of Hell, a title that had been passed down from gypsy chief to chief through the centuries. The Alnwick Romanies were as bloodthirsty and savage as their leader's name suggested. By the time darkness engulfed the fairground, all the gypsies were out in force with those from Alnwick and Lochmaben crowing in delight about Yetholm's Jesse Bailey being beaten in the jumping by a chavi. Well before midnight a series of minor fights had taken place and a good deal of drink had been consumed. Gib Faa was marshalling his men for a proper battle. 'I've just been told it was definitely an Alnwick man who fired the pistol that scared Barbary,' he told his followers. 'We've got to take revenge.'

Jesse, sitting with his arms around his knees on the edge of the conclave, staring into the blazing fire, shook his head. 'Let it be, Gib. The chavi deserved to win for her nerve alone. We'll get the last laugh because I've entered Barbary in the big race at Caverton Edge tomorrow and we'll win it. None of the horses from Alnwick or Lochmaben will be able to catch him – I'm certain of that.'

But Gib was drunk and combative. 'That'll not stop them talking. There has to be a battle,' he slurred.

Jesse stood up angrily. 'Another battle, more murros. Who's to be a corpse this year? You, Gib? Or one of you . . .' His finger stabbed out indicating other men sitting around the fire. 'Well, count me out. I'm not going to make a corpse just because you think that the Alnwick lot have played a dirty trick on you.'

Angrily he strode off, fuming inside. 'Will they never learn?' he asked himself, remembering previous Fairs and previous fights. There was the year his own father was stabbed and later the one when Gib's brother died, with his head bashed in by Lochmaben cudgels. There had never been a year when a Fair did not end with at least broken arms and legs, stab wounds and more festering hatred.

Jesse could not understand why his people always had to react to insult or persecution with deviousness, trickery or burning resentment. They were certainly not prepared to turn the other cheek for their morality was based on different precepts to the Christianity which had been taught to Jesse by the old minister. It was difficult for him to reconcile the two philosophies and the gypsy part of him wrestled hard with the teachings of a man he had admired.

'Oh, what am I going to do?' he groaned to himself again. There were many things to consider, so many confusing elements to be taken into account. His love of the open road and freedom made it impossible for him to consider settling down to a job as a farm labourer, not that any farmer would hire him for gypsies had a bad name. He drew back from the idea of committing a crime that would win him a sentence of transportation to Australia for that idea was risky and convict life was brutalising. Anyway, there was no guarantee that the judge at his trial would not be feeling liverish and decide to hang him instead of sending him to Botany Bay.

During the French Wars, gypsies who wanted to get away joined the Army in place of better off men who had been balloted to go. Sometimes they were well paid for doing so but that escape route had gone now too for since peace had come, discharged soldiers were wandering the roads as tramps and to beg was bitter for a proud man.

Simon Archer's Circus Royale offered Jesse an opportunity. He had done a turn in the ring that evening and knew that it had been well received, though it had not been spectacular. In time he'd be able to build up the act and thought that he might even enjoy circus life – at least it would mean travelling all the time. Yes, he thought, I'll join the circus. After he'd raced Barbary at Caverton Edge the next day, he'd go back to the Archers and offer to join up with them, and then, when he'd saved up enough money he'd strike out for himself. Money, I need money, he thought, and smiled ruefully as he remembered the brown-skinned girl who out-jumped him for the ten pound prize. His stomach gave a queer lurch at her memory. It was as if she'd bewitched him in some way. She looked capable of it.

Ignoring Gib's call, he walked away from the circle of plotting men. Flashes of distant lightning illuminated the deep purple sky over his head and he was halfway down the hill when someone ran up alongside him. A hand stroked his arm and Thomassin's voice whispered, 'Jesse, Jesse, come and sit with me.' She indicated a cluster of women who were sitting around another fire and he allowed himself to be led over to its welcoming circle. When he got there he found that old Rachel was talking about the various people she had dukkered during the day. He sat beside Thomassin with his head half-nodding in sleep when he realised Rachel was telling her audience about the chavi who had won the jumping contest.

That brought him to full wakefulness and to listen intently as the old woman spat on to the ground and said, 'A strange girl won the jumping prize from Jesse. There's a mystery about that one. She thought she'd get away with dressing like a bondager but I could jin her. Her wast was as soft as silk.'

Jesse was about to say, 'Yes, that's because she's a rich

merchant's daughter in disguise,' but Thomassin interrupted him.

'What did you see in her hand?' she asked, in a voice that rose sharply above the others.

'I saw riches, love, hatred, danger, distance . . . voyaging far and near like a gypsy.' Old Rachel laughed. 'It was a fine hand.'

Thomassin leaned forward with her eyes glistening and asked, 'What about her man? What did you see about her pireno? Will she get rommed?'

'Oh aye, she'll be married. To a man that's bangowasted. When I told her that she jumped up and ran away as if she'd been stabbed.'

'You're a faker,' shouted Thomassin, also standing up angrily.

'Meklis, hold your tongue,' said another of the women sharply. 'Rachel's only telling you what she saw.'

Thomassin pointed at Jesse sitting by her side, 'But he's bango-wasted and that chavi was casting the glamourie on him today! I saw her. I felt it.'

He stood up too and glared at the girl as he shouted, 'I can do a bit of dukkering too. I know who that girl is. She's a merchant's daughter from Lauriston. There's no way a girl like that's going to marry a gypsy. Anyway I'm not the only man in the world who's bango-wasted!'

Then he turned and strode away into the darkness. He could not understand why he felt so angry.

Before Canny left the Cross Keys Hotel with Thompson, he had ordered his daughter to go back to Havanah Court. For once she did not argue because there was a look in her father's eye that told her he was in no mood to stand for rebellion.

When she reached home she lay down on her bed fully dressed and waited for news. The oppressive heat promised thunder and made her remember spectacular tropical storms when rain used to beat down on the fronds of the palm trees around her old home and she sat on the verandah with Elma, her black nursemaid, enjoying the thrill of the deluge. The thundering noise of falling rain always made her feel safe and very happy . . .

It took a few seconds to bring herself back to the present when Joe Cannonball knocked on the door and came into the room looking very concerned.

'There's someone to speak to you, Baby,' he said.

'Who is it?' she asked apprehensively.

Joe shrugged. 'I don't know. He says his name's Armstrong – it suits him.'

She followed Joe down to the hall where Mary's swain was waiting, suspiciously eyeing the glories of Canny's interior decoration. Odilie was very glad to see him and her face lit up with a smile as she asked, 'What's happened? Is Grace all right?'

He grinned back. 'A woman with black hair got her out. Now she's gone with Mary and her brother to the marriage place. They sent me to tell you to come.'

Odilie laughed and threw up her hands, her anxiety completely assuaged by the news. 'That's wonderful,' she exclaimed, 'I'll come straight away.'

When she looked around for the shawl she expected Joe to throw over her shoulders, his face was grim. 'You're going no place on your own at this time of night, Miss Odilie. I don't even know this fellow,' he pronounced.

'Oh Joe, but *I* know him. He's Grace's young man's sister's fiancé . . .' She laughed at the intricacy of this explanation and went on, 'He's all right, Joe. I'll be completely safe with him.'

'You ain't going any place without me,' persisted Joe. 'It don't sound like the right time for any wedding if you ask me, but if you're set on going, I'm coming with you.'

In a trio, they marched out of the house with Joe in the middle towering above the other two. 'I'm sure I don't know what Canny'll say about this,' he kept muttering as he strode along.

Patie Mudie had been sleeping on the floor of his tent when Grace and Adam burst in. Adam shook him by the shoulder and cried out, 'Wake up, wake up. We want to get married.'

326

Patie grunted and shook his head. 'It's late,' he groaned, looking at the enormous metal watch he carried on his person.

'Are we too late?' asked Adam but Patie shook his head again.

'You're too late for a pound, though. At this time of the night it'll be two guineas.'

The young man searched his pockets and brought out a handful of coins which he hurriedly counted before saying, 'That's all right. I can find enough.'

Patie stood up yawning. 'Where's your witnesses? You're got to have two witnesses or it's not legal. They've got to see you take each other as man and wife,' he told them.

'They're coming, here's one of them now,' cried Grace as Mary came running up to the tent, her face alight with excitement.

'Jockie's gone to fetch your friend,' she panted out to Grace.

'I hope he hurries up then,' grumbled Patie. 'A man needs his sleep.'

The complaint was hardly out of his mouth when Jockie, Odilie and Joe Cannonball came hurrying over the uneven grass. At the sight of Odilie's manservant, Patie's eyes rolled and the dogs in the tent set up a chorus of frenzied barking which was to continue all through the ceremony.

In spite of her delight for Grace, Odilie's heart gave a stab of envy when she saw the young couple standing hand in hand at the door of Mudie's tent but she immediately reproached herself for selfishness and cried out as she ran towards them, 'How happy I am for you! God bless you both!' Then she embraced them and told Adam, 'When this is finished, come across to our stables with me. I'm going to give you a horse as a wedding present. It'll carry you back to your Cheviot Hills.'

'Come in, come in,' came an impatient voice from inside the tent and they all looked round to see Patie Mudie holding open the flap to allow them to enter. His voice was as lugubrious as if he was about to conduct a funeral ceremony and not a marriage.

His wife, who had been sleeping unnoticed like a curled-up hedgehog at the back of the tent, was wakened too by this time and was writing out a marriage certificate on a grubby-looking sheet of paper that she had propped on to a wooden lectern.

'Is this your other witness?' asked Patie indicating Odilie, who nodded brightly. His tone did not lighten when he said, 'In that case, we'll proceed.'

He smelt of snuff and brandy when he stepped towards the couple, turned them to face each other and took the right hand of each.

'What's your name, lad?' was his first question to Adam.

'Adam Scott.'

'Are you Adam Scott?' asked Patie and Adam looked surprised before clearing his throat and saying solemnly, 'Yes I am.'

'You're no' merrit already, are you?'

'No.'

Patie moved his rheumy eyes to Grace. 'What's your name?'

'Grace Elliot.' She knew what to expect by this time. 'Are you Grace Elliot?' came his question.

'Yes.' Her voice was quavering with emotion in spite of the absurdity of the whole business.

'You're no merrit either?'

'No.'

'You want to marry now?'

'Yes,' sighed the couple looking into each other's eyes.

'You want to marry each other?'

'Yes,' they chorused.

Mudie put Grace's hand into Adam's and then gabbled, 'In that case, according to the law of Scotland and before these witnesses, I declare that you have taken each other as man and wife. That's it, you're married.'

He dropped their hands and turned to his wife saying, 'Where's the brandy bottle, missus? I'm fair dry.'

Odilie stood thunderstruck behind the newlyweds and gave a gasp of disappointment. 'Is that all?' she asked.

Patie turned back to glare at her. 'It's enough. It's all that's needed. They'll get their bit of paper when I get my fee.'

'Are you sure that this is legal?' asked Odilie imperiously.

'As sure as death. It's legal, all right. I've married nobs, lords and ladies and some of them have wished it wasn't legal because they weren't able to get out of it when they changed their minds. So it's legal, don't you worry about that. Scots law's different from English law. As long as two witnesses see the couple take each other as husband and wife, it's legal.'

He held out a grubby paw in Adam's direction. 'Two guineas, laddie. That was the bargain, wasn't it?'

Adam was reaching into his pocket for the money when the tent flap lifted and Alice Archer came rushing in. She ran over to Grace and held her close, one hand on the back of the girl's golden head pressing it into her own shoulder. Both of them began sobbing as they clung together. 'Oh, my dear daughter. Oh, my darling,' cried Alice.

Embarrassed, everyone except Patie and his barking dogs looked away till the two women recovered themselves. Then, wiping her eyes, Alice asked, 'It's not over, is it? I haven't missed it?'

Grace was reeling with shock. 'You really are my mother. You're Lucy Allen?' she asked in a bemused voice.

'Yes, I am, and it's a miracle that we met. Oh, Grace, I'm so proud of you,' wept Alice, holding her arms out again.

'Oh, Mother,' cried Grace, who was weeping too.

They clung together for a long time till Alice loosened her hold on the girl and gently asked, 'Have I missed your wedding? Is it over?'

'Yes, I'm married – Mother,' Grace told her and Alice's face showed enormous disappointment. 'Oh, how I wanted to see you marry. I wanted that so much,' she gasped, and looked so harrowed that even Patie Mudie's stone heart softened.

He stepped forward to offer, 'Och, don't you worry, missus. I'll do it again if you like. Might as well, I'm up anyway. It'll cost you another pound, though.'

'Daylight robbery,' snorted Odilie, reaching into her pocket for a golden coin. 'But here's a guinea. Make it longer this time.'

He did not know any other formula however, and seconds later they were re-married by the same words. Then Patie's mousey wife stepped forward with a broad smile on her face and presented the newly-married pair with a rolled up sheet of paper. Adam unrolled it and read out, 'This is to sartify that on this day of August 3rd, 1816, Grace Elliot and Adam Scott took each other in marriage before Peter Mudie and the following witnesses at St. James' Fair in Lauriston. The witnesses were . . .'

The place for witnesses' names were blank and Patie's wife told Odilie and Mary, 'Here's the pen, fill in your own names or make your marks if you can't write. Then my Patie'll sign it and it'll all be legal.'

As they signed, the atmosphere inside the tent suddenly became almost festive. The lamps' glow seemed warmer and more friendly, making the empty tent undergo a magic change and become a perfect setting for a wedding. In the golden light Alice lost her look of anxiety and bloomed like a rose as she watched her daughter being embraced by everyone. Grace looked really beautiful with her massed hair glowing and her face shining with happiness. She had been transformed from a shy and withdrawn waif into a golden girl and her mother's heart was so full that it felt ready to burst. The tears that trembled in her eyes were tears of happiness. Even in her wildest dreams she had not imagined that something like this would happen on her return to Lauriston.

Joe Cannonball, spying Patie's brandy bottle propped up behind his chair, bent down and grabbed it, drew out the cork, took a drink and then offered it to the person who stood next to him, which happened to be Jockie. 'Here's to your health and happiness!' cried the young blacksmith, lifting the bottle to his lips and quelling Patie's protests with glance of his eye. The bride and groom leaned towards each other in the middle of the tent and though they were exhausted by the rigours of the day and the intense emotions that they had gone through, they rallied the last of their strength and responded joyously to the toast.

Odilie's eyes were glistening with tears of affection when it came to her turn to toast the pair. She had found their strange wedding almost unbearably affecting and kept leaning over to kiss Grace on the cheek or to squeeze Adam's hand and whisper, 'You're so lucky.'

'I know,' Grace agreed. Her face was glowing with happiness as she looked at her husband and her newly-found mother. 'I never could have believed that any of this would happen. Not in my wildest dreams. It's like a miracle. Oh, Odilie, I can't tell you how happy I feel . . .' Her voice trailed off as she saw a bereft look come to her friend's face and the spectre of the Duke hovered between them.

'Let's make plans,' said Odilie briskly. 'You'll have to be on the road before dawn. I wouldn't put it past your father to try to catch you so we must get you a good horse. Come home with me now . . .'

'Before you go, I've something to give you,' said Alice, proferring her bundle of papers. 'Take these with you and read them at leisure. You'll find plenty of interest in them. You're a landowner, my dear. My father thought I was dead and he left you a lot of property that was to be yours on the day you married. I don't want it. When this is over Lucy Allen will disappear again. She's really dead as far as I'm concerned. But the property's the reason why Elliot was so keen to keep you unwed. And there's other things here that he'll not want to get around. You're in a good position to make him do exactly as you want, so don't miss it.'

331

She laid the papers on the chair beside her and smoothed them out flat with her hand before starting to sort through them. 'Yes, it's as I thought – title deeds, wills, letters . . . He's kept everything. That's what a legal training does for you – you never throw anything away, even if it's incriminating. You just keep it under the floorboards where other people can't see it!' She laughed with a bitter note. 'You'll probably find he's been peculating other people's money as well as my father's. He'll have been stealing like a magpie from local folk for years and he won't want the news of it to get around or it'll be Botany Bay for Andrew Elliot. There'd be plenty after his blood if they saw these papers.'

She rolled them up and handed them to Grace. 'So here's your wedding present from your mother, my dear. Guard it well. You'll find in spite of his trickeries and forgeries, you've a good bit of property left. Make him give it to you.' She turned to look fondly at her new son-in-law. 'You'll be a big farmer, my lad. You and your bairns'll be rich. I like the look of you, though, and I think my girl's chosen well. I give her into your care. Fight for her rights.'

He nodded solemnly. 'I'll fight, but what about you? What's going to happen to you?'

She shook her head. 'I shouldn't be here at all. The law's looking for me.' But she turned and held her daughter tight once more as she said, 'I must tell you my story before I go. I was younger than you are now when I married. I hadn't any sense because I believed everything he said to me, the lying snake. I didn't know your father was my maid's lover and had been for a long time.'

Grace nodded and sighed, 'Hester . . .'

'Yes, Hester. I didn't realise it, though. I thought she was my friend. I used to tell her things – what a fool I was! But after you were born Elliot stopped living with me, rarely slept with me. Hester told me he had a lover in the town and I was afraid to tackle him about it because of his temper. I was afraid he was going to kill me but I didn't tell my father though he guessed I was unhappy. Then I met a man, a young fellow. I fell in love and I needed love so badly. We met here at St James' Fair, and we found ourselves under the trees over there by the river. It happened so naturally . . . when I discovered I was having another baby, I was terrified. I knew whose it was and it wasn't Elliot's. He'd know that, too . . .'

Alice paused and stared into the past with bleak eyes. 'I panicked. Hester said I should hide it. The dresses had fuller skirts than now and we were still wearing stomachers – they hid a lot. I didn't share Elliot's bed so he never noticed. When it was near my time, I went to Bettymill with Hester and was delivered there. I had a bad time. When I came round there was no baby and Hester said it had died. It's on my conscience still that I was glad.'

At this Alice gave a sob and clutched her daughter's hands. 'I was really glad, Grace. I thought I'd got away with it. I went home but next day, out of the blue and without saying anything to me, my husband took a party of men out to Bettymill and found my dead baby in a little grave behind the house. It was a wee boy and it had been strangled with my garter. They said I did it. Hester gave evidence at the trial about me being pregnant and concealing it, and about me killing the baby. They believed her. They took me to Edinburgh and the judge there was sorry for me, I think. Instead of hanging me, he banished me. In a way I thought I deserved to be punished for neglecting the baby, for not caring enough – for being glad it died!'

Tears were running down Alice's cheeks as she spoke and Grace put her arms around her mother whispering, 'Don't cry, oh don't cry.'

Then Alice drew back and looked bleakly at her daughter. 'The worst thing was that the baby's father believed I'd killed it, too. He joined the Army and went away. He was killed in Spain, Mrs Anstruther told me.'

After they heard this story everyone was sobered. The time had come for the parting. With fervent promises to meet again, Alice and Grace embraced once more before the older woman slipped off into the darkness and headed back to the freak show. A chastened-looking Odilie ushered the others off to Havanah Court to select a suitable horse.

There were lights on upstairs so the girl knew Canny had returned home. She sent Joe in and headed straight for the stables with the others. The mingled smell of sweet hay and the sweat of horses was, as always, heady for her. There were fifteen horses kept in the big loose-boxes of the main building, most of them lying down now but a few of them slept on their feet with their heads drooping. They blinked their eyes when Odilie took the lantern from its nail at the door, turning up its low wick. Then holding it high, she stepped along the neatly-swept brick passage between the iron-railed boxes and as she walked she told Grace and Adam, 'Come with me, take your pick. Choose any horse you like except my jumping mare because she's not up to the weight of both of you. You need a big horse that can carry Grace on the pillion as well as you, Adam.'

They eventually decided on a well-boned bay with a fine head. His name was Oberon and he had a placid temper as well as enormous staying power. 'Oberon'll carry you to the Cheviots without any trouble at all. He's so careful you can both sleep on his back,' joked Odilie, approving of Adam's choice.

The men saddled the bay and when she was safely installed on the pillion, Grace leaned down to put a tender hand on her friend's cheek. 'Dear Odilie, I'll never be able to thank you enough. I do love you. Don't forget me when you're a Duchess,' she whispered.

Neither of them could say any more but only swallowed and stared at each other with deep emotion, tears sparkling in their eyes. It was Mary who broke the suspense. 'Go away now and may God go with you,' she cried, for she could bear the emotion of parting no longer.

Oberon's reins were lifted and shaken and the couple rode off out of the stableyard with the horse stepping purposefully and Adam's back making a safe prop and bulwark for the girl who laid her head against it as she waved her goodbyes.

CHAPTER 13

Tuesday, 4 August

By the time Jem found Viewhill House, Alice and her party had left. He did not know this, however, and hammered on the door until Hester came down to stand behind it and ask him what he wanted. When he threw his massive weight against the door, she started to scream hysterically and Elliot came running out to threaten the would-be intruder, 'Go away! Go away or I'll fetch the law again. We've had enough of you vagrants in one night to last us for a lifetime.'

'Where's my Alice?' yelled Jem.

'There's no Alice here, go away.'

'She came here with a young lad looking for your daughter.'

There was a sneer in Elliot's voice when he called back, 'You mean Lucy Allen. Hasn't she even told you her real name? She left but she won't get far. They'll soon catch her.'

Alice, oh Alice, what's happened to you? thought Jem in a panic as he went running down the middle of Roxburgh Street. When he reached the freak show again his face was working with emotion and he looked on the verge of collapse. Long Tom was sitting on the steps nursing his aching head and the others were crowded around a blazing bonfire discussing the night's events. They were all very worried and when Jem came bursting in among them they clustered towards him like a crowd of buzzing bees, all speaking at once and reaching out to touch him.

'Did you find her, Jem?' asked Meg. He shook his head but could not speak.

'She's not been back here yet but she'll surely come soon,' Hans assured him, knowing the question was uppermost in his mind.

Jem nodded, 'I hope so. Has anybody seen Billy?'

'Not a sight of him. He's disappeared. We'll have to wait till morning light to look for him,' groaned Long Tom but Jem shook his head again.

'We can't do that. By morning he could be miles away. We've got to find him tonight. I'll run over to the circus and fetch Simon and some of his men. Who else is able to come out and help me?'

A small ill-assorted group gathered while Jem went into his caravan for his pistol and was disturbed to find it gone. When he came out again he told Long Tom and Meg, 'You two wait here. If Alice comes back, keep her with you till I return. I've got to speak to her.'

Simon was closing up his circus for the night when his frantic-looking brother appeared. 'My God, what's happened? You look dreadful,' he said with concern and Jem groaned.

'Billy's run away. He attacked Long Tom and hopped it. And I've lost Alice. The law's after her and I don't know why.'

Simon reeled. It was difficult to know which of the two calamities was the most serious. He asked, 'Did he kill Long Tom? I'm sorry to say it but I've always thought you were taking a terrible risk keeping that lad. He's a real maniac. It's a miracle he hasn't killed somebody by now.'

'No, Tom's all right. Billy tried to do him in but he didn't manage it. Tom's got a hard head. Everybody from the show's out looking for the lad now, but if he gets hold of somebody out there who doesn't know him there's no telling what might happen. It could be a woman . . .' The brothers looked at each other and shuddered.

Simon shook his head. 'Don't take on. I'll come and help you but I don't want to bring my boys because I don't want them hurt. And anyway it would be best not to start too big a hue and cry or every drunken hobblede-hoy in the fairground'll get in on the hunt. That would panic Billy, wouldn't it? You're the only one that can really handle him.'

'That's true. Have you a pistol?' asked Jem shortly.

'Haven't you got one?' replied Simon.

'I went to look for it just now but it's disappeared. It was in the van when we arrived at the Fair but it's not there now. I don't know who's got it.'

'Yes, I've a pistol,' said his brother. 'I'll give it to you. Billy belongs to you and if anybody's going to shoot him it ought to be you.'

'I hope it won't come to that but you're right, I want to be the one to find him. A stranger might just kill him out of hand. He's not capable of managing alone. He's my responsibility – I can't just abandon him.' And then Jem added, 'But, oh God, Simon I wish I knew what's happened to Alice. She's out in the darkness some place. I wish she was safe in the caravan tonight.'

In fact Alice was not far away. After Grace and the others went off with Odilie to Havanah Court, she stood with wrinkled brow working out what to do. She knew that Elliot would not let her get away with his papers without trying to stop her and that he would act quickly. Now that the documents were safe with Grace, it was essential for her to get as far away from Lauriston as possible – but first she wanted to see Jem.

What she did not know was that while she was approaching the freak show from one direction in search of him, he was running off in the other direction towards Simon's circus. They passed only yards apart but unseen by each other because of the darkness and the press of people.

Long Tom and Meg were delighted to see Alice when she stepped into the circle of light made by their bonfire. They both stood up and rushed towards her crying out, 'Oh Alice, poor Jem's almost mad with worry about you. He's been out looking for you and now he's had to go after Billy.'

Alice looked bemused. 'Looking for Billy? What's happened to him?'

Tom shifted his feet in a guilty way. 'I was taking off

his chains to put on his Strong Man costume and he felled me, Alice. Knocked me out cold. I'm lucky to be alive.

Alice turned on him in a fury. 'Couldn't you have taken more care? You know what he's like!'

Angrily she stalked off towards the caravan she'd shared so happily with Jem. A little flame was glimmering low inside the glass bulb of a lamp on the middle of their table and its soft light made the brightly painted interior, which Jem had decorated with such care and artistry, glow like a jewel box. The whole place looked warm and hospitable. This really was her home and she gazed around with a devastated look on her face remembering the happy times she and Jem had shared in the safe little haven.

Then with a shrug of her shoulders, she put one hand into her capacious pocket and drew out the long pistol, putting it on the table so that it pointed at the back wall. 'I'd have used it,' she said aloud. 'I'd have killed Elliot with it if he'd tried anything. He knew that.'

It was a relief, however, that she hadn't been forced into murder for that would have been a certain way of ensuring that they'd hang her. She looked out of the open caravan door and saw that the moon was sinking lower and would soon disappear behind the rearing pile of the ruined castle on the opposite hill. The darkness under the trees in the farthest corners of the field was creeping closer and looked impenetrable. She shivered, thinking of Billy lurking out there somewhere and wished that she could close the caravan door and stay safe inside but that was not to be. She must get away, because in Scotland she knew she could be hunted down like a dog by Elliot and she feared his lying tongue. She would not be safe until she reached the safety of England.

Hurriedly she opened a drawer in the side of the table and took out a sheet of paper, a pot of ink and a pen. She wrote standing up in a hurried scrawl: '*Dear Jem, don't despair. One day soon I'll meet up with you again but in the meantime I have to go to England. I'll take the quickest road. I was banished from Scotland because they said I'd killed my baby but I didn't do it. Tonight I realise how much I love you. Alice.'*

The horses were grazing quietly behind the waggons, unaffected by the confusion that had convulsed the humans. Alice grabbed the halter of a sturdy chestnut with a white blaze on its face that she knew to be quiet and reliable. She led it towards the back of their caravan and pulled out Jem's riding saddle and bridle which was stored in a box there. When the horse was tacked up she clambered on to its back and was about to ride out into the darkness when Meg appeared and asked, 'Where are you going, Alice?'

She turned in the saddle. 'I'm running away. I'm going south. I've got to cross the border before dawn.' Then she trotted off.

While Jem and the people from the freak show were dashing about looking for him, Billy stayed hidden among the trees. From his hiding place he could see the caravan where he'd felled Long Tom and his eyes were puzzled and confused as he crouched down wondering what to do.

He looked over the encampment of the freak show and recognised the people he saw moving about in the glow of the firelight there. He saw Jem come and go; he watched Alice arrive and then ride away again on the big horse. He did not wonder where or why she was going because his brain was not capable of speculation. He watched and he registered, that was all.

Just after midnight, he shifted uncomfortably in his hiding place, for cramp had seized his leg and he decided it was time to move. He sniffed the air. From somewhere came a wonderful smell of roasting meat. His mouth watered and hunger gripped him so he headed in the direction of the smell, tracking it like an animal. As he loped along, it grew stronger. Unknowingly he was heading down towards the Kirk Yetholm gypsy encampment where they were roasting chickens that had been filched from a farmer's yard that morning.

But someone was coming towards him – a man with his hands in his pockets and his head down. Cautiously Billy drew back in the shadows but was able to catch a glimpse of the man's face as he passed and then he smiled for he recognised the gypsy who had ridden the horse in the circus ring that evening, the one who was related to Billy himself. A queer sort of family pride, a longing to belong, a primitive hero worship, seized the big young lad and, hunger forgotten, he turned to follow Jesse.

He walked behind like a shadow as his quarry headed for the river. On the way Jesse was stopped by another man who gesticulated excitedly with his hands and Billy drew back to hide behind some trees. After the conversation was over, the object of Billy's interest turned quickly round and ran back up the hill in the direction from which he'd come. When he reached a circle of men sitting around a fire enjoying the succulent-smelling chicken, he clapped a hand on the shoulder of one of them and said loudly, 'Listen Gib, forget about fighting. I've just heard that Billy, the wild chal Rachel gave away, has broken out tonight. He half-killed a man and escaped. They're all trashe mande in case he kills somebody. He's capable of it, apparently.'

Gib grimaced and bit into his chicken leg. 'He's not our chal now. She gave him away. We've plenty to do worrying about the Earl of Hell. His men attacked Abel tonight and we're going out to get them as soon as we've eaten.'

'That's damned silly. Abel probably asked for it anyway,' snapped Jesse. 'I'm going to help find Billy. He's our concern. He's a Romany, isn't he?'

'Maybe that's why you should let him get away then,' said Gib, who was more than half-drunk and not thinking straight. When he saw that his uncle and the other gypsy men were in no fit state or amenable frame of mind to help him, Jesse strode out of the camp again. Only Billy, who was still following him, saw that the girl called Thomassin rose from her place in the huddle of women sitting apart from the men and followed too.

When Jesse reached the flat ground he paused and thought – what would I do if I were Billy? Where would I hide? He looked along the grassy river bank and started to search about beneath the low hanging branches of the trees. Most of the lovers had gone by this time and only a few were still lying there, cradled in each other's arms. They were not too happy to be disturbed and asked if they'd seen a big fellow go by, but those who did reply to Jesse's questions said that he was the only person who'd bothered them that night.

Eventually Jesse emerged into the open again and stood with his arms crossed over his chest staring across the river. His eye rested on Havanah Court where lights still glimmered in the windows and he wondered which room was occupied by the dark-skinned girl. She had such elegant style! His heart gave a strange leap when he thought about her and he gave himself a shake like a dog coming out of water. 'Don't be silly,' he scolded himself. 'You've better things to do than get bewitched by a girl, especially that one.'

Yet, yielding to impulse, he stood very still on the little peninsula of land staring across to the other bank as if he was summoning the girl up to appear before him.

Behind him Thomassin hid in the bushes, shaking with such emotion that her hands were knotted into tight fists and her face harrowed with a look of unrequited love. She was so intent on spying on Jesse that Billy's approach took her by surprise. All at once he loomed up out of the blackness and stood by her side. 'You're pretty,' he mumbled.

She gave a start and reached for her dagger to protect herself but when she recognised the stranger, she stayed her hand. For a moment she wondered if she should call out to Jesse but Billy was smiling and obviously meant no harm. 'Hello, what are you doing here?' she said without showing any fear.

He pointed across at Jesse, still staring at Havanah Court. 'I'm following him,' he whispered.

'So am I,' said Thomassin with a little laugh. Then she

341

patted Billy's arm confidentially and told him in a low voice, 'That's Jesse. I cast a spell on him today. I gave him a potion to drink and I said "Temon, temon, temon," three times this morning. It's worked all right, but it's worked for the wrong woman I'm very much afraid.'

Billy was flattered that this girl was telling him things even though he could not fully understand what she was talking about. 'I get potions to drink sometimes,' he offered. 'Alice gives them to me. Then I sleep.' He gave a huge yawn at the memory.

Thomassin laughed. 'It'd be no use making love potions for you then, would it? Have you a sweetheart?'

Billy furrowed his brow and shook his head. He liked so many things about Thomassin, the way she laughed; the way she crinkled her slanting eyes and threw her head back so that the hair sailed over her shoulders like a sheet of silk. He put out a hand to touch her scarlet shawl and unlike most women she did not shrink away from his attempted caress but stood firm and let him stroke her arm.

'I'll have to find you a sweetheart, Billy,' she murmured and he smiled trustingly at her.

'You be my sweetheart,' he whispered back.

She looked at him with pity. 'What are you doing here?' she asked.

'I've run away. I hit Long Tom and ran away,' he told her. She drew him with her deeper into the bushes and whispered, 'They're all looking for you. Do you want me to take you back, Billy?'

He shook his head violently. 'Oh no! I like being out. I don't want to go back. I'll stay with you, Thomassin.'

The girl was surprised that he'd remembered her name and her heart was sore for him. 'What am I going to do with you, Billy?' she asked in a musing voice.

He had no suggestions to make but stood smiling at her in the moonlight with hope in his eyes. She glanced around. Only Jesse could be seen, still standing entranced on the river bank. 'Come on. I'll show you a place where you can hide,' she said with sudden decision and grabbed

Billy's arm. Holding on to him as if he was her swain and talking animatedly to him, she led him across the wooden bridge which fortunately was now almost empty of people. They looked just like any ordinary couple and no one gave them a second glance. Instead of following the other late revellers into town when they reached the other bank, she guided him uphill towards the walled park that surrounded Sloebank Castle and soon the thick woods swallowed them up, hiding them from sight. Thomassin was like a sharp-eyed woodland animal and she knew her way about the park because she'd been coming to the Fair every year of her life and when she was younger she'd always gone out poaching with the boys on the evening of Fair Day. The ducal policies were reckoned to be a poaching paradise by the gypsies because they were full of game for travellers' pots.

Billy was intimidated by the darkness and the sounds of the woods but Thomassin pulled insistently on his hand and led him on ever deeper over paths that twisted and twined through the closely-meshed branches of scrubby undergrowth. Above their heads towered much taller trees that sighed in the night breeze. The girl sniffed the air and said, 'Rain's coming. It'll be here tomorrow.'

He was stumbling along because he was not as skilled as she in negotiating his way through woodland paths in the dark. It seemed to him that every raised root was waiting to trip him up and he was uncoordinated because he was very tired and very hungry. 'Come on, don't give up,' she encouraged him. 'There's an old tower in the middle of this wood that most people don't know about. You can sleep in it and stay out of sight when the glim comes. Darkness is the only safe time for you. If you lie low till tomorrow night when everybody's gone home, then you'll be able to run away. I won't let them take you back to chain you up like a dog.'

Billy furrowed his brow. All this was too confusing for him. 'What'll I do? Where will I go?' he asked. All his life other people had taken the decisions – first Rachel and then Jem. They'd made every arrangement for Billy from as far back as he could remember. 'Where will I go? What will I do?' he asked piteously again.

The girl smiled. 'Anything you like. You can take to the road,' she told him. Thomassin did not want Billy to be recaptured for in a strange way, he had awakened a sort of sympathy in her savage heart. The idea of anyone spending their life in a barred cage horrified her. Even Billy's undoubted violence was no justification in her view for such a fate. She disregarded the fact that he was totally reliant on Jem but told herself that he'd soon learn to stand on his own feet. After all, he was a gypsy like herself, a child of the open air, the empty sky and the lonely snaking road. He should be set free to wander even if it was only for a while.

She said little of this to Billy, however, for she knew he would not have understood her words but some sense of her urgency and determination communicated itself to him. 'Tomorrow you'll be free,' she cried, turning to him with her face alight.

He echoed the word, 'Free!' and laughed back at her.

The old tower, when they finally reached it, was even more broken down than Thomassin remembered. The roof had collapsed and night birds were roosting and hunting among the garlands of ivy that cloaked its broken stones. They walked in through a doorway arch that faced an empty fireplace on the ground floor with a big arched mantel that would provide cover in the event of rain. She showed it to Billy who was wearing no coat and was barefoot so the chill of the night was making him shiver. He was glad to huddle into the empty vault of the ruined hearth and when she saw his stricken face, Thomassin pulled off her scarlet shawl and draped it over his shoulders saying, 'Take this. I'll not feel the cold because I'll run all the way back to our camp. Just you stay here and keep as quiet as a mouse so's nobody will hear you. I'll come back tomorrow.'

'Billy's hungry,' he moaned like a child and the girl made an exasperated noise.

'I haven't any food and I can't wait here any longer.

There's plenty of animals about. Catch a few.' But it was obvious he did not know how to hunt so she quickly made a snare out of one of the laces of her boots, set it up in a likely corner of the interior of the tower to catch a roaming mouse or a vole, built a little fire to warm him and left him alone.

But he had never been on his own for long and did not want her to go away so he tried to hold her back, clinging to her hand and saying, 'Talk to Billy. Stay with Billy. Tell Billy about "Temon, temon, temon".'

She looked at him, surprised at his ability to remember that and shook her head. 'No, I'm sorry but I can't. I've got to go. It's late and bad men roam about the fairground at night looking for girls. That's what happened to your mother, Billy. She was caught by one of them and fell with you.'

The Fair never stopped till dawn but during the darkest hours of the night it took on a different, more sinister character from the one of jollity and innocent pleasure that it showed during the day. As Thomassin ran back from Sloebank Park, she took care to stay in the shadows and avoid parties of men who were out looking for women, for this was the time when the whores paraded and decent women stayed at home or in their waggons.

The owner of the Castle always picked his fairtime house guests with the view to making up a congenial party who would enjoy a foray to the after-midnight pleasures. James Fox and his cronies had passed an evening of drinking and dining, played a few hands of cards and then, when the women retired, they foregathered to walk back down to the field where lights still glimmered, and bonfires sparkled like beckoning lures. The Duke walked arm in arm with his special friend Edmund Lacey who had been with him in the Army. For protection, because robberies were always a danger at that time of night, the Duke's manservant walked behind them carrying a pistol.

They were chattering loudly when they passed within

a few feet of where Thomassin was hiding beneath the wooden bridge and she could hear their conversation as they walked along above her head.

'What a pity the black heiress didn't make an appearance today,' said Lacey to the swaggering figure by his side.

The Duke laughed. 'Oh, it doesn't matter. I'll see plenty of her soon enough but she'll be in the party at the races tomorrow – today, I mean. You'll meet her again, Lacey. Smitten with her, are you?'

Lacey laughed. 'She's a little beauty in spite of the colour – or maybe because of it. Exotic – and rich, too. You're a lucky devil, James. When you're tired of her you can pass her on.'

'She'll be used goods by that time. There's an old woman in the gypsy camp making me up a special potion.'

Their voices died away and the hiding girl clutched her arms around her shoulders thinking of the words – 'She'll be in the party at the races tomorrow . . .'

I'll be there too, she promised herself, and so will Jesse. Where he goes I go. Her passion for him was so strong that it hurt like a wound.

The fires were still blazing high as they would all night in the middle of the Kirk Yetholm camp and men were sitting around drinking while women flitted in and out of the shadows fetching and carrying, when the Duke strode into the light and looked around in an imperious way. He made no attempt to conceal his identity for he expected everyone to know who he was.

'Is Gib Faa here?' he asked.

A man stood up from the middle of the crowd. There were bruises and cuts on his face and one of his hands was bandaged showing that he had recently been in a fight. 'He is. What do you want with him?' he asked. He knew perfectly well who was speaking to him but it went against the grain of his pride to grovel to the Duke or address him with an honorific title of respect until he was forced to do so.

'I'm looking for that grey horse,' said the Duke, who was prepared to sweep all before him.

'It's late and it's dark. We've three grey horses but you won't be able to see them properly in this light,' replied Gib.

'That doesn't matter. I want the one that was in the jumping. The price shouldn't be too high because I heard that some countrywoman out-jumped it. I'll buy it from you – take it off your hands,' said the Duke with a laugh.

The gypsies around the fire stiffened with anticipation and pleasure when they realised that the speaker did not know the full story of the jumping competition. The identity of the winner had been kept from him and that gave them an advantage over him. The faces that turned towards him seemed respectful enough but the eyes gleamed with malicious glee showing how they secretly wanted to laugh out loud and no one was more delighted than Gib, who had many old scores unsettled against the Duke.

'I can't sell you a horse that isn't mine,' he said slowly.

'Don't waste my time, man. I know that you gypsies share everything amongst yourselves.'

'That horse isn't mine or ours,' persisted Gib. 'It belongs to my nephew and he's not here.'

'Take me to your horse-line anyway. I want to see it.' The Duke was not used to obstacles being put in his path.

Gib moved out of the circle and some other men rose at his back to follow. 'The horse-line's over here but that particular one isn't for sale, I can tell you that, sir.' He was still pretending that he did not know who the importunate buyer was and the men behind him made muttering noises of agreement.

'I want to see it,' persisted the Duke so they all moved off towards the dark shapes grazing beneath the trees. Some of the horses had piles of hay in front of them and the Duke looked at the fodder with a nasty smile. 'Been raiding hay sheds, have you? I could call the law on you for that.'

Gib looked around as if to check who was listening, leaned closer to the man at his side and said in a conversational tone, 'If you did that, your honour, it would be a great pity for your barns might go on fire and your horses disappear. It's strange how ill-luck plagues people who make too much trouble for the gypsies.'

'Damn ill-luck! It's your thieving hands that cause the trouble, you mean. Which is the horse? Where's that grey?'

With Edmund beside him and the manservant acting as escort at the rear, he walked up the line looking at the animals. Even in the darkness Jesse's stallion was outstanding and the Duke knew his horseflesh. 'This is it. Bring it over to the Castle tomorrow,' he said, clapping its shoulder.

Gib's voice took on a wheedling gypsy tone as he said, 'Oh, it's you, your Grace. I didn't recognise you in the dark. It's some years since we met, isn't it? The last time was when we had the trouble with Becklie as I recall.' He touched his forelock in a mocking way and had the satisfaction of seeing the Duke draw back at the mention of Becklie's name. 'I'll speak to my nephew but I'm not promising anything. I don't think he'll sell his horse,' he continued.

The Duke said nothing but a little of the bounce seemed to have gone out of him and he seemed anxious to leave. He turned on his heel and when he was a few strides off he called over his shoulder, 'I'll expect it tomorrow. It's a good horse so I'll give a fair price.'

Edmund beside him sighed in relief as they hurried away and said, 'They're a rough crew. What was all that about Becklie? It sounded as if he was threatening you.'

'She was some woman or other. It was when I was just a lad – you know what young men are like. They said I'd had her and they tried to foist a bairn she had on to me. Damned rogues. That one with the white hair's their leader: he does all their speaking for them.'

'He's a big man and tough-looking. No wonder people are afraid of them,' mused Edmund.

'It's all trickery,' said the Duke. 'Just trickery.'

'Even the fortune-telling? I hear they're good at that. And if it's trickery what about the potion you're having made up?' asked Edmund, who liked to dabble in the esoteric.

The Duke laughed. 'That's not trickery but the fortune-telling is. The old woman who sells the potions is famous for palm-reading too but it's only guesswork. And as far as her potions go I've still to see the results. If they do what she told my man they can do, I'll be as rampant as that stallion up there.'

'Heaven help your maidservants then,' sniggered Edmund. 'But seriously, I'd like to have my palm read.'

The Duke stopped in his tracks and said, 'All right then, let's go and find her. She'll read your palm for a guinea. They'll do anything for a guinea!'

Eyes glistening, the gypsy woman sat huddled together and watched the strangers patrolling their camp. Some of the younger ones, like Thomassin who had reached the safety of the camp again, recoiled into the shadows when Edmund and the Duke passed but old Rachel was not afraid. She sat smoking her clay pipe and watched them approaching. When he saw her, the Duke's manservant reached forward and tapped his employer on the shoulder, indicating Rachel. She took the pipe out of her mouth and said in her most ingratiating voice, 'Cross my loof wi' siller, gentlemen, and I'll look into the future for you.'

Edmund laughed excitedly and picked some coins out of the little pocket in the front of his waistcoat, selected one and with a flick of his thumb sent it spinning in Rachel's direction. She ignored it but the darting small girl Esther, who had eyes like a hawk, picked it up from the ground.

'A half-guinea, rajah! You'll get a good future for a half-guinea,' Rachel told him though he could not tell how she knew the value of the coin he had thrown to her because she had not touched it.

'But you'd have a better one for a guinea,' interjected the Duke roughly.

Edmund made a shrugging movement with his shoulders and moved towards the old woman. She indicated that he should sit down at her side which he did, holding out his right hand. The flames from the fire dappled their faces as she turned the palm between hers and held it up to the light. A silence hung over them for what seemed like a long time until she sighed and said, 'I see a life of privilege, that's what I see for you. But not a long one. You're right to enjoy yourself, rajah, and make the best of it.'

The young man's face darkened and laughter was forgotten. 'I'm not to have a long life? I thought you fortune-tellers didn't tell people bad things.'

She shook her head. 'I tell people what I see in their hands. If they don't want to hear it, they shouldn't come to Rachel. But your time's not come yet – don't worry. Not yet. There's still some life left for you.'

The Duke peered over his friend's shoulder and nudged him as he asked, 'Does he marry a wife, old woman?'

'No wife. No children. Many friends but few of them true,' she said and dropped the hand.

'Huh, you didn't have much joy for your half-guinea. Satisfied?' the Duke jeered unsympathetically at his companion.

Edmund stood up with an angry look on his face. 'All right, let her see *your* hand. You're not afraid, are you?'

'No, I'm not afraid. I don't believe in the nonsense, that's all. It's trickery for fools.'

'Then anything she tells you won't worry you. Stick out your hand and let her have a look at it.' While this exchange was going on between them Rachel sat staring up at the man with her black eyes inscrutable.

The challenge made the Duke hesitate and the matter was decided when Rachel rose to her feet and reached out for his left hand saying, 'You're Foxy-pawed, aren't you? Your family are all that way. Let me look at your wast.' She did not ask for any money.

Still pretending indifference he allowed her to turn his spatulate hand upwards and trace the lines with her fore-

350

finger. 'Riches, power, pleasure – too much pleasure. . . . you have had them all. A lucky chance changed your life a few years ago. You stint yourself nothing . . .'

Then she dropped the hand so quickly that he was taken by surprise and his arm dropped down on to his thigh as if it was lifeless. 'Is that all you've got to say?' he asked.

'That's all,' she replied coldly and turned away.

He put out a hand to stop her, seizing her by the shoulder. 'Wait. What else is there?'

Edmund chimed in, 'Yes, tell him. He's not afraid to hear it because he doesn't believe in fortune-telling.' There was malice in his voice.

Slowly Rachel turned round and stared up at the Duke's face while she asked him, 'Do you really want to be dukkered?'

'Well, I don't want to leave it like this,' he grumbled, and held his hand out again.

She sighed. 'On your own head be it, then. Cross my palm with money.'

'I might have guessed you'd trick me into paying,' he said with relief in his voice as he handed over a golden coin. Then he extended his left hand once more.

Rachel's face was shadowed as she looked into it and suddenly she started to speak in a chanting voice, almost singing her predictions, 'You are stalked by demons of your own making. There is no running away from them however hard you try. Just when you think you've cheated retribution, it will seize you. Your plans will all tumble like cardboard. Your fate waits for you now. It is in the shape of a man and very close . . . take care.' The last words were hissed and in the silence they hung in the air. Everyone present drew in their breath and held it, as if afraid to let it out again.

The Duke was the first to break the silence and he said in a shaken voice, 'It's mumbo jumbo. It doesn't mean anything. Come on, Edmund, I've had enough of this.'

Rachel put out a hand and held his sleeve as she told him, 'Beware. Your son is a man now, my lord.'

He turned and shouted at her, 'I haven't got a damned son. I've no children. I'm not even married yet.'

Rachel's sloe eyes were fixed on his face. 'I'm only telling you what I see in your hand.'

'You're a wicked old liar. You're like all the others, whispering about the curse. It's nonsense. I'll prove it wrong.'

Grabbing Edmund by the coat sleeve he went storming down the hill.

All through the long night the hunt went on for Billy. Jem looked into every hiding place he could imagine, upturning pedlars' packs and disturbing people sleeping on the ground. There was no sign of the fugitive and no one had seen him. Eventually, Simon prevailed on him, 'For God's sake, Jem, go home and lie down for a bit or you'll drop. If he's still about in the field, someone'll see him eventually. He's easy to spot and if he's far away there's not much you can do about it anyway. We should tell the law officers he's bolted and let them get on with looking for him.'

Jem still did not want to call in the law in their search for Billy. 'They'll shoot him as soon as they see him. They'll be afraid of him and won't give him a chance,' he demurred.

'Maybe it's bound to happen. Go home and lie down,' ordered Simon, pushing his staggering brother off in the direction of the freak show.

On his way there Jem met the dark-haired gypsy lad who was also looking exhausted but he stopped beside the showman and asked, 'Have you found him yet?'

Jem's face took on a guarded look. 'You mean Billy?'

'Yes, have you found him?'

'No, I haven't. There's not a trace of him.'

'Somebody must have helped him,' said Jesse. Then he yawned and told Jem, 'I'm going to sleep for a couple of hours and then I'll start looking again. Let me know if you find out anything.'

Jem put out a hand and detained the young man. 'Why are you bothered about Billy?' he asked.

'He's a member of my family. His mother was one of us,' said Jesse tersely.

When Jem reached his caravan, he paused in the clearing before its door and sent up a prayer asking that Alice would be inside. Then, very slowly he climbed the steps and pushed open the door but his shoulders slumped in despair when he saw that the interior was empty. On the table lay his pistol pinning down a sheet of paper. When he read what was written on it, he threw himself face down on his bunk and wept like a child.

Alice was lost. Though she sat up bravely in the saddle as she rode along, she was quivering with apprehension inside. The dangers of the dark road obsessed her, every rustle of sound, every movement made her blood freeze for she expected to be apprehended any minute. Although he had promised to let her escape without recapture, she knew perfectly well that Elliot was not to be trusted. She had gone off with his precious papers, evidence of the greed and cupidity that had ruled his life. He would want them back. It was true that Hester had admitted killing the baby, but that admission had been made before no witnesses except Alice herself and Elliot, who knew Hester to be guilty anyway for he had put her up to it. The court had not believed Alice the first time when she pleaded her innocence, and there was no reason for them to believe her now.

When she set off south, Alice had decided to take the most direct route out of Scotland, heading in the direction of Yetholm but skirting the villages by a twisting lane that led across the Border and down to Alnwick. She had a good horse which maintained a steady, ground-covering canter as well as a head start, so the chances were that she'd reach the sanctuary of England before pursuers could catch up with her. But she was afraid and she knew she had to hurry.

It was years since Alice had passed along the lane she

was using and even then she'd only ridden it in daytime. There were no signposts on the remote tracks, for the people who used them were only going short distances and knew their way about. Each time Alice came to a fork – and there were many forks leading off to distant farms – she had to draw on the reins and take her bearings from the stars.

At about three o'clock in the morning, when she was giddy with exhaustion, she found herself riding past a steading she recognised. She'd been that way only half an hour previously. Panic rose in her when she realised that she had come a full circle and had no idea how far she had travelled or where she was. When dawn came and the stars disappeared, she would not even have them to guide her.

She spurred her horse onwards, heading for a tall, bell-shaped hill whose outline she remembered from past journeys. It was one of a range that marked the Border.

Keeping it in her eye she drove her heels into the horse's sides but it stumbled forward on its knees. As she pulled it up she realised with a sickening lurch in her stomach that it could no longer trot properly for it had gone lame. Hurriedly she dismounted and lifted the front foreleg. The fetlock was hot and swollen. It was impossible to drive the animal on any further. The pursuers would easily outride her now. In despair Alice let her head drop forward and tears scalded her cheeks. To have come so far, to have accomplished so much and now to be caught so ignominiously. Elliot would be delighted.

She crouched down thinking furiously and eventually decided there was only one thing left to do. She would have to leave the road and take to the rough, trackless country that stretched for hundreds of square miles around her. Leading the limping horse by the bridle she struck off across a wide spreading moor and disappeared into the dawn mist.

Alice was right to mistrust her husband because long before dawn broke Andrew Elliot had made his plans. It was bitter for him to have to accept that nothing could be done about Grace's marriage. If she and her shepherd had gone through a hand-fasting ceremony, as long as they'd done it before witnesses, her father would not be able to overturn it. He would not miss Grace for he had no fatherly feelings for the girl but the reason he had held on to her and wanted to continue doing so was to secure her property. There would be no trouble finding out where she'd gone and he made up his mind when the problem of Lucy was solved, he's seek out his daughter and make an agreement with her. He'd have to hand over some of her inheritance but not all, of that he was determined. A bargain would be struck more easily, however, if he had her mother in his hands. He knew how soft-hearted Grace was and he'd play on her emotions . . . Lucy would be turned over to the law and the scaffold unless some settlement was made between them. But first he had to catch his fleeing wife.

The roofs of the houses were glittering with dew and the grey cobbles were slippery beneath his boot soles when he went down the street, calling first at one house and then at another rounding up his helpers, all of them young men who were eager to earn a guinea or who owed him a favour.

Each was given a description of the woman who called herself Alice Archer; each of them was told where to ride to intercept her if she chose to take any one of the four possible routes out of Scotland. They were to position themselves on bridges or on narrow roads which she would have to use and Elliot was confident they'd catch her if they rode fast and went cross-country to their vantage points. When they caught her, they were to bring her back to him and he would decide when and if she was to be handed over to the authorities. He smiled as he thought of that.

When the mists swirled away from the crowns of the hills, the new day was revealed brilliant and shining. Birds sprang up from the empty moors into the vast upturned bowl of the sky, making cries of outrage because their isolation was breached by two people on a plodding horse. The newly-weds, Grace and Adam Scott, came over the top of the tallest hill and Adam stared down into the valley. The cluster of greystone cottages were huddled together in the middle of a green sward, like scattered children's toys left over from some giant's nursery. He stopped the horse in its steady tread and spoke softly to the girl on the pillion behind him. 'Look, Grace. There it is. We're nearly home. Another half an hour and we'll be there.'

She was dozing with her head against his back and one arm around his waist. His voice made her drift back to consciousness, blinking and yawning. The brilliance and beauty of the world made her imagine that she had drifted from one lovely dream into another that was even better, and little by little she summoned up memories of the events of the previous day. Then she blinked. It wasn't possible. All those things could not have happened to her in the space of twenty-four hours! But there he was, her husband, half-turned in the saddle, smiling at her and saying, 'Look, Grace. That's Fairhope down there. My mother's got the chimney smoking. There'll be a grand welcome waiting for us.'

He was right. When they clip-clopped into the yard, Leeb came dashing out with her face aglow and crying, 'Mam, Dad, it's Adam and that bonny lassie.' Hands reached up and helped Grace to the ground, arms were thrown around her and kisses pressed to her cheek.

'You've come home! Oh, I'm glad to see you,' cried Catherine Scott in genuine delight.

In the dark depths of the wood it took longer for the first

streaks of colour to be seen in the patches of purple above the treetops. When they did appear Billy crept out of his overnight hiding place, shuddering with hunger and cold. Hopelessly he stared around the grassy enclosure within the old tower and started nervously when an own flapped very close above his head. It was making its way home from a night's hunting and he watched it settle itself in a hidden perch among the thick ivy on the walls. He walked over to look at the snare Thomassin had set. A terrified rabbit was thrashing about in it. Billy raised one foot intending to stamp on its skull but it looked up at him out of enormous rolling eyes and instead of killing it, he knelt down, loosed it from the snare and watched it flop away, darting here and there in its mindless terror.

There was a pile of stones on a rise of ground behind the tower and he climbed up on to them. From the top he could see out over the valley. Below him was a big mansion house sitting among green lawns and farther over, across the river, the white tents of the Fair field glittered in the morning light. As the sky cleared the watching Billy began to see people making their way around the field. He felt lonely and wished he was with them, sharing the excitement of packing up to move on, for few stayed more than one day at St James' Fair any more.

Billy wondered why Jem did not come and fetch him. He was down there among the tents, packing, harnessing the horses and urging on the quarrelling freaks. Bread and ale would be passed around among them for breakfast. Billy's mouth watered with hunger and he longed for the sound of a voice to tell him what to do. Even the iron bars of his cage and the shackles that used to be locked around his ankles did not seem so bad any longer. He scratched his leg reflectively. The sore on his ankle was healing and he no longer felt any desire to open it again and watch it bleed. He did not leave his hiding place because he remembered that Thomassin had told him to wait there until she came back and he trusted her. She would come, he was sure of it.

In his isolation there was nothing to do but sit among the stones with hunger hurting his stomach and spy on what was going on below him. He was frightened of being alone, and wished that the girl with the slanting eyes would hurry. Her shawl around his shoulders smelt of her and he sank his face into it. He loved her. He'd never met anyone so beautiful who did not treat him as something to be feared. 'Come back, Thomassin,' he cried aloud in a voice of despair.

It was as if she'd heard him calling, for within minutes her slim figure came towards him, slipping through the trees, over walls and ditches, under thickets of shrubbery and into the deepest part of the woods of the park. When she reached the tower she was breathless and panting and her green skirt was stained with patches of wet where the dew had soaked it.

'Billy,' she whispered, gazing at the empty vault of the chimney-place. 'Billy, where are you?'

A rattle of stones announced his presence as he came clambering down from his eyrie. He was smiling with pleasure at seeing her again.

'I've brought you food and some clothes. You're going on an outing, Billy,' she said, holding out a dark bundle and a basket that contained a loaf of bread and a piece of cheese that she had stolen from another traveller's caravan on her way across the field. The clothes turned out to be a long black cape, a big-brimmed pedlar's hat and a pair of heavy boots – all stolen, too.

She put the food into his hands and urged him to eat. Then she said, 'Now Billy, you're going to have an adventure with Thomassin.' She told him to sit down while she slipped the boots on to his feet. 'We're going to the races – you'll like that. You'll have to behave, though, and keep very quiet or someone will recognise you and put you back in your cage. You don't want that, do you?'

When she woke up that morning wondering what ought to be done about Billy, she had finally decided that the best thing to do was take him with her to Caverton Edge. Poor thing, he had never had any pleasure and she was sure that she could control him. She'd give him some money – it would be easy to pick a couple of pockets in the race crowd – and then he'd be able to slip away from the course in the press of people when the racing was over. When she told him this plan, she was rewarded by the look of sheer delight on his face. He jumped to his feet and held out a hand to her, wanting to start that very minute but she shook her head. 'Not yet. We'll have to wait till it's busier on the road. You stay here in the tower for a bit longer and I'll come back to you when it's time to go to see the horses racing,' she told him.

His face fell and he wanted her to remain with him so he tried to detain her by grabbing at her skirt with his huge hand but she prised open his fingers and mastered him by the force of her personality and through his love for her. 'Let go, Billy. I'll come back soon,' she promised and then she ran off, darting into the depth of the woods like a fairy.

Only a short distance away from the tower, her sharp eyes heard the sounds of something moving about among the undergrowth. The girl paused and shrank back behind a tree trunk. Someone was coming into the clearing before her. A man appeared waving a stick and shoving it into the thick shrubs massed beneath the trees. She sighed with relief when she saw it was Jesse.

She ran out towards him crying, 'What are you doing up here?'

He was surprised to see her but he explained, 'Billy's escaped. He's simple and might hurt somebody. I'm looking for him. I'm going to search that old tower up here – remember, the one we used to play in as bairns? Billy came with us sometimes and he might have remembered it, too. There's no telling what goes on in his head.'

Thomassin nodded. 'Yes, I remembered that as well when I heard about Billy running away. I've just been up to the tower and had a good look round. He's not there, Jesse. Maybe they've found him by now anyway,' she told him.

He sighed. 'They probably have. It's easier looking for someone in the daylight.'

Thomassin lied with a guileless look, 'I heard people down on the field shouting out a little while ago. Let's go back to the Fair.' She took his arm and added, 'It's the races today and you've entered Barbary, haven't you? I'm laying a guinea on you to win.' She clung to him, looking up adoringly as if her cup of happiness was full and arm in arm they made their way back down the hill together.

When they came within sight of the field where the Fair had been held, he paused and looked down at her with a solemn expression. 'I want to tell you something, Thomassin.'

Her smile glittered at him but her eyes were wary. 'What?' she asked.

'If I win that race today I'm going away. There's a prize of fifty pounds and if I win it, I'm going away.'

'Take me with you,' she pleaded.

'No.' He was definite. 'I'll give you half the purse but you must let me go free. I'm not ready to settle down. I'm sorry, but I've made up my mind.'

'But if you win the fifty bars and don't give them to our people, Gib'll cast you out . . .'

'I don't care if he does. I'm going away. I'm tired of faking, choring and killing.' Jesse's face was set with determination.

Thomassin stopped and cried, 'It's all the fault of that minister. He shouldn't have made you into a pol-engro. He cursed you.' But when she saw that he really meant what he said, she turned on him like a wild cat and hissed, 'And it's because of that girl with the black skin. You've been bewitched by that one. If she asked you to take her with you, you'd do it. Why won't you take me?'

She was clinging with both hands to his shirt-front and he had to shake her off. He clasped her hands in his and implored her, 'Don't act like this, Thomassin. I want a new life and it's got nothing to do with that girl. I'm going away and that's the end of it.'

CHAPTER 4

In Havanah Court everyone was late in rising. Canny felt very old and tired after his exertions of the night before and lay in bed looking bleak while he thought about Elliot's machinations. What a good thing it was that he had been prevented by Odilie from having Grace committed to the madhouse. Even the cynical Wattie Thompson had been horrified by Elliot's duplicity and had not hesitated in telling him so. But when Lucy Allen appeared that was the most astonishing thing of all. Canny and Thompson had agreed between themselves to say nothing about it – they'd not seen her, hadn't recognised her, for as far as they were concerned, the poor soul would go free.

When he thought about Elliot, Canny reflected that he'd chosen his lawyer because of his sharp mental ability, but if he could behave like that towards his own wife and daughter, what was there to stop him from cheating his clients?

'I'd better get myself another lawyer when this marriage business is over,' was his predominating thought as he rose from bed. Another busy day lay ahead of him for Odilie's engagement was to be announced, and the Rutherfords were to accompany the Duke to the race meeting at Caverton Edge. Only yesterday the idea of such an outing would have filled him with glee. Today it made him feel tired. He wished that it was already over.

Odilie was also dejected when she woke up. She turned her face into the lace-fringed pillow and groaned because her head was aching. The light showing between her bedcurtains told her that the day she dreaded was well advanced and she shivered because during the hours to come she felt that she would be carried along by events like a twig on a flooded river. By nightfall her fate would be well and truly sealed. She'd be affianced to the Duke, caught in a situation from which there was no escape.

As she sat up in bed and pulled one of the curtains aside, she saw the sun gleaming on the silver and crystal dressing table ornaments. The necklace she had worn on the previous night lay sparkling beside them and memories of Grace's wedding came flooding back. How wonderful that had been, like a romance in a storybook. She wondered if the newly-wedded pair had reached Fairhope and wistfully envied them their wonderful happiness which seemed even more like a miracle in the full light of day than it had been last night.

She lay back smiling as she remembered the scene in the tent with the chorus of howling collie dogs. It was so incongruous! Then she thought about the vivid, yearning face of Grace's mother, who had the air of someone to whom a hundred fantastical things had happened. That woman looked as if she had truly lived.

Odilie reflected that her own wedding would be very different. Certainly there would be music and pomp, anthems, flowers, prayers and pageantry but it would lack the ingredients that had made her friend's impromptu ceremony so memorable – it would lack love and commitment and above all it would lack passion.

These thoughts were interrupted by Aunt Martha who came bustling into the room crying out, 'It's nearly ten o'clock, Odilie. I thought you were never going to waken. What are you going to wear? We're setting out for Caverton Edge with the Duke's party in an hour.'

'I've a headache, I feel ill,' groaned Odilie.

'That's what you get for wandering about half the night. I heard you come in but I never said a word to your father though it was almost as late before he came home. That Wattie Thompson was always a bad influence on him. He's nursing a headache as well and that's Thompson's fault, pushing drink on him all last night I'm sure. But I'm not asking what you were doing out so late . . .'

'I'll tell you anyway,' said Odilie, who was standing

362

before her glass in her nightgown. 'Last night I went to a wedding. Grace got married.'

'Heavens bless us!' cried Martha, clasping her hands. 'Grace Elliot married! Where – when – who to?'

'In the marrying tent at the Fair, that's where. In the middle of the night, that's when – and to a shepherd called Adam Scott, that's to whom!'

'Well that's one in the eye for Andrew Elliot,' laughed Martha.

'I think her father'll be a quieter man from now on,' predicted Odilie, remembering Grace's mother's triumph when she gave her daughter the wedding present of a bundle of deeds.

'Good. It's about time,' said Martha, who had never liked Elliot.

Odilie had more news to impart. 'You'll be interested to hear this bit, Aunt Martha. Grace's mother, Lucy Allen, the one you wouldn't talk about, was at her wedding. She's not dead after all.'

Martha's face registered shock. 'Oh, bless me! Elliot said the poor soul died years ago. That's how he could marry again! I didn't want to talk to you about Lucy because folk in Lauriston never really believed she'd killed that bairn, especially after Hester upped and married Elliot. Oh, I'd like to see her again She was a sweet lassie.'

'You couldn't call her that now, I'm afraid. She looks formidable. She must have changed a lot,' said Odilie, remembering Alice's bleak face. 'She was obviously happy to see Grace getting married to such a good young man, though. She really glowed at the end. It was as if she'd achieved the most important aim in her life.'

Martha nodded sagely. 'She loved that bairn, did Lucy. I told you how she carried on when they took her away. The screams of her were terrible. They went through me like knife thrusts. The bairn was all she got from that marriage. Where's she now?'

Odilie sighed. 'I've no idea. If she's any sense she'll be far away from here.'

'I hope you're right because if he knows anything about her coming back Elliot'll do his damnedest to spite her,' Martha predicted.

'Oh, he knows all right,' said Odilie.

'Poor Lucy. I hope she's changed enough to outwit him this time,' said Martha with a heavy look on her face as she began sorting through Odilie's clothes in the wide-open wardrobe. 'But what are you going to wear today, my dear? This is an important day for you. Everyone'll be looking at you,' she said, pulling out first one gown and then another and holding them up for Odilie's scrutiny.

'I know, don't remind me. I'll hate it.' Odilie's voice was cold.

'None of that now. You're going to be the most striking-looking girl on the course. Are you going over in the Duke's carriage or in your father's with me and Canny?'

'Neither. I want to ride my mare across. All the men ride so why shouldn't women . . . I'll wear my new habit!' was Odilie's brisk reply.

The habit had been delivered only a few days before from a London modiste. It was made from pale cream linen and the tight-waisted jacket emphasised Odilie's slender figure. A deep fluted peplum flowed out over the hips and the bodice was cunningly darted and fastened down the front with military-style rosettes of plaited braid. There were gathering puffs on the tops of the sleeves which tapered tightly down to the wrists and the skirt swept the floor in a majestic swirl. When the girl put it on her aunt raised her hands in speechless admiration. 'A picture,' she sighed.

'And I'll wear my new brown boots and my silk hat with the feather,' announced Odilie who was slightly cheered by her pleasing appearance in the new outfit.

Martha pulled out a hatbox and reverently took out a high-crowned top hat made of beige-coloured stiffened silk. A jaunty feather was sticking up from one side of the ribbon around its crown. When it was perched on Odilie's head and the big-meshed brown veil dropped over her dark eyes, Martha said proudly, 'You look a perfect Duchess, Odilie, a lady of style! You're beautiful. Now I'll ask the gardener to make a nosegay for your buttonhole. Roses, perhaps?'

Odilie shook her head. 'No, not roses. Ask him for a gardenia, one of the big ones from the glasshouse. I love their smell – they remind me of Jamaica.'

From early morning Jem and Long Tom had been out searching for Billy. As the field in which the Fair had been held gradually emptied, their despair increased for no one they spoke to had seen the fugitive. There was not a trace of him.

Jem went to speak to his brother Simon who was loading his circus. 'I'm going south and if I see your Strong Man on the road, I'll take him in with my folk,' Simon promised. 'They'll watch he doesn't run away again and I'll send you a message to say we've got him. Where are you going now?'

'I don't know. I'll look around here a bit longer for Billy and then I'll head for Wooler too because Alice said she was taking the road south. My God, this has been some Fair, Simon. I feel as if the world's collapsed around me. I've always been afraid I'd lose her again,' groaned Jem. A sleepless night had made him look older than his age and his shoulders sagged dispiritedly.

His brother put a hand on his shoulder in comfort. 'You've not lost her for good, lad. She's real fond of you – I could see that.'

After he left the circus, Jem headed for the gypsy encampment but most of the Romanies including old Rachel had already left. A dark-haired, flashing-eyed girl in a scarlet shawl was still there, however, and he asked her, 'Where's the big man with the white hair, the one they call Gib?'

She told he, 'He's gone to the race course. We've a horse running for the Duke's cup today.'

'I wanted to tell him that Billy's run away,' said Jem.

She did not take the news very seriously. 'He knows

about that but Billy can't have gone far,' she said in an indifferent voice.

'Maybe not, but he's dangerous wherever he is. He gets violent,' replied Jem.

'Oh, he looked like a big bairn to me. Maybe you're worrying about it too much,' said Thomassin, 'but I'll tell Gib to look out for him.'

Finally, in despair, Jem went to the authorities' tent and reported that his Strong Man had run away. They did not take him very seriously, either.

'Oh aye,' said the craggy-faced provost of Jedburgh, 'and what are we meant to do about that?'

Rubbing his tired face with his hand Jem explained, 'He's a bit simple and he can get rough sometimes. He's very strong . . . he could kill somebody by mistake.'

'No' like some o' them that go around killing folk and meaning it,' said Turnbull, who had spent an arduous night trying to quieten the scrapping gypsies and whose only wish was to see the lot of them off the field and go home himself. His most pressing problem now was to ensure that his town's share of the Fair profits, nearly four thousand pounds in bank draughts and coin, was safely transported to Jedburgh without let or hindrance. Some of the old soldiers who had been hanging around the Fair looked rough customers.

'His name's Billy and he's like a big bairn,' explained Jem again. 'But he's stronger than five men put together.'

'We'll keep an eye out for him,' said Turnbull briskly.

'You'll not shoot him?' asked Jem anxiously.

'No' unless he needs shooting,' was the brusque reply.

At noon, staggering with exhaustion, Jem made his way back to the freak show and sat down heavily on the half-demolished platform surrounded by the litter and debris of Fair Day. One by one the worried freaks came and clustered around watching him anxiously as he sat with his head in his hands. The bearded lady patted him gently on the arm and handed him a slice of beef laid on top of a bit of bread. 'Eat that, Jem. You've not had a bite I expect,' she said. He bit into it and chewed slowly, eyes on the ground, the picture of dejection.

'You've not seen or heard anything of them then?' Hans' voice was tentative. When Jem shook his head, Long Tom looked shame-faced because he still blamed himself for Billy's escape.

'I'm afraid in case he kills somebody – or somebody kills him. Nobody but us really knows what he's like,' Jem told them.

'Aw, poor Billy,' sighed the dwarves in unison and Meg gave a strangled sob clutching her baby to her heart as she did so.

'Any news of Alice?' asked Long Tom and Jem groaned even more loudly.

'Not a cheep. If we could get on the road soon, we might meet her at Wooler or Alnwick. I hope she waits for us there. Simon's got a booking at Wooler the day after tomorrow and he'll keep an eye open for Billy and Alice too.'

'What about us, Jem?' asked Meg anxiously.

'I can't leave here till I find Billy. He's my responsibility. The old woman gave him to me,' he said, then added, 'but if you want to go on alone, get started. I'll follow later.'

They looked at each other in dismay as one by one they drifted back to their waggons to discuss the turn of events. Jem was not left alone to brood for long, however, because a young man on a rough carthorse came riding into their circle leading a big chestnut with a blaze on its nose. 'Somebody said that you're Mr Archer. Is this horse yours?' he asked the slumped figure.

The big man looked up and furrowed his brow. There was a bemused look on his face.

'Is this horse yours?' repeated the young man. 'I found it half-drowned on our farm this morning. There was a note tucked into the saddle-flap saying it belonged to Jem Archer, at St James' Fair, Lauriston. The folk in the circus said that's you.'

'I am. It's my horse right enough. Thank you for bringing it back . . . Where did you say you found it?'

'In a moss above Mowcop. It'd got itself bogged. Up to the withers in glaur it was – look, you can see the mark. I searched around to see if the rider was lying about but I didn't find anybody, but that's some bog we've got up there. It swallows up a cow a year. I hope there wasn't anybody on the horse when it got in there . . . it's a bad bit, that.'

Jem shuddered and put a hand up to the horse's face stroking its nose. 'It's the horse Alice took,' he said half to himself.

'So it's yours then,' said the young farm lad impatiently. 'I'm glad I found you. I'll have to be getting back . . .'

Jem knew what was expected of him. He went into the caravan and came back with a half-guinea which he handed to the young man, saying in a deadened sort of voice, 'Thanks for bringing him back. He's a good horse and you could easily have kept him. I appreciate it . . . Do you still have the note that was in the saddle-flap?'

The lad shook his head. 'No, sorry, I lost it but it told me where to bring the horse, didn't it?'

Jem nodded silently. His face was griefstricken.

The races were a much more High Society occasion than the Fair. While they attracted a large number of the same people as had attended the more vulgar attractions of the previous day, they also drew a large following from more snobbish people. From mid-morning, fine highly polished carriages and gigs could be seen driving through Lauriston on their way to Caverton Edge on the southern side of the town where a previous Duke had laid out a race course which was still under ducal patronage.

Like all race courses it was a melting pot where crooks rubbed shoulders with gentlemen and, the innocent walked with the scheming. Coups were hatched, plots were laid and the presiding gods were the horse and fortune.

The Duke's party set off early from Sloebank in a line

of carriages, with Lady Augusta queening it over the women and the men riding behind on prancing thorough-breds. They thrust headlong and uncaring through the crowds converging on the course, scattering them into the hedgerows as they went.

Thomassin and her tall companion, who was dressed as a pedlar, had to run hurriedly off the road to prevent themselves from being run down by the ducal entourage. They were barely settled into their stride again when another group were upon them. This time it was Canny Rutherford and his sister riding along in a carriage with their black manservant sitting in the high box behind them. Canny's daughter mounted on her beautiful chest-nut mare followed behind the carriage. She was attended by a liveried groom who looked infinitely proud of her for she sat her horse with majesty and on the road people paused to stare up in admiration, nudging each other as they whispered, 'That's the lassie who's going to marry the Duke, that's her!'

When she passed Thomassin, the gypsy girl also nudged her companion and whispered, 'Look at her. What do you think of that lass, Billy?'

His eyes followed her finger but his expression was confused. 'I'd rather have you for my sweetheart,' he told her. She took his hand and smiled at him.

The white-railed race course was laid out in a circle on a green plateau overlooking Lauriston. A low greystone building with two windows and a green-painted door stood staring out at the road and behind it was a railed-off enclosure positioned at the point in the course where both the starting gate and the finishing post were located. In this enclosure, horses and their grooms were clustered and they all looked up when the cavalcade of horses and carriages came sweeping into the race course gate.

The riders were led by the Duke himself – dark, upright, overweeningly proud and glowering. His head towered above his companions and the fact that the prancing horse on which he rode looked like a charger added to his despotic appearance.

He dismounted and was immediately surrounded by a group of fawning friends, who all stood staring in the direction of the entrance gate when another party arrived followed by a mounted woman on a chestnut mare that was curvetting coquettishly, turning sideways like a playful kitten. Its antics did not upset the rider who sat securely in the saddle staring straight ahead. She looked slight and willowy but the sinuous movements of her body and the assurance that exuded from her made many a man catch his breath. Her face was expressionless behind the mesh of her veil.

Involuntarily one of the men in the paddock straightened as she passed and the movement made her glance his way. When he stood upright the open neck of his shirt fell forward and showed strong collar bones and a brown chest beneath it. No sign of recognition showed in either of their faces and no one could have guessed that Odilie's heart had made a disturbing leap at the sight of Jesse. Its beating quickened so much that she felt her head swim, and her fingers convulsed around the reins. A strange yearning seized her. 'Stop it. This is madness,' she told herself and deliberately turned her head away.

The Duke was waiting for her and held a hand up to the girl on the chestnut. 'Come, Miss Rutherford. I'll escort you to the viewing stand,' he said. When her boot toe touched the ground she gave him her gloved hand and then carefully shook out her skirt. She knew that the eyes of the people all around were fixed on her. Among them was her father and she hoped she was doing him credit. With more disquiet she also knew that the handsome, dark-eyed gypsy was watching her too.

The Duke was acting the part of a devoted suitor most effectively. Quelling her distaste she took the arm he extended to her and walked in pace with him up three shallow stone steps into a damp-smelling hall. 'There's two big events on the card this afternoon. I'm running horses in each one,' he told her.

'Which is the biggest race of the day?' she asked.

'The first – it's a sprint, twice round the course. There's

370

fifteen runners so it's going to be run in three heats,' he informed her. It was gratifying to him that this girl was interested in horseflesh. They'd at least have something to talk about when they were married. He smiled down at her and asked, 'Would you like to present my cup to the winner of that race?'

She glanced up at him from behind the provocative veil. 'Yes, I would,' she said.

'Ha, then you'll probably have to present it to me! I've a good horse running. Perhaps you'll give me a kiss with it.'

She dropped her head in the fetching hat to avoid catching his eye. 'Perhaps,' she agreed. It was the first lover-like suggestion he'd made towards her and she was not prepared for how much it upset her to hear him talk like that.

The corridor through which they were walking led past the weighing room which was crowded with people, among them jockeys in brightly-coloured silks. they were all chattering together, assessing each other's chances. The owners of their mounts were there, too, gathering information and making secret deals.

Everyone fell silent when the Duke went past for he was well-known among them although he had no intimates. They respected the horseflesh he owned and it was common knowledge that he liked to win at his own Caverton Edge meeting. This year he had a woman on his arm and the watchers guessed that meant he would be even more anxious than usual to pull off a victory. The visiting owners suspected that things could be fixed for him to do so and there was a great deal of speculation about which of the horses he had entered in the day's card would be the successful one.

Indifferent to their interest, he led Odilie up a shallow flight of steps to a raised stand roofed with green canvas to protect the spectators from the glare of the sun which had taken on a strange coppery sheen as it blazed down from a purple sky. White-painted benches were arranged in lines facing the course and black iron railings closed it off from the crowds of ordinary people on the other side. Servants in livery bustled around with glasses of wine and the girl lifted her veil as she accepted one, sipping it gratefully for the heat was indeed tremendous. Then her host showed her to a seat and she settled down in the middle of the front row while a servant ran up with a cushion which was placed at her back.

There she sat, looking supremely elegant against a pile of braided cushions on the white bench, and it would have been difficult for anyone to discern what was in her mind. In fact Odilie was bleakly wondering if this was the way the rest of her life was to be spent. She realised that the only way she could cope with the events of the day was by cutting off her mind altogether, by moving, speaking and smiling automatically. The moment she stopped acting a part and allowed herself to be fully conscious of what was going on, she would be overcome with dread and disappointment.

From beneath the green shade of the canvas roof, her eyes followed the Duke who was pushing his way in an ungainly and discourteous manner through the crowd on the other side of the railings. He was heading for the horses in the paddock and it was obvious that he'd forgotten all about her. As she watched, she wondered with a sort of sick despair how often she was fated to observe him with the distaste of someone watching a bumbling and bothersome bluebottle.

With an abrupt movement, Odilie turned her head aside and directed her gaze across to another part of the crowd. Something made her stiffen in her seat and she became disturbingly aware of eyes on her. To her dismay and surprise, she saw that she was being watched by the girl who had threatened and accused her of 'casting the glamourie' on the handsome gypsy at the Fair. The girl, garishly robed in scarlet and green, was staring over at her with the same cold fixity as Odilie herself had used when watching the Duke. The girl was accompanied by a tall bulky man dressed like a pedlar in a long black cloak and big hat. How stiflingly hot he must feel in those clothes today, thought Odilie who was suffering enough herself in her tight-fitting riding habit. The heat was so oppressive that she wished she had agreed to Martha's suggestion that she wear muslin and ride in the carriage.

Even beneath the shade of the awning, the atmosphere was oppressive and because there was no breeze, the air seemed unnaturally still and heavy. An advancing army of dark clouds could be seen massing above the rolling outlines of the Cheviot Hills and the light had a violet tinge to it. Over the course hung a strange feeling of anticipation, like the frisson that sweeps through a theatre audience sitting on the edge of their seats in the seconds before the curtain rises. At Caverton Edge that day there was a promise of more than an afternoon's racing in the air.

From the middle of the press of people, Thomassin's eyes were intently fixed on Odilie and she did not bother to hide that she was burning with jealousy so strong that she had trouble containing it. 'She's taken the power of my spell into herself, she's taken my magic,' thought the gypsy girl in impotent rage for she was sure that the potion Rachel brewed had worked right enough but it had done so for Odilie Rutherford who did not want it. Thomassin felt that her heart had turned to stone in her breast and she hissed like an angry cat, so loudly that Billy, who was watching the wonderful goings on around him, looked down at her with the frank amazement of a child. 'What's wrong?' he asked.

She turned her head up towards him and said piteously, 'Jesse doesn't love me, that's what's wrong Billy.'

He shook his head. 'I love you,' he said.

She took his hand. 'Yes, you're my sweetheart,' she told him and Billy felt something strange happen to him. It was if a balloon had been blown up inside his chest and he swelled with pride and love as Thomassin bestowed her smile upon him. He was bemused and bedazzled by the love that ached in him like a fire. Thomassin had helped him escape from the freak show; she'd shown him how to live on his own; she'd fed him and given him clothes and

373

now she'd brought him here to watch the horses racing . . . Billy was in heaven and to have Thomassin standing beside him with her hand on his arm was the most sublime experience he could imagine. She noticed that he was standing straighter and feared he was preparing to run away, 'Stay with me, stick to my side and keep quiet, Billy,' she warned.

The Duke did not return to sit beside Odilie during the running of the heats of the big race but she was not alone for she had the company of her father, Aunt Martha, and a proudly pacing Joe Cannonball who was that afternoon over-acting the part of the faithful manservant. While Martha stood up gazing around at all the fashions on display, Canny perched on the bench beside his daughter and fanned his face with a folded piece of paper, making exclamations about the oppressive weather.

'It'll thunder tonight. Look over there,' he said pointing towards the horizon to where clouds were massed into what looked like a huge pile of dark-coloured pillows.

'That's the way Grace has gone. I hope she's reached Fairhope by now,' said Odilie. Then she asked her father, 'Have you seen Elliott today?'

'Not a sight of him, thank God. I'm glad because it would be hard to be civil to the man. I saw Wattie Thompson and that young architect fellow Playfair out in the crowd and Wattie's going on about Elliot's devilish effrontery. He said he'd probably have signed the paper committing Grace if you hadn't stopped him. He's coming to speak to you later, my dear.'

'I'm glad he didn't do it,' said Odilie absently but her mind was not on what her father was saying because she was staring out at the crowd again. The gypsy girl and the pedlar had come closer to the enclosure rails and there was something peculiar about them that disturbed her. She told herself not to be silly. The girl was just another of those bold-eyed gypsy women who always gave her a chill with their wheedling voices and pretence at seeing into the future. Her heart sank when she remembered Rachel and her prediction that Odilie's husband would be bango-wasted. The Duke was the only left-handed man she knew . . . there seemed to be no way of avoiding her fate.

She diverted herself by noting the activities of the gypsies in the crowd. They were slipping about intent on their nefarious ways, picking pockets, whispering into ears, tipping winners, telling fortunes, casting spells. At the back of the crowd she picked out the big man with the white hair who had presided over the jumping competition. Again he had a gang of men like a bodyguard around him but the handsome gypsy who had so unexpectedly moved her heart was not among them.

A loud blast of a trumpet announced the third heat of the big race. By this time Odilie was beginning to tire but suddenly she sat up straighter and her whole attitude changed from dejection to sharp interest for Jesse Bailey appeared in the paddock mounted on his beautiful grey stallion. He was to be one of the runners in a field of five horses.

She sat forward in her seat with her eyes coming vividly alive as she watched the line-up. The runners had to complete one circuit of the course and Jesse and Barbary tore away from the start with a magnificent plunge establishing a lead which they managed to sustain. While the crowd yelled encouragement, they stayed in front till the finish. The whole thing was over so quickly that Odilie had barely time to realise what had happened before it was announced that Jesse had won.

The best race was still to come, however, and a shiver of anticipation swept the crowd as the names of the entrants in the final were called out. It was to be run in half an hour's time when the winners of the three heats would race against each other. Betting became heavy; people ran to and fro while Odilie, pretending indifference, sipped chilled white wine, made polite conversation with other members of the Duke's party and willed the time to pass. At last came the announcement . . . 'This is the final of the big sprint, ladies and gentlemen. The winners of all three heats will compete against each other.

The prize is a purse of fifty guineas and a silver cup generously presented by His Grace, the Duke of Maudesley, our patron and owner of this course.'

Her father who was sitting beside Odilie, perked up because he loved to bet. Turning to Joe he said, 'This is it. There's two possibilities out of the three, I think – the grey and the Duke's horse Flying Demon. They both won their heats easily. Which do you think?'

Joe wrinkled his ebony brow. 'I'm for Flying Demon, boss. The Duke's out to win his own cup, I hear.'

'Go into the ground and lay ten guineas for me then,' said Canny. Both of the men then looked at Odilie who said nothing. She would make no bet though she was willing the grey horse to win.

From her well-positioned seat she watched the horses going out to the starting gate, all prancing and preening on tiptoe with excitement. First came Flying Demon, a huge black animal with rolling eyes and a flowing curly mane. The gypsy and his grey stallion followed next. Jesse was the only rider not clad in brightly-coloured racing silks and instead wore a plain white cotton shirt with a red scarf tied around his neck. Her throat tightened at the sight of him. It seemed ungracious to let him race without putting her money on him. Standing up she called to Joe's disappearing back, 'Put a guinea for me on the grey horse. The one with the white mane and tail.'

With a laugh her father seized her hand and squeezed it tight, so pleased was he that she was recovering her spirits enough to want to bet against him, for he had been acutely conscious of her depression during the earlier part of the day. She smiled back and suddenly was surprised because unrehearsed words trembled on her lips. At that moment she wanted to tell him that no matter what happened, she would always love him, that there was a special bond between them that nothing would ever break. But the chance of communication between them was taken away when Martha rushed up and told Canny, 'I hope you've backed Flying Demon. Everybody's saying the Duke's fixed the race so's he can win and Odilie will present him with the cup. If she does, that'll be when he makes the announcement of his engagement!'

Odilie shivered and her black mood returned. 'There's many a slip between the cup and the lip,' she said without a smile. Now she hoped more than ever that the gypsy would win the race, for his victory would at least postpone the announcement she dreaded.

She rose from her seat and walked across to the railings, gazing across the course to where the horses were lined up at the starting rope. Tense-muscled and nervous the riders hunched in their saddles, hands lowered and eyes fixed on the man at the side of the course whose duty it was to drop the red starting flag.

Time seemed to stand still and the crowd held its communal breath. 'Are you all ready?' the starter called out, his voice loud in the silence.

No one answered but three heads nodded. 'One – two – three!' shouted the starter and, at the last word, the flag dropped. The horses plunged forward together, muscles rippling in their silken flanks. Heads jerking up and hooves flashing, they passed from the watchers' line of vision.

Flying Demon got away first and his jockey, a tiny scrap of a man who looked like a midget on the horse's back, was standing high in the stirrups holding the animal back because it was raring to go and kept swinging its neck about as if trying to wrench the jockey off and toss him over its head. Before the horse covered any distance at all its sides and neck were coated with a white lather of foam that looked like soapsuds. At the sight of them Canny sighed, for he knew that a horse which exhausted itself with nerves before the race was half run would have little energy to spare when the real testing time came at the finish.

For the final there were two circuits to run, and when the runners passed the viewing stand for the start of the second circuit, the Duke's black horse was still in front and still wrestling with its bit. The grey was tucked away in third place, galloping on steadily with its rider looking neither to right or left. At this stage Odilie noticed an unusual amount of activity among the gypsies and saw that the man with the white hair was gathering in a large amount of money. She hoped that Joe had managed to lay her bet because she could tell that the grey horse still had plenty of stamina left.

When they emerged on to the long straight at the back of the course, the grey had crept up into second place and its only rival was the Duke's horse. Now they would have to battle it out between them. Though she wanted to, Odilie found that she could not shout encouragement for her fancy like the people around her because her throat was too dry. Inside she was quivering with emotion and silently she willed the gypsy to win. Somehow his victory meant a great deal more than just a horse race to her.

The noise rose to a crescendo as the crowd started to shout in unison when the horses came charging round the last bend. Now they were putting on speed and the Duke's jockey, who had been told that he was to win the race come what may, took out his whip laying a cruel cut on his mount's flank. From the side of his mouth he bawled at the gypsy riding beside him, 'I've got to win this. The Duke's expecting it. You'd better haul on your reins or you'll be in trouble.'

The other man only grinned and roared back, 'If you're going to win, you'll have to beat me fair and square!' Then he leaned forward and whispered words of encouragement to his horse that stretched its gallop even wider.

When the long straight opened up in front of them like a green infinity, dwindling away to a distant finishing post, Jesse turned his head slightly and saw that the two of them were alone. The third runner was left far behind. 'Come on Barbary, show them,' he whispered again and his horse responded beautifully. Its stride lengthened and it stretched its neck out as if reaching for the winning post. The two horses streaked past it a length and a half apart, with Barbary in front of the Duke's Flying Demon. The crowd were screaming in excitement and throwing their hats in the air. Though many of those who cheered

378

had lost their money, they dearly loved to see someone take away what the Duke had clearly expected to be his triumph.

Odilie watched Jesse winning the race with her heart thudding and her hands gripped so tightly together that her fingernails cut into the soft flesh of her palms. She stared hard at him as he flashed past the starting post and saw resolution evident in the set of his chin and the hard stare of his eyes but when he saw that he had won those grim expressions were swept away by a smile of such triumph and exhilaration that it made her want to run out and throw her arms around him.

Every exciting race that is closely fought to a finish ends with a strange sense of anti-climax. The spectators, who in the thrill of the finish have been yelling in unison and thumping each other on the shoulders like old friends, suddenly draw apart again, embarrassed at letting down their guard. They revert to being islands.

The crowd who watched Barbary outrun Flying Demon shouted and yelled like mad things while the horses streaked towards the finishing line but when it was over and their calls echoed away over the fields and hills, they sighed in unison and made bland comments like, 'Good finish, capital race . . . If the Demon's jockey hadn't taken out his whip he might have won it . . . That grey's too good for the Duke's horse to beat.'

The Duke, standing at the winner's entrance, was a deeply disappointed man and didn't bother to hide his feelings. After accepting the commiserations of his cronies, he shouldered his way through the crowd and mounted the viewing stand with a face like thunder. 'Damned gypsy,' he grunted to his friends there. 'I was sure my horse was going to win. Still, mustn't appear a bad loser, have to put a good face on it.' He turned brusquely to Odilie. 'Can't bring myself to present the cup personally. I said you'd do it and I'm sorry it'll have to be to that dirty Romany but I want to buy that horse off him so I'll need to keep him sweet. Come on, Miss Rutherford, we'll make this business short.' When he put a hand on her elbow and helped her to her feet, he did not notice how much she was shaking.

Thomassin was watching intently, however, and saw how excited Odilie looked. She knew it had something to do with Jesse for all the time the race was being run, her eyes had never left the other girl's face. When the Duke led Odilie away Thomassin also grabbed Billy's arm and pulled him along with her. 'Come on, come on, let's follow them. Keep your head down in case somebody sees you and recognises you,' she told him.

Towed along by the Duke, Odilie saw the crowd opening in front of her like a sea and had to fight off a feeling of giddiness as he ushered her along. She put one hand up to her hat to keep it on her head but he did not slacken his pace which was upsetting for someone of her short stature since she could not see over any of the heads around her or make out where she was going. At last they came to a halt alongside the shoulder of a sweating grey horse and she put up a hand to stroke it gently. 'You've a big heart, you did magnificently,' she told the horse, ignoring the Duke's lowering disapproval.

People all around were talking and someone was making a speech above her head. She heard her name and, 'Miss Odilie Rutherford of Havanah Court will present the winner with his cup!' There was a burst of cheering and hands around her began clapping. It sounded to her like thunder echoing in her ears and she feared that she might faint but fought off the weakness. An enormous silver cup with handles on each side was thrust into her hands and the weight of it made her stagger. Then the Duke dropped a purse of clinking coins inside it and the increased weight pulled her hands down even farther.

Then all the people clapped again and she looked around in panic, wondering what to do. Her father and Joe Cannonball were standing close beside her, both beaming broadly and Joe nodded encouragingly, flicking his eyes above her head to tell her to raise the cup. She smiled shakily, then very slowly and reluctantly looked up and found herself staring at the gypsy rider.

He was sitting very still on his horse's back and the first thing she saw were his strong muscular hands lying lightly on the saddle pommel. Her stomach clenched but she fixed her eyes on these hands because she was terrified to look any further. But she had to give him the cup and awkwardly tried to heave it up towards those beautiful hands. When a man in the crowd stepped forward as if to help her she realised how gauche she must look, presenting a cup without looking at the man who was to receive it. And so, slowly and deliberately she raised her head. Her eyes behind the mesh of her veil met his challenging black ones again and the miracle happened between them for a second time.

She gave a little gasp as if she had been winded and he blinked like a man who is temporarily blinded. In that instant the crowd all around, all the rest of the world, disappeared leaving only Odilie and Jesse staring at each other as if they had experienced a glorious revelation. Both of them found it impossible to look away and they had no idea how long they went on staring. It could have been seconds or it could have been an hour but neither of them knew nor cared.

The Duke was saying something at Odilie's elbow and she shook her head as if she could not understand his words. He said it again more loudly, 'Give him the cup, Miss Rutherford. Hold it up. Do you want me to help you?'

She shook her head and stepped closer to the grey horse with the prize held up, cupped between her palms. Gasping as if for breath she licked her lips and managed to say, 'I – I – I thought you ran a wonderful race.'

Jesse leaned forward and put out one hand to receive his prize. The hand he proffered was his left. Her heart sang. His eyes were still fixed on hers and he smiled, a smile that wrinkled the skin around his eyes. She felt as if she was drowning in his gaze and blinked in a futile effort to ward off the effect they were having on her but it was no use. If glamourie meant magic, it was certainly there between them and too strong to be denied.

The spell was broken by a shout from somewhere behind the Duke. It made Jesse glance up over Odilie's head and what he saw brought a look of astonishment to his face. Thomassin, her face working with fury, was pushing her way through the crowd. 'Get away from my man. Leave him alone, leave him be!' she was crying out. The crowd watched in horror and involuntarily drew back when they saw the knife in her hand.

In his adventurous past Joe Cannonball had survived many dangers because he was almost supernaturally quick in his reaction to any threat. When he noticed the intruder pushing her way into the party he leapt to Odilie's defence and threw out both arms to envelop Thomassin in his grasp. Jesse was equally fast and, like Joe, his instinct was to protect Odilie, while Joe grappled with the furious, fighting gypsy girl, Jesse dropped his silver cup and purse of money and grabbed Odilie's up-reaching hands. Straightening in his saddle he hoisted her into the air at the same moment as Billy rushed out of the crowd and felled Joe to the ground with a single swing of his arm. His eyes were staring in his head and he was uncontrollable in his fury at seeing someone hurt his Thomassin.

While Joe fell backwards with Billy on top of him, Odilie's feet left the ground. Jesse leaned sideways from the saddle and hooked an arm around her waist. In a trice he pulled her up on the horse's back where he propped her in front of him like a doll.

Neither of them paid any attention to the struggling mêlée going on around the horse's feet. Like someone entranced Odilie stared into the gypsy's face as he asked her, 'Are you my prize?'

'I think I must be,' she said.

'Thomassin's out to kill you. We'd better get out of here. Hang on tight,' he told her as he drove both heels into Barbary's sides. Without arguing she leaned on to his chest and slipped both hands under his armpits, clinging close to him as he urged the horse forward. With three gigantic strides, Barbary headed for the white-painted fence of the enclosure and cleared it in a massive leap.

While the astonished crowd cried out, the galloping horse carried the runaways off over the course until they disappeared behind the farthest hillock.

Joe Cannonball was lucky. He was lying on the ground with his assailant's hands around his throat when a struggling Thomassin broke away from the men holding her and hauled at Billy's shoulder screaming, 'Billy, Billy, leave him alone, Billy! Come with me!'

For a miracle, he listened to her. Even Joe was unable to master Billy by strength but Thomassin dominated him through the force of her personality and his love for her. She had become the only person apart from Jem that Billy would obey.

When he heard her frantic voice calling him, he stopped pounding Joe's head up and down on the ground and let her haul him to his feet. She grabbed his arm and pulled him along with her as they fled off through the crowd that parted for them because no one was brave enough to challenge Billy. Hand in hand they ran at full tilt out of the racecourse and down the road towards Lauriston while a straggle of shouting men ran after them. It took a little longer before others leapt on horses to join in the pursuit and by the time they had organised themselves, Billy and Thomassin had dived into a thick wood where she knew mounted men would find it impossible to penetrate.

Panting they huddled in the depths of the undergrowth, staring out at the road which they could see away below their hideaway. 'We'll wait here for a bit,' Thomassin told Billy, 'then we'll make up our minds what to do.'

On the course they had just left everything was in chaos. The Duke was scarlet-faced with fury and shouting, 'Follow them, follow them!' while men ran around in circles not knowing whether he meant they should go after Thomassin and Billy or Jesse and Odilie. Joe Cannonball lay half-conscious and ignored on the ground. When he started to come to, he fingered the cuts on his face and was trying to rise when Canny rushed up and bent over him asking, 'Are you all right, Joe? My God, you saved my Odilie's life. That lassie would have killed her. Now she's disappeared with the gypsy. What on earth is going on?'

He helped Joe to stand up and together they stared out over the countryside. Neither of them gave a fig for Thomassin's or Billy's whereabouts. It was Odilie who was the object of their concern. Joe consoled his employer. 'He saved her, not me. He'll bring her back. He's a decent lad though he's a Romany,' he said, groaning and rubbing his woolly head with one hand.

Canny, however, was frantic. He stared wildly around crying out, 'Come on, we've got to find her. There's some of his people over there. Come with me.' He ran across to where an astonished-looking Gib was standing among his men. Grabbing him by the front of his jacket Canny demanded, 'Is that lad who took away my girl one of yours?'

Gib nodded. 'He's Jesse Bailey, my sister's son.'

'Get the word to him that if he brings her back unharmed, I'll pay a ransom,' snapped the agitated man.

'Jesse won't hurt her,' said Gib with dignity. 'We treat our women with respect, better than Giorgios do. I saw what happened: he took her away to save her. Thomassin would've stabbed her sure enough.'

'Yes, yes, I know that but there's a lot of money waiting for him when he brings her home,' snapped Canny. 'And he's left his prize cup and money behind!'

Then he turned to Joe and said in a stricken voice, 'Oh God, I'm feeling bad, Joe. I've a terrible pain in my chest.' With those words he buckled at the knees and fell into a heap on the ground. With an exclamation of horror, Joe knelt beside him and saw that Canny's face was turning blue. Without pausing for a moment, the big black man scooped up the inert body in his arms and ran with it towards the carriages, shouting as he went, 'Get Dr Thompson. Bring him to Havanah Court at once.' Then he laid Canny's limp figure on the carriage floor, pushed the coachman aside, jumped into the box and, cracking the whip over the heads of the startled horses, drove pell-mell off the course.

Before Canny's carriage reached Havanah Court the rain started. The confusion on the course became worse as the sky darkened and enormous raindrops started plumping down, bursting like miniature explosions as they landed on the parched earth. The grass and the trees seemed to reach up gratefully towards the rain, drinking it in and the dry earth gave off a warm, humid smell. People were drenched in minutes but they, too, turned their faces up to the sky in relief at the realisation that the suffocating heat was gone at last.

The rain had become a deluge when Joe carried Canny from the carriage to his front entrance. The maid opened the door to find them wringing wet on the step. Joe pushed past her carrying the body of his master in his arms and ordered, 'Fetch the brandy bottle.'

Canny was only just settled among his pillows when there was the sound of a voice shouting in the hall and Walter Thompson came charging up the stairs two at a time. He burst into the bedroom and leaned over the bed scanning his old friend's face anxiously.

'He's not dead. I've sent the maid for the brandy,' Joe told him.

'I'm the doctor here and I'm aware that he's alive, thank you,' said Thompson shortly. Then he said more softly to Canny, 'How're you feeling, old man?' Slowly the patient opened his eyes as Thompson repeated, 'Are you feeling better, old fellow?'

'Not really. Where's Odilie?' was the reply and Canny closed his eyes again.

Thompson tried consolation. 'You're going to be all right. Don't upset yourself about Odilie. She'll be safe enough with that gypsy. I saw by the way she looked at him that they know each other.'

Canny wished he was strong enough to shout, 'Is that meant to be a consolation to me? I saw that, too, and it makes things worse. I never dreamed she'd do anything so rash.' But all he managed to whisper between dry lips was, 'I hope to God he brings her back safe.'

While Thompson was ministering to Canny, Joe stood impassively watching what was going on and wondering what to do about Odilie. The moment he could get away he was determined to go to the gypsy camp and find out about the lad who'd abducted her. Then, if necessary, he'd go and find her himself. He didn't give a damn whether she married the Duke or not, but he knew that Canny would never have a moment's peace of mind till his daughter was restored to him and it was to Canny that his first loyalties were directed.

After Thompson had dosed his friend and sent into town for the apothecary to come and apply leeches to Canny's forehead, Martha arrived home wringing her hands in horror at the day's events. She did not know whether her brother's illness or her niece's disappearance was the worst calamity and she hovered beside while the patient, looking and feeling more comfortable after he'd been bled, lay ashen-faced against his pillows. To their distress he kept asking over and over again, 'Is there any news of Odilie?'

'Not yet – soon,' said Joe each time he was asked.

'What was she thinking of? To run away like that! To take off with a ragged gypsy!' Canny groaned.

Martha interrupted, 'She didn't take off. He saved her from the girl with the knife. She'd be lying here a corpse if it wasn't for that lad.'

Canny weakly shook his head. 'He saved her right enough but he didn't need to run off with her. Didn't you see how she clung to him like one of those leeches. Even if she comes back, she'll be a fallen woman.'

Martha snapped irritably, 'Lie back and rest, you old fool. You were a wild man yourself in your time if all they say is true. It's maybe not the lassie's fault. It's her inheritance. You can't breed tame geese out of wild geese eggs.'

Canny closed his eyes and heaved a sigh. 'Trust you to take her side, Martha.' When he was about to fall asleep he opened his eyes again and groaned, 'What's the Duke going to say about this? He'll clean me out. To do it at the races . . . Oh my God, maybe it'll be best if I die.'

Martha and Joe looked at each other in consternation and she attempted to reassure the patient. 'You're not going to die, Canny. Wattie Thompson says you've had a shock, that's all. If you lie quiet and do what you're told, you'll be fit as a fiddle soon.'

But Canny groaned even more deeply. There was no comforting him.

Although Andrew Elliot did not go to the races, he'd spent an exhausting day working out what he ought to do about his various problems. When there was no news of his runaway wife, he grew more and more irritable so that when Hester came bursting into his study, full of excitement, he threw a book at her and yelled, 'Get out, leave me alone. I'm trying to think!'

She didn't leave, however, but stood her ground with her hands on her hips. 'You'll want to hear what I've to say. I've just got it from the grocer's laddie who heard it in the square. Rutherford's girl's eloped with a gypsy at the races – right under the nose of the Duke. He's mad with rage, raving and shouting like a maniac. You'll be having a summons from Sloebank any minute I'll be bound.'

Elliot sat back in his chair with an astonished look on his face. Then his expression cleared and he actually laughed as he said, 'Well, well, good for Miss Rutherford. She's saved me! Canny has only himself to blame. Serves him right.'

Hester looked puzzled. 'But how can she have saved you? You're her father's lawyer – the Duke'll be mad at you as well as at him.'

'No, he'll not, because I'm going to help him. Get my coat and my good shoes, saddle the horse. I'm not waiting for any summons, I'm going up to Sloebank before he sends for me. Hurry, woman! There's no time to lose.'

He looked positively pleased with himself when he went

out, so pleased that he did not even mind the downpour of rain as he headed for the gates of Sloebank Castle.

CHAPTER 15

By the time the rain started the field where the Fair had been held was almost empty. The only sign that life had returned to old Roxburgh for a day were the piles of litter, huge areas of beaten-down grass, lengths of rope or bedraggled bunting lying snaked in whirls like coiling cobras, and the unvarnished pine footbridge, empty of people now and waiting for demolition. The tents had been struck, horses harnessed and caravans loaded for the long trek to the next stopping place. Simon and Bella Archer's Circus Royale was one of the last to leave.

'I'm worried about Jem,' said Simon to his wife when they were finally aboard their van and heading for the gate. He pulled on the reins of his straining horses and said, 'Hold on here a little while I go and take another look at him. I don't think he was listening to me earlier when I said we were going.'

He found his brother sitting in the shelter of a tree with the other members of his freak show clustered in a panicstricken huddle, watching him from a distance. Jem's hunched attitude showed that utter dejection and inertia had overtaken him. It was difficult to remember that this was normally an energetic and enthusiastic man. When Meg saw Simon approaching she bustled up to him and squeaked out anxiously, 'He'll not eat. He'll not speak. He's just sitting there . . .'

The younger Archer knelt down beside his brother and said gently, 'You'd better pack up and get out of the field before this rain bogs the ground, Jem. We're off to Morpeth. Come with us. We'll wait till you're ready.'

Jem looked up with eyes that were rheumy and exhausted. 'All right. Long Tom can take the show and follow you but I can't travel till Billy's found – and till I know something about Alice. Her horse was brought back this morning. The lad who found it thinks the rider may have been swallowed up in a bog. I'm going up there to see if I can find any trace of her.' He sank his head in his hands to hide his tears and stared silently at the wet ground around his boots.

Simon shuffled his feet and said awkwardly, 'I heard the horse had been brought back but it's not certain she's drowned is it? There wasn't a body with the horse, was there?'

Jem stared up at him with angry eyes. 'But how could she manage up there on those moors without a horse? How'd she get away on foot? The law'll catch her sure enough even if she's not been swallowed up by the bog. Oh God, Simon, everything's gone wrong for me. I wish I'd never come to St James' Fair.'

His brother persisted, 'Come on Jem, this isn't like you. Have you told the law that Billy's missing? You can't go on searching for him yourself. If he's anywhere close he'd have been seen by now. Let the law find him, Jem.'

The seated man nodded. 'I've told them once and they aren't interested. Anyway I don't trust them not to shoot him out of hand. Folk are scared of Billy and they'd kill him rather than risk taking him alive. That's why I wanted to find him myself but maybe I'm not going to manage it.'

'I'll come with you and find the law and tell them again,' offered Simon but Jem stood up and clapped him on the shoulder.

'No, off you go with Bella and your family. You're all packed up. Long Tom can follow you. Keep an eye on him because he's giddy-brained. Don't worry, I'll come as soon as I can.'

Simon looked anxiously at his brother. 'You won't do anything silly if – if – something's happened to Alice, will you?'

Jem shook his head. 'I'll look for Billy and then, if I've heard nothing about Alice, I'll see what I do. Don't worry about me.'

The law officers of the Fair were still patrolling the field

with long staves in their hands. This time the one that
Jem stopped listened carefully to what he had to say and
then gave a shout to summon others of his company. Soon
a cluster of men were standing around listening intently.
One of them was carrying a gun. Jem looked at the
weapon in a worried way and pleaded, 'Don't just shoot
him on sight. Give him a chance. He'll be cold and hungry
so he'll come quietly. I'll go on looking too but if any of
you find him first, send for me and I'll take him for you.
He knows me and he won't hurt me but if you frighten
him, he could turn difficult.'

'He's got to be stopped,' said the man with the gun
who had a coarse, cruel face.

'He's not done anything wrong and he's been away
since last night without hurting anybody. That proves
he's not a troublemaker if he's left alone,' pleaded Jem
but the guards were not convinced and it was obvious
that they were afraid at the idea of having to tackle Billy.
Most of them had seen him perform his act and had a
good idea of the strength and violence contained in him.
Just looking at their faces told Jem that it would be best
if he found Billy first.

In a short time the news got round the town that the
wild man had escaped. Terrified mothers ran out to round
up their children; doors were closed and locked and the
most intrepid looked anxiously over their shoulders as
they hurried home to safety. Wandering drunks preferred
to walk in groups for not even the most inebriated were
bold enough to take any chances. Billy's reputation grew
in the telling.

In the rain Jem strode up and down the streets and
alleys of Lauriston questioning everyone he met. 'Have
you seen a big lad with a sort of bairn-like face? Have
you seen my Billy?' but no one had. Poor Billy, he
thought, you'll be wet and you must be hungry. I've got
to find you. Yet he had an even more important concern.
He must discover what had happened to Alice before it
became too dark to search the place where her horse was
found. When he drew a blank over Billy, he decided to

let other people worry about him for a while, mounted his horse and rode off through the driving rain towards the distant hills. His soul was mourning inside him like a wailing wind. He had barely left the square when news of the amazing happenings at the races arrived from Caverton Edge.

The arrival of the rain pleased Thomassin; it would dampen the enthusiasm of the people who were hunting Billy and herself. To her delight the deluge grew heavier, sweeping through the wood in which they were hiding and battering the trees, making saplings and branches bend before its onslaught. Billy had fallen asleep – panic and fear did not last long with him – but the noise of the rain woke him and he shuddered, clapping his arms across his chest in an effort to bring some heat into his body.

He had eaten Thomassin's bread and cheese long ago and was starving again. Like an animal, his stomach was his clock and now it rumbled with emptiness telling him meal-time had come around again. He sat up with his eyes fixed on Thomassin, waiting for her to provide what he needed.

As she huddled beside him, she propped her chin in her hands, brooding about Jesse and the girl who had clung so closely to him as they rode away. She was sure their elopement had been pre-arranged and when she thought of Jesse's arms holding that girl, a spasm of jealousy clutched her throat with such strength that she feared it would choke her. Billy saw her grief and put an arm around her. She did not reject him but turned and said, 'We've got to get out of here. We'll go back to the tower where you slept last night, and when things quieten down we'll head for England. I'll take you to the Romanies at Alnwick. They're our own people even if we're from Kirk Yetholm. Come on, there's no time to lose.'

Billy did not understand all she was saying but nodded as if he did and stood up to follow her. She led him through the wood to a stretch of open fields over which she ran like a deer, slim and lithe, hair flying out behind her. He pounded along at her rear and they ran for about two miles until they emerged at one of the Teviot fords. One look was enough to tell Thomassin that by this time it was too swollen by rain for them to cross.

She could hardly speak for disappointment when she saw the height of the river. 'We'll have to cross the bridge. I hope the toll-keeper's kept in by the rain,' she said, taking Billy's hand.

But luck was not with them. When they tried to crawl under the toll-bar, a noise made the keeper look from his window. He came charging out, grabbed Thomassin and though she wriggled and fought, she could not escape from his clutches. Billy, about to attack the man on her behalf, was quelled when she shouted at him, 'No, let it be, Billy. Let it be,' for she thought she could talk her way out of the problem. What she did not know was that a party of the Duke's men who were been out looking for Billy and herself, were in the toll cottage sheltering from the downpour. They came tumbling through the door and shouted in delight when they saw that their quarries had literally landed in their laps. They pounced on Billy first and pinned him to the ground. He was so tired, wet and hungry, that the fight had gone out of him and, mindful of Thomassin's instructions, he lay without struggling as they tied his arms behind his back.

He made a pathetic sight when they led him away with tears slipping hopelessly down his perplexed face. He could not understand what had happened or why, and he had no idea what he should do. Thomassin, her hands tied too, was walking in front of him and she turned her head to call back to him, 'It's all right, Billy. Don't worry. Gib'll hear about this and he'll come to get us.' But Billy could only sob. His mind was full of confused questions. 'Where's Jem? Where's Alice?' By now he wished with all his heart that he was safely back with the freak show. Even chains were better than the cold confusion and gripping hunger.

Andrew Elliot arrived at the Castle shortly after the furious Duke had gone storming inside with his entourage trailing behind him. The manservant who answered the door was rolling his eyes and tried to close the door against the visitor. 'No callers, no callers!' he exclaimed.

The soaking wet lawyer passed in his card. 'Tell his Grace that I'm Canny Rutherford's man of business. I'm sure he'll see me.'

The Duke did. He was already shouting when Elliot appeared at the far end of the big salon, 'Go back and tell, Rutherford that there'll be no marriage now. I'm going to keep the ten thousand and damn the girl. She can't make a fool out of me! Bolting with a gypsy in front of all those people . . . You're wasting your time if you've come to plead with me.'

Elliot kept on walking steadily towards the furious man. 'I've not come to plead for Rutherford. I've come to help you. I can do you a service, your Grace.'

The Duke stared bleakly at the bedraggled lawyer and asked in a scornful tone, 'What service can *you* do for me?'

'I can get you a quarter of a million pounds – the whole dowry or damned near it. I presume you'll keep the first instalment anyway but I can get you the rest as well.'

'How?'

'I'm Rutherford's legal adviser. I've all the papers to do with the marriage in my possession. I drew them up.'

'Get on with it, then. I've better things to do than stand here listening to you.'

Elliot did not bat an eyelide. 'I'll add a clause saying that if the contract is broken the one who is let down should be suitably recompensed for their disappointment and loss of prospects. I seem to remember that Rutherford wanted something like that written in at the beginning but your people wouldn't have it. But you won't be at any risk of paying up now, will you? Who's going to expect you to take damaged goods? Who's going to expect a Duke to marry a gypsy's doxy even if she does come back? It's only Rutherford who'll suffer and it's up to you how much he pays. It depends on how badly you feel you've been treated . . .'

A glint came into the Duke's eyes then and he felt a rush of excitement at the thought of so much money. The reconstruction of Sloebank Castle would be secure after all and Playfair would be able to get to work straight away. What was even better was that he, the Duke, wouldn't have to go to the trouble of marrying that insolent chit of a girl in order to get his hands on the funds.

'Why should you bother to do this? Rutherford's your client, isn't he?' he asked suspiciously.

Elliot coughed discreetly and looked down at the wet hat he held in his hands. 'I'm sure that you'd be a good patron to anyone who helped you in such a way, your Grace. You own a fine house and park along the road to Coldstream that I've always admired. And I have a score to settle with Miss Rutherford anyway.'

'It must be a big score since it's going to cost her father so much,' sneered the Duke. He turned on his heel to walk away but before reaching the salon door, he paused and threw back at Elliot, 'Get to work then and there'll be that house and five thousand in it for you.'

'The house and ten thousand,' said Elliot politely.

The Duke merely nodded, 'Very well.' Then he snapped his fingers at a waiting servant and said, 'Send for Playfair – he's in the Cross Keys. Tell him I want to see him first thing tomorrow morning.' He was smiling broadly when he disappeared.

His smile was even broader later that evening when a servant came in to tell him that the gypsy girl and the man dressed as a pedlar who'd caused the trouble at the races had been caught and were presently confined in his stableyard.

By this time the Duke and his cronies had been drinking claret for several hours and his anger at having his bride filched from under his nose was well softened, especially by the lawyer's insinuations that he might be able to hang on to the whole dowry. Now it was only his pride, not his heart or his pocket that were affected, and loss of pride was easily soothed by the flattery of friends and the oblivion of good wine.

'Keep them locked up for a bit. I'll decide what to do with them later,' he announced grandly and reached for his third bottle.

Later the servant appeared again. 'There's a gypsy outside. He's asking to speak with you, your Grace,' was the message this time.

'Not the gypsy with the grey horse? Not the one that ran off with the girl?' asked the Duke, looking blearily up from his cards.

The servant shook his head. 'Another one, but he's very insistent.'

'Oh, show him in. I hope it's about the horse. I sent Faa a message to say I'd pay a hundred guineas for it.'

Gib stood erect in the doorway and looked dispassionately at the elegantly dressed but dissolute-looking men sprawling in chairs around the room.

'What's your business?' asked the Duke from a winged chair by the fire.

'It's about the girl Thomassin and the idiot Billy. I've heard you've got them. They're our people: if you give them to me I'll take them away and we'll deal with them ourselves,' said Gib slowly. He'd been wondering how to phrase his request ever since the news reached him that Thomassin and Billy had been captured.

'I've not seen them yet myself,' said the Duke.

'I'll take them off your hands, your Grace. They've not done anything bad . . .'

'The girl looked as if she was intent on murder and he's the wild man from the freak show, isn't he? If he's one of your lot what's he doing there?'

Gib stared bleakly at his questioner. 'The girl's only a little wild. She wouldn't have done anything really. As for Billy, he was given to the freak show by his grandmother because he was too strong for her to handle. He's simple. His mother had a difficult birth with him. You maybe remember his mother, sir. Her name was Becklie. I came to see you about Becklie when Billy was born.'

The Duke stood up, slamming his hand of cards down on to the table top. 'Not that again. The girl was a damned liar like all you gypsies. It wasn't me. It was my brother,' he spluttered.

'Becklie said it was you. Your brother was smaller than you, not so big and heavy. She said it was the big one who caught her in the park . . .'

The Duke's face was scarlet and he roared in anger, 'Have you come to drag all that up again? Is this just another ploy for money? Get out of here before I have you run out. I'll make up my own mind in my own time what to do with the girl and the idiot. Get out, damn you!' He was badly shaken and his half-drunk friends could not understand why.

There had been many hard times in Jem Archer's life but he could not remember such misery as the hours he spent looking for Alice in the lonely bog.

While he searched, turning back the branches of trees and bushes, peering into ditches and little river beds, he was in agony dreading that he would find her dead with her hair floating around her face.

He worked his way to and fro around the moss in this grim and isolated place covered with scrubby birch trees. Bottomless viridescent pools, covered with what looked temptingly like green velvet sward, dotted the landscape. For a while the farmhand who'd found the horse helped in the search but he soon gave up and drifted away, telling Jem, 'You're wasting your time. If this moss gets a body it doesn't give it up.' When evening came there was nothing for it but to retrace his steps to Lauriston. Though he did not want to believe it, he was sure Alice was dead.

On his way down the hill towards the Tweed, Jem met a big black man riding hell for leather southwards on a heavy horse. Jem held up a hand to stop him and called out, 'Have they caught the Strong Man from the freak show yet?'

The rider nodded as he cantered by, 'Yes, they've got him. He's up at the Castle. You haven't seen a man with a girl riding pillion on a grey horse, have you?'

'No, I haven't.' It seemed to Jem that everybody was

looking for somebody. At least one anxiety was removed
– Billy was no longer at large. Jem felt deathly tired and
decided to go back to his caravan, change into dry clothes
and have a meal before he went up to Sloebank to claim
his charge, for he saw no reason why Billy would not be
given back to him.

Meanwhile Billy and Thomassin were shut up in adjacent loose-boxes of an empty stable building at the Castle.
There was plenty of straw on the floor so they were able
to lie down and sleep. After a while a man brought them
each a mug of ale and a chunk of bread. Billy was dis-
traught and he lay, hungry, wet and lonely, with childish
tears of misery slipping down his cheeks but when he'd
eaten he fell asleep and Thomassin heard him snoring.
She lay awake thinking out ways of escape but the loose-
box door was padlocked on the outside and there were
iron bars along the top of the dividing enclosures. She
and Billy were as securely held as tigers in cages.

It was dark when she heard a noise outside the building
and the outer door swung open. She shrank back against
the wall when she saw the figures of men filling the doorway. They were shouting and laughing and with terror
she realised they were all drunk.

'Where are they, then? Get them out and let me have
a look at them,' came a voice which Thomassin recognised
as belonging to the Duke. She shrank even deeper into
the shadows as the padlocks were rattled. Then the door
of her box was thrown wide.

'Out you come, my pretty!' said a man as he stepped
in and hauled her to her feet. She hung back with her
eyes flashing and her fingers curved to scratch him but
he only laughed and pushed her through the door in front
of him. 'Here she is – a little wildcat by the look of her,'
he announced.

The noise woke Billy and he was rising to his feet when
a man came into his loose-box and prodded at his ribs
with the toe of a boot. 'Come on, come and join your
ladyfriend,' he ordered. Billy rose, shaking himself as he
did so.

When the two of them were standing in a paved walk-way between lines of boxes, a voice ordered, 'Take the girl up to the house and bring the idiot as well. We'll have a little sport with them.'

The Duke, completely drunk, staggered in front of the cavalcade that dragged Billy and Thomassin to the house, now ablaze with lights. A few moments later they found themselves in a brilliantly lighted room that seemed to their confused eyes to be filled with men. Thomassin, her hair flowing wild, stood in the middle of the floor with a frightened look on her face. When he came in behind her Billy ran over and took her hand.

The men jeered at the sight of the two of them and the Duke's voice called out, 'A lovers' meeting, eh? Let's see what you're like beneath all that gypsy finery, girl. Take it off.' He was full of claret-induced bravado, determined to ignore Gib's insinuation that Billy was his son.

Thomassin folded her arms over her breast and pulled her red shawl tighter. 'I won't,' she said defiantly.

'Take it off or we'll tear it off,' he ordered her.

She still shook her head and the Duke nodded to a young man who dashed forward and took hold of Thomassin's thin cotton skirt, ripping it as he pulled it away from her waist. They all cheered when they saw she was naked beneath it and she gave a cry of anguish as she tried to cover herself with the shawl. 'Oh Billy,' she cried, 'Don't let them do this to me!'

Billy, who had been watching what was going on with a bemused expression, leaped forward with his face work-ing, a terrifying picture of anger. His eyes flashed and his mouth was drawn back in a fearsome rictus. Unable to control himself he gave a terrible shout that echoed around the room like a wolf howling.

Immediately all the men who had been staring at Tho-massin stopped sniggering and looked at the creature who had made the awful noise. The Duke shrank back and pointed his stick at Billy, calling, 'Look at the lunatic, her lover. By God what a pair they make. That's no son of mine, no matter what the gypsy says.'

As he turned his eyes to Billy there was a gleam of sadistic cruelty in his gaze, and when he saw that three of his companions had the Strong Man securely held, his courage grew. 'So you're the Strong Man, are you? You don't look very frightening to me. Do a turn for us before we take you back to your keeper. Show us how strong you are. Break that.'

He pointed to a thick brass poker that stood in the hearth. 'Go on, break it,' he ordered. Billy looked at Thomassin who was weeping with her head hanging low and her silken skin showing beneath her tattered clothes. She was sexually modest and for the first time was terrified of what was about to happen to her.

The Duke pointed his stick at Bill again and ordered, 'Break the poker.' Then he turned towards Thomassin and told her, 'And you take off that filthy blouse. I want to see you naked.' He nodded to his watching friend Edmund. 'Do you want her? You may have her first. The others can take their turn after you.'

Thomassin, all bravery gone, was sobbing heart-brokenly and lifted her head to appeal to Billy. 'Oh, don't let them, Billy. Stop them, kill them if you have to.'

The words 'kill them', sparked something in Billy's dull brain. Flexing his muscles, he lifted his head and snorted, staring at the Duke who aware of the watchers, laughed out aloud and lifted the long poker, pointing it in Billy's direction. Billy grabbed it in both hands and bent it into a loop as if it was a green twig. Then he advanced closer on the man in the chair who stood up in a panic and reached behind him for another fire iron which happened to be a long fork.

He jabbed it towards Billy's face and that was his fatal mistake. Billy lifted his head and stared directly at his tormentor out of bloodshot eyes. It always took some time for his fury to be roused when he performed and he only achieved his most astonishing acts of strength when worked up into hysteria. Now with his beloved Thomassin sobbing behind him and this man threatening him with a fork, a red tide of rage rose in his brain. Though he did not comprehend the full meaning of all that was going on, he knew only too well that he was being jeered at, and what was worse, his beloved Thomassin was weeping and in danger.

He shook off the men who held him and then, with a roar like a lion, he reached for the fork and tore it out of the Duke's hand. Though the other men tried to throw themselves on to him, he shouldered them all off again like ants and strode forward, upturning the wing chair and reaching for the screaming man who cowered behind it. He seized his tormentor with both hands, gave a terrible howl, threw his head back and lowered his brows over his eyes till he looked like an ape. Then he squeezed and squeezed the Duke in a suffocating embrace.

'Get him off! For God's sake get a gun, somebody!' cried Edmund as the Duke's scream ended in a horrible gurgle but Billy never loosened his grip though men pummelled at his back and hammered him over the head with anything that came to hand. He stood like a rock mangling the body in his hands. When he had finished he shook it like a terrier shaking a rat. Then, taking advantage of the panic around him, he followed a fleeing Thomassin from the room.

Because he was so exhausted, Jem fell asleep when he went back to his caravan but did not remain so for long. The moon had only just risen when he set out for the Castle to fetch Billy. As he stepped off the footbridge, he was startled to meet a half-naked girl flying down the path towards him. Her face was distorted with terror as she ran and when she neared him she veered aside but he called out to her, 'I won't hurt you. What's going on? Has somebody hurt you?'

'It's Billy,' she sobbed, pausing a good way off from him. 'It's Billy. He attacked the Duke and they're out looking for him in the woods. None of them could stop him. He ran away after he'd done it.'

Jem was horrified. 'Has anybody hurt Billy?'

401

'No,' cried the girl. 'It's the Duke that's hurt. They're out with guns looking for Billy.'

'With guns!' cried Jem. His worst fears were coming true.

The girl ran on and he hurried onwards to Sloebank, arriving in the stableyard where an astounded crowd had gathered. Everybody was talking at once. 'The Duke's all covered with blood. They've sent for a doctor from Lauriston. He's in there now . . .' The talkers were fired by the relish that a disaster evokes in bystanders.

'Where's Billy? Where's the man that did it?' Jem asked anxiously.

Arms waved in every direction. 'Over there, that way, downhill, uphill . . .'

Search parties were organised and volunteers told to fan out and comb the area. Some of them brought dogs from the Duke's kennels and went off into the night with the slavering animals straining red-eyed on their leashes. Because Billy was dangerous everyone was armed with a firearm or a thick cudgel. They'd hit first and ask questions later.

Jem waited until they had all left and stood wondering where Billy would go. His guess was that after such a traumatic night, the poor confused soul would head back to security, back to the fairground. So he struck off downhill again taking the shortest, quickest way and heading for the river that gleamed in the moonlight like a silver snake. He ran along the side of a hedge, crossed a field and found himself at an old ford which was high with rainwater but by now he was oblivious to danger and waded through although he was wet to chest-height when he emerged on the other side.

Jem's was the only caravan left on the field. The old green van with the patient horse grazing alongside it looked lonely. As Jem drew near, however, he saw that the horse's head was up and its eyes were rolling in fright. Something had scared it. He hesitated and stared at the caravan door. Then he called out in a low voice, 'Billy, Billy. It's Jem, Billy.'

A sound like a bear snorting came from inside and that was followed by an almighty crash. Crockery was being broken inside the van. There was another smash and a series of terrible thuds which told Jem that Billy was berserk and beaking up everything within reach in a frenzy of violence. Wearily the burly man climbed the steps and kicked the door open. Billy was standing facing him with his back against the rear wall of the caravan. Broken dishes were piled around his feet and his hands were held out in front of him with the fists open and reaching like terrible claws. His eyes were rolling as if he was about to have a fit.

'Billy, it's me, it's Jem,' cried the man at the door in a soothing voice but this time his power did not work. Billy had been driven completely insane.

He lunged towards Jem, hands reaching for his throat, but with a groan Jem dodged round him and reached for the table. Miraculously, the pistol Alice had left was still there. He held it out rigidly in front of him and pulled the trigger. The ball hit Billy in the middle of his forehead and threw him back with tremendous force. His body sprawled against the wall before slipping down to the floor in a welter of blood.

With a terrible cry, Jem threw down the gun and covered his face with his gnarled hands. 'Oh God, Billy, I didn't want to do it. I didn't want to kill you but I'd rather I did it than anyone else!' he sobbed, dropping to his knees beside the lifeless body on the ground.

Cruel sheets of rain came driving across the open moor, cutting into the two young people who clung together on the brave grey horse. The deluge made them gasp with the ferocity of its onslaught but it did not stop them because on they galloped, not thinking about where they were going or what they were doing except that they were escaping from the rest of the world. When the gallant Barbary dropped his head and faltered in his stride, however, Jesse finally realised that the horse could endure the storm's onslaught no longer: it was time to look around for sanctuary. Through the swirling sheets of rain he saw an ancient stone building with a steeply pitched roof standing isolated in the middle of the expanse of moorland ahead of them.

He turned the horse's head in that direction and the building turned out to be a barn used for housing animals during the winter. The entrance door was open showing that inside it was dry and snug with a paved stone floor. In one corner was heaped the residue of last autumn's turnip harvest and the loft was full of sweet-smelling hay. Jesse smiled in relief when he realised there would be plenty of fodder for Barbary. He was more concerned about that than about food for himself and the girl. The horse could drink too because a stone water trough with a wooden bucket hooked above it stood at the side of the doorway.

When they clattered into this shelter, Barbary gave a whicker of pleasure as he sniffed the hay. The rain could be heard beating on the stone-slated roof and when he jumped down to the ground Jesse realised he was soaking wet to the skin. He held up his arms for the girl to fall into them. She stood shivering but smiling as she looked up at him with raindrops clinging to her lashes. 'Why did you do it?' she asked. It was the first thing she'd said since they left the race-course.

He shrugged and laughed back. 'I don't know. Why didn't you stop me?'

'I don't know that, either. What are we going to do now?' she asked.

His hands were still loosely holding her around the waist and he half-hugged her to him as if he was reluctant to let her go but he knew he had to break the spell and did so by saying briskly, 'We'll have to get dry first or we'll die of cold. I'll build a fire, there's plenty of wood around. Then you'll be able to dry your clothes while I see to the horse.'

She put out a hand to detain him before he turned away. 'What's your name?' she asked.

He laughed out loud. 'You ride off with a man whose

name you don't know! You're a wanton one. I'm Jesse Bailey. At least I know who you are. You're Miss Rutherford and your father's the old pirate from Lauriston.'

She took off her hat and shook water from it, then she shook herself too like a wet dog as she replied, 'Not Miss Rutherford. I think we can be on first name terms. My name's Odilie.' She paused and then another thought struck her. 'Oh heavens, they'll be looking for me everywhere. We must be mad to have bolted like that.'

He shrugged. 'You could have stopped me or asked me to let you down but you hung on tight enough.'

She looked haughtily at him. 'How could I fight you off? It was all so sudden . . .'

'Are you saying you want to go back, then? When Barbary's fed and watered and rested a bit I'll lend him to you if that's what you want.'

'I'll think about it but I must get dried first. I suppose the harm's done now anyway,' she said. She felt strangely light-hearted and could not decide if she wanted to go back or not. She was torn between pity for her father and the magnificent excitement generated in her by this daring man and their thrilling ride. But now, in order to think more clearly, she deliberately moved away from Jesse as if to remove herself from his aura and sat down on the dirty floor to take off her boots. The leather was so wet that they clung to her legs like an extra skin and she could not shift them.

He watched her struggle for a little while before he stepped up close again and said, 'Here, let me help. Stick out your foot and I'll pull the boot off for you.' He wrenched off first one boot and then the other, hauling her along the floor a little way because of the effort required. When her silken-clad feet were revealed, he curled his hands around her toes and said, 'They're so cold, like ice on a winter's morning. I'll light the fire and you can warm them.'

His voice was gentle and she felt her whole body thrill at his touch. It was impossible to control the shivering that seized her when she looked up at him. Their eyes met and this time she did not want to draw away. He stared back entranced and then, very slowly, sat down beside her and leaned forward to brush her lips with his. Their kiss was tentative at first but then grew more urgent. They held it for a long time.

'That's why I did it,' he said when they finally drew apart, still staring at each other.

Odilie was having difficulty in breathing and was afraid that she might faint. She put a hand to her head and sighed, 'I'm giddy.'

'You're chilled through,' he told her in the brisk tone again, which he could adopt so swiftly. 'Look, while I'm making the fire, climb that ladder to the hayloft, take off your wet clothes and throw them down to me. I'll spread them out before the heat and they'll dry soon. You can stay up there till they're ready.'

'You're wet too,' she told him.

'I've to look to the horse before I dry my clothes but you do as I say. I'm used to hard weather but it's not good for you to wear wet things. You're not used to it.'

A rickety old ladder led up to the open loft and he held it while she ascended. 'Throw your clothes down as soon as you're ready,' he called when she was safely settled among the piles of sweet-smelling hay. Then she heard him bustling about beneath her making the fire and seeing to Barbary.

With stiff fingers she battled with the frogging of her tightly-buttoned jacket and slowly untied the drawstring of the long skirt that clung wetly to her legs. Standing in her petticoat she squeezed its lace-edged hem and water dripped to the ground. She was soaked through to the skin so she divested herself of her underwear as well and was finally wearing only her chemise. When she felt it, to her dismay she found that even it was wet. There was nothing for it but to strip completely and she pulled the thin cambric over her head with upraised arms hoping that he was not spying on her. When she was naked she crept to the edge of the loft and, lying on her stomach in the hay, peered into the semi-darkness of the barn below.

Jesse was away in a far corner, rubbing down his horse with a wisp of hay and crooning lovingly to it. Confident of him now, she smiled as she dropped her clothes one by one on to the floor below. From her eyrie she soon heard him coming back to pick them up and she watched as he carefully spread them out on a makeshift arrangement of posts to dry before the fire. When he had finished, she still lay quietly watching everything he did.

When he called up, 'Are you asleep?' she didn't answer because she was half-mesmerised by exhaustion and the dancing flickering of the flames reflected on the greystone walls around her. Through the half-open door of the barn she could see that darkness had gathered outside while below her the fire blazed up in a circle of light. She felt safe and happy as she lay with her head cradled in one arm watching him. The hay prickled her aching body but she did not mind for she was warm and comfortable and safe. I trust this man, she thought. He'll do nothing to hurt me . . . and little by little she dropped into a comforting state of half-consciousness, drifting in and out of the sleep of exhaustion.

Once, around midnight, she opened her eyes and looking down into the vault saw that he too had stripped. His clothes were hanging beside hers and he was crouched facing away from her and staring into the fire. The long brown back that was turned towards her looked muscular and strong and there were two raised lines of muscle running down each side of his spine. His broad shoulders and slim waist made her thrill and she wondered what he would do if she crept down the ladder and slid her fingers up that enticing indenture in his back . . . In her half-conscious mind she wondered too what he would do if she called to him. I want to, she thought drowsily, I want him up here beside me among this soft hay with the darkness outside and the fire glowing down below. I want him to make love to me. She closed her eyes as a glorious shudder swept through her at the forbidden thought but she drove it away because she knew that gypsies, in spite of their vagrant ways and lax behaviour about other people's property, were very moral in matters of sex and rarely slept with their wives before they married them. He'd be shocked if I suggested such a thing, she thought, and with a sigh fell asleep again.

CHAPTER 16

Wednesday, 5 August.

A terrible scene met the eyes of Professor Thompson when he hurried into the Duke's bedroom at Sloebank Castle. By the light of candles dripping wax from silver sconces on the walls he could see bloodsoaked rags piled on the carpet at each side of the bed. A crowd of onlookers, male and female stood around in their nightclothes gaping in horror while servants went rushing in and out, elbowing everyone out of the way in their haste to bring more bandages, ewers and basins of hot water.

The injured man lay in the middle of a huge bed with a coronet finial on its dome-like roof and richly embroidered curtains looped up at each side. His face was as yellow as beeswax and strips of white material that rapidly took on a terrible reddish stain were bound roughly over his wounds.

Thompson, who had been summoned by a servant who knew that the famous Professor was staying at the Cross Keys, took one look at this hellish tableau and banished most of the onlookers. 'Get out of here and let me get on with my work! Go away. I'll send for you if I need any of you,' he raged, driving them out before him. Then he climbed on to the vast bed and knelt beside the gasping man. The Duke's eyes were open but he could make no sound.

Gently Thompson started to unwind the blood-drenched dressings and blanched when he saw the damage that Billy had inflicted. The Duke's ribs were crushed, and deep lacerations covered the patient's face, neck and chest. His arms and legs were broken in several places as if he'd been stamped on by a giant and judging by his breathing and the rasping sound in his chest, his lungs had been punctured.

When he climbed back on to the floor again, Wattie looked sombrely at a white-faced Edmund Lacey who had been allowed to stay with the patient. He told him, 'There's not much I can do except wait for the end. I'll give him opium to ease the pain. Will he be wanting a minister of religion, do you think?'

Edmund shook his head. 'He had his fortune told by an old gypsy on Monday night. She said he hadn't long to go,' he said in a quavering voice.

'Coincidence,' snapped Thompson. 'Who's the heir?'

The Duke's friend told him, 'It's going to be a matter of dispute. He's only got cousins, all pretty distant and all with a claim. That's why he was planning to marry and settle the business.'

'He left it a little too late,' said Thompson, looking at the body on the bed.

The women of Gib Faa's family were on the road outside Kirk Yetholm when Thomassin caught up with them. They were horrified by her nakedness and angrily questioned her, ignoring the fact that she was sobbing and hysterical. Then old Rachel stepped forward and ordered, 'Let her be. Cover the girl. What's happened to you, Thomassin? Tell old Rachel.'

The terrible story poured out while the women listened in horror. 'Is the Duke dead?' they asked at the end of it.

'I don't know. I didn't wait to find out.'

'Oh aye, he'll be dead,' said Rachel shaking her head. 'I saw it in his hand. I knew it was coming and I told him he wouldn't be able to avoid the curse.'

'But this Duke has no son,' said one of the other women.

'Oh, but he has a son right enough. Poor Billy's his son. That poor demented soul's the Duke's bairn. My grand-daughter Becklie was caught in the park by two young bucks one night and the one who got her with child was the Duke. It was before his brother died so he must have thought he was safe enough. Gib went to see him

410

about it but he denied it. He said Becklie was a liar . . .
My Becklie never lied about that.' Rachel's voice was
chilling and the women were unable to conceal their shock
as they listened to her.

'But it's Billy that's attacked him. He's been killed by
his own son!' cried out Thomassin. Rachel's eyes were
full of tears and she nodded as the girl groaned, 'Oh,
what a cruel fate for poor Billy, my poor Billy.'

It was daylight when Odilie woke in her nest of hay.
What brought her to consciousness was the smell of roasting meat that wafted up to her soft bed of hay. She rolled
over and leaned on her elbows so that she could see into
the void of the barn. Jesse, fully dressed once more, was
crouching over a spit on which something was being
turned. She drew back, for with daylight her modesty had
returned and at that moment she noticed that her clothes
were lying in a neatly-folded pile beside her. A blush
swept her as she thought, 'He's been up here beside me.
He stood over me and saw me naked.' The thought made
her furious and she dressed quickly so that she could go
storming down the ladder and accuse him of spying on
her. When she reached the ground she said haughtily,
'You should have called and told me that my clothes were
ready. You should've given me the chance to hide before
you brought them up. You spied on me! That was a
shameful thing to do.'

He looked up from the rabbit he was roasting. 'I didn't
spy but yes, I looked outright at you and I think you're
the loveliest thing I've ever stolen. I hope I don't have to
give you back. Does that annoy you?'

She looked at him, made uncertain by her feelings for
him. In the morning light he was even more devastatingly
handsome than he'd been in her dreams. She longed to
rub her cheek against the dark stubble that marked his
chin. In an instant her rage disappeared and he recognised her awkwardness as he said, 'Sit down here. I
caught a merrylegs this morning and we've good clear

water to drink. The rain's stopped and it's time we left. Have you made up your mind what you want to do?'

She sat down as she was told and accepted a piece of rabbit. It was delicious and she ate more, washing it down with the water. She had never enjoyed a banquet better. While she ate he sat watching her with a smile on his face. Then he said, 'Thomassin was right even though she tried to stab you for it. You've really cast the glamourie on me, Miss Rutherford.' She looked at him, shifting in her seat as she did so and he held out a hand to stop her. 'Don't come any nearer. I don't know what I'm doing when I'm close to you.'

'Was that why you ran off with me?' she asked, putting down the rabbit bone she'd been nibbling.

'It must have been. I don't know. I looked at you and thought that I had to take you with me.'

'Well, you've made sure about one thing at least. The Duke won't marry me now,' she said in a laughing voice.

Jesse turned on her in surprise. 'What do you mean?'

'I said the Duke won't want to marry me now . . . not after I've run off with a gypsy.'

His face was thunderstruck. 'You're not the girl that he was meant to be marrying, are you?'

'You mean you didn't know? You must be the only person in the district who didn't.'

He stood looking at her with a strange expression. 'Does it worry you that he won't marry you?' he asked.

She bit into her piece of rabbit. 'No, but I'm worried about what my father's going to say. He was so set on the marriage.'

'He'll find you another rich man,' said Jesse sharply and, as if her remarks had returned him to reality, he stood up abruptly and poured water on to the embers of the fire from the wooden bucket that stood on the floor beside him. While the flames hissed and spluttered, Odilie stared at the blackened ashes with a deep feeling of disappointment for she realised that their extinguishing meant the idyll was over. The sexual excitement that crackled between them seemed to be as brusquely dampened as

412

the flickering flames. The dark-haired young man stared down at her and coldly asked, 'So what do you want to do? Are you for going back?'

'What would happen to you if I did?' she asked.

'Nothing. They might come looking for me of course but they'll not find me. I was going away from my people anyway. I'm tired of choring. I was thinking of joining up with Archer's circus. I did a turn for them because their trick rider's ill and they've offered to take me with them. We're not far from Wooler and they'll soon be there. If you ride Barbary back to Lauriston, I'll walk over and meet them.' He was burning up with a strange mixture of emotions which he could not really analyse now he had learned that this girl was the Duke's fiancée.

'You'd really give me your horse? But he's so precious to you,' Odilie breathed.

His reply was, 'You're precious to me, too, but I'm no competition for a Duke. Take the horse. One day I'll let you know where to leave him so I can get him back again.' Before she had time to react he added with a set face, 'And when you go back, you must stay away from me for ever more, Miss Rutherford.'

She stood up and said softly, 'Don't be so angry. Please take my hand.'

Slowly he accepted the hand she held out to him and they stood together looking at the smoking pile that had been their fire. Then he groaned as if in pain. 'Oh, go away. I don't want this.' But she leaned towards him and rose on the points of her toes to kiss his lips. This time their embrace was both passionate and angry and Jesse was the one who broke away. 'Stand back!' he ordered her. 'Keep away from me. What are you trying to do?'

'I don't know. I really don't. Let's ride down together to the road and meet the circus. Then I'll decide what to do,' she told him in a chastened voice.

In the breaking dawn, Jem Archer took Billy's body into town and then returned to the caravan where he fell into an exhausted sleep. He was wakened an hour later by hammering on his caravan door. When he opened it, a group of men stood there and their leader, the big gypsy, asked, 'Where's Billy? We've come for him.'

'He's dead. He's in the town death-house. I took him there early this morning on the back of my horse. They're burying him tonight.'

Gib did not ask how Billy came to die. He had heard the story already. He shook his white head and said, 'No, they're not. We'll take him. He's one of ours and we'll bury him our way. You knew he was the Duke's son, didn't you? And that he killed his own father.'

Jem was genuinely shocked. 'No, I didn't. That's a terrible thing. So the Duke's dead, too! When I went up to the Castle last night I heard he was bad but I didn't know he'd died. When did it happen?'

Gib shrugged. 'Early this morning. He'll not be missed. He couldn't cheat the curse. You must come with us now to get Billy's body. You were his guardian because Rachel gave him to you and you have the say about what happens to him. They won't give him to us without your permission.'

Billy's corpse lay in the town mortuary, a chilly stone-walled room at the back of the Town Hall. Jem and the gypsies filed into the half-darkness and stood silently surveying the body which looked huge on a scrubbed deal table. The dirty bare feet sticking out under the edge of the covering blanket looked pathetic and innocently defenceless. Jem put one hand over his eyes to hide his tears and moaned softly, 'Ah Billy, I'm sorry lad, but I had to do it. They'd have hanged you anyway especially now that the Duke's dead . . .'

Gib standing behind him put a hand on his shoulder and said, 'We don't blame you. It was his fate, that's all.'

The Provost of Lauriston, who was supervising the sad business, also patted Jem on the back and told him, 'Don't take on, it was inevitable. There'll be no case about this – just get out of town as quick as you can and take him with you if you want so we can forget the whole thing.'

While the gypsies were loading Billy's corpse into a

414

little blue cart with the tailboard down. Professor Thompson came running over from the Cross Keys and grabbed Jem by the shoulder. 'A hundred pounds for the body. My offer still holds good.'

With a grimace of distaste Jem shook him off and Gib stepped up to tell the Professor, 'We've not done well by Billy but there's no way we'd sell his corpse. He'll be sent off in our way like his ancestors. Go away with your hundred pounds.'

Jem mounted his horse and watched the final scene in the life of his protégé with tears pouring down his cheeks. The last sight he got of Billy was an arm trailing from the back of the cart that carried him away. Then he stood alone, shoulders bent. With a shake of the head he returned to his caravan where, moving like an old man he backed his horse between the shafts. Slowly he gathered together his scattered, broken possessions and packed up the green van which was full of heartbreaking reminders of Alice – her shoes, her straw hat, her winter shawl, the dishes she ate from, the pillow she slept on. By now Jem was sure she was dead and his heart was aching. He felt as if his life was finished; all joy in living had been snatched away from him.

When he finally climbed up onto the box, and laid the pistol with which he had killed Billy on the floor by his feet. He was determined that when the pain became too bad to bear, he'd use it on himself.

At last his caravan lurched over the field towards the open gate and when he reached it he paused, not knowing in which direction to go. It didn't matter any longer. Simon and Bella were on their way to Wooler with the freak show in their wake but he could not face any more questions or sympathy. Neither did he want to ride back to the bog where Alice had disappeared. The memory of its sinister pools would haunt him forever. 'Oh Alice, Alice,' he mourned aloud.

Along the road to his right was the place he had taken her when she wanted to see her old home again. It had been pleasant and shady, a peaceful place. He'd take his farewell of her there. Jem headed the horse in the direction of Bettymill.

The lumbering waggons of Archer's Circus Royale travelled slowly along the rutted road that snaked through hill passes to Wooler. As they rolled along, they were overtaken by faster vehicles and speeding horsemen who relayed items of news. In this way a good story travelled faster than a stagecoach along the roads to the south. It was from a dealer in flax, returning with a load from St James' Fair, that Simon heard how the gypsy with the grey horse had stolen the Duke's bride at Caverton Edge races. The news of the Duke's death had still not got about.

Simon laughed. 'I liked that lad! He'll go far if he doesn't get hanged first.'

He laughed even louder when they reached a hump-backed bridge and he recognised the couple who sat waiting on a grey horse by the side of the road. 'Bella,' he said to the wife at his side, 'we're in luck. I think the gypsy dare-devil might be going to join us after all, and he's brought his equestrienne with him!'

Jesse was smiling too as he held up a hand to halt the waggon. 'Can we ride along with you for a spell?' he asked.

'You're welcome,' was the reply. Simon had a glint of merriment in his eye and Bella too was beaming at the couple as if they were newlyweds. She moved along the bench seat to make a place for Odilie and called out, 'Come up here and ride with us, lovie. Your horse can't carry two all day.'

Odilie clambered aboard the cart and told them, 'I'll only ride a little way. I've got to decide what I'm going to do. I haven't made up my mind yet . . .'

'We heard about what happened,' Bella interrupted her. 'My word, but it's created a great sensation round about.'

Odilie looked shocked. 'Has it got so far already?' she asked.

416

'It'll be in London by the day after tomorrow,' laughed Simon. 'It's moving faster than the King's messengers.'

They rolled on towards Wooler and when they were near the turnpike toll-cottage at Milfield, they saw another mounted man waiting by the side of the road. As they drew nearer to him, he rode into the middle of the carriageway and held up his hand. Odilie, on the box with Bella and Simon stood up with a gasp and cried, 'It's Joe Cannonball! It's my father's man.'

When the waggon stopped she leapt down from her seat and ran towards Joe. His face was working with emotion when he saw her, then he leaped from the saddle and asked, 'Are you all right, Baby? Are you safe? I only stopped the circus to ask because I heard the gypsy was going to join it. I didn't think he'd have got here so soon.'

'I'm quite safe, Joe, but you look awful! Did Father send you after me?'

'No. Poor Canny, he couldn't send anybody any place. He collapsed when you took off. He's ill in bed with that man Thompson drawing blood off him as if he's plenty to spare. He's in a bad way, Miss Odilie. If you don't come back, I don't think he'll live.'

The girl's colour drained away and she looked over at Jesse. 'Did you hear that? My father's ill. I must go back to Lauriston right away. Please lend me your horse.'

The young gypsy's face was expressionless as he dismounted from Barbary. Without speaking he cupped his hand so that she could put her foot into it and be hoisted into the saddle. All Jesse then said was, 'I expected you to go back. Barbary's easy to ride if he knows you're not afraid of him. Treat him well. He's a prince among horses.' He made no effort to try to change her mind. By the way he acted it was as if he was taking leave of a casual acquaintance, so little did he reveal of the turmoil raging within him.

She gathered up the reins and looked down at the man in the road. His words cut her to the quick and she could not hide her disappointment at his reaction. There was so much she still had to say to Jesse but his distant manner

417

and the presence of Bella, Simon and Joe restrained her. All she managed was, 'I'm sorry. I have to go. It's got nothing to do with my marriage. My father's ill and it's all my fault.'

Jesse clapped Barbary on the shoulder and said, 'All right. Goodbye, old man.' Then he added, 'I'll send for him one day. Take good care of him, Miss Rutherford.'

She blushed scarlet and with a touch of her heel urged the horse forward. Soon all that could be seen of her and Joe was the flying mud sent up by their horses' hooves. Then Jesse shrugged heavily and shook his head before he climbed into the waggon beside the Archers. 'Do you still have a place for a trick rider without a horse?' he asked laconically.

The lane down to Bettymill looked even more like a secret pathway to heaven than before because the rain had brought out a fresh crop of brilliantly-coloured wild flowers. The tree branches, lacy with leaves, arched down low and made a damp green tunnel for Jem to walk through when he jumped down from the caravan. Leaving it at the head of the lane he set off, walking very slowly between the thickly clustering trees. He felt that he was stepping into Alice's youth. There was no sound except for the crackle of dried twigs and last year's beech mast beneath his boots. The sun dappled the path and there was a sweet smell of flowers and damp moss. This must be what heaven's like, thought Jem with a strange sense of peace.

Half way up the lane he realised he'd left the pistol on the box so he had to run back for it. It was hanging loosely from his hand as he turned and retraced his steps deeper and deeper into the all-embracing greenery. When he reached the mill, half-hidden in its mossy clearing, he gave a sigh of satisfaction. The broken stone walls looked warm in the sun, the dusty windows seemed to smile upon him.

A sense of timelessness enveloped him. He walked into the middle of the patch of green opposite the mill door and looked around. A faint trickle of falling water came to his ears like distant music from the stone-walled lade, and a little breeze was making the fronds of a clump of ferns growing out of the wall above the broken millwheel wave gently to and fro like beckoning hands, leading him onwards to the waterside.

Holding the pistol carefully, he sat down on the mill-lade bank and stared into the stream that swirled beneath his feet. A fat brown trout was slowly circling in a deep pool floored with multi-coloured pebbles. Big yellow buttercups drooped their heads into the water and wild mint scented the air. Jem raised his eyes to the scraps of sky showing between the treetops and thought of Alice. She'd grown up here, she said. How often she must have played here as a girl, how often she must have sat where he sat now, her head full of dreams. He spoke his thoughts aloud, 'Oh Alice, I can't live without you.'

A gentle hand stroked his shoulder and a voice whispered, 'You're not going to use that gun on yourself are you, Jem? I love you. I'm glad you knew where to look for me.'

Without turning he laid the pistol down on the grass and raised his left hand to his right shoulder, grasping her hand in his. 'Is that you, Alice?' he asked as if he was blind.

'Turn round and see,' came her voice. When he turned they reached out for each other like young lovers clinging together with fervour. It took a long time until all their tears were shed and they had assured each other of their love. Then, holding hands, they walked together back to the caravan while she told him what had happened to her.

'I knew I couldn't risk being taken by Elliot's men so when the horse went lame I set it free on the moors. I had no idea it was going to get itself bogged down. Then I found my way back here. It was the only thing I could think to do because I was lost and I knew the other roads into England would be watched. I wondered how to get a message to you so I sat here and thought and thought. I tried to send a message to your mind. I thought if I concentrated hard I'd make you understand – and perhaps it worked. If you hadn't come I don't know what I'd have done . . . but you did come, didn't you?'

'I nearly didn't,' he admitted. 'When your horse was found in the bog everyone thought you were dead. I thought so as well. I came here today because you loved this place, that was all.'

She clung to his arm and said, 'I'll never leave you, Jem. Never, never. You must believe that now.'

He nodded his head with crystal tears standing in his eyes. He could not trust himself to speak. A long while later he told her, 'We've got to get away from here. Nobody's looking for you any more because they're all too taken up with the Duke getting murdered. If anyone tries to bother you, I'll shoot them.'

Alice had not heard about the Duke's death and that story had to be told. She held Jem in her arms while he cried tears of remorse for Billy. By the time this recital was finished, it was evening again and they decided to drive the caravan deeper up Bettymill Lane and camp the night by the river. After all the emotion that had engulfed them, they felt cleansed and very peaceful. When the moon rose, Jem sat by the old mill holding Alice's hand and said, 'I feel as if I've come through Hell into Heaven.'

She nodded. 'I feel that way, too, but we'd best make tracks out of Scotland as quick as we can. I don't trust Elliot. I'm sorry to leave here and I'm sorry to leave Grace but she's going to be very happy and she'll be rich as well. I've done all I can for her. I've settled my old scores.'

Jem stroked her hair and whispered, 'I'll be glad to go. I don't know about you, Alice, but I've had enough of St James' Fair to last me a lifetime.'

The town was clamorous with gossip when Odilie rode across the Rennie Bridge with Joe Cannonball and the sight of her started a new wave of excitement. Little boys ran from shop to shop calling out, 'She's back! Rutherford's lassie's back, and she's riding the gypsy's big grey horse!'

Before she reached the gates of Havanah Court, people were peeping out of their front doors to gaze down the street in the hope of catching a sight of her. All the heads nodded at once and tongues wagged, for there hadn't been such goings-on in the town since the Provost stood in the square eleven years ago and, amid the ringing of bells, announced the death of Nelson and the victory at Trafalgar.

Stevens the head groom was idling in the stableyard when Odilie rode in under the stone arch. He ran forward with his hands held out to greet her. 'My word but I'm glad to see you, Miss Odilie! Your father's in an awful state. That's a fine horse you've got there – isn't that the one that took the big race?'

She threw him the reins and said, 'Look after it well, Stevens. It belongs to a friend.' Then lifting her skirt she ran towards the house.

Inside, everything was unusually still and silent as if time had stopped. Odilie paused in the hall with her heart pounding in terror for it seemed like a house of mourning. Even the dust-motes in the sunlight slanting through the window looked suspended, motionless and waiting. Her father was not dead, surely? Oh no, he couldn't be dead! She took the stairs in a most unladylike way, oblivious of the scandalised faces of the servants watching her from the door to the kitchens. In the upper hall, she kept on running, heading for her father's room and burst in without knocking. Aunt Martha was sitting by the bed and she turned around, her mouth making an 'O' of disapproval, but this changed to a gasp of delight when she saw that the intruder was Odilie.

'Odilie, dear lassie,' gasped the old woman and surprised even herself by bursting into tears. It was the first time that stoical Martha Rutherford had wept since the year her mother died when she was twelve years old.

Odilie ran towards her with her arms extended, calling

421

out, 'How's my father? How is he? Joe rode to Wooler to tell me he'd been taken ill.'

'And no wonder he's ill,' scolded Martha, recovering herself quickly. 'Seeing you jump into the arms of a gypsy and ride off like that was enough to give him an apoplexy.'

'An apoplexy! Is that what he's had? Is that what Thompson says?' asked Odilie.

A voice came from the bed and the women turned towards the patient whom they thought to be asleep. 'He says that I'll live – and I certainly will now that you've come back,' said Canny Rutherford weakly.

Odilie ran towards him. 'Oh, Papa, I'm sorry I rode off like that without thinking. It wasn't the gypsy's fault – I willed him into it, I think.'

'I guessed as much. I know you, Odilie. Wild geese eggs . . .' Cannie's voice was feeble but his eye was brighter.

'I've come back. I'll do whatever you want. I'll even marry the Duke if he'll still have me and not say a word of protest. The gypsy was honourable. He never touched me, I promise you that . . .' said Odilie fervently.

Martha was standing facing the bed with both hands up to her mouth as she listened. Then she spoke solemnly. 'You needn't worry about marrying the Duke, my love. That sinner is dead. The wild man from the Fair tore his heart out.'

'At least he tried to, but he found he hadn't got one. I'm sorry I got you into that situation through my stupidity, lass,' said Canny.

Martha went on, 'Dead as mutton is our Duke, and they say there's going to be a court case about who's to inherit the title.

'In any case, there's not going to be a wedding,' sighed Canny and closed his eyes again.

Odilie looked at her aunt in bewilderment. 'The Duke is dead? Oh dear, my legs feel wobbly. Does that mean that the betrothal arrangement's null and void – Father doesn't lose my dowry?'

Martha nodded. 'That Elliot's been here already, all

sly and confidential, saying Canny can have the whole lot back – all except what's gone into the pocket of that young architect from Edinburgh.'

'That's not too bad. At least I liked *him*. Thank goodness Father won't be ruined. Elliot told me he would be utterly destroyed if I backed out and I was so worried about that.'

'It's Elliot himself that looks like being ruined. Folk are saying Grace'll take most of his property now she's married. But let's hear what's happened to you – where's the young gypsy for a start?' said her aunt.

'He's in Wooler with the circus. But I've come back, Aunt Martha, isn't that enough for you?'

'I suppose so. Sit down by your father and talk to him for a while. You half-killed him, you ungrateful girl!' Odilie sat down looking abashed for Aunt Martha had rarely been so hard on her before.

She was quietly holding her sleeping father's hand when a maid entered and announced that a Mr and Mrs Scott were in the hall asking to see Miss Odilie.

'Go down and tell Grace what's happened,' whispered Martha. 'She probably doesn't even know about your gypsy elopement.'

'Oh Aunt Martha, don't talk about it like that,' the girl protested but Martha was not interested in the romantic aspect of the affair.

'Go on down, miss,' she scolded and Odilie ran downstairs to the salon where she found Grace and her young husband who looked ill at ease among Canny's grand furniture. Adam brought the air of the moors into the elegant drawing room and made everything there seem artificial and unsettled.

Grace, however, was beautiful. The old fear and tension had gone from her face and she looked relaxed and tranquil which meant that her real beauty was magnificently revealed. It was as if a curtain had been dropped from before her and she smiled on Odilie like a Madonna when the girls embraced, hugging each other tight. Grace told her friend, 'I've just come from my father's house. It was wonderful to be able to tell him what to do for once! I really laid down the law, stipulating which farms I wanted and what I'd allow him to keep. He didn't utter a word of protest, did he Adam?' She laughed and then her eyes searched her friend's face. 'But he said you've had quite an adventure – running away with a gypsy. Oh Odilie, you're so daring!'

'It wasn't me that was daring. It was him,' said Odilie who felt a sharp pang of pain when she remembered the dark young man who had swept her off her feet. It all seemed to have happened long ago to someone else.

Now that she was back in Havanah Court such things seemed only to be the stuff of storybooks.

'But why did you come back?' asked Grace suddenly. What a strange question from Grace who's always been so amenable, thought Odilie looking at her friend. But there was something new in Grace's eye. She had been wakened up by the silent young man who was watching them so intently from the other side of the room.

'I came back because of my father. I heard he'd been taken ill . . . I felt as if it was my fault.'

'But he's all right, isn't he? He's going to recover. And the Duke's dead – nobody minds that, at least nobody that I've heard about. So what are you going to do now, Odilie?'

'I don't know. I can't seem to be able to think clearly.' The answer was a whisper.

'Then I think you must be in love,' said Grace gently. 'Don't lose it, Odilie. Whatever you do, don't lose it.'

CHAPTER 17

Thursday, 6 August.

On the following day, Canny Rutherford was sufficiently recovered to rise from his bed and be dressed by Joe. Then he reclined in a chair on the terrace overlooking the river while his sister and the servants danced attendance on him. His constant companion was Odilie who would not leave his side.

In the afternoon, Professor Thompson called and examined Canny. 'You're on the mend, old friend. Lead a quiet life for a few weeks and you'll be as good as ever,' he pronounced and shot a look from beneath his grey eyebrows at Odilie. 'Don't you go running off with any more gypsies, Miss.' He was only joking but she did not laugh.

When Wattie Thompson had left, her father told her, 'Why don't you go out for a ride, my dear? You ought to take some exercise because you've been sitting here all day. I don't mind.'

As Stevens saddled her chestnut mare he sang the praises of the stallion that was standing in a box at the far end of the stableyard. When Barbary saw the mare being led out he set up a tremendous whinnying and started kicking at the box door. 'He's in love,' laughed the groom.

'Has no message come about him yet?' asked the girl.

Stevens shook his head. 'I hope we don't hear anything either because that's a valuable animal. If the gypsies don't fetch him back, we'll have a real treasure.'

Odilie's face was angry as she told him, 'We can't keep him. No matter what happens I won't keep him. When they come for Barbary, you must let him go at once.'

The town was hushed as she rode out. The excitement and gossip of the previous two days was dwindling and

425

because of the Duke's death, the tolling of the town clock was muffled. Black crêpe ribbons were looped over house doors and garlands of mourning ribbon were displayed in shop windows. People going about their day to day business seemed to walk on tiptoe and their voices were hushed. The dead man was lying on his bier in the Castle and it was arranged that his funeral was to take place inside the nave of the ruined abbey in a week's time. Workmen were already digging his grave when Odilie passed and she hoped that she would not be expected to attend the ceremony. There had been no communication between Sloebank and Havanah Court since the race meeting afternoon so she reckoned that she was not on the guest list and gave a sigh of relief; the prospect of attending the funeral or pretending to mourn appalled her.

Members of the Duke's family, every distant second cousin and third nephew from far and near, were gathering in Lauriston, and servants' gossip informed the town's people that many of the relatives were hopeful of their chances of succeeding to the title, despite the curse. There had already been several disputes about genealogy and at least three court actions were threatened. There was obviously potential for several years of town gossip brewing up at the big house.

Odilie looked sombre as she rode along, acutely aware of curious eyes on her. She knew the women were wondering if she'd been ravished by the gypsy and speculating what Canny would do with her now. The men looked on more kindly because they felt grudging pity for Jesse Bailey at having to let such a prize slip out of his grasp – lovely as a summer rose and rich as well!

The summer rose was thinking, 'I could go back to Jamaica to our estates there. My mother's sisters and all my cousins will be pleased to see me again. Father won't object if I tell him that it's impossible for me to stay here after this. People in this town will never stop gossiping about me. Father might come back to Jamaica as well –

but he's happy here and what about Aunt Martha? She'll never leave Lauriston.'

She sighed in perplexity as she set the horse trotting to the top of a hill on the road to Ednam. From its eminence she had a good view of the surrounding countryside spreading before her in a luscious and fertile panorama. Fields of corn were turning bright yellow like squares of brilliant patchwork and any day now harvesting would commence. After that the year would be on the turn, scarlet and purple fruits of autumn would start appearing in the hedgerows and the summer birds would fly off to warmer climates; leaves would go yellow, russet, gold and orange before they dropped from the trees. Odilie felt melancholy and shivered as she remembered the sight of Jesse Bailey sitting naked before the fire in the barn. Why didn't I climb down and put my arms around him? I wanted to, oh how I wanted to, she said to herself. Why had he turned on her so savagely when he heard she'd been about to marry the Duke? Why had he allowed her to leave the circus with so little protest? He had accepted that she was going and never once said, '*Stay*.' Tears welled up in her eyes at the memory of his indifference.

I wish I could stop thinking about him. I wish I could drive the memory of his face, his laughing mouth, the line of his throat, his broad shoulders and those incredible hands out of my mind, she thought – but to no avail. She was obsessed by him. By the time she turned to go home again, Odilie had convinced herself that the only way to be cured of her passion was to sail to Jamaica as soon as possible.

Canny and Martha were taking tea when she returned. Her father's appetite had almost recovered and he was managing to despatch a considerable amount of food. He waved a fork at her and exhorted her to try a piece of sponge cake but she refused. 'I'm not hungry,' she said dolefully.

Canny then glanced in a significant way at Martha who rose and left the room. At this, Odilie realised the move had been pre-arranged. Her father wanted to talk privately to her. He waved her to a chair.

'You're looking very sad. Something's troubling you – what is it? Everything's worked out for the best. My stupidity in trying to marry you to the Duke could have cost me ten thousand pounds but I escaped that, though I deserved to suffer a bit for my foolishness. I'm sorry, my dear, I should never have done it. I knew you didn't like the man and to be quite frank with you, neither did I. It was stupid snobbery and ambition that made me do it. Can you forgive me?'

She nodded, 'Of course, Father. I understand. I don't know why I'm so upset. I made up my mind to come back . . .'

'Why?' His eyes were shrewd.

'I heard that you'd collapsed. I couldn't ride on with the gypsy and leave you.'

'Would you have done so if I was well? Now that you find that I'm not dying after all, are you sorry you came back?'

'Of course not. I love you.'

'Would you go back to him now if I said you should follow your heart?'

She stared at him in surprise with tears welling up in her eyes. Canny leaned forward and took her hand. 'Listen to me. This may not sound like the advice that most fathers would give their daughters but I've followed my own inclinations since I was eleven years old and rode out of this town on the back of a wool merchant's cart. I don't regret any decision I've ever made and one of the best was when I saw your mother at the other side of a room and decided there and then I was going to marry her. You know when something like that happens to you: It hits you like a blow.'

She nodded. She knew what he was talking about.

'Go back and see your gypsy again. Make up your mind if you want to stay with him or not. He must be a remarkable lad to have snatched you the way he did. You'd make an interesting couple. I should have fine grandchildren! Go back to Wooler. Martha and I'll stay here and you can come back to us whenever you choose. It's not as if you're going to the other side of the world – you won't be as far away as Jamaica, anyway.'

The last sly remark made her realise that he had anticipated what she was planning as a way out of her unhappiness. With a tearful laugh, she threw her arms around his neck and kissed his cheek. 'Thank you Papa, thank you,' she said and ran from the room.

It was dawn on the next day, Friday, when they started. Odilie was mounted on the chestnut mare but Stevens was having such a hard time trying to control Barbary who pranced, reared and arched his neck in such a furious courtship display that the girl remounted on a placid gelding.

They took the road south through Coldstream and it was almost deserted for it had returned to its normal condition after the last of the Fair traffic had passed that way. The only other travellers they saw was the occasional pedlar toiling along under the burden of his pack, or a couple of riders going from farm to farm.

It was afternoon when they reached Wooler, where a large poster fastened to the door of an inn informed them that Archer's Circus Royale was due to perform in the field by the river that night.

The tents were pitched and people were bustling about when Odilie rode up. No one challenged her as she dismounted and went in search of Simon.

Under the scrutiny of a convalescing El Diavolo, Jesse was rehearsing in the circus ring, circling its circumference over and over again, brows bent in concentration. Sometimes he rose on to the saddle, standing on one leg with his arms outstretched, at other times he put the horse into a gallop and leaned down from the saddle to sweep objects off the ground. He did not notice a group of people enter at the back of the tent and settle down on one of the benches. It was only when he drew on the reins and stretched his legs out that he was startled by the sound of clapping.

'Well done!' cried Simon. 'You're as good as El Diavolo already, isn't he, Pat? What you need is a good partner, though. There's a girl just come in that I'd like you to see. Do you want to have a look at what she can do?'

Jesse shouted, 'All right, send her in,' and sat still on his horse in the middle of the ring as the canvas curtain was lifted and a black circus horse swept in at the canter, head down, neck arched and going at a steady pace. The girl on its back was dressed as Britannia and she made the horse pirouette, prance, canter backwards and go sideways crossing its legs in a scissor motion. When she came close to him she lifted her head and smiled at him from under the tall cockade of feathers she was wearing in her hair.

He gasped, 'Odilie!'

She smiled again and held out a hand in his direction. His horse plunged forward and he grasped her fingers. Together they circled the ring, cantering in step and in perfect harmony, so close that their stirrup irons clanged together. When they finally stopped Jesse reached out an arm to encircle her waist and hugged her close. The horses stood immobile while the couple clung together staring at each other in delight.

It was Simon who broke the spell.

'Will she do as a partner for you then?' he called out laughing.

'Indeed she will if she'll have me,' was Jesse's reply.

More Compulsive Fiction from Headline:

A Liverpool saga in the great tradition of Catherine Cookson

ELIZABETH MURPHY

'Better is a dinner of herbs where love is than a stalled ox and hatred therewith.' Proverbs 17

When her Mam dies in childbirth, little Sally Palin becomes a second mother to her two brothers and baby Emily, the apple of her eye. Sally is determined that her sister shall leave the mean streets of their Liverpool home and enjoy a better life, but the success of her dream is bittersweet.

To escape a fever epidemic that ravages the city, Emily is sent away to her rich, childless Aunt Hester, to grow up in the healthy country air with luxuries the Palins could never provide.

But despite these material advantages, Emily fails to find happiness, and settles for a loveless marriage to an elderly widower, while Sally enjoys love and fulfilment with her husband and children, even though they must struggle against unemployment, illness and tragic loss . . .

'. . . an evocative novel of life behind the scrubbed doorsteps at the turn of the century. Gently paced, it nonetheless conveys the grinding miseries of poverty and making ends meet in the pre-welfare days . . .'
Books

'Elizabeth Murphy draws on her knowledge of her home town Liverpool to conjure up a cast of colourful characters . . . in a family saga that you just won't be able to put down.' *Prima*

FICTION/SAGA   0 7472 3192 3

A selection of bestsellers from Headline

FICTION

HUNG PARLIAMENT	Julian Critchley	£4.50 ☐
SEE JANE RUN	Joy Fielding	£4.99 ☐
MARY MADDISON	Sheila Jansen	£4.99 ☐
ACTS OF CONTRITION	John Cooney	£4.99 ☐
A TALE OF THE WIND	Kay Nolte Smith	£5.99 ☐
CANNONBERRY CHASE	Roberta Latow	£4.99 ☐
PRIDE	Philip Boast	£5.99 ☐
THE EYES OF DARKNESS	Dean Koontz	£4.99 ☐

NON-FICTION

A CHANCE TO LIVE	Marchioness of Tavistock and Angela Levin	£4.99 ☐
THE GREAT DONKEY TREK	Sophie Thurnham	£4.99 ☐
THE JACK THE RIPPER A TO Z	Paul Begg, Martin Fido, Keith Skinner	£6.99 ☐
HITTING ACROSS THE LINE	Viv Richards	£5.99 ☐

SCIENCE FICTION AND FANTASY

BUDDY HOLLY IS ALIVE AND WELL ON GANYMEDE	Bradley Denton	£4.99 ☐
BRAINCHILD	George Turner	£4.99 ☐
A BAD DAY FOR ALI BABA	Craig Shaw Gardner	£4.99 ☐
DESTROYING ANGEL	Richard Paul Russo	£4.99 ☐
ALBION	John Grant	£4.99 ☐

All Headline books are available at your local bookshop or newsagent, or can be ordered direct from the publisher. Just tick the titles you want and fill in the form below. Prices and availability subject to change without notice.

Headline Book Publishing PLC, Cash Sales Department, PO Box 11, Falmouth, Cornwall, TR10 9EN, England.

Please enclose a cheque or postal order to the value of the cover price and allow the following for postage and packing:
UK & BFPO: £1.00 for the first book, 50p for the second book and 30p for each additional book ordered up to a maximum charge of £3.00.
OVERSEAS & EIRE: £2.00 for the first book, £1.00 for the second book and 50p for each additional book.

Name ....

Address ....

....

....